The Strange Case
of the Pharaoh's Heart

The Strange Case of the Pharaoh's Heart

Timothy Miller

SEVENTH
STREET
BOOKS®

Published 2024 by Seventh Street Books®

Cover image © Shutterstock / Rvector, artform,
Liudmila Klymenko, RATOCA, Vlada Young, Roberto Castillo
Cover design by Jennifer Do
Illustrations by Terry Ward
Cover design © Start Science Fiction

Inquiries should be addressed to
Start Science Fiction
221 River Street
9th Floor
Jersey City, New Jersey 07030
PHONE: 212-431-5454
WWW.SEVENTHSTREETBOOKS.COM

10 9 8 7 6 5 4 3 2 1

978-1-64506-081-9 (paperback)
978-1-64506-082-6 (Ebook)

For Jim and Asa,
who have gone before.

"It is neither decent nor safe to take from their resting places the bodies of old kings. The Egyptians knew much more about the occult than we do today. This must have been a peculiar element of an Egyptian curse.

"The ancient Egyptians were very anxious to guard the tombs of their Kings, there is reason to believe that they placed elementals on guard, and such may have caused Lord Carnarvon's death.

"An evil elemental may have caused Lord Carnarvon's fatal illness. One does not know what elementals existed in those days, nor what the form might be.

"These elementals are not spirits in the ordinary sense, in that they have no souls.

"An elemental is a built-up, artificial thing, an imbued force which may be brought into being by spirit means or by nature."

—Sir Arthur Conan Doyle, April 5, 1923

Chapter One:
Dr. John Watson

T he seventh of April 1923 was the day I formally repudiated Sherlock Holmes. It was like plunging a dagger into my own heart, but I had stomached all I could of his spiritualist rubbish. Even in the embarrassing case of the Cottingley fairies, in which he had actually championed the claims of two young girls to have photographed pixies at the bottom of their garden, I had stood by him, making labored excuses for him to the press and the public. But when he told the London papers, on the very day of Lord Carnarvon's death, that it was elemental forces protecting Tutankhamun's tomb from desecration that had laid him low, I could no longer in good conscience defend my old friend. I called upon Holmes publicly to retract his statement and make his apologies to Carnarvon's grieving widow, the lady Almina. I waited but received no reply from Holmes, either in public or in private. He cut me dead.

Thus ended a friendship of forty years' standing. Of course, I still owed a profound debt of gratitude to Sherlock Holmes, which I am ever ready acknowledge and which can never be repaid. My entire reputation as a man of letters rests on my association with the man and my accounts of his extraordinary investigative methods. But more than this, he was the great friend of my life. Often irascible, supercilious, unsympathetic, he was the truest friend a man could have.

But the man who spat on Lord Carnarvon's grave was not the Sherlock Holmes I had known. First the death of Professor Moriarty, and then the uncanny events of 1912, which I have chronicled elsewhere, had affected the man profoundly. Once a dyed-in-the-wool skeptic whose world was as elegantly constructed as a Euclidean theorem, he had come to embrace not only spiritualism, which had once again slithered into vogue, but all manner of supernatural hogwash.

The spiritualists, in return, embraced him with open arms, as one might imagine. Every speaker's dais, every testimonial dinner, every lecture circuit shot an engraved invitation to the villa in Sussex where Holmes's quiet retirement had been elbowed aside for his new obsession, punctuated by a series of notorious séances. I could only shake my head in dismay. I immersed myself in my practice and turned my back to the world. I was too old to engage in the matter—and too wounded.

Which brings me to the events of January 1924, beginning with a visit I received from a lady. On the telephone she had presented herself as a new patient seeking medical advice, though she was maddeningly vague as to her symptoms. New patients are, to say the least, a rarity in my practice in these latter days. Most of my clients have been with me since I first hung out my shingle on Queen Anne Street. The lady's name was Eve Herbert. It embarrasses me to admit that I didn't recognize it immediately. But I recognized her face the moment she stepped into my office.

And why not? I had seen her face blazoned in the press for months, first accompanying her father, then by the side of his coffin, and, most recently, arm in arm with her fiancé. The heart-shaped face, countenance serene as a Madonna's, careful, weighing gaze from heavy-lidded eyes. She was a little thing in stature, and barely in her twenties, but so self-contained and straight that she threw a much longer shadow.

"Lady Evelyn!" I exclaimed.

Lady Evelyn Leonora Almina Herbert, the only daughter of the late Lord Carnarvon himself, discoverer, along with Howard Carter by his side, of the tomb of Tutankhamun, thirteenth pharaoh of the eighteenth dynasty of ancient Egypt, the archaeological find of the century. She was still dressed in mourning—the most fashionable mourning one could imagine.

"Dr. Watson. Thank you for seeing me on such short notice."

"Lady Evelyn," I stuttered, "please allow me to extend my deepest sympathies on the loss of your father. The entire kingdom mourns his passing."

I took her coat—it was a frigid day outside, with the wind scudding along the street, searching out the keyhole in every door, every chink in every window. (I noticed a brown maple leaf caught in her hair but dared not remove it or even bring it to her attention; besides, I found it charming.) I ushered her into my consulting room, which looked decidedly shabby in contrast to her elegance. I made a mental note to have the housekeeper beat the rugs to death that very afternoon. It was at least quite warm, for I had a fire blazing on the hearth. I find as I've grown older that the cold wants to lodge in my bones.

"You're very kind, Doctor," said Lady Evelyn. "I'm sure you've guessed I'm not actually here seeking medical attention."

I nodded, waving her to my best chair. "Please do sit, my lady. Would you care for some tea?" I was painfully aware that young ladies of Lady Evelyn's crowd were more at home with martinis in the afternoon than oolong, but I could no more mix a martini than I could pilot an aeroplane to the moon.

The lady demurred. "In fact, Doctor, my father's death is the reason I'm here today—or at least part of the reason."

"Let me apologize, then, for the untoward remarks of my associate Mr. Holmes. My former associate, I should say. This mania for spiritualism has clouded his judgment in his latter years."

"Yes, he told me you would say something of the sort."

"I'm sorry, my lady, who told you?"

"Mr. Holmes. It was he who sent me to you."

"I'm afraid I don't follow you."

"No, of course not. Please allow me to explain. Have you heard the story of Hugh Evelyn-White?"

I most certainly had, though I was loath to admit it, for it touched upon this selfsame "curse of the pharaoh."

"I may have seen something in the papers about it," I admitted reluctantly. The papers had had a field day with the sensational suicide. Once they'd discovered that he'd been a member of the Metropolitan and had been one of the first inside Tutankhamun's tomb, they went into paroxysms, for he had written his suicide note on the wall of his study with his own blood—"I have succumbed to a curse that forced me to disappear"—and then hanged himself. If talk of a curse had died down in the last few months, this certainly threw enough fuel on the flame to make it burn merrily.

"Well, to be brief," she began, "Evelyn-White was one of our pre-eminent scholars in ancient Greek, a lecturer at University of Leeds. He was also a talented Coptologist and a translator of hieroglyphics who had done some work for us on Tutankhamun's tomb. After leaving a suicide note, he got into a taxi and requested to be taken to the house of Dr. Maxwell Telling, a well-known physician. Just before reaching the doctor's house, however, the driver heard the report of the gun—it must have deafened him—and turned back to find Evelyn-White slumping forward. He had shot himself. The driver raced to a nearby hospital, but Evelyn-White was pronounced dead an hour later. Terrible enough on the face of it."

This was somewhat milder than the lurid tale I had read in the press. Therefore, far more apt to be correct. But—

"The suicide note?" I probed carefully.

"You've hit upon the nub of it. This was the note he had left upon his desk." She took a slip of paper from her bag, unfolded it, and handed it to me. I read:

"I knew there was a curse on me, though I have leave to take those manuscripts to Cairo. The monks told me the curse would work all the same. Now it has done so."

Not written in blood, perhaps, but certainly problematic.

"What are the manuscripts he speaks of?"

"No one has the slightest idea. Nor who the monks are. Have you heard of Prince Ali Kamel Fahmy Bey?"

She certainly liked to jump from one subject to another. I humored her.

"Egyptian chap, wasn't he? Created quite a stir this summer. Wife shot him, didn't she? At the Savoy. Rum business. These Orientals often let their passions run away with them."

"His wife—his widow—is French."

I might have argued that the Orient begins at Dover, but I decided on discretion. She went on. "You're familiar with the story of my uncle, Colonel Aubrey Herbert?"

I frowned. "Didn't know you had an uncle. Not that there's anything strange in that. Your having an uncle, I mean, not me not knowing about it. Although that's not strange, either, come to that. Don't really keep up with the society section."

"He was my father's half brother. He died in September."

"In Egypt?"

"In London. Of blood poisoning. As did my father."

"Bad spot of luck." No, that wasn't the right way to put it. I put a finger to my temple, trying to reorder my thoughts. "You mentioned Holmes sent you to me?"

Lady Evelyn smiled. "I don't mean to be mysterious, Doctor. Colonel Herbert and Prince Ali and Mr. Evelyn-White share a very important distinction with my late father. All four, at least according to Mr. Holmes and his spiritualist associates, were victims of the pharaoh's curse."

"Would you care for a glass of port, my lady?" I asked, for I felt myself in desperate need of a restorative at that point, and billy-be-damned if it were improper etiquette. Lady Evelyn nodded sweetly.

"Pardon me, my lady." I took up the thread, pouring with a shaky hand. "But we have already established that the prince was shot to death by his wife. How exactly did your uncle die?"

"He had every tooth in his head pulled out."

"Good Lord! Was he tortured?"

"No, he was given frightfully bad medical advice by a quack doctor. He was trying to stave off advancing blindness and was told that it could alleviate his symptoms. Instead he contracted blood poisoning."

"It sounds like criminally bad medical advice. And your father, I believe, died of an infection caused by—what was it?"

"A mosquito bite."

"Yet the great detective Sherlock Holmes looks beyond these trivial facts to the eternal wrath of a boy king buried three thousand years ago in Egypt, and cries, 'Aha! Here we have our culprit!'" I trumpeted, unable to keep the bitterness from my voice.

"Yes," agreed the girl, accepting the port from me and taking a sip, "but he is the great detective, after all, is he not?"

Was he? Was he still, in spite of the séances, the table turning, the floating ectoplasmic visions, the mediums possessed by their spirit guides, was he still Sherlock Holmes?

"Yes," I was forced to concede, "he is."

She drank her port with relish, as if she had the reassurance she had come for. But I was wrong on that count. She had come for more.

"The truth is," Lady Evelyn said, with just a hint of a tremor in her voice, "the deaths do have one other thing in common. You see, Prince Ali and Colonel Herbert both visited the pharaoh's tomb within days after it was opened, just as Evelyn-White did."

"Along with how many others? Dozens? Scores? What of Mr. Carter? Or yourself? Have you suffered any ill effects? My lady, don't tell me you believe this nonsense about a curse?"

"My brother Henry seems convinced of it. He said my father's dog Suzy at home began howling the moment my father died, three thousand miles away."

"But what do you think?" I pressed her.

"I want to know, to be frank. I want to be certain. I want someone to examine all the evidence and either put the rumors to rest or confirm them. I want your help, Doctor."

I was flattered, but not enough to lose my head. "What you want, my lady, is a detective. A proper detective, not some superannuated old army surgeon."

"I've already hired a detective. Sherlock Holmes."

I had a sudden vision of myself throttling the girl till she made some sense, but I believe I only stood there blinking. "But Holmes has already reached his verdict on these incidents!" I finally got out. It sounded like a yelp, even to me.

"Is there another detective you would recommend over Mr. Holmes in the case of a suspicious death?" she returned, unruffled.

She was going to drag it out of me. I had to admit there wasn't. Even in his sunset years, even in the fog of his spiritualist beliefs, there was no more penetrating mind than that of my old friend, at least once he was on a case.

"Mr. Holmes presumes supernatural influence. I have challenged him to investigate. He has accepted my challenge. I will accept his findings. No one could debunk Sherlock Holmes with authority but Sherlock Holmes himself."

I looked at her with new eyes. "You're a gambler, my lady," I said admiringly.

"I take after my father in that regard."

It was well-known that Lord Carnarvon had lost a fortune gambling, especially on horse racing, a fortune that had only been recouped by his marriage to Lady Evelyn's mother, Almina Wombwell, the illegitimate daughter (so it was bruited about) of the millionaire banker Alfred de Rothschild, the first Jew appointed director of the Bank of England.

"Well, then," I said. "The only question is, why have you come to me?"

"Mr. Holmes was extremely reluctant to take this commission, as you might guess. He swore he had not taken a case in twenty years, though I'm well aware of his secret work for military intelligence during the war. He tried to fob off some Belgian mountebank with a waxed moustache on me. At one point he even called himself a doddering old fool. But I persisted. Finally he agreed, on one condition.

He could do nothing, he insisted, he would not take step one, unless his old partner John Watson were by his side."

There was no hiding my astonishment. It must have been incised upon my face like glyphs on the Rosetta Stone. He had asked for me. He had demanded me! Could it be that he was somehow unaware of my barrage of censures? Or had he simply brushed them aside as unimportant?

"Well, Doctor," asked Lady Evelyn, with a smile I can only characterize as seductive, "will you help us solve the riddle of the pharaoh's curse once and for all?"

Chapter Two:
Mrs. Estelle Roberts

I kissed my beautiful girls goodbye before they left for school that morning, hugging them so tightly to my breast that they complained they could not breathe. I tried in vain to keep the tears from flowing. I felt as if I were going to the ends of the earth, never to return. I would not be long at all, I kept telling myself, a fortnight perhaps, but it was farther than I had ever dreamed of voyaging in my life. And there was Terry, the baby, with the croup. How could I leave him? Yet I knew that I must. Sacrifices had to be made.

My husband, Arthur, and I had thrashed it out repeatedly, till we were sick of hearing each other's voices. Of course, Arthur colored it as high adventure, which I suppose it was, in a certain light. He said they would be fine without me. Which did not comfort me one iota. Bea, the hired girl, would take perfectly good care of them. I agreed, quelling the anxiety in my voice. And of course Mrs. Slade was just next door. I admitted the soundness of it. But I didn't have to like it, not one bit.

I had a much shorter journey ahead of me that afternoon. The Aeolian Hall in Bond Street, where I had a long-standing invitation to perform a psychic demonstration for the Spiritualist Association. Sir Sherlock had neglected to inform me of little niggling details such as where and when I should meet my escort. He always expected me to simply know. I don't think it was because of my clairvoyance, which is anything but infallible; he always expected everyone to anticipate his needs. Little wonder he had never married.

I should have to bring my bags along with me to the demonstration. More bother. And I was feeling nervous as a cat. Arthur saw it and did his level best to calm my jitters. Dear man. He would have his hands full for two weeks, even with Bea to cook and clean and tend to the baby. He reminded me to pack for warm weather. I hadn't noticed what I was shoving into my bag until he mentioned it, and I had to unpack all my woolens. Did some of my warm-weather clothes still smell of smoke? I sniffed. Well, it couldn't be helped.

I would probably be seasick for most of the journey and confined to my cabin, anyway. No dining at the captain's table for me. Of course, we might be booked in steerage, for all I knew. For all I knew, we could be booked aboard a tramp steamer and be forced to swab the decks for our passage. But then, I was certain to be more familiar with the business end of a mop than Sir Sherlock was. He had mentioned a boat, or I might have pictured us in a camel caravan, bouncing our way across the deserts of North Africa all the way to the pyramids. I wondered how long our voyage would really take. The man was so secretive. Ah, well, all would be revealed. It was no use fretting. I fretted. Oh, it was starting to rain.

At that time I was still quite new to public exhibitions and prone to butterflies in the stomach at the best of times. But I always settled myself with the thought that my audiences were not there to hear me. They were there to hear the spirits who jostled round me. They were always eager to communicate, to be reunited with their loved ones still on this mortal shore. Nor was I the guide; that was the province of Red Cloud. I was no more than a conduit. My only mandate was to be sensitive, to be receptive, and to be honest.

It was still raining, the kind of cold, thin early-February rain that creeps into the crevices of your collar and drains into your shoes; the spirits seemed to huddle together as if for warmth. The audience was restless, with the rain pelting steadily against the roof. Mr. Penderecki held the floor; I was weary of him. He had been a morose type during his life, but now that he had crossed over, he nattered on incessantly, mostly about the haberdashery he had left behind and especially his fine cambric handkerchiefs; his wife seemed thrilled merely by the sound of his voice, or at least Red Cloud's impression thereof. The sentences drained away like dishwater. No one ever admits it, but the task of a sensitive can often be dreary. Red Cloud had not put me into a full trance; how I wished that he had! But perhaps you're not familiar with Red Cloud? He is my spirit guide, an American Indian who lived some four or five hundred years ago. No, I don't know which tribe he belonged to. Does it matter? We are all part of one tribe.

Where was I? Oh, yes. As the Pendereckis continued, a man scuffled into the back of the hall, and at the mere sight of him an electric thrill went through me—not because of his looks, for he was plain as a poker in that stolid little Englander fashion that was mercifully fading away after the war, and he was old enough to put me in mind of my father. But my skin burned in a flash fire and went icy cold at the same time. I had only experienced such a powerful emanation twice before, but I had not forgotten her, no, not for a second: Madame Louise. Though I had only encountered her twice, each time far away in the rolling meads of Sussex, there was no mistaking the commanding force of her anima. Nor was there any forgetting in whose name I had summoned her.

Madame Louise swept Mr. Penderecki aside effortlessly as royalty. She pinned my gaze to the newcomer. He had taken a seat at the back of the room, with his rain-spotted trilby pulled down to his ears as though trying to remain inconspicuous. Yet I felt drawn to him like a magnet to true north. I was compelled to move down the steps toward him. He was hardly prepossessing as I drew nearer: an old man in his sixties, with a bushy white moustache and a look of alarm in his rheumatic eyes. Not a believer, that much was obvious. What could Madame Louise want from this sad specimen?

I stopped before him.

"There is a lady named Madame Louise," I told him. "She has red hair framing a heart-shaped face and eyes grey as rain. The light from a fire flickers in her face. She speaks with a slight accent—a French accent. She wishes to speak with a doctor. His name is John ... Dr. John Watson." I looked for affirmation in his eyes.

He stiffened. Then he rose and doffed his hat. Rainwater dripped off onto the floor. "I was supposed to meet a Mrs. Roberts here. Please don't tell me you are Mrs. Roberts." He was a bluff old campaigner with the air of a professional man, but his face was tomato-red with indignation.

"Are you Dr. Watson, sir?"

"I'm Dr. John Watson, but I'm sure you knew that," he said with asperity.

"Have we met before, Dr. John Watson? Have you come seeking a loved one, perhaps your wife? Mary, is that her name?"

He stepped back as if I had struck him. I had hurt him somehow. I immediately regretted it. He was a man of deeper feeling than I'd taken him for.

"Did Holmes tell you that? Look here, what kind of flummery is this? I came because Sherlock Holmes wired me, told me to come to this address and introduce myself to you, if you are Mrs. Roberts. I didn't expect an audience."

"Ah." I was beginning to see my way clear. All the while, she was drumming insistently at the back of my mind. I was reluctant to give up control to her. The pain when Louise took over was dreadful. Her death had not been a peaceful one.

"You could have met me in a tearoom. Did he not tell you more?" I inquired.

He took a telegram from his pocket and unfolded it. "He said you would introduce me to a woman named Louise. He said to follow this woman Louise's instructions. To the letter. Although it seems a round-about way of going at it. Don't know why he couldn't just wire instructions himself. Or have this Louise step round to my office."

"No doubt all will be made clear." I felt an upwelling of emotion, which was difficult to tamp down. She was dangerous, I remembered all too well.

"Where is this Miss Louise?" he questioned, casting about in his ignorance.

"Louise is here. She is anxious to finally meet you, Dr. Watson." Indeed, the pounding in my head was becoming intolerable. "There is a message coming through. She says that you are about to embark on a long journey. Her instructions are that you will take me with you."

His voice cracked. "This is entirely preposterous. And an unsuitable request. By the ring on your finger, I take it you're a married woman, are you not?"

This evoked a salacious titter from the crowd.

"She says we are to leave here and go straight to Victoria Station. I hope you mean to take me somewhere warm. I haven't packed for cold weather."

"I know no one named Louise. Who is she? Where is she?"

"She is a spirit, one who knows you quite well, though you don't know her."

"Oh, a bit of hocus-pocus, is it? She seems quite high-handed for a dead person. What happens next? Do you go into a trance? Levitate? What humiliation does Holmes have in store for me? I should just go home." He plumped his hat back on his head.

"Sometimes I do go into a trance. But this spirit is so commanding—"

There was no holding her. She flung me aside. A film came over my eyes. I could hear my own voice, but soft and deep, with a melodious French accent, curling up my throat.

"You do not know me, John, but well do I know you. I am Madame Louise Vernet-Lecomte Holmes. You are the intimate friend of my only living son, Sherlock."

He blanched. His eyes went blank. At last, he found his voice, and he roared his anger:

"What kind of blasphemy is this? Louise Holmes has been dead these twenty-five years. Cease this playacting at once, Madam!"

"Please, I come from far away to speak with you and have little time allotted me. I know you are a skeptic. But my son is going into great danger—not merely of his life, but of his soul. He needs you by his side—at the Reichenbach Falls."

I knew nothing of the Reichenbach Falls then. I had followed little of Sir Sherlock's career before he became the great champion of the spiritualist movement. Indeed, I had only a shadowy idea at that point who this Dr. John Watson was. But I could see in his face that the Reichenbach Falls was a name of evil omen to him. I could feel the evil myself as the words passed my lips, like sharp shards of glass.

"The Reichenbach Falls! Now you've gone far too far with this game, Madam. Madam! Sherlock Holmes will never set foot upon that accursed path again."

"Need will drive him, and he will need you there. You must swear not to leave him."

Now he looked insulted. "I have already given my word to accompany him. I don't give my word lightly. I don't need all this tomfoolery to convince me. Quite the opposite."

"To Reichenbach he must go, and he will need you by his side," she said insistently.

"Yes, yes, yes! What I tell you three times is true!" he fairly spat.

I could feel her presence beginning to withdraw, like the tide drawing back from the shore. I was gasping for breath, groping for the stones on the beach. But still she said in a desperate whisper:

"Don't leave him!"

"I won't leave him," said Dr. Watson irritably, as if he were being nagged at by a tram conductor for his ticket.

"Merci. And you must take Mrs. Roberts with you."

And without another word, she had sped away like a falcon making for the distant reaches of the sky. I nearly fainted as I felt her abandon me. Dr. Watson had to reach out and steady me. My demonstration was definitely concluded for the day. I felt hollowed out. My mind was a blank. I dismissed the crowd with a wave of my hand and sank into an empty seat. Though there was much grumbling and protest, I think mainly because of the rain, the crowd slowly filed out. My course was clear.

"But this is madness!" exploded the doctor. "Yes, I was to meet a woman here named Louise, but not the Louise who burned to death twenty-five years ago."

I leaned over, my face in my hands, still trying to clear my head. "Burned? Yes, that explains the flames. Sir Sherlock never told me. I suppose I was meant to introduce you to her, and she in turn to introduce me to you. And you're to take me with you. I assume we are going on some sort of trip."

"You mean you don't know where we're supposed to go?" A vein in his forehead started to throb.

Of course, I knew perfectly well, but it wasn't my habit to share secrets with the acquaintance of a moment. How much had Sir Sherlock confided in him? Ah, but here was someone . . .

"Perhaps he can tell us," I replied.

He wheeled round to find a telegraph boy standing directly behind him with a note in his hand, as if I had conjured him out of the air. The light frosting on his overcoat and uniform cap told me the rain was turning to snow.

"Dr. John Watson?" asked the boy timidly.

Watson gave me a sidelong look, as though he suspected skulduggery on my part. "Only coincidence," I told him. I had no intention of embellishing the truth. I am a seer, but I do not lay claim to magical powers.

He read the note and took out two railway tickets. "It appears we're to meet Sherlock Holmes at Dover. That almost certainly means a trip to the continent. I hope you can pack quickly. We have little more than an hour before our train departs."

"I'm already packed. My bags are in the coatroom."

Again he gave me the look of one who has swallowed too much bilge water. But after all, there were two tickets. There was no time for further niggling. Dr. Watson still had to pack. He dashed into the street, heedless of rain or snow, while I collected my bags. Sooner than I would have credited, he had secured a taxi. He tossed my bags in the back, a trifle cavalierly, I thought. They were old valises made of canvas, and I had a horror of them splitting open and my unmentionables tumbling out. Next he handed me in and called out his address to the driver. He lived on Queen Anne Street. A medical address, though not quite Harley Street.

Apparently he had instructed the driver to go at breakneck speed. There were corners we took so sharply that I sucked in my breath, sure we would overturn like turtles. The taxi threw up walls of water on either side, leaving drenched pedestrians shaking their fists in our wake. I noticed that Dr. Watson gripped the seat with all his might, as if he feared being thrown out the window. Soon we lurched to a stop at his Queen Anne Street address. The doctor slid out with a celerity that belied his age.

I thought I would catch forty winks while he packed since I had been up early that morning packing myself, but I had hardly closed my eyes when he returned with his bags. I've since educated myself on their exploits and learned how often he and Sir Sherlock had stuffed their valises with the necessities and galloped to the station. He was an old hand at packing at a moment's notice.

And in fact, he seemed to relax among the crowds of the railway station, as though the coal soot were a tonic to him, the clouds of steam were a spring shower, and the din of humanity a lullaby. Once we were boarded in our compartment and properly situated, he kept his eyes glued to the window like a ten-year-old boy on his first train trip. Or perhaps he was simply avoiding meeting my eyes. He seemed a bit shy, which I found oddly charming.

But my nerves were still burning after my encounter with Louise. I recalled the first time I had been confronted with her personality. I had been invited to Sir Sherlock's villa in Sussex, a great honor for such a novice medium as I was. She was so powerful I nearly drowned in her. What I hadn't known was that she had never appeared to him before, though some of the greatest sensitives of the age were put to the test. He was grateful beyond words, and we bonded immediately. He was a remarkable man.

And yet this man, who Madame Louise had pronounced Sir Sherlock's intimate friend? Ordinary enough. Yet even in the awkwardness of our silence I could sense something comforting about the doctor, something solid. I could see perhaps why Sir Sherlock wanted him by his side. They were alike somehow. Not that he was sharp-edged and alarming in the way of Sir Sherlock, but he was protective and solicitous—a very parfait knight, as they used to say. That was what they had in common, I guessed.

The rain cleared and the moon rose. I began a letter to my husband briefly sketching out the events of the afternoon. I missed him terribly already, even as I looked forward on tenterhooks to the journey.

As the hours ticked by, Dr. Watson became restless, again like a little boy. I suggested he take a stroll down the aisle. (I might have suggested dinner, for I felt a sudden growl in my stomach, but I'm sure he would have felt himself obliged to pay. I had no wish to impose upon him.) He seemed immediately released by my words. I think he had felt responsible for me, as though I were a package he was delivering to Sir Sherlock. I confess I felt something of the same. And I could not help but sense we were going into danger, and it would take all our talents to defeat it—if we could.

Chapter Three:
Dr. John Watson

———— ◆◆◆ ————

The cold air in the passage hit my face, rousing me from my torpor. I made my way toward the observation car. I will admit Mrs. Estelle Roberts had set me on edge with all her chicanery. Why all these ludicrous attempts to convince me of her powers? What would be her next trick? Did she have a deck of marked cards? And then there was her constant cold-eyed stare, as though trying to examine my insides. I wondered how far she would accompany us; indeed, how far would we go. Surely not—

"Well, what do you think, Watson?"

I turned slowly. I was floored. It was him. His hair was thinning and what there was had turned snow-white. A pair of rimless glasses was perched upon his nose. One almost expected him to tear off his disguise and reveal the Sherlock Holmes of forty years ago. Yet he had the same hawkish profile and fierce, concentrated gaze.

"Holmes! Where did you get on?" I cried.

"London."

"What? What farce is this now? I've had enough—" And indeed my temper was boiling over. I perceived that I was being treated shabbily.

"I wanted you to get to know Mrs. Roberts on your own. A charming woman, is she not?" he asked lightly.

"Why on earth did you saddle me with her?"

"She's magnificent. Psychic, medium, clairvoyant, clairaudient, healer, psychometrist—there's nothing she can't do."

"A mountebank, like all the others. When will you drop this nonsense? How far must we drag her along?"

"All the way."

"All the way to where, for God's sake?"

"Didn't I tell you? All the way to Luxor."

"Luxor, Egypt?" I asked, incredulous.

"Of course. Where the curse originated," he stated matter-of-factly. "The tomb of Tutankhamun."

"But . . . but no one died in Luxor. Most of your victims seem to have shuffled off this mortal coil right here in merry old England. Have you interviewed Lady Almina? Or Princess Marguerite? Wouldn't that be much the simpler course? We certainly know how Prince Ali died, however the jury cocked up the verdict."

Had I mentioned that Princess Marguerite had been acquitted of murdering her husband, even though she had certainly done the deed? You probably remember the case as well as I do—fraught with improprieties from the defense, including counsel pointing a gun at the jury, which the court let fly by as if it were the Gloucester cheese roll.

"Idle minds are the devil's playthings, and we are hemmed in by devils. The lady Almina has wed that scoundrel Colonel Dennistoun before her husband is cold in the grave and has no time for anyone else. As for Princess Marguerite, she played me like a concert grand. She'll get her comeuppance eventually, but for now she is inviolate."

This was a remarkable admission coming from him, who had always been able to enlist the ladies to his cause without ever becoming entangled with one. Well, those sleepy bedroom eyes, full lips—how old was the princess? Probably thirty? And Irene Adler would be sixty by now if she had lived. There was more than a passing resemblance. Yes, it could be. Stranger things had happened.

But to the matter at hand. "Thus we journey three thousand miles or more to a barren desert, where no one at all has died, save the savage natives forced to subsist there?" I was still out of sorts.

"No, no one died there, but the one commonality the victims share is that they were all at the tomb of Tutankhamun shortly after it first was opened. And that 'land of savages' you imagine is the cradle of civilization."

"But there have been hundreds of visitors to the site."

"Which is precisely why we must find out why these particular victims were cursed. What did they do at the tomb that set them apart for punishment?"

"Holmes, I beg of you—"

"Did my mother not speak to you?"

"No. Your Mrs. Roberts put on a very bad French accent and tried to frighten me."

"She's superb, isn't she?"

He wasn't listening to a word I said. "Holmes, what if the deaths were merely coincidence?"

"I can countenance coincidence up to a point. But three people have already died. You don't call that coincidence."

"I can certainly call it coincidence before I call it the curse of some moldering pharaoh," I persisted.

"And there was the death of the canary."

"What, some tattletale?" This was a story I hadn't heard.

"Carter, the archaeologist in charge of the dig, owned a canary—a marvelous singer by all accounts. The workmen all considered her a lucky omen. On the very day he first opened the tomb, a cobra slithered its way into his house and killed the bird in its cage."

"The pharaoh revenging himself on a canary bird!" I chortled.

"The cobra, as I'm sure you know, is a symbol of protection for pharaohs. Four cobras bearing four suns crown his forehead. The *uraeus*, I believe it's called."

"Really," I stated flatly, never in my life having heard of a *uraeus*. "Well, I suppose that proves it."

"Excellent. Your obdurate skepticism is exactly why I need you. Hold tight to it."

He was infuriating. "And why do you need her? Her gullibility?"

"If you like. Come, let's go find her. Mrs. Roberts's talents will be indispensable."

"In that case, what do you need *me* for?"

"My dear Watson. For what purpose does the flame need the flint?"

At least he had not run out of cryptic aphorisms. I tried to brush that one aside and put a cheerful slant on the affair.

"Well, we won't need a fire in Egypt, if it's as hot as they say. And I have always wanted to visit the pyramids."

"Do not speak so glibly, my friend. We're not embarked on a holiday. Egypt is on a knife edge, fraught with danger. The fall of the Ottomans has made that whole part of the world a tinderbox."

"The military is still in control, is it not? Old Allenby still at the tiller?" I asked.

"The Egyptians believe they've gained independence under the new treaty."

"But they haven't really, have they?"

"Of course not. Which they are just coming to grips with. And when they do, there'll be blood watering the sand," he declared ominously.

"It's nothing to do with our little errand," I said, looking for assurance.

"I wouldn't be so confident of that. Tutankhamun's tomb is opened, and straight off all of Egypt is a powder keg? His influence lies everywhere on the land of the Nile."

"You make Tutankhamun sound as dangerous as Moriarty."

"Moriarty's spirit is more malevolent, but Tutankhamun's power is the more pervasive."

"Moriarty's spirit? Have you been in touch with him, too?" I lifted an eyebrow.

"He is never far from my thoughts."

Were his teeth chattering? It was then I noticed the bluish cast of his complexion. Here we were on an open platform in February with the wind whipping about at a good fifty miles an hour. I have always been a warm-blooded man, and was well upholstered against the wind to boot, but not so my companion, whose hands were stuffed into his ulster. I led the way back to our carriage, eager to see the lady's face when I sprang Holmes on her unawares.

I was disappointed.

"Sir Sherlock, how wonderful to see you." She didn't blink as she glanced up from her letter writing to greet him. She didn't bother to ask where he had joined the train. Her face was at any rate not one for betraying surprise: with deep-set eyes, a sharp nose, and prominent cheekbones, framed by close-cropped black curls, she was the model of the mysterious woman, giving nothing away—not that I had ever been especially proficient at reading women. Had she known all along that Holmes was on the train? Probably. Certainly. They had arranged this little play between them. This was her deck of marked cards.

Holmes asked after her health.

"I'm afraid I may have picked up a head cold dashing about in the rain. It will definitely be a welcome change going from the London downpour to the warm Luxor sun."

Holmes offered her no dire warnings about Egyptian blood. She'd led me to believe she had no knowledge of our destination, though I will admit as the days went by it would become obvious that she had packed for the warm weather—as I had not. I thought uncomfortably of my woolen suits and, worse, my woolen underclothes.

"This time of year in Egypt is fairly moderate," remarked Holmes, probably sensing my discomfort. If there were a mind reader aboard, it was Holmes.

And was she really going to call him "Sir Sherlock"? He had been knighted after the war for services rendered to his country, though those services were secret, and he always claimed that it was for championing the spiritualist cause. He swore he had facilitated a séance in which the king received invaluable advice from Queen Victoria.

I could only pray he was joking. I remember the king intoning his name, "Sherlock Dantes Holmes," at his investiture while touching his shoulders with the blade. No one noticed me wipe away a tear with my sleeve. I fancy "Dantes" came from some French relation. I still called him "Holmes" and always would. I doubt he would have called me "Sir John" if our roles had been reversed.

"I can't believe we are going to Luxor to explore the tomb of Tutankhamun. My husband is eaten up with jealousy. He's read every word the papers have printed about it," Mrs. Roberts said.

"I could hardly invite your husband and children along. I shall need your undivided attention to the task."

"You will have it, of course," she replied brightly.

I had already noted that she was a married woman but had given little thought to her responsibilities therein. Now there were children to be considered as well? "Of course?" That was all she had to say? She had simply abandoned her children for a fortnight's holiday? She must be wedded to a truly understanding, not to mention long-suffering, husband. Of course, there were many times I'd left Mary alone when Holmes needed me to traverse afield at a moment's notice on some dangerous affair, and she never complained. But I was, after all, a man.

I fell into tender remembrances of Mary, which I would not share, even with my faithful readers, for the world. Holmes and Mrs. Roberts occupied themselves with shoptalk, if spiritualists can be said to talk shop.

It was nearing one, and all of us were drowsing, when we arrived at Dover to board the channel ferry at the Marine Docks. It seemed almost like old times, the ocean spray crusting our faces as we stepped out of the station, crowding onto the ice-caked Admiralty Pier, the heavy fog muffling our tread, save that this time the apricot scent and swirling skirts of Mrs. Roberts intruded. Strange that I still remember her scent after all this time. If she was at all disquieted about abandoning husband and children, she did not show it. She seemed wrapped in serenity as securely as in her burgundy duster.

Once we were settled in for our crossing, Mrs. Roberts produced some knitting from her bag. I wished she had introduced it earlier, for the endless clacking of her needles had me so drowsy so that I soon fell fast asleep—only to wake with a start, groggy and bleary-eyed, some three hours later to the garbled sounds of a loudspeaker in French and English (or it may have been Swahili for all I could make of it), announcing our imminent arrival in Calais. In response the passengers were slowly shifting, like stone made flesh, gathering their belongings about them.

Mrs. Roberts was asleep—those unsettling eyes closed, her mouth slightly open, looking vulnerable as a child, her knitting resting upon her lap. "Sleep, that knits up the raveled sleeve of care" inevitably passed through my mind.

I daresay Holmes had not slept at all. Though he had removed his spectacles, his eyes seemed turned inward upon himself, searching for answers to questions I would not even think to ask, as I had seen him do many times in our youth. We all do with less sleep at our age, just at the point in our lives when we have fewer concerns to fill our waking hours. Besides, Holmes had long ago trained himself to go for days on end without sleep.

Still, I think we were all bone-tired when we shuffled down the gangway into a grey mist to await the continental train at Calais. It was mere steps to the station, the Gare Maritime, but they were slow steps with the crowd around us gawking—as if Calais had any sights whatever to boast of, even in the daytime. At this time of the morning there were only inquisitive dock lamps frowning down on unfriendly, crouching buildings.

"France doesn't look very much different from England," observed the lady, looking about forlornly.

"Calais was actually built by the British, back in the 1300s. It never seems to have lost its English accent," said Holmes.

"It'll look different when we reach gay Paree," I assured her.

"When will that be?" she wondered, stifling a yawn.

"Our train leaves at one," Holmes informed us.

"One o'clock!" I groaned in dismay. It had just turned five in the morning by my watch. The sun would not venture forth for another two hours if it decided to make an appearance at all. "Surely there must be an earlier train."

"I think you'll find the wait worthwhile."

"I think we're all dead on our feet and would rather take the first train running," I complained.

"Perhaps, but I have business to attend to here. Personal business." His face was set in stone, unreadable.

"What? Whom do you know in Calais?" I grumbled mutinously.

"An old friend. No need to concern yourself with the matter. The fog should lift by nine, and then you may glory in the sight of the white cliffs of Dover, Mrs. Roberts."

"And what shall we do in the meantime?" I wailed, put out by the entire arrangement.

"The Chatham has just added a restaurant, I understand. Also there is a lounge, and a reading room. Even a casino if you'd like to take a flutter. It should be very much to your liking. Almost the entire staff speaks English as perfectly as Oxfordians. Should you require anything, ask for Edgerton. He knows me of old."

Well, there was nothing to say to that, although the lady needed constant reassurance that her luggage would be transferred to the correct train. She seemed to have heard tales of hatboxes winding up in China and having to be ransomed. But the mists looked to want to increase to a drizzle, so we parted with Holmes and hurried our way up the dark, still street to the Chatham, a quarter mile distant along the coast. At least it was a well-lit, cheery-looking target.

We decided to try the restaurant, although the lady had misgivings as to French cooking. I myself looked forward to a galette complete, a sort of pie filled with egg, ham, and cheese that I had read about. But my courage failed me, and we both ordered English breakfast, with tea. One would never have known we'd left London behind. We ate in a dead silence that became increasingly awkward.

Finally, Mrs. Roberts looked up from her meal (and there was nothing ethereal about her appetite) and said plainly, "You'd like to ask me a question."

I don't suppose it required any extraordinary powers to divine that.

"Perhaps one or two," I replied cautiously.

"Ask. I'll answer."

Her curt tone sounded so much like a gypsy fortune teller that I wondered if she expected me to cross her palm with silver.

"Well . . . how did you get into this line of work? Mediuming, that is. Mediumship. How long have you been at it?"

"Only a couple of years. If you mean public readings, that is."

"Did you study with someone?"

Mrs. Roberts laughed.

"I'm sorry, have I asked an untoward question?"

"There are many paths. I heard the voices of those who have passed over from a very young age. I learned to hide my abilities, because no one would believe me. It was three years ago when I attended my first spiritualist meeting and met Mrs. Elizabeth Cannock, who told me I was chosen by the spirit world. Once I was convinced, Red Cloud sought me out."

"Red Cloud? Is that a spiritualist organization? Or congregation?"

She smiled at this. "He is my spirit guide. An American Indian."

"Oh—you mean he's—"

"Passed over, yes."

"What, uh, what tribe was he with? Or is he with?"

"He does not speak of his past. 'Know me by my works,' he tells me."

"Didn't Jesus Christ say something of the sort?"

"Perhaps. Perhaps he heard it from Red Cloud."

I laughed heartily at this, until I realized she was serious. Her eyes bored into mine. The conversation once again became awkward.

"And you really think the pharaoh's tomb is cursed?" I said delicately.

"I'm certain of it. Any time an ancient Egyptian relic is disturbed, someone ends up paying. You have only to look at Cleopatra's Needle to be convinced."

"What, the obelisk on the Victoria Embankment? That's been there fifty years or more," I pointed out.

"And in that time it's seen more suicides than any other spot in London. There's talk of a dogheaded man who haunts it. There's your real Jack the Ripper," she declared. "It should be returned to Cairo without delay."

I could see this trip was going to be excruciating.

I passed the rest of my time in the reading room, luxuriating in all the English newspapers. The weather having cleared, as Holmes had predicted, Mrs. Roberts elected to go for a walk along the shore, taking in the white cliffs, dodging the sea gulls, and no doubt freezing her toes off.

We were to meet Holmes at the Gare Maritime for luncheon. He was already waiting for us in the canteen. The smile etched on his face meant he had secrets he was hoping we'd try to winkle out of him. If there was one language I could read perfectly well, it was that of Holmes's facial expressions. I was little in the mood for such games unless he had solved the case and we could return home. None of us ate much. I had a *croque monsieur* and pretended it was a galette complete.

But when it came time to board the train, I will admit my day brightened considerably.

"The blue train!" I exclaimed when it came into view, the cars all glistening blue with gold trim like an admiral of the fleet. "You cannot be serious, Holmes." *Le train bleu* was only the most luxurious form of transport on the continent. It was known as the millionaires' train. None of us were millionaires, I was fairly sure.

"I'm not certain that Lady Evelyn knows there are any other means of accommodation available," Holmes posited.

"Remind me not to tell her."

Even for Lady Evelyn, it seemed an outsize order. From what I'd been led to understand, the blue train was sold out sometimes months in advance, and February must be the height of the Mediterranean tourist season. Exclusively first-class, white-gloved stewards, and cordon bleu dining. If this were a foretaste of our journey, I might be able to overlook any ancient curses.

"Well, I suppose we'll have to forgive a few hours' delay." I finally gave in and inquired of Holmes how his meeting had gone, but he only nodded and his mouth went up at the corners a trace. Secrets were worth more to him than pounds sterling.

We boarded. The lady was agog (as was I, I'll admit) at the appointments, luxuriant blue velvet upholstery trimmed in mahogany, beds to sink into forever, stewards all in blue and gold, with entire banks of gold buttons winking across their chests. Then, once the train started, it was as silent as if we were flying. I've always had a fondness for trains of every kind, but if all trains were like the blue train, I should spend my days simply riding back and forth across the continent, at peace with the world.

Of course, this train could hardly carry us all the way to Luxor, more's the pity. We would wake in the morning to disembark at Marseille, and board a steamer that would carry us to Alexandria. Even if it were as luxurious as the train, it would yet be tedious, and the rocking of the sea would do terrible things to my insides. And Alexandria, from what I had heard, made Calais look like paradise. From there we would make our way to Luxor—hopefully by train and not by camel. We had many weary days in each other's company ahead of us. Was I already regretting my promise to Lady Evelyn? There was no turning back.

I was looking forward most to the sleeping car on this leg of the journey. But I had promised to join the others for dinner, and certainly the prospect of a full five-course dinner with the Selle de Veau Orloff was alluring, if I could just keep from falling asleep with my face down in the oeufs frites Catalan.

"How many hours to Marseille? When does the ship depart?" I asked, once we had given the waiter our orders and toasted each other with real French champagne.

"We are not taking the ship at Marseille," said Holmes.

"What? Aren't we going to Luxor?"

"Indeed, but first we must proceed to Monte Carlo, where my lady and her newly minted husband await us."

"What? They're accompanying us? Why, for heaven's sake?" I protested.

"Be sure that we would get nowhere near Tutankhamun but for the good graces of my lady. My understanding is that Carter is a touchy subject and takes a dim view of our project."

Well, I certainly couldn't blame Carter for that. I took a dim view myself.

"Why are they waiting for us in Monte Carlo and not, say, Cairo?" I asked.

"My lady does not want the press to get wind of our expedition. She is ostensibly on her honeymoon in Monaco."

"And where then? Rome? Venice? The grand tour?" The champagne had somewhat restored my good humor.

"My lady has not shared her itinerary with me. We shall accompany them no farther than Luxor. But she does not want her visit to Egypt bruited about. Remember that."

"As soon as she boards the boat to Alexandria she'll be recognized," objected Mrs. Roberts.

"She has an aeroplane waiting for us in Monte Carlo. We shall be whisked from thence to Cairo in an instant, in complete secrecy."

This news made me slightly apprehensive. As one went farther east, the planes were rarely maintained, and the pilots very rarely adequately trained. Or so I had heard.

As soon as the consommé du volaille aux something-or-other came, I fell to, rather greedily. Of course I hardly knew what I was eating as we marched through the dishes. I kept hoping Mrs. Roberts would ask Holmes or the waiter, but she never did. I can say this: it was glorious, whatever it was. And glorious, too, was the French countryside passing by the window, with the sun slowly melting like butter all over the green horizon. Not that the English countryside wasn't every bit as glorious, but it was a bit mildewed at that time of year.

But it was not only fresh strawberries and the view of the rolling

French pastures that was on the menu. I was about to bear witness to Mrs. Roberts's sleight of hand at its most ingenious.

I was just wondering where I was going to put the Charlotte Russe when our tranquility was invaded by the approach of a stranger, a big fellow with a broad, open face and a toothy smile that put me in mind of an American—or a huckster. So has my association with Sherlock Holmes bent my mind toward mistrust. He stopped short right in front of us. As it turned out, he was not an American.

"Sherlock Holmes! You are Mr. Holmes, aren't you? Or Sir Sherlock, I should say."

So it still happened. He still had fans who recognized him. Sometimes he cursed me for his notoriety and cursed my stories in the *Strand* as the cause of it. But his eyes always lit up at these encounters.

This, however, was no ordinary fan, I'm sorry to say.

"I'm Geoffrey Hodson!" he practically bellowed.

This pronouncement had an immediate effect on both Holmes and Mrs. Roberts, although Holmes seemed far more enthusiastic than the lady. I was completely in the dark.

"Of course, I should have known you from your picture! This is quite the fortuitous occasion! I would never have expected to find you here," said Holmes.

"Do you know Gerald Murphy? No? Awfully good chap," Hodson said, as if he had just scored one for the team. "American, but trying to live it down. I've been invited to his place in Antibes to give a lecture to some of his friends. Cole Porter, Scott Fitzgerald, Picasso . . . ."

"Anyone I would have heard of?" asked Holmes.

The fellow seemed to have had some wind taken out of his sails but recovered himself. "Well, and of course there's the sun and the sea."

"What do you have to do with those? Are there fairies?"

At this point I was quite sure Holmes had gone mad. Alas, I was only a little wrong on that score. It would prove to be the case that I was the only sane one of the group.

The fellow Hodson stuttered, "No . . . you go there to swim in the sea and lie in the sun. Get tanned."

"It sounds like a perfectly good way to acquire sunstroke," said Holmes with some disparagement.

"Yes . . . well . . . what about yourself? A speaking engagement somewhere?"

"Something of a more confidential nature," Holmes replied with his usual tight smile.

"What an amazing coincidence running into you like this." Hodson was apparently trying to start the conversation over. Of course, this meeting would prove no coincidence at all.

"Hodson, this is my longtime associate Dr. Watson, and the lady is the renowned medium Mrs. Estelle Roberts."

The fellow gave me a glance before his eyes came to linger on Mrs. Roberts.

"I'm gratified to make your acquaintance," said Hodson, taking the lady's hand. For a moment I thought he might kiss it continental style, but she withdrew it before he could follow through on the threat.

"Mr. Hodson is perhaps the foremost authority on the fairy phenomenon," said Holmes.

"Yes, I've read your book," said Mrs. Roberts.

Mr. Hodson, I was to learn, had authored a book called *Fairies at Work and at Play*. Yes, that was really the title. You are forgiven if you are not familiar with it. I myself, to this day, am not familiar with it.

"His chapter on the Cottingley fairies is particularly illuminating," Holmes said.

Oh, God, not the Cottingley fairies again. I thought that had died its natural death. Fairies! The man who was once known as the sharpest mind in England was now known for his championing of fairies—fairies, needless to say, on which he had never set eyes himself. I'm afraid my cheeks went red with shame.

Holmes had no such shame. "Where would you say fairies in England are most plentiful?" he asked matter-of-factly, as if we were discussing the best climate for vegetable marrows. I wondered whether the two little girls who had taken photos of the fairies had been invited to talk to Gerald Murphy's celebrated guests.

"Well, I've toured England quite extensively in search of fairies, as you're aware, together with my wife, Jane. I would have to say the Cotswolds trump any other both for number and variety."

"Ah, yes, the Cotswolds, they do seem to congregate there," Holmes agreed.

Moths. Moths congregate in the Cotswolds. I must have made a face.

"I see someone is not a believer," tsked Hodson, earning my ire twice over.

I cleared my throat. "Tiny little supernatural beings frolicking at the bottom of the garden are simply not my cup of tea."

"Oh, but they're not supernatural. They're entirely natural. And they are not all tiny," responded Hodson.

"I've never seen one, in point of fact. But you'll say they're shy, I suspect."

"Not in the least, though they exhibit little interest in our human world. But one must train oneself to see them. They operate at much higher frequencies than we are accustomed to."

"What, like hummingbirds?" I asked, goading him.

"A very apt analogy. Or dog whistles. Would you deny the existence of sounds at higher frequencies than our ears are attuned to?" he asked, shooting his cuffs. "It's the same with our vision."

I sighed. Once again I had allowed myself to be dragged into one of these ridiculous, exasperating conversations that had so strained my friendship with Holmes. But I noticed something unexpected. Mrs. Roberts looked as unimpressed as I. Was there a rift here I could exploit?

"What do you think, Mrs. Roberts?" I asked, hitting the ball to her. "Are there fairies on the other side of the great divide?"

She was slow to answer. All three of us were staring at her. "There are nature spirits. I have never been in contact with one. But that doesn't mean—"

I followed up quickly. "Why not have a go at it?" I said. "Between your talents as a medium and the gentleman's remarkable eye for spying out fairies . . ."

"Why, Watson, what a tremendous idea!" said Holmes. "This is exactly the pair to pull it off."

Mrs. Roberts, for her part, now seemed nervous as a rabbit, searching for a politic answer. But before she could think how to worm her way out, Hodson chimed in. "Capital idea! Shall we say midnight? I've always found the fairy folk to be most active at the witching hour."

I think that was when I lost my taste for Charlotte Russe.

Chapter Four:
Mrs. Estelle Roberts

I had never seen a fairy before and was, frankly, skeptical. But Sir Sherlock seemed animated by the idea. As for Dr. Watson, he had attended to most of Mr. Hodson's little dissertation with his head in his hands. But he popped up with such a cunning look in his eye when he made his suggestion, his manner so unlike himself—at least as he had presented himself—that I had to wonder what he had in mind. Skeptics are always trying to trip me up.

The doctor swiveled back toward me. "Have you never spoken to fairies before?" he demanded.

I repeated, rather sharply, that I had not. I don't like being badgered.

"But you're a clairvoyant, like Mr. Hodson, are you not?" he continued.

"I'm confident she's up to the challenge. Her powers are phenomenal," said Sir Sherlock.

I was, you'll agree, in a tight corner. Different sensitives are attuned to different vibrations. Fairies might simply not be on my harmonic. I was reluctant to give in to the request, but now all three men seemed thrilled by the idea; there was no graceful means of backing out. A moving train far from the seat of my power was hardly the ideal setting for attempting such an unusual séance. But as I suspected Dr. Watson of wanting to embarrass me, I found myself keen to display my prowess. Besides, if my abilities should prove themselves diminished here, of what use would they avail me in faraway Egypt? I found myself agreeing reluctantly, to the delight of Sir Sherlock and, I suspected, the secret joy of Dr. Watson.

We agreed to meet at midnight, though for my part I ascribed no special merit to that time or any other. I would simply be sleepier. In fact, I did try to nap. When nothing came of that, I ordered a pot of chamomile and resumed my letters, which, at the rate I was plodding along, I was afraid I would never finish.

We met that night in Mr. Hodson's compartment. To my surprise, we were greeted by Mrs. Hodson. He hadn't even mentioned that his wife was on the train with him. I was relieved to have a friendly woman's eyes to gaze into. More, it would mean no more oh-so-genteel kissing on the hand or, worse, kissing on the cheek. Hodson was positively distant with me in her company.

He did not introduce her, so we introduced ourselves. The lady's name was Jane. Where he was expansive, she was contained, with brown skin and boyish bobbed hair, which was the style that season. She put me in mind of one of the brownies I'd read about in Hodson's book, or perhaps it was Peter Pan. Oh, so many races of fairies in his world! Elves and gnomes and undines and sylphs and devas, all with their peculiar manifestations and rituals. His book was frankly quite maddening, although the girls enjoyed it, especially Ivy.

"But do fairies die?" Dr. Watson started in, out of nowhere, as we were assembling. Oh, now he was cooling to the idea? He probably just wanted his bed. He hid a yawn behind his sleeve.

"Death has no meaning for such creatures. The question is whether they can penetrate to the other side and what their purpose may be for making such a crossing in the first place." There, I'd staved him off with a confident-sounding answer. Just at the moment I was more concerned with whether Red Cloud would even deign to make his appearance in such an unfamiliar and possibly hostile atmosphere. He is a sensitive soul.

Hodson had us sit around a tiny table in the middle of their compartment, our knees practically knocking together. Utterly unnecessary, but I didn't like to spar with him.

"You work through a spirit guide of some sort?" Mrs. Hodson wanted to know.

"Red Cloud."

"Another American Indian, eh? They seem popular this year." Hodson grinned as if amused. I did not care for his insinuation. Not at all. A man who wrote about fairies!

Mr. Hodson had scared up candles from somewhere. He closed the curtains tight and turned down the lights while his wife lit the candles. I must admit that the clack of the rails and the wavering of the candles set a certain sonorous rhythm, which was actually meditative. I took a deep breath. Our hands found each other's round the table.

"Red Cloud? Are you near? Do you hear me?"

There was nothing, no sensation. I felt a wave of panic rattle through me.

"Come to me. I am far from home." My voice was trembling. I had to take a breath. I opened my eyes. Everyone was staring at me expectantly, Hodson eyeing me almost hungrily.

Then Dr. Watson winked at me. It was such an unexpected gesture that I nearly laughed out loud. I felt a familiar warmth tingle through me, a lightheadedness. It felt just the same as if I were in the heart of London. My pulse slowed. I was ready for whatever came next—I thought.

"Good evening, Estelle," I heard my voice saying, an octave lower in pitch. Red Cloud had taken up residence. "You are indeed far from home. But I am not." Red Cloud had always exhibited a puckish sense of humor.

"Yes, Red Cloud, I am traveling to Egypt." As soon as I said it, I remembered Sir Sherlock did not want our destination disclosed. I was still a bit nervy.

"For what purpose have you summoned me tonight?"

"This is Mr. Hodson. He wants to contact someone."

"What is the name of the person you wish to contact?"

"A fairy," I added hesitantly.

"What is the name?" returned Red Cloud without a moment's qualm, as if it were the most ordinary request in the world. Perhaps it was?

"A name, please, Mr. Hodson?" My gaze fell on the man. He looked befuddled.

"Can't you simply . . . ask for a fairy?" he fudged. There was the trace of a whine in his voice.

"How many fairies are there?" I asked patiently.

"The fact is, I'm not sure they have individual names," he said. "I've never spoken to one. I'm not certain that they do speak."

This appeared to rouse Dr. Watson's aggravation. "How do you expect to communicate with them if they can't speak?" His sentiment chimed with mine.

"Well, don't they knock on walls and such?"

Jane Hodson spoke up abruptly. "Winnie," she said. Her husband cast a confused look her way.

"The brownie who lives in the kitchen cupboard," she explained.

"You have spoken with it?" asked Sir Sherlock, who had been silent up to this point.

"I've spoken to it. I named it Winnie. It seems to like the name." She blushed prettily at the attention she drew.

"Well, then. Winnie," I said, addressing Red Cloud. Splendid that it was a brownie, I thought. I recalled from Hodson's book that they were domestic creatures, more or less tame.

I could feel Red Cloud spreading out in all directions, searching the etheric.

"Look!" hissed Hodson. I opened my eyes to lights—small lights, dancing on the walls. Fairies? But Red Cloud was still searching. Could they have been called simply by uttering the one name? I could sense no consciousness in them, no guiding force. They were only . . . lights.

"Behold the fairies in their true form, prior to taking on their thought forms," Hodson said in that sermonizing tone. "Now one is changing, taking on the form of a manikin."

"I see nothing but little lights," said Dr. Watson.

"You are not attuned to their frequency," snapped Hodson.

"Perhaps you'd best describe him, dearest," admonished Jane softly.

"Oh, well then—he is about fourteen inches tall, raw red face and hands, beady eyes, sheathed all in green. Ah, now here's a brownie with the face of an aged man, a long beard nearly down to his bare toes, a tall conical hat on his head—and, yes, he has a fairy with him!"

He drew a deep breath. His wife was tense by his side.

"The fairy is a female, dressed in white, or pink—"

Wait, was I seeing it? I could almost anticipate what he would say next—

"... a clinging, sheeny material, fine textured—"

Then I recalled it—Ivy reading to me by the firelight, from Hodson's book:

> ... dressed in a white, or very pale pink, clinging, sheeny material of exceedingly fine texture ...

"... drawn in at the waist and shining like mother of pearl. The wings are oval," he continued, his voice thrumming. He was quoting himself, from his book! It was all a patter! Was Jane a part of it, too? What were they up to? I felt like flinging the woman's hand away! Just at that moment, unexpected words formed on my lips:

"Jane? Geoffrey?" My voice was treble, slightly hoarse, and trembling like a leaf.

"Who speaks?" demanded Sir Sherlock.

"I am Winnie," answered the voice.

There was a hush all around the table.

"Speak to her," I coaxed.

"Yes, Winnie, we're here," murmured Jane.

"Winnie," said her husband cutting in, "what is my mother's name?"

Of course, the bully *would* try to test me. "Constance," Winnie answered flatly.

He smiled sheepishly. I decided to ask it a question myself. "How did you get the name Winnie?"

"Winifred was Jane's great friend in childhood. She died in 1911."

"That's true," said Jane, sounding exultant but a bit scared.

"Would you like to speak with her?" Winnie asked amiably.

"No . . . no, thank you," stammered Jane, flustered.

We had established Winnie's bona fides to both their satisfactions.

"You are not at home. I've searched for you," Winnie's voice said accusingly.

"No, we're on a trip," Jane answered gently.

"To find more fairies?"

"Are there fairies in the south of France?" Hodson smirked. He thought I was as much a fraud as he.

"Coco will be there," Winnie shot back.

"No. You're mistaken," said Hodson hurriedly.

"I do not mistake. Coco is there now."

Jane cast a swift, furious glance at her husband. "You told me positively she would not be there."

Sweat broke out on his forehead. "Not positively. I mean, you never know who'll turn up at the Murphys'. She said she would be at Cannes—"

He realized he'd said too much.

"You've spoken with her," Jane concluded.

"You should not go," Winnie contended. The brownie was evidently intent on making mischief. Or perhaps shielding against it? Who could know a fairy's purpose?

"You made a fool of yourself over her the last time," Jane reproached.

"I didn't—"the protest began.

"You should come home," Winnie said insistently.

"Were we really invited?" Jane demanded to know.

"I told you, I misplaced the invitation. Gerald and Sara are expecting us. You like them."

"I don't like the people who hang around them. Bohemian poseurs. I want to go home." She was suddenly miserable.

"You should come home," repeated Winnie implacably.

The lights had disappeared. Jane stood abruptly and bolted from the compartment.

Instead of following her at once, Hodson had the gall to ask, "Does Coco want me to come?"

I had had enough. I shut myself off from all voices—one of the first defenses a medium learns. I wanted to disappear from this world as well. "Mr. Hodson"—I swallowed a sob—"go find your wife. Beg her forgiveness. Forget Antibes. Go home."

"It's not that I have any great feelings for Coco—"

"Please, just go!" I put my face in my hands, exhausted.

The big man looked uncertainly at Holmes, who nodded and waved him toward the door. He shuffled out.

"I'm sorry," I said, trying to keep the tears from my voice.

"What on earth for?" Sir Sherlock said. "You did exactly as he asked and told him precisely what he needed to hear. I expected some such denouement when I observed his cavalier treatment of his help-meet."

It did my sense of self-worth no good to hear that Sir Sherlock had anticipated logically what it took Red Cloud to lay out before me. I could be sure I hadn't impressed Dr. Watson, who was looking at me askance.

"Who's Coco?" he asked of no one in particular. Sir Sherlock shrugged.

"Coco Chanel. A Parisian couturiere," I supplied.

"Never heard of her," he said gruffly.

"She has a reputation." I did not add that her reputation was borne as much on her many love affairs as her dress creations. I drew myself up, trying to look dignified.

Dr. Watson opened the curtains, which restored an air of normality to the room, though the candles still guttered, refusing to give up. No words were spoken.

"Good night, gentlemen," I said dully, leading the way out of the compartment. Where the Hodsons had vanished to, I had no idea. I felt as terrible as if I had done injury to my own marriage. Of course, they should have known that summoning a fairy would lead to mischief. Didn't every fairy story involve mischief and loss?

That thought did not make me feel any better. I had been the medium of that mischief. I had caused a rift between them that might not be mended this side of—well. The fact that I loathed, yes, *loathed* Geoffrey Hodson from the first moment I met him made no difference. I had made clients cry before, but those had always been tears of joy. They were able to communicate to their dear departed the love that too often went unspoken while they lived. Red Cloud usually ended a séance with "If I have made some of you happy, then I am happy." There had been no such benediction tonight.

I sat in my compartment writing to my husband, but I kept tearing up my letter and starting over. A bit later Dr. Watson came to my door, yawning his head off, to invite me to have a cup of tea. It was kind of him. But I could not yet face him or Sir Sherlock, so I begged off, pretending a headache. I kept reliving the whole night over and over in my imagination till I *did* have a headache. I had taken on this Luxor project too blithely. What if I were simply not up to the task? I had been unable to control the most harmless of elementals. What chance would I have against the age-old power of the elementals that had been released from Tutankhamun's tomb? Doubt gnawed at me. At last, I decided on a course of action.

Chapter Five:
Dr. John Watson

We sat across from each other, painfully aware of the absence of Mrs. Roberts, watching the moon slowly slink away.

"I'll admit, it wasn't the usual spiritualist song and dance," I finally said.

"The reality of it rarely is," said Holmes gently. "If you weren't so muleheaded—"

"You said yourself you could predict what would happen merely by observation and logic. Perhaps she simply shares your gifts of observation to some degree."

"Or perhaps I share her psychic gifts," he posed.

"Rubbish. You've never claimed to have an American Indian in your back pocket. Or spoken with the dead, at least not before—"

"No, I speak with a bullheaded general practitioner, and the dead speak to me through clues. You've often striven to determine the source of my abilities; perhaps I've made a deal with the devil. He, like God, is in the details."

"Balderdash. I've seen your work close at hand. I'll pay tribute to your talents, but not to supernatural predicates."

"You still deny the existence of the supernatural after what you witnessed tonight?"

"Smoke and mirrors!" I insisted doggedly. In truth, I was puzzled by the whole event, but I was certain sharp practice was at the heart of it.

"Well, I didn't bring you along to convert you, though you may yet see things on our journey that you cannot explain away so peremptorily. But I'll leave that to your conscience, my starchy friend."

"Then tell me truly, why do we journey to the Valley of the Kings? What do you hope to find there? Fairies?"

"Witnesses. The chief archaeologist, Carter, is still there, with his crew largely intact. I fear it was no accident, Lord Carnarvon's death. But let us posit that it was not due to the curse. Perhaps it was your simple garden-variety murder, the kind you so relish. His associates will know of anyone who wished him dead. And who had the means to accomplish it."

"Now you're talking sense. Although how murder can be attributed to a mosquito bite—" I heard a note of petulance in my own voice that stopped me. I didn't want to discourage his current line of thinking.

"We've seen stranger occurrences. I simply keep an open mind, as ever, until I have enough data to form a complete theory. Dark spirits at times possess the minds of men and employ the hands of men for dark purposes. There are any number of documented cases throughout history. You may call it sickness or corruption if it sets your mind at rest. You have witnessed a not-entirely-benign example tonight. What are elementals but another kind of fairy, full of mischief, which may be beneficent or malignant?"

It must be trickery, or illusion, even delusion, I was determined. The alternative did not bear scrutiny—that the woman's mind was deep and dire and endless as an ocean, that one could descend, weightless yet weighed down, past light, past sound, past breath, past all understanding until—what did Shakespeare call it? A sea-change. Yes, a sea-change. "Into something rich and strange." Bah! It was all folderol and fiddledeedee.

The hour was late. We turned in. I thought that I would be asleep as soon as my head hit the pillow. Instead, I stared at the ceiling, feeling the passing miles radiate through my frame.

I admit that my confidence was shaken. Perhaps Mrs. Roberts did possess Holmes's gifts, though I had never witnessed anyone with his uncanny talents save his own brother, Mycroft, who had died of apoplexy some years before. (Indeed, he had died in his favorite haunt, the Diogenes Club, famous for its rule of silence, stricter than a Trappist monastery. Which meant unfortunately that it was several hours before anyone suspected he had deceased, even though the room was full of his fellow members.) Had Holmes ever tried to contact his brother after death? Or did Mycroft believe himself still in his old club, forbidden to speak? Such speculation was fruitless.

I turned over fitfully, punching my pillow.

What would it mean to be surrounded by the dead, to hear their riot of voices like the punters cheering on the colts at the three-quarter mark? I could not but think of all those young men, thousands of good lads, who had died in the Great War, blasted to kingdom come. What would they say if I could speak to them again and their tongues were loosened—those I had tried furiously to save, had failed to save, soaked in their blood, hands wrestling with their living viscera, what would they say? Would they profess contentment in laying aside the cares and burdens of living, or would they be bitter at their fate? I know I'd be bitter, and I had lived to a ripe old age. By thunder, I'd be bitter if I died right now, before I have the chance to finish this tale. I'd be elated to be reunited with my precious Mary, of course, but to be faced with my father and brother once more? I'd said all I wanted to say to them in this world or the next.

Then I heard violin music coming from the compartment next to mine. Holmes had brought his Stradivarius! As I listened, I realized a change had come over his music. No longer did he play the wild improvisations of his youth. Instead, he had chosen a melancholy gypsy sort of tune I had heard before but could not place—Sarasate, perhaps? Mrs. Roberts was in the compartment on his other side. I hope she enjoyed being serenaded.

I lay back. It had been too long since I had fallen asleep to the violin. My doubts still nagged at me, even as I was sinking into sleep, but I did not let them nag for long. The solution to the puzzle was near at hand.

I woke at six to the radiant sun of Provence. I pulled down the window shade and managed to sleep again until ten. I've grown civilized in my waning years. Thus it was that I was just making my toilet when we rolled into Antibes, a barely populated spit of sand with its toe in the Mediterranean. The attraction escaped me. I had heard that wealthy Americans liked to come and lie in the sun until they were lobster red. The idea made me appreciate my London pallor all the more.

Then my attention was arrested by a sight glimpsed through my window: the Hodsons and their baggage. Not terribly strange in itself, since I recalled they had mentioned Antibes as their destination. They had obviously managed to patch things up. They were gazing at each other like lovestruck newlyweds. Then the riddle unraveled before me. Mrs. Roberts approached them—not like someone who had stirred up a hornet's nest between them, not with a look of contrition, but like an old friend. She spoke to them for several minutes in a comradely fashion, then actually hugged the wife and kissed the husband on the cheek. I heard the call to board, and she disappeared inside.

I had seen enough. What a cunning little vixen! To have brought these two confederates here all the way from England to stage their little play. Well compensated for it they were, I imagined.

All to convince Sherlock Holmes. No—to convince *me*. Holmes was already well hooked. But why did she want to accompany Holmes and Watson all the way to Luxor? There would be an honorarium, perhaps but surely no more than a pittance. Merely for the notoriety? Was Holmes still so well-known?

Among the spiritualists, I suppose he was. He and his pharaonic curse. Yes, it was fame she was seeking by strapping her name to Holmes's.

I tracked Holmes down in the dining car, feasting gluttonously on pain au chocolat. Should I tell him what I had witnessed? But what *had*

I witnessed? Not enough to sway him in his calcified beliefs. Better to hold this card close to my chest, to collect more, until I had a stronger hand. Holmes's own strategy. And surely she would attempt further demonstrations of this sort—the mark once lured must be constantly reassured. I would watch her every movement and catch her out. In the meantime, I would feign complete faith in her powers. I would seem as convinced as the most innocent of naïfs. And then I could convince Holmes not only of her wiles, but of the insincerity of the entire spiritualist movement. Now there would be a triumph!

She joined us at breakfast with a secretive smile on her face. She made a half-hearted stab at an apology for the doings of the night before, but Holmes dismissed it with a magnanimous wave of his hand. "The humbug got his comeuppance," he pronounced.

"Humbug?" I repeated in amazement.

"You weren't taken in by him, were you, Watson?"

"Of course not. But there were the lights."

"Smoke and mirrors," he said, with delight in his voice. He did not elaborate further. Could he be aware of Mrs. Roberts's role in the deception?

"Then fairies do not exist!" I said triumphantly.

"Of course they exist. You heard one speak yesterday eve. And expose Hodson as a base philanderer." He was, regrettably, serious.

I literally bit my tongue. After that refreshing demonstration of Holmes's acute powers of deduction, I had thought we'd had a breakthrough. I was sore mistaken.

"One question. Do all fairies speak English?" That should tie her in knots, I thought.

"I couldn't say. I've only met the one. Hers was a very strange tongue. But Red Cloud translated for me."

"Red Cloud is a . . . translator?" I asked, despairing.

"Oh, yes. He's translated for me from German, French, even Greek. All languages are one on the other side, of course." Which made no sense when you thought about it. Which I was the only one doing, curse her.

"Mrs. Roberts is a most talented female," Holmes reminded me for the umpteenth time.

"Red Cloud has all the talent," Mrs. Roberts reminded him for probably her umpteenth time.

I nodded agreeably, holding my peace. "How ever did you ever find her?" I finally rasped. It was only meant rhetorically. Holmes took it literally.

"You're aware that I had been trying to contact my mother for years."

I knew nothing of the sort, though I was privy to the tragic tale of her life in Colney Hatch and death in the terrible fire. I let him go on.

"I'd tried numerous mediums without success. My mother, they all concluded, did not wish to be found. Then Mrs. Cannock, whom I had worked with during the war, introduced me to her new discovery, prophesying that she was destined to do great things."

Now I desperately wanted to know the story behind Mrs. Cannock in the war, but I knew well that Holmes's wartime activities were a closed book—when he so chose.

"But Mrs. Roberts was able to succeed where others had failed?"

"Admirably. My mother and I had a long and very intimate tête-à-tête."

"Did you find your mother bitter toward your father?" I asked. (Of course, what I was really asking behind this convenient fig leaf was whether *he* was bitter. It had always been too risky a subject to broach.)

"You're encroaching on very private matters," warned Mrs. Roberts.

"No, no, it's all right. I've never concealed anything from Watson. He knows that Squire Holmes had my mother committed."

Mind you, it had taken me ten years to wrangle that titbit of information from him. Holmes had always been an oyster in regard to his private life. I will admit that I had never been exactly forward with details regarding mine, either. One of the reasons we got on so well together, I expect.

"I think, yes, she was very angry at first and for some time. They had been ill-suited from the start, he stolid and she so fiery. But there is balm in Gilead, and she had left those feelings far behind by the time I was able—or Mrs. Roberts was able—to contact her. Now she has only the best interests of her sons at heart. I think being joined in the afterlife by Mycroft must have helped to reconcile her."

How long had it been now since Mycroft's death? Twelve years? How long had it been since Holmes's father had died? I hadn't the vaguest. Holmes never spoke of him. Never.

"Have you ever contacted your father?" I wondered aloud.

He was reluctant to answer. Finally, he nodded.

"His real father," she cooed, placing her hand on his.

I must have jerked back as if bitten by a swamp adder. My chair may have been ejected into the aisle, causing a waiter to trip, spilling a pot of coffee all over a silver-haired matron whom the conductor kept referring to as "Duchess" while offering his profoundest apologies. I am not quite sure of all this, I was so dazed. Mrs. Roberts must have intuited that this was a secret I had *not* been privy to, one she had just betrayed.

Holmes's eyes were slitted in the way that I knew danger lay therein. Mrs. Roberts stared at the floor as if hoping it might open and swallow her up. I signaled the waiter for more coffee and engaged him in talk about trains, his bad back, his wife's spending habits, and his role in the war—anything to keep from meeting Holmes's eyes. Mrs. Roberts slipped away, claiming another headache, the all-purpose excuse of the modern female. Holmes merely slid away. I remained and consumed enough coffee to give me the shakes.

Were Sherlock and Mycroft only half brothers? Was Sherlock the love child of Louise and—who? Did Squire Holmes know? Was that the real reason he had her put away? The reason Holmes was so distant from his father and even his brother? The reason he had inherited nothing but his wits? It would explain a great deal.

In the afternoon, we had another shock. Holmes was late for dinner, but when he came in, he slammed down a newspaper on the table. It was *Le Figaro*, but the headline blazoned across the front was one even I could translate—*Maggie dit qu'elle est enceinte!*—and of the picture there was no mistaking. Princess Marguerite, who had been found innocent of murdering her husband even after she admitted putting three bullets in his back, now claimed that she was pregnant by her late husband—presumably while he was still alive, although the article did not make that clear. When he died, several unscrupulous papers had actually laid the blame on Tutankhamun. (They had visited the tomb on their honeymoon. I might have murdered him for that reason alone, had I been her. But he was an Egyptian, after all. I daresay he thought it was all in the family.)

I couldn't help but speculate at the time whether the jury had been swayed by talk of the curse of the pharaoh. What other mischief might be perpetrated in the name of this codswallop?

"I thought he . . . liked men," offered Mrs. Roberts demurely. "That was what the defense said. That he treated her . . . as a man."

"I've no doubt it's simply a ploy to strengthen her claim to the prince's fortune," said Holmes.

"I still can't believe she was exonerated," I said. "A bloodsucker through and through."

"And that is why she was exonerated, or at least why the evidence damning her was never brought to light. Prince Ali Kamel Fahmy Bey was not the first prince she'd snared."

"Whatever do you mean?" asked Mrs. Roberts. I leaned in eagerly to hear as well.

Holmes seemed to find it distasteful to go further. But he had led us thus far. "The Prince of Wales."

"You mean he—?" Mrs. Roberts could not finish the indictment.

"And what was monumentally stupid, he penned her letters. Which she very judiciously kept by her."

"My word, it's the scandal in Bohemia all over again," I uttered.

"With the important distinction that you shall not be writing up any accounts of it."

"How came you to hear of it?" Mrs. Roberts asked.

Holmes fell silent.

"By Jove, you negotiated for the return of the letters!" I cried.

"Very good, Watson. That onerous task fell to me, yes."

"I wonder if all royals are such ninnies when it comes to women," Mrs. Roberts mused.

"All men are. The royals simply make the morning edition," I answered firmly.

"Oh, please," said Mrs. Roberts rather haughtily. "Next you'll be saying that all women are bloodsuckers."

"Not necessarily just women. We shall be crossing into Monaco soon, where we'll meet with Evelyn Herbert and her new husband, the Baronet Brograve Beauchamp. Another wastrel wed for money and no doubt burning through her fortune as quickly as ever he can get hold of it," I said with profound distaste.

"You've grown a prickly hide in your old age, Watson," said Holmes reprovingly. "The baronet served in the Life Guards with distinction during the war. It's Lady Evelyn who has the itch for gambling. She inherits it from her father, I'm sure. He was the real wastrel who married for money."

"Any man who marries for aught but love is a bounder," I fumed.

"Really, Doctor, would you refuse the woman you loved just because she had money?" chided Mrs. Roberts.

Holmes could not keep silent at that. "John Watson has already passed that test with flying colors, my dear. He would not have proposed to the love of his life save that her fortune sank into the Thames."

It was true that the sight of a chest full of fabulous gems going into the drink had made my heart light and freed my tongue. For how could I, a virtual pauper at the time, have dared to ask for the hand in marriage of an heiress? But I shot a warning look toward Holmes, and he wiped the mirth from his face. If Mrs. Roberts was waiting for a story, she would not get one. My darling Mary's name was not to be bandied about.

"Speaking of gambling, Lady Evelyn's wagered a thousand pounds that I would find no proof of a curse," Holmes said.

"A thousand pounds! He should rein her in," I remonstrated.

"It should mean a nice little nest egg for me—or my ruin."

"You mean you took her up on it? Good gracious, man."

"According to your lights, it should be easy money for her. After all, that's why she insisted you come along. She has complete faith in your probity."

"Then I'm to officiate?" I blanched at the thought.

He gave a nod. A brief smile flickered across his face.

That shone a whole new light on the endeavor. True, I longed with all my heart for Holmes to abandon spiritualism, but I had no wish to humiliate him publicly, much less ruin him. Backing him up in a dangerous situation was one thing, but this put me in virtual opposition to my old friend. It was an uncomfortable position, especially knowing Mrs. Roberts would be whispering in his ear every minute, trying to fill his head with her Pandora's box full of superstitions. And there was the revelation that Holmes had not insisted on me; Lady Evelyn had. I felt that the earth rock beneath my feet.

The sun was just cooling its toes in the wine-dark sea when we chugged into Monte Carlo, the easternmost bastion of Provence (though officially part of the dollhouse city-state of Monaco, the tiniest in the world). It's a charming town that climbs from the water's edge to the high hills guarding it from prying eyes like a player guarding his cards from blacklegs. Of course, we saw none of this. The Monte Carlo train station, for some inexplicable reason, lies underground, so we were greeted upon alighting by dim lamps and concrete floors, walls, and ceilings, which created a deafening echo. We might as well have been in the Marylebone tube station toward the end of the workday.

Except for the dress, of course. Everyone in the corridors was outfitted to the nines. Holmes had dropped the news on me at the last minute that evening wear was de rigueur at the casino. No exceptions. At which I dropped the news on him that I had brought no evening wear, since I had not been informed that we would be going anywhere within a hundred leagues of Monte Carlo. At which he pulled another one of his conjurer's tricks, saying that he had foreseen that eventuality, and produced a tuxedo "in your exact size" on the spot.

Well, it was not my exact size. I suppose I had put on a few pounds since Holmes had last sized me up, so it was a tight fit. I cut quite a dashing figure, however. Holmes looked rather like a scarecrow in his, I thought.

But the real eye-opener was Mrs. Roberts. I am not unaware that ladies' dress styles have changed rather drastically since the war. Outfits that would have been considered scandalous before the war were now commonplace, and bustles, petticoats, and corsets had all vanished as if they were candy floss. But Mrs. Roberts had always presented herself in a matronly fashion, which I thought very becoming to her years. So you can imagine my shock when I saw the evening gown she had selected for the casino. I'm no good at describing women's clothes these days, but it—plunged—well, everywhere, back and front, with no sleeves at all, sort of a Greek affair, very loose and low-waisted, except it had a sash at her hip, and the color of it was, well, I don't recall.

When he set eyes on her, Holmes said, "Mrs. Roberts, you look ravishing," which made her blush—all over—and frankly set me back, since Holmes was not in the habit of meting out compliments to the fairer sex. I mumbled something in agreement, but I was really thinking that she must have known all along about our coming to Monte Carlo, as well. (Or do women always pack their finest gowns when they go abroad, on the off chance they might be invited to a royal wedding? Perhaps they do.) It occurred to me, too, that mediumship must be more remunerative than I had deemed. That dress was worth a pretty bit of pounds, shillings, and pence, if I was any judge.

We stepped away from the train into the churning sea of humanity. We were nearly swept along with the crowds making their way eagerly—to what? I couldn't spy the exits for the crowds pulsing toward them. We held our ground with some difficulty, trying not to become either flotsam or jetsam, waiting to be rescued by Baronet Brograve Beauchamp. He was promised to meet us here if all things had gone as scheduled—that is to say, if he had sailed into Port Hercule yesterday or this morning at the latest. He always moored the yacht at Monte Carlo for the winter, or at least the yacht was always moored there by its owner—most recently Lord Carnarvon, I presume. Rarely does one moor a yacht in the dead of winter, but I suppose he had been delayed by two deaths in the family and his own nuptials.

Holmes relayed all this to me above the hum of the crowd as we tried to locate Beauchamp. But if he were there in the crush of excited gamblers streaming away and dejected losers waiting to board (though probably not on *le train bleu*), he was nowhere to be seen. If he had encountered rough seas anywhere along the way, he could be days behind, especially if he were not a skilled sailor. Anticipating just such a scenario, and finding that Holmes had no way of contacting the Lady Evelyn in case of a snag in our plans, I had made sure to ask a steward about nearby hotels, and he had jotted down a few. I started looking through them.

"There is the Hotel de Paris, the Hotel Metropole," I began reading aloud, not that anyone paid me the least attention, "the Hotel Hermitage—that one sounds your cup of tea, Holmes." No response. There was a time when I could expect that Holmes had planned for any eventuality, but these days he seemed to drift along serenely, expecting everything to work itself out. Mrs. Roberts assured us that we would be met. Small comfort. I don't know whether she had consulted her Indian on the subject or not.

We were foundering in the tide of humanity, surrounded by our bags. Porters swarmed around us, but there was no one to meet us. I was about to consult my list of hotels once more to discover which was nearest when Mrs. Roberts said, "Wait," and strode away purposefully.

She approached a singular young woman with blinding blonde hair, dressed in a grey tunic and trousers, leaning against a pillar smoking a cigarette. This was obviously one of the light women we had been warned about by our steward on the train, creatures of ill repute. Monte Carlo was infested with them, he had warned. I should have gone after Mrs. Roberts and stopped her, but I will admit that I didn't much mind her looking a bit foolish. She marched right up to the girl and barked out, "Are you with Baronet Beauchamp?"

The girl gave her an icy look. She had delicate, porcelain features, yet somehow there was a mannish air about her. I am not used to seeing a lady in trousers. She dropped her cigarette and stamped it out, rather viciously, I thought.

"Ja."

"Well"—Mrs. Roberts seemed as disconcerted by the answer as I was—"I'm here with Sir Sherlock," she said, pointing back to us as proof.

The blonde flipped her long, straight hair out of her face, peered in our direction, and nodded. "Ja, ja, ja," she said in a rat-a-tat tone. She snapped her fingers and issued rapid-fire orders in what sounded to me like especially guttural German (it was Dutch, I was later to learn). A cloud of porters congealed around her. She collected our baggage tickets from us and dealt them out to the porters like so many aces. They pounced on them.

"But . . . where is Beauchamp?" I asked.

The girl looked at Mrs. Roberts quizzically. She repeated the question more slowly.

"Ah! *Boven*," she said, pointing to the ceiling.

Mrs. Roberts looked back at us helplessly.

"I believe she means up," Holmes supplied, amused.

The girl nodded energetically, took Mrs. Roberts by the shoulders, and pointed out the way to the escalators, which were now visible since the crush of people had thinned out a bit. Who on earth was this woman? Beauchamp's first mate? The Lady Evelyn's duenna? She gave Mrs. Roberts a little shove, then headed off in the opposite direction.

"Wait," I cried. "Aren't you going with us?"

"*Nee, ik ga naar de auto*," she said, pointing at our fleeing bags and giving me a look she obviously reserved for idiots.

"I believe she's seeing to our bags," said Holmes, who had apparently added Dutch to his repertoire in the last five minutes. So we left her behind—I hoping she wasn't simply an opportunistic thief—and followed the dwindling crowd to the escalators.

Here we came up against an unexpected obstacle. Mrs. Roberts refused to ride. She had never been on an escalator before, it seemed, but she had heard hair-raising stories of innocents eaten by the monsters beneath. No amount of cajoling could induce her to set foot on one.

"Elevator's to the right," slurred an American fellow who had seen our predicament. He had also seen the bottom of a whisky bottle. But we acknowledged his suggestion with relief and made our way to the lift, which Mrs. Roberts seemed to be on friendlier terms with. It was probably better that we had been delayed, or we would have been packed into the lift like herrings in a barrel. As it was, we had little breathing room, although a great miasma of alcohol fumes rose about us. Our fellow passengers had apparently begun imbibing on the train.

The lift doors opened, and the entire company in the elevator let escape a gasp as one. We had arrived at the casino terrace at the setting of the sun, and it was magical. We found ourselves gazing on an immaculate greensward, a courtyard dotted with dainty cocktail tables, a colorful promenade, and a sparkling purple sea crowded with ships like swans. The facade of the casino could have passed for the prince's palace. I stood blinking in the red-gold light while others pushed past me, grumbling, till Holmes laid a hand on my back and I stepped out onto the terrace of the Casino de Monte Carlo.

The casino at sunset was a powerful crowd magnet. The lights were just blinking on as all the world strolled past in the glorious fashion of the jazz age, light skirts fluttering about bold knees, straw boaters being chased in the sea breeze, the lovely laughter of young ladies without a care in the world. Oh, to be twenty-one again. (Although I recall when I was twenty-one, I was freezing in Edinburgh, studying for my degree.)

And, of course, no Beauchamp. Or at least—well, Mrs. Roberts was leading the way, and since she had become our bloodhound, we followed obediently.

And sure enough, she led us straight to him—a man whose face was burned by the sun and the wind, who had a trim military moustache, not a hair out of place, a straight-backed military frame, but deeply asleep at one of the small tables, shaded by a giant umbrella. He was dressed to kill, in his white tie and black satin collar, but his open mouth took some of the shine off him. The journey must have taken the wind out of his sails, literally. At least he wasn't snoring.

Holmes rapped on the table in front of him with his stick. I will admit that I have never seen a man go from a semirecumbent position to standing ramrod straight at attention so swiftly. Nor seen him relax and put a frown on his face so speedily when he recognized the interrupters of his dreams.

"Mr. Holmes," he said, casting a weather eye on him but not extending his hand. "I trust you had an enjoyable trip."

Holmes nodded in that curt military manner he had picked up from dealing with officers during the war. He had never got in the habit of saluting. "More restful than yours, I deem," he replied.

Baronet Brograve Beauchamp did not acknowledge me nor even Mrs. Roberts. We were merely entourage, or perhaps peonage. Status hath its privileges, if not its manners.

Mrs. Roberts was having none of it. "Why weren't you there to greet us?" she snapped. "Your girl had no idea who we were." Here was the face of a lion tamer she hadn't evinced before. I liked it.

"Anna? With your reputation as a mind reader and Mr. Holmes's as a detective, I had no doubt you would find her out."

I wondered how often Mrs. Roberts was tested in this way. I did not dwell on the fact that she *had* identified the girl. That was merely . . . well, fortune.

"And your bride?" inquired Holmes.

"Is inside, losing my shirt at the roulette wheel."

"Shall we join her?" I asked, tired of being ignored.

"I'm afraid you'll have to fill out these forms first, old man." He held up a sheaf of papers.

"What's this for?" I objected. "I have no intention of gambling."

"Dr. Watson, is it not? Have you ever been in a casino before, Doctor? No?" he asked scornfully. "Then don't say you'll not gamble. Famous last words and all that. But these papers are simply to be admitted, even if you've sworn to dear old mater never to give in to the devil. Monte Carlo is extremely security conscious. I had to use all my pull just to be allowed to bring these out here for you. There's quite a queue inside."

I did not feel the urge to disabuse him of the notion that I was such an innocent as he thought. It was none of his business that I was at one time a heavy plunger on the turf. I had put that devil to rest long ago.

So we sat down and proceeded to fill out forms. They were simple enough: name, birthplace, place of residence. I was relieved to find that they didn't ask for an estimate of my wealth. I might have been barred forthwith. I tried to steal a peek at Sherlock's; after all these years, I still didn't have the foggiest where he was born. Did it say "Montpellier, France"? He put his hand over his answers. So many secrets, still. And now one more: Who was his real father? Could he be French? After all, his mother was. To think that this most English of Englishers might be pure-blooded French was—well, *parbleu!*

Beauchamp rose. "Are we all finished? I'm anxious to rejoin my wife. Depending upon how much she's lost at the roulette wheel, we shall either continue on to the hotel or I shall have to abandon you on the side of the road and let you make your way home as best you can."

If he were joking, I did not appreciate his sense of humor, and I decided to close my ears to any further harangue and get on with filling out my form, which I had *not* finished, as we had only one pen between the three of us and I had been waiting my turn. Lady Evelyn was certainly known for taking a flutter, though not to the extent that her father had. Was Beauchamp worried about his bride exhausting his fortune or her own? He would not be the only baronet to marry with money in mind. With the shocking taxes imposed after the war, every young nobleman with a country estate had been packed off to America to fish for young heiresses. Beauchamp simply had not had to go so far afield.

He was still droning on. "Monte Carlo is well on its way to recovery from the war, largely due to the steady guidance of René Léon, who's transformed it from a winter resort to a year-round playground. Villas sprouting up like mushrooms in the hills crowding the old city. Money feeds on money, you know, and then all the frills that come with money. Now, Evie prefers the older casino, the Casino de Monte Carlo, and I don't much blame her, although I prefer the Sporting Club for its baccarat tables. But I'm sure you're all fagged out, and I'm a tad bit gassed myself. So we'll kidnap her away to the Reine d'Azur, which is not only a well-appointed hotel but safely off the main drag, so that she can't scratch the old itch to gamble if it comes on her sudden in the night. Unless she bribes Anna, of course."

"Anna?" questioned Mrs. Roberts.

"Anna van V., our driver. Bit of a pet."

The baronet seemed to have rather free and easy way of speaking about women, even his wife, but I refrained from mentioning it. I've learned that oftentimes it's the couples who quarrel the most that are the most steadfast. And from what I knew of Lady Evelyn, she could hold her own.

He whipped back on us again. "And speak to no one, particularly the press, about our little dash over to Luxor. My wife and I are wintering in Monaco. That is all anyone needs to know of the affair."

He seemed somewhat abashed at raising the subject. I could certainly agree with the sentiment. I felt foolish enough going on this harebrained expedition without seeing it splashed about in the penny press.

I handed him back my entry form. By the time we were prepared to take the plunge, there were already some coming out whom I recognized from the train, with the dejected and destitute looks of those who had bet their fortunes on one turn of the wheel. And lost.

I rose. "Shall we go in?" I offered Mrs. Roberts my arm.

"Oh, no," she said timidly. "I think I'll just wait out here. Watch all the grand people."

"No, you shan't," said Beauchamp determinedly. "My wife is most eager to meet you—inside."

It seemed couched as an ungentlemanly demand, but after a swift glance at Holmes, she decided not to contest the matter.

Beauchamp studied us with a critical eye. "We'll have to get beyond the dress police first."

"The what police?" I blurted.

"Once you enter the casino, you're part of the show, or at least part of the backdrop." He had the effrontery to straighten my tie. "You stick close to the lady and they might not notice you."

I could see we were going to get along swimmingly.

Chapter Six:
Mrs. Estelle Roberts

I stepped through the doors of the casino and was absolutely shattered. First of all, it was immense: rows of creamy columns topped by Greek capitals, supporting a high gallery that wrapped around the entire space, lit by countless electric globes, and a heaven-stretching skylight spilling the last golden rays of the sun on everything and everyone. Looking down from the gallery were slender men in swallow-tail coats and swan-necked flappers kept from flying away only by the weight of their jewels. It reminded me of a fairy tale—and I was only seeing the atrium as yet.

Perhaps Sir Sherlock and Dr. Watson were accustomed to this sort of magnificence. They seemed perfectly blasé as to the surroundings, although their tuxedoes did seem a trifle outdated compared to the perfectly tailored evening clothes most of the men wore, with their slim silhouettes and spectators instead of boots. The doctor had turned a peculiar shade of purple; I think the baronet had cinched his tie too tight.

We entered the roulette salon, a room that seemed to stretch to the horizon, lit by chandeliers as massive as anchors. It thronged with people, most of whom seemed to be milling about looking for someone they expected to meet. My cheeks flamed when I saw the women draped in silk and chiffon, dripping with diamonds and pearls. I had felt like Cinderella in the spangly black gown I wore with the rose-colored sash (picked out and paid for by the Lady Evelyn, Sir Sherlock had assured me), but I felt decidedly dowdy by comparison with the bejeweled and bedecked beauties all around me. The only bit of jewelry I wore was my plain wedding band. I felt invisible.

Yet most of the women moved across the room restlessly, like antelopes across the veldt, peering in at the gaming tables, trying to understand why the men were fixated on play rather than on themselves. They seemed more a part of the decor than actual living, breathing human beings. Perhaps that was by design.

There was the scent of wealth everywhere, and not just in the delicate perfumes, the peppery cigar smoke, or the walnut smell of expensive whiskies. The scent of something strangely like a gathering storm filled my nostrils, crackling with electricity and yet weighed down by heavy air at the same time. There was a whisper of prayer in the air, in which the only deity was Mammon.

Well, I was not here on holiday, but on business, even if it were only ancillary business. Thanks to the baronet's description, I had a horror of having to drag Mrs. Beauchamp out by her hair, with her heels leaving little grooves in the exquisite carpet.

In the center of the vast room were three green baize tables like islands in the storm, stacked with winking tiles. They were lined with players so intent on their games I could feel the baritone hum of anticipation and smell their burning cupidity. I had no idea what roulette was all about, but the wheels were spinning, the play was fast, and the croupiers seemed ruthless, those bright tiles clawed away as fast as they were shoved out onto the field of play. My entire savings could be devoured in five minutes. I clutched my pocketbook to my bosom.

The Baronet Beauchamp scanned the room for a few seconds. Then he said curtly, "Ah, center stage, of course," and made a beeline for the table at the very center of the room. Holmes and Watson dove in after him. I came behind at a distance, eyes still dazzled.

There was a clutch of women at the table, but it was obvious which one was Lady Evelyn. She was not draped over some man but sat with furrowed brow and flashing eyes concentrating on her tiles before her. The baronet's stern look gave way to something resembling pride. There was nothing diffident about her—heavy-lidded eyes, a prominent nose, a mobile mouth. She wore a floor-length cocoon coat of stretch velvet in royal blue, gathered at the waist with a silver butterfly, which I would have died to wear—not that I could have pulled it off. On her forehead was a beaded fascinator, much more practical and far more stylish than my vagabond hat. Of course, I had seen her in the papers before, but they had not conveyed the set of her chin, nor the domination in her eyes. Here was a woman to be reckoned with. What did she want with me?

The man next to her, I realized, was not merely next her, but with her. Quite a handsome man. Fair hair, blue eyes, complexion brown as mahogany. Wearing his RAF uniform, he was quite dashing, if a bit rumpled. It was a shame he was no taller than my twelve-year-old, Iris. The two were deep in consultation. I was surprised to catch no hint of jealousy in the baronet's eyes.

As soon as she saw us, she dropped her tiles and swam into the baronet's arms like the beaming bride she was. But she did not stay there long, for soon she was greeting us with effusion and introducing her companion.

"This is Captain Tom Shaw of the RAF. He flew me down here from Croydon. I think we should buy a plane, darling."

"Sir Sherlock, I can't tell you what a pleasure it is to meet you. And, of course, the redoubtable Dr. Watson." Captain Shaw shook both their hands warmly. Dr. Watson reciprocated just as warmly. Sir Sherlock was more reserved, but then, he always is.

"Shaw, you said?" he asked with a curious look in his eye.

"That's right, Shaw as in George Bernard."

"Oh, are you related?" Dr. Watson asked.

"Possibly. He's Irish, I'm Irish. We're an inbred population." He didn't sound Irish. He sounded like an Oxford don. But he had the Irish sense of humor.

"What do you fly?" asked Sir Sherlock.

"Avro 504K."

I had no idea what they were talking about.

"All the way from Croydon?" Sir Sherlock sounded dubious.

"By easy stages," he replied smoothly.

"It was thrilling," volunteered Lady Evelyn.

The granite look did not leave Sir Sherlock's face. What could it mean, I wondered.

"Captain Shaw is a great fan of yours, Mr. Holmes. He even threatened to leave me behind and carry you instead," said Lady Evelyn. Then she turned to me. "You look simply marvelous, Mrs. Roberts. Thank you so much for coming." Of course, she was too tactful to mention that she had chosen the dress, and paid for it. I could only guess how much it cost. I was half afraid I might be waylaid in some alley by dress thieves and forced to hand it over.

She gave me a long going-over, but it was not the look of a superior to an inferior, merely a look of curiosity and perhaps assessment. She finally said, "These people with all their hopes and fears must really set a psychic buzzing."

I didn't know quite how to answer. I'm no mind reader as such, but I am sensitive to people's moods and could feel the waves of anxiety in the crowd pressing round. I would imagine anyone could feel it. I reminded myself that I was here solely at Sir Sherlock's behest. I had no idea whether she was sympathetic or teasing me. I nodded my head in a noncommittal way and let her make of that what she might.

"You're not really going to ask her?" said Captain Shaw, his face lighting up.

Oh, no. Too often people want me to perform like a circus animal, even believers. I thought back to Mr. and Mrs. Hodson. I had spent the whole night reconciling them, explaining how fairies loved to tease mortals and cause trouble between them. Me, lecturing Hodson on fairies! It was only by several anecdotes (largely passed on to me by my old nanny, I'm ashamed to say) and most of a bottle of sherry that I was able to put them in a receptive mood and leave them smiling at Antibes.

The lady took my hands in hers, leaned in, and whispered to me, "You're just in time."

I was taken aback. Just in time for what?

"Just whisper the numbers in my ear." Her eyes sought mine out, looking for some sign of complicity. "You can do that, can't you?"

"You're asking for the moon, Eve," Shaw chided her. I thought at first he was referring to my role in Luxor. I felt slapped.

But what would she have me whisper to her? Then I realized. Oh.

She gave him a look of annoyance and sat back down and spread her tiles again.

"How much have you lost, darling?" Beauchamp asked casually. Too casually.

"My luck is about to change," she rejoined confidently and gave the briefest toss of her head in my direction.

She had made herself plain. She wanted me to help her, to be her confederate. To use my powers. I was flattered, and to my dismay I felt a sudden surge of warmth. I *wanted* to help her, to prove myself. But it was wrong; it was cheating. I didn't even know whether I had the ability—

For one thing, I didn't have the slightest idea how to play roulette.

How quickly could I learn? The game was played, as I said, on a long green table. The table was sectioned out into three columns of printed numbers, from zero to thirty-six, some in red, some in black. The wheel, situated at the center of two tables, had the same numbers marked around its circumference, in the same colors. There was one man with a white ball poised in his hand ready to launch it onto the wheel, and another fellow with a long rake next to him, both as serious as undertakers. There were, besides the Lady Evelyn, six miserable-looking men on either side of the table in perfectly tailored swallowtail coats, boiled shirts, and brilliantined hair. They smelled like a patch of lavender. Each had a stack of tiles in front of him, and each slid his tiles onto various numbers jerkily, as if he would much rather be sliding them back to safety.

That was all I could grasp of the game. If only I had been warned this would be expected of me! It was also far warmer than was comfortable, even with my shoulders and arms bare. No wonder the ladies doused themselves with scent.

I closed my eyes and breathed deeply. I felt the undertow of the spirits, but there was nothing unusual in that. I gave myself up to them, drifting in their wake. It was only with their help that I could succeed. I heard the ball drop onto the wheel. And felt myself falling, whirring. Dizzy, the ball clattering, so dizzy.

I sank to my knees on the soft carpet. No one seemed to take the least notice. The next thing I knew I was curled up in a ball, seeking solace in the protection of my own limbs. All I could hear was the white ball tumbling, tumbling, tumbling, never coming to rest. All I could feel pressing in on every side was anticipation and fear. Notes of triumph and failure. If only the ball would stop, stop, come to rest! The clattering was driving me mad.

And then I heard my name called. Had Red Cloud come to me at last? Lead me away!

No. I heard my name again and realized it was a man's voice, from across the table. I opened my eyes and found that I was still standing upright, just behind Lady Evelyn's chair. A little man with a French accent was trying discreetly to get my attention. He wore a pince-nez and had a large, carefully waxed moustache flourishing hedge-like on his upper lip. He seemed almost a caricature of a Frenchman. In fact, he put me in mind of Max Linder, the film star. His hands moved in the air as though he were conducting an orchestra or perhaps fighting off a swarm of bees.

"You are Madame Estelle Roberts?" How long had he been calling me?

"Yes, yes. Oui," I spoke up. How did he know my name? Who was he?

"I am with the casino. Might I have a little word with you?"

I looked around at my cohorts, but everyone seemed focused elsewhere, as if they had not heard—perhaps as if they had not seen him! Could he be from the other side? I stepped forward uncertainly.

"Just the one word. In private," he coaxed.

Sir Sherlock cast my way a look of reassurance, which calmed me. The man was flesh and blood. I followed where he indicated. I thought I might be led to some to some secret chamber deep within the entrails of the casino, perhaps to face accusations of stealing my spangly dress, but he only guided me to a quiet corner and halted peremptorily, so that I found myself uncomfortably close to him. I could smell the garlic on his hot breath.

"I will be brief. You are Mrs. Estelle Roberts of Londres, Angleterre?" He had my entry form in his hand.

I nodded. Wide-eyed. "Born in Kensington," I said.

"The medium psychique?" He whispered it as if it were something shameful.

"Yes, I'm a medium," I said loudly and clearly to show that I was thoroughly unashamed.

"Ah, yes. A thousand pardons, Madame, but in that case, you must depart the casino. *Tout de suite.*"

"What? I don't understand."

"I shall endeavor to explain. Your . . . gift places you at an unconscionable advantage here. These are after all the games of chance, not of skill, no?"

I must have turned scarlet. His imputation was obvious. "Oh, but . . . but I'm not playing. I'm only here with friends."

"Oui, I am witness to your friends. One of them, I believe, is the lady Evelyn Herbert, is it not?"

"Beauchamp," I corrected him. He paid no heed.

"A long-standing patron of our club. I believe you English say, a very good sport, is it not?"

"We've only just been introduced," I countered.

"Ah, very likely. I cast no aspersions. But our rules are our rules, Madame, surely you see that?"

I was about to make a strong objection when I remembered that I had just been attempting to do exactly as he'd implied, tipping the scales toward Lady Evelyn. That I had failed miserably hardly cleared me of culpability. I'm afraid tears were starting in my eyes.

"All right," I said, subdued. "May I have a moment with my friends, to explain to them?"

"But of course. You are free to go wherever you please, Madame."

That was hardly the case. I started back, then turned. "How did you know who I was?"

"I have studied your picture, Madame. We keep dossiers on all the celebrated psychiques."

You will think me silly, but I could not help being flattered by his portrayal of me as *celebrated*. I had thought myself rather obscure at that point in my career. But apparently my reputation had spread to the continent. I tried to keep a smile from my face.

As soon as I had rejoined the party and explained my predicament, the baronet seized the opening to carry his wife away from the gaming tables, insisting we were finished for the evening. I apologized profusely to Lady Evelyn while her husband scooped up her tiles, but she took it in stride.

"You were marvelous," she said. "We would have broken the bank at Monte Carlo had that odious little man not intervened."

"What . . . what are you talking about?" It sounded like she was making fun.

"The way you took over with such assurance, placing those plaques on all the right squares. Magnificent."

"No, I—"

"I'm none too nimble at converting francs, but I think you must have made three hundred pounds on those three spins," Captain Shaw said with a charming smile that won my heart.

"I believe I shall have to share some of my winnings with you. How much does one tip a medium?"

She was serious. While I thought I was lying on the floor in dread, I had apparently been throwing around her tiles with wild abandon.

It must have been something akin to automatic writing. My God! My legs shook thinking of what could have happened. I nearly fainted to imagine it. Now I understood what had alerted Max Linder, or whatever his name was.

We stopped in front in front of the cassier's cage. The baronet shoved the plaques in front of a bored-looking cassier, who sorted them swiftly and methodically.

Well, I thought, at least I had won her confidence. I had no idea the performance I was yet to put on that night for the Beauchamps' benefit.

His chips cashed in (I say *his*, for Beauchamp pocketed the winnings, at which his wife made not a peep), we proceeded to the exit. Leaving the casino was a much more arduous task than getting in had been, however. We were stopped every few feet by old friends of Lord Carnarvon who wished to pay their respects or relate some amusing anecdote about him. There were even some who recognized Sir Sherlock and wanted some aspect of a long-ago case explained in detail. I thought it curious that none of them appealed to Dr. Watson, since he had recorded, and no doubt embroidered on, the adventures in question. But he deferred to Sir Sherlock, which I gather was his customary role. The baronet stood by, tapping his foot, visibly exasperated. He did not strike me as a stoic. If he were incommoded, he would make certain the world knew it. He traded commiserating looks with Captain Shaw, who was relegated to the shadows as well—although for his part, he seemed quite content with his role. He even seemed to prefer it.

And from afar I glimpsed the manager, or detective—he never had said which, or even given his name—watching my every move, seemingly equally anxious at our slow parade toward the exit. What did he think, that I might pick a pocket or two along the way?

Just as we were about to make the door, we heard a mournful, mooing voice.

"Going so soon?" he asked.

"Ah, Monsieur Léon!" Lady Evelyn perked up.

He was a dull-eyed, mild little man with the obligatory close-clipped French moustache. (Beards had positively disappeared since the war.) He looked more like a waiter than a casino mogul.

"I'm afraid one of our party was asked to leave," she told him.

The little man's face darkened. "On what grounds?"

"Mrs. Roberts is a spirit medium." She indicated me with a nod.

He did not even look my way. "And so?"

"Well, according to your monsieur . . . What was his name?"

"Max . . . no. He didn't give it," I said. I turned. The man who had watched me so closely had disappeared in a puff of smoke.

"Such professionals are apparently banned. Are they not?" said the baronet.

"Of course not. Every gambler in the casino has his good luck charm. If we banned them all, we should be destitute. If you'd like to go back in—"

The baronet shook him off. "We shall be here all season. Plenty of time for you to drain our bank accounts."

To that, our host could only nod and bow. I kept my lips sealed about the insult of being compared to a lucky rabbit's foot.

"Bonne nuit, Monsieur Léon," said Lady Evelyn, a little wistfully.

At last we emerged into the open air. The night air was sweet and pure, the sky the color of turquoise. A sea breeze set the palm fronds ashiver. There were still as many people outside as in. These, however, were paired off now, their faces alight in the moonshine, their voices warm and whispering. I had no idea where the baronet was leading us, but I was content to follow at his heels. Sir Sherlock put my arm in his. I felt safe.

I came back to earth as the stillness was broken by the voices of the baronet and the Dutch girl in the grey uniform—a very military sound. She had apparently been guarding the car the entire time we'd been inside. What a dull job! There were cigarette butts all around her feet. I could only hope that none of our luggage had been left behind. I didn't have the nerve to demand an inspection.

"This is where I take my leave of you—à bientôt," said Captain

Shaw, with a sweeping, courtly bow. He had something of another century about him, perhaps the court of Elizabeth. I could picture him laying down his coat over a puddle so the queen could cross without wetting her toes.

"How do you plan to pack us all into a two-seater Avro?" Sir Sherlock asked pointedly, bringing me out of my reverie.

"That would be a jolly trick. No, I've managed to acquire another kite, a Handley. It'll carry all of you without a strain, plus fifty-pound packs if you're planning on trenching."

"Is it safe?" I couldn't help but ask.

"Safe as houses," he submitted confidently.

"It did admirably landing five hundred troops in Kirkuk to fight the Kurds," Sir Sherlock added.

"Right you are," said Captain Shaw, obviously surprised by Sir Sherlock's ready knowledge. "It's been through its baptism of fire."

"Ripping, old man. That'll get us there in no time, and without all the prying eyes of the press. Where shall we meet you in the morning?" asked the baronet.

"I'm staying at the Hermitage," said Shaw.

"Then we shall see you on the morrow, Captain Shaw. Sweet dreams," said Lady Evelyn.

"Shaw?" the driver echoed, looking puzzled.

"Anna, get the car started," said Lady Evelyn sharply.

The girl looked as if she were about to argue but thought better of it and complied with her mistress's command.

"Quite a girl. This is the racer you told me about?" asked Captain Shaw.

Lady Evelyn answered. "Anna van Vredenburch. She would have won the 1912 Rally if she'd had a better auto."

"I'm sure you can provide that," he said in a teasing voice.

"Oh, I shall."

It seemed the Lady Evelyn had her fingers in all sorts of pies.

It struck me then, as the moonlight caught his face, that I had seen Captain Shaw somewhere before. But I had not the slightest idea where. A spiritualist meeting? Doubtful. He had the kind of swagger that denies death altogether.

Then he kissed Lady Evelyn on the cheek (rather daringly) and strode away. I was left with the conviction that I must be mistaken. It was not as if I hung about any RAF barracks. Perhaps he just had one of those faces. I put it from my mind.

Dr. Watson had the rear door open, waiting for me to slide in. The auto was a complete beauty, a long, sleek saloon car. I'm afraid I have no idea what kind of car it was, but I remember it was quite luxurious and roomy, even with three of us sharing the back seat. The engine roared to life, which gave me goose pimples. The tonneau was down, and the air was brisk as we leapt away from the curb. I checked my hatpins to make certain they were secure.

Lady Evelyn turned back to us, shouting over the wind. "I'm sorry, we stay a bit out of the way, at Hotel Reine d'Azur. My husband doesn't like me to be too near temptation."

"It's the finest hotel in the South of France," came the voice of the baronet gruffly.

"But we are not in France. We're in Monaco," corrected Sir Sherlock.

The baronet ignored his comment. His wife merely sighed and laid her head on his shoulder. We climbed into the hills away from the seductive lights of the harbor. I was a bit apprehensive about a woman driver, even though I was sure she was perfectly competent. She was a racer, after all. Not that I wanted her to do any racing. We ascended higher into the hills. Now was the time to voice my concern.

"I . . . I heard a rumor today on the train. That Dr. Carter is ill."

"Never refer to him as Dr. Carter," said Lady Evelyn, practically reprimanding me.

"Why not?" I asked.

"Firstly, because he's not a doctor. Secondly, he hates being reminded of the fact. He has no formal education. He literally learned in the trenches."

That I found interesting, if somewhat unsettling.

"And thirdly," she continued, "you need not concern yourself with Mr. Carter's health. He's more than a match for any curse."

There was still the moon trailing behind us, but the road before us was a pitch-black river, shrouded on both sides by pitch pine and cypress with the occasional narrow lane winding precipitously down the hill to nowhere in particular that I could see. But then, I didn't have benefit of a window seat. I kept wishing the driver would go just a bit slower. The constant rocking back and forth was making me bilious.

Then it hit me like a thunderbolt, splitting my mind wide-open.

"Stop!" I cried. "Stop now!"

The car came to a screeching halt, and the two men on either side of me were thrown against the front seat. But I remained motionless, held rigidly in place by the summons.

"Mrs. Roberts! What's this about? Are you ill?" Lady Evelyn's face was in mine, full of concern. Indeed, their eyes were all fixed on me, with varying degrees of concern, the driver with a look of spasmodic fury. My face felt flushed, but not because of embarrassment. The pull was too strong. I could not speak, could barely breathe. My rib cage was constricted, my tongue filled my mouth, so thick it almost choked me.

The baronet scowled with impatience. He turned his back to me and nodded to the driver, who started the engine. The wheels turned beneath me.

I found my voice again. "No, you must go back!" With every moment the feeling was more pressing—literally, pressing against my bosom.

"Stop the car at once," said Sir Sherlock in such a commanding tone the driver reluctantly slowed the car to a halt a second time. Robins were kicking up a fuss in the trees above us, disturbed by our headlamps. The only other sound was the ticking of the engine.

"I'm sure whatever it is, we can deal with it more effectively at the hotel," the baronet said, thoroughly aggravated.

"No, I think not," shot back Sir Sherlock. "What is it, Mrs. Roberts? Take your time."

"Something down that road we just passed. Something urgent."

He turned to the front. "Where did that road lead?"

"Cap Martin, a little coastal enclave. Very exclusive," volunteered Lady Evelyn.

"Do you know anyone living there?" asked Sir Sherlock.

The baronet shook his head.

"Well, that's not exactly true, darling. Didn't Mr. Gould say he had a place there?" interjected his wife.

The baronet threw her a confused look.

"George Gould, the American, darling. You remember, we met him at the tomb. Villa Zoralde, he called his place."

"Gould, the American railroad magnate?" asked Dr. Watson, sounding impressed. The name stirred a memory in me, but I could not place it, with all the turmoil in my mind.

"Yes, but he's really a very nice man. Not like most Americans. You remember, dear, he had that fantastic boat, the *Vigilant*, that won the America's Cup. And that lovely new wife, Guinevere, I think she was called."

"Gwendolyn. I don't believe he's receiving tonight," said the baronet, frowning with his whole body.

"But we must go," I said. "Tonight. Tomorrow he'll be gone."

"How do you know that?" asked the baronet, eyeing me curiously.

"I can't explain. I just know."

Pure disbelief registered on his face; I'd seen it often enough to know. "He's already gone. In point of fact, he passed away last May."

"Oh, that's right. I'd forgotten," said Lady Evelyn. "Pneumonia, wasn't it?" She sounded disappointed.

All eyes slid away from me. But then Sir Sherlock laid his hand discreetly on my own, patting me. "Where did you meet him, Lady Evelyn?" he asked softly.

"At the tomb, when . . ." Lady Evelyn trailed off. Sir Sherlock let it sink in.

"He's waiting. With a message," I said doggedly.

"Beauchamp, you've gone to a great deal of expense to include the lady in our expedition. I should listen to her, were I you," said Sir Sherlock.

The reminder did not please the baronet overmuch but, muttering, he instructed the driver to turn around. "Go where she tells you," he instructed her, fluttering his hand as if I were perfectly capable of taking them to Wonderland, or Neverland, or the Land of Nod.

All at once I felt foolish. What if we went to this Villa Zoralde and found nothing at all? I was gambling a great deal on the pricking of my thumbs. I might lose the credibility I had gained so serendipitously at the casino. But there was no turning back now. And as we reached the turnoff, there was a rushing in my ears, like a full-throated lament, though no words were discernible. I shouted out directions as they came to me, and we wound our way downhill.

"So you believe Gould's death was caused by devils out of the tomb?" asked the baronet, his voice laden with sarcasm.

"He took ill just after he visited the tomb, did he not? And never recovered," said Sir Sherlock.

"More likely he was poisoned by his wife," chirped the baronet.

"Brograve!" Lady Evelyn chided.

"Don't pretend you haven't suspected it. His mistress for seven years and he was right as rain. He marries her and a year later he's dead. That's not suspicious?"

Mr. Beauchamp, it struck me, was really rather a crude fellow.

The way wound down past towering villas of pink and white, like elaborate wedding cakes with too much frosting, likely to tumble over any moment. I only glimpsed them through the crowding tree cover, mind you, whereas the winking lights in the distant harbor below us were perfectly visible. The sea air rifled our lungs. None of us had actually been to the house before, of course, so they depended on me to point out the way, and somehow I did.

"It's like having Toby on the leash," said Sir Sherlock; Dr. Watson laughed. I did not know who Toby was. But I was glad to see them merry. It relieved the pressure.

"Turn here," I directed.

There was a narrow gravel path, nearly invisible in the dark, but I knew it was there, between fragrant junipers. The driver turned onto the road. It slowly widened out before us as the gravel crunched under our tyres.

And we were there, just at the zenith of the moon. Luckily, the driver stopped before she pitched us into the swimming pool. Why there was a pool in front of a house not a stone's throw from the sea I can't imagine, but the rich, I've heard, are not like you and me. It was a simple place, really, if a house with too many windows to count and colonnades on either side of the door can be called simple. But the walls were white stucco, and the roof was red tile, quite rustic. There were window boxes in every window, filled with flowers.

The flowers were all dead.

The house was dead. There was not a light to be seen, not a whisper to be heard. There was no one there. I had expected no one. The widow Gould was probably far away in America. And yet... there *was* a presence.

Silence filled the car. "I take it this is the Villa Zoralde. Are you satisfied?" the baronet asked in a caustic tone.

"Italian Renaissance. Quite handsome," said Dr. Watson. I think he was trying to be helpful. That was his role.

"I'm sure it's for sale if you're interested, Doctor," said the baronet, almost spitting the words.

"What now?" asked Lady Evelyn. She was looking to me for direction.

"Do you still sense what brought you here, Mrs. Roberts?" Sir Sherlock asked.

"More strongly than ever," I whispered.

"Then let us see if we can find this message." And with that he was out of the car, with Dr. Watson at his heels like a terrier. I slid out behind them.

From the car I heard her say, "She does speak to ghosts. At least according to Mr. Holmes."

And he retorted, "I hope she speaks on a trunk line. He's buried in New York."

Well, I would let them argue it out between them. But I heard the car doors snick open behind me. What else were they going to do?

I touched the handle on the gate. It creaked open. I realized with a shiver that I had expected it.

"Unlocked?" said the baronet querulously. "Demmed careless."

It wasn't carelessness. It was an invitation.

"We're at the back of the house," said Lady Evelyn. "Shouldn't we be at the front?"

Sir Sherlock ignored her. He passed me by and strode up to the back door of the house. He tried the handle. It was locked. That was not the way.

Where, then? *Let your mind go free, Estelle.*

"Watson, it appears we shall have to take a more direct approach."

"Have you your lockpick with you?" asked the doctor, as if he were asking whether he had a pocket watch on him.

"You're not really going to break in?" asked the baronet, horrified at the thought.

"Nothing so drastic. Witness all these lovely flowers."

"They could do with some watering," Dr. Watson pointed out.

It was then that I began to drift away from the conversation. Not physically, no, I did not take a step. Not mentally, either, but spiritually. It was as if their voices were coming from a distance, from the other side of an ever-widening chasm. Therefore, I cannot vouch for the accuracy of my memory of the discussion that followed.

"You're going to climb?" asked Lady Evelyn, looking up at the windows.

"I am no longer as lithe as in my earlier days. No, I was noticing the urns of climbing roses on either side of the door. One pink, one white. Those are well tended and flourishing."

"Helen Shepard, Gould's sister, is a well-known expert on growing roses. I believe she even has a breed named after her," Lady Evelyn instructed.

"A hybrid tea, I believe. That does not, however, answer the riddle of why these are the only flowers so well tended. I believe the Helen

Gould is one of those rare breeds without thorns. I think you'll find the key in one of those urns," Sir Sherlock confided.

The baronet impetuously plunged his hand into the nearest urn, with the white roses. "Well—demm me, that's got thorns!" he cried, pulling back his pierced thumb and sucking on it, mortified.

"No, the Helen Gould rose is a pink blend, if I recall correctly. Watson—" He pointed toward the other urn.

Without hesitation, Dr. Watson plunged his hand into the other urn—to no ill effect—rooted around for a bit, and with an "aha!" drew forth what must have been the house key.

I suppose this was the cleverness Sir Sherlock was so famous for. It would be profitless in this instance.

"A pretty little trick." Holmes took the key from Dr. Watson and applied it to the lock. The door swung open, and a cold wind rushed forth that danced along my spine. There was nothing in that house. I would not enter.

"Good evening!" called the baronet, poking his head inside.

He knew no one was there, but he seemed chary of entering first. He was perhaps worried that a ghost would leap upon him and turn his insides out. Unbelievers are usually scared witless by the slightest hint of the uncanny.

Sir Sherlock produced a pocket torch. What didn't he have tucked away in his pockets? He flashed it across the back hallway, revealing a few coats and hats on their pegs, which the wind stirred to life. The others crowded around him as they entered.

But I was not there at all. I was on a tennis court. There were couples playing tennis, laughing, flying past me in their tennis whites, virile and alive. They passed right through me, calling out the score. Tennis in the moonlight made for a raucous game.

There was another gate before me. It, too, was unlocked. I heard the scrape of a boot. I stopped and looked behind me. The Dutch girl, Miss van Vredenburch, had followed me, the moon bleaching her fair skin white. Well, what of it? She flashed me a thumbs-up. What of it? I had nothing to fear here.

The garden was bathed in golden moonlight, revealing an eerie sight. It was a chessboard of fantastic proportions, manned by chessmen taller than me, all shaped of gleaming marble. I remembered reading somewhere that Gould had been a chess fanatic. I could feel his presence. I wanted to call out, but I sensed that I should let him come to me. I waited, stilling my heart.

He stepped out from behind the black king. Whether he was composed of moonlight from above, or mist rising from the tall grass and tangled riot of flowers, I could not say—perhaps both. When he moved, his body trembled all over, as if he were exerting himself to maintain the illusion of corporeality.

He wore an immaculate white suit. His hair and carefully curled moustache were likewise snow-white, though he hadn't been that old, barely sixty. His flesh was alabaster, almost translucent. His grip on this world was tenuous. A breeze might blow him away.

I had read about his death in the papers, of course. Some sort of fever. Gould had something to tell me. When was it he had died—May? He had been waiting here all these months to speak to me. A lonely vigil.

"Speak," I said, though I was shaking.

"I've waited for you."

"I know. Soon you will be at peace."

"I've waited ever so long."

"You have a message for me, do you not?"

On hearing that, he let out a bloodcurdling scream. I nearly fainted dead away.

He was gone! I had come too late.

Then, slowly, the moonlight congealed into his form again, but now as though he were woven from nothing more substantial than spider webs, flung between the black king and queen.

"She has the name," he said.

"What?" I asked. "Who has the name?"

"She has the true name."

I wished that Red Cloud were with me, but he was silent. George

Gould didn't want anyone speaking for him. But what did he mean? I could sense him slipping away already.

"Your wife?" But I knew it was wrong as soon as I said it.

"She stole it."

"The name? Can you tell me her name?" I was straining with every fiber of my being to hold him. He opened his mouth, but his lips fell away, his jaw dropped to the ground and rolled away in the grass. His face crumbled into ash.

Then a light blared behind me. Sir Sherlock? I looked back.

It wasn't Sherlock. It was a man in a forage cap and tunic, a dark, lanky man with a large electric torch shining in my eyes, yammering at me in French. I didn't know the language, but he was upset, that I gleaned right off. Did he see Mr. Gould? I turned. No, he was gone! And not only gone, but every bit of spectral energy that had drawn me here had been scattered to the four winds. I felt suddenly weary, oh, so weary. I leaned against a white rook. I went through it and nearly fell on my face. It dissolved into the ether, along with the whole grand chess set.

Miss van Vredenburch began talking excitedly in French. It did not seem to pacify the man. He drew a gun. He almost dropped it pulling it out. He aimed it at her, then at me. He was nervous.

So was I.

Chapter Seven:
Dr. John Watson

Thank the stars for Holmes's fluent French and his easy ability to lie on the spur of the moment. And that the watchman knew Lady Evelyn, or at least knew of her—it was difficult to understand him even when he spoke in fractured English, he was so agitated.

Well, and he had a large bump on the back of his head where the chauffeur had nearly split his head open with a sap. That had probably been unnecessary. But at least I was warned now not to upset her.

She stood by her actions, too. She did not like guns, she said emphatically. She repeated it so many times with such energy that "*Ik nou niet van wapens*" may be the only Dutch I will ever remember. No one likes guns, of course, though I was glad I had my service revolver secured in the waistband of my trousers. I thought it wisest not to divulge that fact to her.

The watchman finally calmed enough to holster the weapon he'd been waving about. He escorted us back to the auto, as gracelessly as possible, his eyes full of suspicion. No one volunteered the fact that we had been inside the house, nor that we had been through every drawer we could find, searching for a message that said we knew not what.

Any trace of George Gould was long gone, of course. Mrs. Roberts, we discovered too late, was not even with us but along with the chauffeur had been tramping through the flower beds on the side of the house. What had Mrs. Roberts been doing out here to put the watchman in such a furor?

And what had her so pale and drawn? What had she seen? She kept harping on about some giant chessboard. Holmes had found a concrete chess table in a corner of the garden, nearly overgrown with marigolds. Not giant.

"Did you find anything, darling?" Lady Evelyn asked her husband, when we were once again on our way, the watchman and the house receding in the distance.

"Of course I didn't find anything," growled Beauchamp. "And I think it were best that we drop the entire project right now, before we make bigger fools of ourselves."

There it was. Cards on the table, as it were.

"You know, the British Museum is being inundated with Egyptian relics that people had lying about at home. Everyone is worried to death that they may contain evil spirits," said Lady Evelyn.

"Everyone's a fool. What's that have to do with it?" he blasted.

"It's not just my brother, Henry. The whole kingdom's in a state of panic."

"You can blame the fellow in the back seat for that," snapped her husband.

She turned away from him with a sigh. "Mr. Holmes, do you have anything to report?"

"It was not so much what I did find as what I didn't," replied Holmes at his enigmatic best. Holmes had no cards to play. But he always had a joker up his sleeve.

"What do you mean?" asked Lady Evelyn, intrigued.

"Mrs. Gould must have had the body transported immediately, and no one has returned to the villa since. That much is obvious."

"Why obvious?" groused Beauchamp, for whom, I suspected, nothing was ever obvious.

"The furniture was not covered. And the dust on the furniture is at least six months deep." Only a man with Holmes's reputation for wonders could have gotten away with such an outrageous lie. At least I assumed it was a lie. (That I was largely responsible for that reputation did not occur to me at the time.)

"So she had to get back to her American lawyers. If you think there's not going to be a battle royal among the heirs—"

"What wasn't there?" asked Lady Evelyn, determined not to get sidetracked.

"You noticed that all his clothes were still in the wardrobe, and a large part of hers. His personal effects were still there, including some personal papers."

"Utterly uninformative papers," said Beauchamp.

"Yet they had not even bothered to throw them away."

"What wasn't there?" said Beauchamp irritably.

"My dear sir, the Goulds had just come from Egypt, where they had honeymooned at the tomb of King Tutankhamun, just as you are doing. That suggests a more than passing interest in Oriental culture. And yet there was not a single item of Oriental souvenir in that house. Not a trinket. Does that seem likely?"

"Then she must have taken it with her—if it existed at all."

"Perhaps, but why was it so important that she would remember it, and not her wedding ring, which was on her dressing table?"

"Because it was *gestolen*," said Miss van Vredenburch out of nowhere.

There was a tactful silence.

"Stolen? How did you come to this conclusion, Miss van V.?" said the baronet, very slowly, as to a child.

"It is . . . logical, no? Is that what you say? *Logisch?*" She glanced over at Mrs. Roberts. She followed with a spate of Dutch, which no one understood. Then she retreated into silence.

Mrs. Roberts finally spoke up. "It wasn't a thing that was stolen. It was a name."

"Who said this? The watchman?" asked Beauchamp.

"No," replied Mrs. Roberts. "Mr. Gould said it."

This caused a tumult of voices, all vying to be heard at once. Finally, Mrs. Roberts's voice cut through, distinctly: "It was Gould. George Gould. He spoke to me."

"You've met him before? I knew his wife was interested in spiritualism," said Lady Evelyn.

"No, I never met him in his lifetime. I spoke to him just now. On the chessboard."

This caused further consternation. The questions flew, and I thought the driver would put us in a ditch. Mrs. Roberts's face was a fine shade of crimson. At last Sherlock Holmes silenced us all. He took Mrs. Roberts's hand in a way that I once would have called too familiar and asked simply, "What did he say?"

Well, after all that to-do, of course it turned out that he hadn't said much, and no one could make head or tails of what he *had* said, including Mrs. Roberts herself.

"She stole it? Stole what?" asked Beauchamp.

"The name," said his wife for the twentieth time, irritation creeping into her voice.

"I would rather know who *she* is," said Holmes, speaking my own thoughts. "He gave no clue at all?"

Mrs. Roberts shook her head wearily. "The watchman interrupted."

"I say she imagined the whole thing" was Beauchamp's verdict.

The car jumped as the girl shifted into high gear. She was a racer indeed! I clamped my hat on my head before it flew off.

"Damn the watchman for showing too soon!" I erupted, which earned me turned heads and blank looks. "Well, I mean . . ." I had been swept up in the moment.

"At least we know who unlocked the gate. It must have been the watchman," said Lady Evelyn.

"No, that was why he was so livid," Holmes said. "He thought Mrs. Roberts had managed it somehow."

"Mr. Gould unlocked the gates," Mrs. Roberts said.

The baronet barked a laugh. I myself was inclined to dismiss her claims. But if the watchman hadn't unlocked the gates, who had? Mercifully, Beauchamp decided to put it from his mind and push on to an entirely different subject.

He turned back to his wife. "Well, tomorrow we'll be in Cairo, well quit of Gould's ghost. If Shaw can actually scare up a plane for us."

It seemed to me that as long as Mrs. Roberts was with us, we would have more than our share of ghosts.

"Is this Shaw a dependable fellow, would you say?" Holmes asked.

"He's the most resourceful man I've ever met," said Lady Evelyn.

"I hope we're not taking him away from his duties," I said.

"He's on leave, awaiting a new assignment," she assured me.

"He seems to be assigned to you," her husband edged in.

Was there a bit of friction between man and wife over the dashing pilot? (I say *dashing*, though he barely came up to my chest. There wasn't much of him, but what there was he carried off with panache.)

"Shaw seems an interesting fellow. He must have seen action in the Arab campaign?" asked Holmes. He seemed inordinately curious about this Shaw fellow.

"Oh, no!" said Lady Evelyn hurriedly. "He was a . . . fighter pilot. In France."

Holmes's face registered puzzlement. Apparently, his ability to read a man's past had faded with the years. Not much chance to exercise his talents in the solitude of Sussex, I expect.

"And now he's stationed in Cairo? Or Damascus? Does he speak Arabic?"

Lady Evelyn did not answer. "A bit. Enough to get by in the souks, you know," supplied Beauchamp.

Quiet seemed to steal upon the group, or perhaps it was simply sleepiness. Thankfully, we soon arrived at our hotel. I wasn't sure by that point whether we were in France or Monaco or Italy. I don't imagine it mattered.

But it was a perfectly splendid establishment, the Hotel Reine d'Azur, though not much larger or grander at first sight than the

Goulds' villa, but the entrance was braced by palms and the view of the bay was magnificent, and the wide verandah was welcoming. The service was typically surly, like all the French, except for the occasional obsequious Italian or proud Monegasque, but the rooms were spacious, and the bed looked perfectly alluring. If there was one fault with the blue train, it was that the beds were, perforce, rather narrow. This one could have done for a football pitch. This, of course, would have been the time for me to confer with Holmes over a pipe and brandy, but now Mrs. Roberts was included in our tête-à-tête, and she commandeered the most comfortable chair. And, of course, we could not smoke in front of a lady.

"Now then, Madam, what did you see? Exactly," Holmes began.

What she recounted next sounded like a ghost story. It *was* a ghost story.

But she had a strong feeling, she said—although she hadn't said before, and was probably only dressing up her story—that she felt whatever had been stolen had been stolen from Tutankhamun's tomb, which she knew as well as I did was exactly what Holmes wanted to hear. She was an artful creature.

"What did he mean, she stole the true name? Did Gould have a new mistress, Watson? I know you follow the society pages," said Holmes.

"I don't. I only take the *Mail* to follow the royals. And whatever she saw, what's it to do with our case?"

"Why, did you not hear Lady Evelyn? They met Gould and his wife on their honeymoon at Tutankhamun's tomb. A week later he arrives at the villa on the sick list, according to the watchman, and four weeks later he is laid to rest. He is obviously the fourth victim of the curse."

"Ah. Then why isn't his wife dead as well?" I demanded.

"A point that cannot be overlooked. Why are some subjected to the curse while others are spared? I suspect that is the key to the riddle. What say you, Mrs. Roberts?"

Was he being deliberately obtuse? Conspiracy never seems to afford any place to coincidence.

Mrs. Roberts was at least discreet enough not to voice an opinion on the matter. She would leave the sleuthing to Sherlock Holmes.

"Now we have our first clue," he crowed, clapping his hands together. "X stole Y. From where? From the tomb. I think we can safely infer that much. We must simply fill in the missing variables."

Of course. Though there was no evidence of it whatsoever. Mrs. Roberts had either made it up out of whole cloth or hallucinated the entire episode. It was really only a question of whether she was a fraud or a lunatic. But I would play along. "Why not from the house? The widow, perhaps, has absconded with something not hers? Papers in his name?"

"Now you sound like the Baronet Beauchamp."

"It wasn't a thing, it was a name," Mrs. Roberts reminded us.

"How does one steal a name?" I objected.

"That is the problem we must solve," Holmes pronounced, continuing in his algebraic vein.

It was all very well for him to say so.

"So she, whoever *she* may be, steals something from the tomb, yet the tomb reaches out and kills Gould? And what's his name, Carter, who's packing up the entire tomb lock, stock, and barrel and hauling it away like the Elgin Marbles, remains healthy as a horse. It doesn't make the least bit of sense."

"We must determine what was stolen," said Mrs. Roberts decisively, as if she had just made the deduction of the year.

"Then Howard Carter is the person to ask. According to the papers, he keeps an exact record of every mouse and housefly that goes out of that tomb," I flung back.

"Then we are on the right path. What is it, Watson?" asked Holmes.

I had opened my mouth and shut it again. I had a million questions, a million objections. I wanted to say how barmy it all was, but if I did, I could simply pack my bags and go home. If I wanted to play, I would have to play by their rules. I had been co-opted.

Holmes leaned toward us, spreading his hands out. "One more

thing—this pilot, Shaw. Don't let's share any of this with him. Keep your distance from him tomorrow," he cautioned.

So I *had* noticed him giving the slant eye to our tiny captain. Why? I wondered.

"I'd rather we weren't flying to begin with," said Mrs. Roberts. "Wouldn't a ship be far safer?"

"Never been in the air before, Mrs. R.?" I said. "It's not so bad—rather exhilarating, really. And a sight better than humping our way through the desert with all that ancient dust. But what's wrong with this Shaw, Holmes? Lady Evelyn seems to think he's a pukka sahib. And he seems to worship you."

Holmes chose his words carefully. "Perhaps there's nothing wrong. But he seemed a bit *too* eager to meet me. There are still some of Moriarty's old henchmen in the remote wastes of the world, and all quite eager to make my acquaintance."

That cast a different light on the matter. Holmes had had an old raven named Moriarty, if it still lived, but I had not heard that name uttered as a threat for thirty years. Moriarty's men were known for holding long grudges. "Should I keep my revolver at the ready?"

"No, but keep your eyes open." Then a look of concern enveloped his face. "Not that same service revolver you've been carrying around since 1881, I hope?"

"No, I procured a new one after our encounter with Mr. Hyde."

"Ah, an elephant gun." That drew a laugh from me.

"If you shoot him, how shall we land?" Mrs. Roberts's face paled with the thought.

"We might have to call on your Red Clown," I said, which drew a laugh from Holmes.

"Red Cloud!" she snapped.

"Yes, you'd best not mock him if you expect him to save you from the vasty deep," said Holmes, but there was mischief in his eye. All was right with the world, at least for the moment. Mrs. Roberts bade us good night, perhaps a bit miffed with us.

Holmes seemed wide-awake.

"Holmes . . . the fellow at the casino . . ." I ventured.

"Yes, I thought you'd catch that. I don't believe anyone else did. I felt Mrs. Roberts needed something to bolster her confidence, especially after the Hodson debacle. Completely unnecessary, as it turned out. Her performance at the roulette table was astonishing."

"And her performance at the villa was even more astonishing."

"I sense the old doubt creeping up on you."

"Miss van Vredenburch was with her. Why didn't she see anything? Why didn't the watchman?"

"I'd like to question the Dutch girl further. But she's a close one, I think. We'll learn the truth of the matter soon enough. If something of consequence is missing from the tomb, will that suffice to convince you?"

I didn't answer, considering what other tricks Mrs. Roberts might have up her sleeve.

Chapter Eight:
Mrs. Estelle Roberts

We were up early the next day, with the sleep still in our eyes, when we hustled into the car to meet Captain Shaw at his hotel. We were to meet him in the Belle Epoque room for breakfast. I was determined not to gawk at whatever I saw this time, but pink marble columns and crystal chandeliers and ceiling frescoes and hats with a hundred plumes like an aviary tried my resolve severely. I have no idea what I ate, save that it was buttery and creamy and French. Not ideal for the figure.

Dr. Watson seemed to have thawed toward me somewhat, and the talk flowed like wine. *The talk flowed like wine.* I'm not usually so poetic, but the South of France—or Monaco, whatever—does something to you. Even the baronet seemed in good form that morning. We studiously avoided discussing the events of the night before.

"Mrs. Roberts," the baronet asked, lighting a cigarette, "how do you intend to deal with these elementals if you do come across them? How will you even recognize them?"

The question was fair enough. I responded shortly, "Revulsion." Then I realized that was not explanation enough for neophytes. "I've dealt with something similar before. Have you ever heard of a psychic rod?"

"Something wicked this way comes," muttered Sir Sherlock.

"Exactly. A psychic rod may appear anywhere there is a strong concentration of wickedness."

"How will you destroy this wickedness?" pressed the baronet.

"I shall do nothing, but Red Cloud, using my hands, will send purifying vibrations through the elemental until it loses all cohesiveness. It will simply cease to exist."

I was surprised to see everyone hanging on my words. I had at least not lost my ability to command attention.

"Well," said Lady Evelyn at length, "I'm glad we have you with us."

And then we were joined by Captain Shaw, and everything went awry. He looked quite romantic in his flight jacket and scarf. Oh, he was an engaging little devil, full of compliments and sly little barbs, meant to prick but not to puncture. Not the kind of badinage the baronet seemed inclined toward, which was always sharp and often hurtful. His mannerisms were pleasantly old-fashioned and stately, as if he might share a drop of blood with the royals. And he knew how to charm with just a twinkle of the eye, as if he were sharing a secret joke with you. I couldn't imagine what made Sir Sherlock so wary of him. Had he not warned us against the man, I would have warmed to him instantly. I noticed Beauchamp took his wife's hand firmly in his own; I think he was perhaps a tad jealous after all.

Then Sir Sherlock proceeded to roast him over a slow fire.

"So you fought in France during the war, I understand. Were you in Arras in '17?"

"Bloody April? I was in reconnaissance."

"A bad business. Sopwith Snipe?"

"You know your aircraft."

"Yes. I do." He drummed his fingers on the table.

Captain Shaw lost his smile at this rejoinder.

Wait. I had worked in a Sopwith factory in Kingston-upon-Thames during the war, sewing fabric onto the ailerons of aeroplane wings. There was no Sopwith Snipe in 1917, I was almost certain. They were both mistaken. But I didn't want to add fuel to the fire.

"You were in Intelligence during the war? One hears rumors," said Shaw, trying to turn the conversation away from himself.

Sir Sherlock fobbed him off. "Oh, strictly behind-the-lines stuff. Too old to go adventuring far afield. And now you're assigned to Monaco? Are we preparing to assault the roulette wheels?"

That stung a bit, if the captain's tight-lipped scowl was anything to go by. What was all this fencing about? Was Captain Shaw really in league with this sinister fellow Moriarty? What if he wasn't really a pilot at all? But he had flown Lady Evelyn all the way from London. Heavens, I hoped he was a real pilot.

"I made some small modifications to the engine in my Avro. Needed to test them out. Monte Carlo seemed as good place as any to aim for. Always sure of finding petrol for refueling. And I'm attracted to bright lights. Like a moth."

"What were these modifications you made?" prodded Sir Sherlock.

"My job is to make planes go faster. On less fuel, preferably."

"And whose bright idea was it to go mucking with the engine? French manufacture, isn't it? Don't trust them myself," railed the baronet.

"No, she's outfitted with a Bristol Lucifer. Hundred horsepower. As for whose idea? It was mine, expressly. Tinkering with engines is a bit of a specialty. During the war, speed became something of an idée fixe for me. So I mucked with the engine. Funny thing, then they expected me to test it, too."

"I'm not sure I want to subject myself or my wife to any of your tests," said the baronet stiffly.

"Good man. A gentleman defends his lady to the death. But be of good cheer—I wouldn't subject a passenger to any ride I'm not one hundred percent confident in. Certainly not your lady. 'And there I made promise unto your lady that I should yield me unto you.'"

"*Le Morte d'Arthur*," said Sir Sherlock.

"Very good, Mr. Holmes. But then, I would have expected you to be a devotee of Malory."

"I knew a pilot during the war who carried Malory with him on every mission. What was his name?" Sir Sherlock searched his memory. "Ross, I think."

Shaw gave him a black look. Then he did something funny, if *funny* is the word for it. He unbuttoned his jacket, pulled out a book, and threw it on the table. It was *Le Morte d'Arthur*. He threw it down as if it were a gauntlet.

The table filled up with tension. Why, because of a dog-eared book? A coincidence, nothing more. When men talk, why is it they always talk about everything but what they mean? Banal talk about machines and books and sport—it all seems charged with hidden meaning. Women are clear as glass. Men see through a glass darkly.

"It appears to be a custom that's spreading," said Dr. Watson, trying to lighten the mood.

"It should be required reading for anyone who challenges the skies. 'For herein may be seen noble chivalry, courtesy, humanity, friendliness, hardiness, love, friendship,'" quoted Shaw.

"'—cowardice, murder, hate, virtue, and sin,'" added Sir Sherlock. Captain Shaw had understandably shied away from that part of the quote.

"Always with your mind turned to the dark side of human nature, Mr. Holmes? I suppose it's inevitable in your line of work."

"Where is this plane, anyway? There can't be an aerodrome for a hundred miles around here." Dr. Watson, too, seemed tired of double-talk.

"You're correct, Doctor. Not an aerodrome, but Etienne Romano has an aircraft plant just west of Cannes, less than an hour away by automobile, with the crew of skilled mechanics I needed to fine-tune my adjustments. Which leaves me free to borrow another plane for a few hours to fly you to Cairo. If you're finished with your breakfasts, we should take our leave. No more than fifty pounds a person, though, unless you seek a watery grave."

"Watson and I pack light," Sir Sherlock threw in.

"Bully. She should be gassed up and ready to fly"—he checked his wristwatch—"just about now. On to the Aeroport Côte d'Azur."

"I'm not sure I don't have more than fifty pounds," Lady Evelyn hedged doubtfully. I could imagine!

"We'll take our chances." His dazzling smile came into play. All my misdoubts were quelled.

So we took our leave of Monte Carlo. A place so full and yet so empty. A whipped-up froth that would dissolve into nothing if ever given the chance to settle. That was my verdict, at least. Others might disagree.

It would have been far simpler to take the train over to Cannes, but it was a glorious day for a drive with the wind in your face. And we did have a driver, after all, though she was an odd one. I kept catching her at breakfast, staring at me from under her dark lashes, as if hoping she might catch me at something.

Once we were out of Monaco, a forbidding wall of granite rock rose up on one side, and the glittering sea lay flat and calm on the other. Occasionally trees sprouted horizontally (cheekily, I thought) from the bare hillsides. The hills diminished gradually until tamed. Palm trees marched on our left side, cypresses on our right, like debutantes and their escorts, shy of each other, never meeting to dance. Of Nice itself we only got a briefest glimpse: Monte Carlo without the glamour and dash.

In less than an hour, we were at our destination. What Shaw had grandly called the Côte d'Azur Aeroport turned out to be a row of aeroplane hangars and a single airstrip in the middle of nowhere, situated on the only flat ground for a hundred miles in any direction. The sign over the office door read *Chantiers aéronavals de la Méditerranée*, which sounded like a wonderful French dish, but the interior of the hangar was dark and musty and smelled of oil.

I had never seen an aeroplane quite so large before (I'd seen few of any size), but it seemed so delicate, patched together from wood and wire and canvas. I wondered who had sewn the ailerons. Were they conscientious? Did they realize that lives depended upon their stitches?

Three assistants—three layabouts filled with the self-importance that seems to attend anyone having faintly to do with the science of flight—were giving the vehicle a last check under Captain Shaw's watchful eye. I noticed that the cockpit was open and separate from the interior. Nothing to fear from Captain Shaw. He wouldn't be able to get to us even if he did mean mischief. Of course, if he were to jump out over the sea—

"It is a Handley Page 0400—'bloody paralyzer,' they call it. They used them as *bommenwerpers*—what you call bomber, I think—during the war. Now they convert them to civilian aircraft." It was Miss van Vredenburch who spoke, in better English than I had credited her for. Was there anything with an engine she didn't know about? I didn't like that name, "bloody paralyzer," at all. I hoped there were no bombs left lying about on this aeroplane.

Miss van Vredenburch stood very close to me. Uncomfortably close.

"I hear him," she whispered.

"You hear who?" I asked.

She gestured for me to keep my voice low. "Mynheer Gould. I do not see him, but I hear him. He say she stole, she stole the name."

I was struck dumb. Was she serious? Why hadn't she said anything before?

"This mean I am like you? Psychic?" she asked, in an almost pitiable way.

I could glimpse her then, not as she was, beautiful and daring, but as she must have once been, a plain little towheaded thing, probably the only girl among all brothers, ignored by everyone, wanting to be told she was special. I would have to be very cautious with her. She was more fragile than she appeared.

"Have you ever communicated with the dead before?" I asked.

"I do not think so. Could I have forget?"

"Perhaps. I suppose it is possible." It was not possible. My first experience with the departed still burns in my mind, though I was no more than three at the time.

"What do I do?" she asked.

"Do you want to be a seer?"

She nodded.

"Wait. Pray. Be receptive. If they choose you to speak through, they will make it plain."

"May you teach me?"

Oh, my. Well, it wasn't the first time I'd been asked that question.

"It doesn't work that way. You see—"

But her face had already fallen. She had already turned and was walking away with jerky, self-conscious little steps. So much for taking care. I would have to make it up to her somehow.

I watched the assistants start to wheel the plane out. It seemed to wobble. I feared it might simply collapse under its own weight.

I hung behind. There was Captain Shaw, directing them from the back of the plane. I had a question for him; I forget what it was. Perhaps it was something to do with *Le Morte d'Arthur*. Or perhaps it was whether the plane would go up in a fireball.

I never got my chance to ask. Just as I approached him, Sir Sherlock appeared out of the very shadows and said, "Lawrence."

Shaw whipsawed around and had his hands on Sir Sherlock, driving him to the wall. Sir Sherlock grunted with the impact. Shaw jammed his arm against Sir Sherlock's throat.

"I knew you were here for me. All this talk about mummy's curses was just a sham," he hissed.

It was all so unexpected, I didn't know what to do. Should I shout for help? Throw myself into the fray? Summon Red Cloud? What could he do? Nothing. There was a spanner hanging on the wall near at hand. Should I—? All these thoughts ran through my mind in a blur.

Sir Sherlock peeled the arm from his throat as if it were a stray twig in his path. There was still strength in that arm. "Keep your hands from my person, Airman Ross," he said contemptuously, though it came out as little more than a whisper. "I'm not here for you. I was demobbed from the service a year ago. But how long do you think you can go undiscovered this time? It doesn't take a Sherlock Holmes to sniff you out. Especially if you're stirring up trouble among the natives again. Most especially if you've your sights set on Egypt this time. Too valuable to let you fumble it away."

"What am I supposed to do, grow a moustache and wear an eyepatch?" He stepped back from Sir Sherlock, just inches, did Tom Shaw—or Lawrence Ross.

"It might do for a start. Not meddling with the Arabs would be another excellent measure. They're a coiled viper, ready to strike. They'll bite you as soon as anyone else."

"I'm finished with the Arabs. That book is closed."

"I beg to differ. I've read your book."

"What the devil do you mean? My manuscript? It was you who purloined it?"

"Not precisely. But did you think the government would ever let you print it? Oh, it's largely fable, but you did leaven it with a bit of fact, most of it quite embarrassing to His Majesty's government. And some of it embarrassing to you."

"I don't care about my reputation," Shaw flung back.

"Sometimes I think it's all you do care about. What would Emir Faisal say if he knew about your double dealings?"

"You're unqualified to speak about Faisal. You're unqualified to speak about the Arabs. A brave, honorable race. Don't you see these people deserve the liberty that is every man's God-given birthright?"

"They have the same freedom and protection I enjoy under the beneficent sway of George the Fifth. They aren't your desert nomads, scrambling from one water hole to the next, afraid they'll have to drink camel's blood if the oasis has gone dry. Left to their own devices, they're a lethargic, biddable people."

It was obvious that Sir Sherlock had known Captain Shaw—or Aircraftman Ross—all along. Indeed, they seemed to be rehashing a debate they'd had many times before. Regional politics bores me stiff and hardly seemed the sort of thing to come to blows for. Men are mad.

"Do you intend to notify GHQ?" Shaw—or Ross—asked.

"That depends entirely on your intentions."

"I only want my privacy. I wish to God I had never met that huckster Lowell Thomas."

"Indeed, it's never wise to let a journalist get close. You couldn't find privacy at Oxford? What is this mania for the RAF?"

I was right! He *had* been to Oxford.

"Where can a man find more freedom than in the skies alone? It's even purer than the vastness of the desert."

Sir Sherlock seemed to weigh his answer.

"I have no brief for you. But you won't be able to hide. You're no good at it. And if you want to liberate your honorable people, just ask your friend Carter about all the royal tombs that have been looted over the centuries."

"You mean the masses of gold that were dug for centuries to fill the tombs of the powerful while the people were kept poor and starving? I don't blame them for feeding their children by theft if it were the only way to keep them alive. I'd have stolen the bishop's candlesticks for bread."

They could have gone on with this strange and pointless debate for hours, I suppose, but now the mechanics intervened to tell Shaw that the aeroplane was in position and the checklist gone through. Shaw gave a little gesture to them that might have been the beginning of a salute and strode off. His voice floated back: "I'll hold you to your promise of silence."

I tried to recede farther into the shadows, but Sir Sherlock, without even looking my way, said, "Come, Mrs. Roberts, we have an aeroplane to catch." I joined him where he stood. He locked his eyes with mine and said, "I know, though you promised him nothing, that I can count on your discretion."

"Of course," I stuttered, "but is he—?"

"There will be a time for questions later." He took my arm, but I stood my ground.

"Is he an actual pilot?"

He merely sighed and led me out into the sunshine.

When I was helped into the—car, cabin?—I registered at once it was not like a train, with luxurious seats, a dining car, or an observation platform. Not that I had actually expected such amenities, but—it had pull-down wicker seats facing each other, bolted to the walls, and the whole thing echoed like a drum. If it had been converted for civilian use, it still had a great deal of converting to go. I wished I had brought a pillow. I did make sure I could not see out of a window by sitting right next to the front wall—er, bulkhead—directly behind the cockpit, hoping I could hear or sense if anything went wrong with the pilot. I smelt oil and leather and disinfectant. It was only supposed to take a few hours to Cairo, which seemed altogether too short a time to me. I would just as soon have taken it at a more leisurely pace. Sir Sherlock was in a terrible hurry to reach Luxor, but I really couldn't fathom why. The elementals had been bound to that tomb for three thousand years. They weren't likely to go anywhere soon.

Miss van Vredenburch was seated next to me, rigid and relaxed at the same time. Could she pilot an aeroplane? When I mentioned to her that I would just as soon we took our time, she informed me blandly that if we were still in the air after dark, we would surely crash and die. She was still peeved with me, I think.

I was surprised she had come along at all. I had already begun to suspect when she brained the watchman that she was more than simply a chauffeur—but a female bodyguard seemed a perfectly preposterous idea. Especially since she had traded in her uniform that morning for a crepe georgette in blue, complimenting her eyes. Very fetching.

Dr. Watson was across from me, grinning his fool head off. Yet somehow he still seemed comforting. Then he unbuttoned his coat, revealing a shiny silver pistol, and all my fears came flocking round again. I hoped Anna had not seen it. I closed my eyes and tried to shut out the world, but I could feel the juddering everywhere. I could tell when the plane was taking off; there was a delicious feeling of weightlessness coupled with a horrid feeling of gaining weight at the same time. The wind was so loud I felt it would soon beat in the walls of the cabin and squeeze us all to death.

"Headwinds," commented Sir Sherlock, as if that explained anything.

Then it began to get cold, and colder as the flight went on. I began to think I had the chills, but when I appealed to Sir Sherlock, he said no, that the higher we went, the thinner the air, the colder it would be. All this had to be shouted over the wind.

"You might have warned us about that," harrumphed the baronet to his wife. He was huddled in his lightweight morning coat.

"I did warn you, but you pooh-poohed me," said Lady Evelyn tranquilly. She was, I noticed, wrapped quite snugly in a fox fur. She definitely hadn't warned *me*.

"Oh, come, you've been to the Valley of the Kings, Beauchamp." Sir Sherlock rubbed his hands together briskly. "You'll be inveighing against the heat as soon as we land."

"I've been, yes. Have you?" said the baronet, positively glaring.

"With Hogarth in 1906 at Asyut. Unfortunately, I did not discover the find of the century," drawled Sir Sherlock.

"But you didn't stir up any elementals, either," Lady Evelyn pointed out rather sharply.

"No, just a few potsherds. I did cut my finger rather badly on one." I expected a chuckle, at least from Dr. Watson, but there was only silence, or else the sound was drowned in the roar of the engines. Lady Evelyn had taken on Sir Sherlock, and even Dr. Watson and myself, to investigate these elementals. But did she believe in them? Sometimes the whole affair seemed a lark to her. Other times it seemed deadly serious. She was a volatile sort.

It was Sir Sherlock who discovered the blankets under our seats, which made the cold just tolerable. There was also a bowl beneath each seat, purpose unclear. Did they usually serve meals on board? The thought made me queasy.

As for Dr. Watson, he still had that grin plastered on his face like a rictus, and I realized he was scared to death. Did he know something dire about our pilot? I crossed, wobbling, to him, leaned over and, whispering, asked him whether he knew a Lawrence Ross.

"Ross? Hmm . . ."

"Airman Ross."

"Is he a friend of yours?"

So Dr. Watson was not in on the secret. Indeed, he seemed at times the most incurious man I had ever met in my life. I wondered that he and Sir Sherlock were such great friends. Perhaps it was only the cold getting to me. I tugged the blanket tighter around myself.

Soon we were descending, and I began to feel easier. That hadn't been that bad after all.

"Cairo?" I asked hopefully.

"Pisa!" shouted Sir Sherlock.

"Italy? What are we stopping in Pisa for?"

"Refueling."

Well, then. I looked out, trying to find the famous leaning tower but saw no towers at all. When I expressed my disappointment, Dr. Watson said something about our flight path, which made no sense at all. We were in the air. We could choose any path we saw fit.

We were hardly on the ground more than a few minutes before we were in the air again. We were barely in the air again before we touched down in Rome and then Crete (the landing strip there was in a dormant volcano, which left me extremely unsettled) and Athens. They all looked alike to me. Air travel was dull.

We were out over the sea again, headed for Libya, when the plane nearly dropped out of the sky and I nearly lost my breakfast. I remember being helped back into to my seat by someone. I thought we were about to crash. No, someone explained (I had my head in my hands and didn't see who), it was a perfectly normal thing for a plane to do. Something to do with air currents. I knew about ocean currents, but air currents were an entirely new concept. I resolved never to ever fly again. A promise I was unfortunately to break, and sooner than I ever would have expected.

Then I heard a sound that did make me look up. Only for a

moment. Dr. Watson had discovered the use of the bowls. He had his head hidden in his but could not hide the awful retching sounds he was making. That explained the smell of disinfectant. I cowered under my blanket.

In the end, the sun was red and the sky purple before we were circling over Cairo. Why we were circling and not landing was not at all clear.

"Headwinds," said Dr. Watson. I think I would have slapped him had he not still looked so green.

We were all relieved when we did land. As I stepped off the plane, I felt the dry heat hit my face. It was a relief. I felt the grittiness of sand in my mouth. But the reason I passed out was none of these, but the overwhelming press of thousands of dead souls.

Chapter Nine:
Dr. John Watson

rs. Roberts came around after a cold compress was applied to her forehead. I was able to get some aspirin down her throat. She had been acting out of character all day, probably distraught by anticipation of her maiden flight. First there was that question about her friend Lawrence Ross, and then something about "spirits." If she wanted spirits, I suppose Egypt could supply aplenty. Half the city of Cairo was a necropolis.

We registered at Shepheard's Hotel, where we would stay the night before taking an auto to Luxor. We had been slated to take the train down, but Holmes kept saying that haste was necessary, and we *had* brought the driver along. Whether it was faster through the desert by train or auto was a moot question. Our pilot, sadly, was on his way to Damascus.

Shepheard's was certainly opulent enough to make me wish our stay was longer than just one night, which is to say it had all the Western amenities with just enough Moorish arches, splashing fountains, and perfumed terraces to remind one that he has been transported to the Orient. The "long bar" unfortunately turned out not to have been named for its size but for the amount of time it took to be served. It seemed to be a favorite watering hole for military types, with which Cairo was bursting.

But the next morning Mrs. Roberts had a high fever. There was no question of our taking a train or auto anywhere. Holmes fretted, but I absolutely forbade it. She wasn't up to any tricks this time. She spent much of the time in a delirium, talking to people who weren't there. Or perhaps they were.

"What about a boat? Could she travel by boat?" asked Lady Evelyn on the third day of Mrs. Roberts's malady, when she seemed no better and Holmes was wearing a rut pacing the floor.

"Boat to Luxor? That could take a week!" complained her husband, always the cheery soul.

"I suppose a boat would do no harm. So long as there's a cabin that's light and airy," I opined. "It might even be beneficial."

"A boat it is, then," said Holmes. "Better to travel slowly than not at all."

"I'll see to the arrangements immediately." Now that we were in Egypt, Lady Evelyn had begun to assert herself more authoritatively. We were in her territory. In short order she had secured a dahabeah, which was explained to me as a sort of private sailing houseboat, the traditional mode of navigating the Nile before steamers had entered the picture.

Also in short order she had us each assigned to procure the necessaries for our journey, which meant we would have to do battle with the vendors of the myriad bazaars the city was burgeoning with. But I was relieved when she insisted that no one go out alone—here she looked pointedly at Miss van Vredenburch—the streets were too dangerous for neophytes, which apparently included everyone except herself, though both Holmes and Beauchamp acted slighted by the insinuation.

I looked up dahabeahs in *Cook's*. According to that traveler's bible, it would take us forever to reach our destination, if indeed we ever reached it at all. That was not encouraging. But apparently calms and contrary winds are rare in February, and our nights were cool once the sun set.

We could evidently count on nothing, or nothing decent, from the boat's owner, so we should have to furnish our own blankets, sheets, pillows, towels, mosquito nets (a must!). The beds were provided. Very decent of him.

We would have to seek out a decent chemist for quinine, chlorodyne, brandy, calomel, camphor, emetic of ipecacuanha, rosewater, zinc, (for ophthalmia, as my eyes were already feeling gritty as the desert), and common soap.

Also provisions, of course—a great deal of fresh fruits and vegetables, rice and mutton, butter, flour, sugar charcoal, and coffee. (No tea? I'd take it upon myself to procure tea.)

Lastly, we could not forget presents. Over and above the usual baksheesh, certain local types would need to be mollified further: gunpowder (!), watches, telescopes, shawls, and pipes might be expected to smooth the way. English gunpowder was better than gold, I was informed. No wonder Egypt was a powder keg.

The streets wound about so willy-nilly that I could wish we had bread crumbs to strew to find our way back to the hotel. Of course, I was afraid they would all be eaten by the ragamuffin little beggars pulling at our coats wherever we went. If we'd stayed a week in Cairo, Holmes would have developed a fine little set of irregulars.

All this took haggling. It wasn't that we required everything of the cheapest, but the local merchants would be insulted if we did not bargain them to the edge of death. I had learned how to say, "How much?" in Arabic—*bekam dee*—but since I could not even guess at the answers, the phrase proved of limited use. One item we discovered was a blessing: sunglasses, like the film stars wear. Of course I had prescribed them for years for cases of syphilis, but they turned out to be the exact thing needed for desert sun and sand. We bought a dozen pairs. I was even able to buy some lighter clothes for practically the price of a song.

"Shouldn't we pay a visit to the Continental-Savoy since we have the opportunity?" I asked Holmes one day when we stumbled upon the hotel in our travels.

"Whatever for?"

"It's where Lord Carnarvon died. We could search for clues."

"His Lordship died there nearly a year ago. Did you think they'd sealed up his rooms all this time? Or that the maids didn't dust under the bed?"

"Well, what do you plan on doing, going to the tomb and asking the elementals politely who it was that stole whatever it was? Don't tell me that gibberish wasn't all made-up. She's playing you for a fool!"

"Did I tell you that Miss van Vredenburch came to me with a confession?"

"What, has she been bilking Lady Evelyn on the petrol fund?"

"She says that she heard Gould as well. She didn't see him, but she heard him. Heard him say, 'she stole the name.'"

"Do you believe her?" I questioned.

"Do you?"

"I don't know—I'm not Sherlock Holmes, blast it!"

"Oh, my dear Watson, neither am I anymore. I'm just old Sir Sherlock. I spend my time messing about in the garden and listening to the gramophone. I'm here as much to feel the warm sun on my bones as to solve a mystery."

I couldn't tell whether he was having me on, but he looked somber enough.

"Mrs. Roberts could have been throwing her voice. It's not a difficult talent to cultivate from what I understand," I claimed.

"Once more unto the breach, dear Watson," was all the answer Holmes gave. I had scored a point, I was sure.

I would rather not go into my visit to the Great Pyramid at Giza. Oh, the pyramids are colossal, and the Sphinx mysterious and grand, just as they'd been advertised. But I made the mistake of entering and summoned my own kind of curse. You see, one enters, virtually crawling, through a long, dark, narrow shaft that leads down to the subterranean chamber—also a dark, narrow shaft, filled with dozens of children skittering back and forth playing tag as if they were in Brunswick Square. About halfway down, I experienced an acute attack of claustrophobia—I was in a grave, mind you—and turned around and crawled out as fast as my hands and knees would carry me. Not my bravest moment.

But, excepting that, Cairo was a charming city. Especially in the evenings, the call of the muezzins to prayer from a thousand minarets, the splashing of the fountains, the lamps lit through high stained-glass windows, turned every door into a secret invitation to a thousand and one nights. No, not the thousand and one nights of the books. It was more muscular, more rooted. It was only for a short time, at twilight, that the night weighed anchor and one could, if one had a mighty enough oar, cast off for distant shores. Perhaps twilight is like this everywhere, but the sudden rain of stars and the exhalation of the lotus made it more imaginable in Cairo.

We were four days preparing for our journey up the Nile; I could have wished it were four months. Not that I was glad Mrs. Roberts had taken ill, you understand. I *was* glad Miss van V. had come along. We took turns watching over our patient. She was attentive but did not cosset her, which made her an excellent nurse.

We also received an honor we could not possibly have accepted had we not been stranded in Cairo. The lady Evelyn announced that we were invited to dinner with the sirdar, Sir Lee Stack (*sirdar* being an ancient Persian title adopted by the governors-general).

The dinner was to be held in the Sirdaria, the aptly named compound ruled by the British on the isle of Zamalek in the Nile.

"An oasis, with lovely gardens and fragrant trees," promised Lady Evelyn.

"And completely impenetrable," added her husband.

I wondered why it was necessary that it be so impenetrable. I learned that night.

The Sirdaria was indeed attractive, a great stretch of verdant parkland, fanned by a cool breeze, with clusters of tall trees—and even thicker clusters of armed guards, some English, some Egyptian, all of whom seemed to mean business.

The dining room was like something out of a sultan's palace, except that the soldiers lining the arched bays along the walls were equipped with Enfields, not wicked, cruel scimitars. But I'd wager that if they fixed bayonets, they could have killed just as swiftly and silently as mamluks. It almost put one off one's feed.

We were introduced to quite a distinguished group. Besides Sir Lee and his wife, Flora, there were the High Commissioner Lord Allenby and wife Adelaide, H. H. Asquith, the newly created earl of Oxford (ostensibly retired from politics, but who believed that?), as well as his son Herbert, who was something of a poet. The last member of the party was Stack's aide-de-camp, Captain P. K. Campbell of the Black Watch, which had spearheaded the lion's share of the battles in the Turkish campaign.

Sir Lee was a splendid example of British soldiery. The sirdar, governor-general of the Sudan and commander of the Egyptian army, was a square-jawed, square-shouldered, clear-eyed exemplar of manhood, and his wife, Lady Flora, was just as trim and well turned out as he.

Then I noticed a dark fellow in a tarboosh all alone in one corner, holding himself aloof but absorbing every word and gesture of our group.

"Who is that gentleman?" I asked discreetly.

"Sa'ad Zaghlul," Stack answered shortly.

"Zaghlul Pasha?" asked Beauchamp, alarmed. "Isn't he the leader of the insurrectionists?"

"And now premier of Egypt," rejoined Stack. "The sands here are constantly shifting. The trick is to keep the scales balanced."

"And to keep the Sirdaria well guarded," Campbell emphasized.

"Well, perhaps, but does that mean you have to invite him to dinner?" Beauchamp's sense of decorum was obviously offended.

"I prefer to keep an eye on him. Besides, I wanted your opinion of him, Sir Sherlock."

"My opinion?" said Holmes, somewhat taken aback.

"Yes. In the accounts I've read, you seem able to fillet a man after only a glance."

"Ah, that is due more to Watson's poetic license than to my abilities."

I was about to defend my fidelity to facts when Holmes touched me on the sleeve to stop me.

"The fact that he wears a tarboosh places him squarely in the Turkish camp, even as his immaculate evening wear proclaims him thoroughly westernized. I suspect that he has comfortably straddled both camps all his life. He is somewhat ascetic, which gives him advantage over his foes. You'll notice he wears no jewelry or even a handkerchief square."

"But he does have a tie pin," pointed out Lady Evelyn.

"I was getting to that. A coral tortoise. His time in the Seychelles was vital to the forging of his ideas. Perhaps most troubling is the perfectly groomed spread-eagled moustache, which points to an overweening vanity. He will have his way, no matter whether an entire people suffer for it."

I was about to applaud but caught myself in time.

"You've confirmed my worst fears. He wants to provoke me to violence, creating an outcry among the people. Egypt is a powder keg," pronounced Sir Lee solemnly, echoing Holmes's phrase uncannily.

Egyptian politics was apparently more complicated than I had given it credit for. Of course, the Oriental mind is deep and often devious. I would not step into Sir Lee's shoes for the world.

But dinner began shortly, driving away any thought of political turmoil. The dishes were tiny, but there was such a multitude of them! I remember ta'meyah, labeh, ful nabed, and hummus—though I have no idea what the ingredients were, I wrote them all down and intended to find them out once back in London. I was well satisfied. That is, until I realized that they were only meant as appetizers and there was still a whole army of entrées to follow. I groaned. Luckily, I was not overheard. Thank heavens for capacity.

I was seated next to Colonel Campbell (with the phlegmatic Zaghlul on my other hand), so I began asking him about his campaigns. Once started, he did not stop. I'm sure he was fascinating, but a native band began playing, so I never understood a word he said. They were not so awfully loud, but terribly distracting. They played authentic native instruments, but the music they played was American jazz, which was disconcerting to say the least. The drone of the oud dragged at the tempo. Jazz always seems to me to be just skirting toppling into chaos, and I thought certain it would collapse like the tower of Babel this time. But they struggled on manfully. The Beauchamps actually got up at one point and danced the Charleston, which I put down to a surfeit of martinis. And yes, I did sample a martini. I shall never do so again.

It was over coffee, with the musicians dismissed, that the talk became general again.

"How goes the Gezira Scheme?" asked Lady Evelyn of Sir Lee.

"The Sennar Dam will finally be completed next year. The Sudanese will be able to cultivate cotton."

"Which should be quite a boon for the British textile industry," said the earl.

"The Sudanese will sell only to the British?" asked Holmes.

"We built the irrigation canals. We built the dam. If they even try to sell to anyone else, we'll shut down the Suez," proclaimed the earl.

"And what if the Egyptians lay claim to the Suez?" I asked.

I was greeted by a general look of amusement. "Britain will never give up control of the canal," said the earl with finality.

"Ha, no," agreed the baronet. "Can you imagine the canal in the hands of the natives?"

Zaghlul Pasha's onyx eyes seemed almost closed in sleep. Apparently the conversation troubled him not in the slightest, which was worrisome in itself.

"I'm sure some Little Englanders would be more than willing to give up the Canal," Holmes remarked. "What if a Lawrence of Egypt arose in the vein of Lawrence of Arabia?"

"Best not to mention Lawrence in polite company," Captain Campbell advised with a wink.

"But Lawrence is a hero!" Lady Evelyn burned with sudden vehemence.

"Lord Allenby, what say you to that?" Holmes asked.

"He was useful, but he went right off the reservation. We had Arabia nicely carved up between ourselves and the French until he started making all kinds of promises to Sharif Hussein and his progeny."

"But surely that was only to secure their cooperation," said Lady Evelyn, still defending the man.

"You should have seen him at the Paris talks, all wrapped up in his white robes, following Emir Hussein around like a puppy dog. He so badly wants to be an Arab prince himself," Allenby answered with asperity.

Well, you'd think T. E. Lawrence was a personal friend of theirs, so stricken were they. The Beauchamps both put on glum faces, and conversation dwindled to perfunctory talk about the weather back in England. The earl seemed to think the cold weather was a plot devised by the Russians to bring us to our knees.

Miss van V. had elected to stay at the hotel and keep an eye on Mrs. Roberts. We found them both asleep, the girl in a chair next to the bed. She awoke when we came in.

"How is she?" I inquired.

"She is fretting all night. Say someone is *in gevaar*, in danger," pronounced the girl somberly.

"Danger? Who?" asked Holmes.

"Sir Lee. She say he is in terrible danger."

Holmes raised an eyebrow. "When she said these things, was she asleep or awake?"

"How is one supposed to know the difference with her?"

"You should go to bed yourself, my dear," I counseled.

"I *ben comfortabel* here."

She would not be gainsaid. We soon came away. I could see that Holmes's brow was knotted with concern. I turned to him. "Do you intend to warn the sirdar?"

"As long as he has Zaghlul Pasha at his elbow, he has all the warning he requires. But I suspect the elementals are restive."

"Sir Lee seems a reasonable fellow. I'm sure he takes reasonable precautions," I said.

"Reasonable, yes. That may be his downfall."

The following morning, we set sail for our final destination: Luxor and the Valley of the Kings.

The dahabeah was an ungainly looking creature on first sight, sort of a Pushmi-Pullyu, with tall lateen sails fore and aft. I had to wonder which was the prow and which the stern. There were four cabins only, meaning Holmes and I would have to double up. Mrs. Roberts was showing signs of improvement but would undoubtedly need a cabin to herself, what with my constant coming and going, changing her mustard plaster and lemon socks at all hours of the night. Miss van V. offered to sleep in a cot at her feet, but I vetoed that idea. The girl had obviously contracted a bad case of hero worship. I did not intend it to go any further.

It was on the first night of our voyage that I made a singular discovery. I was stretched out on my bed, fatigued with all the preparations. Holmes should have been worn to a nub himself, but he was pacing the tiny cabin, a well of nervous energy. I noticed then the absence of a familiar odor.

"Holmes, where's your pipe?"

"Oh, I haven't smoked in ages. Had to give it up. Emphysema."

Well, I was glad to hear that he had heeded medical advice, for so it must have been, but I did wonder what he would do if faced with any three-pipe problems. I wrapped myself in my mosquito netting and fell asleep to the splashing of night creatures on the Nile.

Holmes had been in a tremendous hurry to get to Egypt. Now that we were nearing our destination, however, he seemed to feel that we (meaning Mrs. Roberts) needed some time to acclimatize ourselves. He withdrew into himself, taking his cue from the constant river.

Whatever the cause, I was glad for the change—Holmes may have visited Egypt before (another adventure he had never told me about), but it was all new to me. The occasional splash of a waterfowl diving for its dinner made a soothing sound, and the vegetation was sweet and greenly fragrant on either side, reeds high enough to hide the infant Moses—though just beyond it one could glimpse the ragged teeth of hard-packed red earth, ancient beyond weariness.

It was truly a different world on the river. The mornings seemed to unfurl and grow taut with the swiftness of sails, while the night was one long, vast purple twilight, unable to close its eyes and sleep. Steamers passed daily, and small boats of every description flitted in and out of sight like dragonflies. We even met a dahabeah or two, which we greeted with great excitement and much hallooing, as if they were cousins.

The third day out, we were all seated on the deck, as tranquil and shiftless as if we were on holiday with old friends. The conversation was desultory. I might have dozed, I don't recall, when I noticed both the tone and the import of the conversation had shifted.

"Lady Evelyn, you met George Gould when he visited the tomb?" I recognized the inquisitorial tone in Holmes's voice.

"Actually, I met him first in Cairo. You remember, darling. The newlywed dinner?"

Beauchamp was distracted, watching the pilot trim the sails.

"Newlywed dinner? I don't understand. You were married just this month," said Holmes.

"It was an idea of my uncle Aubrey's. We were going to be married in March, but Father's death made that impossible. And Uncle Aubrey wouldn't have been able to make it—well, in the end he didn't make it, any more than poor Father did—" I could hear the catch in her throat. She stopped, gathering herself.

"And he invited Gould?" prompted Holmes.

"And his wife Guinevere. They had been married less than a year. Prince Ali Fahmy Bey—he wasn't really a prince, you know—and his wife, Marguerite. We were all, more or less, on honeymoon. Well, there were some marriages that didn't last."

"Wait," I interrupted, "you knew Ali Fahmy Bey?"

"Didn't I mention that before? Well, that was the only time I met him. Or his wife—I suppose I should say his widow. Does one address a gentleman's murderess as his widow? They seemed very much in love at the time. Uncle Aubrey loved to rub shoulders with the rich and powerful, no matter their reputations. Of course, half the time it was merely a device to pump someone for information. The rich and powerful do know things, sometimes things they are not even aware they know. He was always deep into ferreting out nuggets of information for Intelligence. He loved storing up secrets."

"Wasn't he a member of the Egyptian intelligence unit?" asked Holmes. "Along with T. E. Lawrence?"

"Mr. Holmes, you know your intelligence better than I. Yes, Lawrence and my uncle, Stewart Newcombe, and Lloyd, all under the command of Clayton. A group of wild men, my father called them."

"Was he trying to gather information from someone at your dinner?"

"I really couldn't say. His methods were often so convoluted. There were always wheels within wheels. I certainly wouldn't doubt it."

"Was Mr. Shaw there that night . . . or Mr. Lawrence?"

Lady Evelyn blanched. I stared at her witlessly. Only Beauchamp was calm, though I noticed a tightness in his jaw.

"I see now why you hired Mr. Holmes," he remarked.

"I'm sorry if I haven't been entirely forthcoming," she said, her eyes darting everywhere.

"You didn't answer my question."

I had missed something while I was drowsing. What had I missed? It seemed of some importance.

"No, there were just the seven of us at dinner that night. Three men are now dead. All visited the tomb shortly after it opened. I don't want to lose Brograve."

"You won't get rid of me that easily, my dear."

I went to check on Mrs. Roberts, still musing over the conversation, though I could not make heads or tails of it. The nap is the enemy of the mind in age, shrouding the most salient of facts in the clothes of a dream.

She seemed somewhat revived, although she was fretful again. Perhaps she had begun to worry over how she would convince the group of the presence of elementals when the tomb came up empty. Even Holmes was bound to expect some sort of proof. Wasn't he?

On the fourth day, when I was changing her plaster, she asked me a question that brought me up short.

"Doctor, what is the Reichenbach?"

"The falls? Have you never heard the story of his struggle with Moriarty over the abyss? It was in all the papers. I myself—"

"I never had time to read in the old days. My first husband died and left me with the three girls to raise."

"Ah. Of course. Well, then, Moriarty was the Napoleon of crime, as Holmes christened him. A mathematician, a genius, and the tortuous mind behind half the crimes in London. Holmes fell afoul of him, and we were forced to flee to the continent. He caught up with us in Switzerland, in a little resort town near the falls. There Holmes and Moriarty came to blows, and there both fell into the abyss and perished, or so I—and the world—believed.

"But I learned—the world learned—three years later that only Moriarty had perished that day. Holmes had gone into hiding."

"Sir Sherlock killed a man?"

"It was kill or be killed."

"Of that I have no doubt. But it must have left its mark on him."

"It did, although he concealed it, of course. But I think in part that was why he disappeared. He visited the Dalai Lama in Lhasa, the Mahdi in Khartoum, and I believe the bishop of Rome. Rather amazing for a man who barely knew the Buddha from a baptistery. I think he sought answers to questions that had never before occurred to him. I'm not sure he found answers that satisfied him. His mien had changed. He softened, became less remote. More fallible, more human. As if he were Pygmalion and Galatea both."

"It sounds an improvement."

"It would seem so, I suppose. Unless it's the result of being burdened by guilt."

Lady Evelyn had somehow got hold of a bath chair, so Holmes and I wheeled Mrs. Roberts out into the sun the next morning and lifted her up the steps to the upper deck, which stretched the length of the vessel, and we sat down on either side of her for another conference.

(I had finally talked Miss van V. into taking a nap in her own bed. Otherwise, I warned her, I might have two patients on my hands.) Beauchamp and the lady Evelyn were no doubt sleeping late after spending the night counting stars. It was difficult to remember that they were essentially newlyweds, since neither seemed comfortable with open displays of affection. The landed class has always been fastidious about that.

"And now—how are you feeling, Mrs. Roberts? Your color has improved remarkably," observed Holmes.

"It was difficult at first, like a swarm of . . . You don't know how many wanted to tell me their tales, how many want to pass on messages to loved ones who themselves died thousands of years ago, but I've made peace with them now. I think I have them under rein. Of course, many thanks must go Dr. Watson's ministrations. And Anna."

I may have colored at this praise. "Not much I could do in this backward place. Had to fall back on old-fashioned remedies. But I think it's these cool river breezes that have helped most of all." I did not entertain talk of nagging voices from the dead.

"You know, you are liable to face some powerful emanations once you enter the tomb," Holmes warned, studying her intently.

Mrs. Roberts nodded slowly, even dreamily, but did not speak. Her lips were pressed tightly together. If she was an actress, by George, she missed her chance on the boards.

"Dr. Watson and I will be with you every step of the way. If you feel danger drawing near, you must tell us at once."

"Er . . ." I asked, "how exactly do we deal with these elementals? Can they be seen or felt . . . or harmed?"

"Reserve yourself for the more mundane threats, my friend. There may be those who would rather we not discover certain secrets," Holmes counseled.

"You mean those already in the thrall of the elementals. Yes, they are powerful. I can already feel their tendrils reaching out to me from the tomb." Mrs. Roberts's eyes grew eerily bright, a habit of hers when she pretended to communicate with the dead.

We might have been telling Christmas ghost stories, for the

delicious thrill that went up the spine when such tales were well told, but I'm afraid all I could think was "Bah! Humbug!" Not that I discounted the danger posed by human hands. There was enough gold in that tomb to whet a man's mind to murder many times over.

As the days went by, the landscape changed around us as the banks rose and became stony behind tall palms. Pitted caves dotted the shoreline—whether natural erosion or ruined fortresses, I could not guess. The silence grew around us; no bird sang. I could not conjure fogs ever shrouding these banks in their forgiving blankets, nor swallowing voices so that shouts became whispers. Everything had always been just as it was, solid and immovable. No stones were simply rolled away from tombs in this country. No wonder the ancients' dreams conjured up lions with men's faces, and dogs with men's bodies, or crowned serpents. The starkness was enough to make men dream open-eyed.

We were coming to the Valley of the Kings. I began to be curious about the original discovery of Tutankhamun. Obviously the papers had been full of accounts, but I knew well the mishmash of exaggerations and errors the papers were liable to. I sought out Lady Evelyn. She and Beauchamp had taken shelter from the noonday sun in the cool of the lounge below deck, where the only idols were gin and tonics.

"We always knew we would find the tomb, given enough time," she said. "But we never thought we would find it intact. I suppose that's what gave rise to the talk of a curse. What else could hold the tomb inviolable those thousands of years, when so many surrounding it were looted?"

"Perhaps they were simply fortunate in its hiding place?"

"Oh, no, the tomb was found. It was definitely disturbed. Why it was not looted is the great mystery of Tutankhamun."

For the first time on our journey, I felt the hairs prickle on the back of my neck. I thought of going down, down into the darkness of the tomb, sealing my fate by greed and folly. Would it be like the pyramid at Giza? I took my leave and went up on the deck to try and wipe the spell from my mind. Yet there was the brown murk of the Nile, the banks sliding by, the foliage screening any prying eyes from my sight. *Foolishness, foolishness*, I repeated to myself.

At last the day came. Ten days for a dahabeah was record time, I was told. Mrs. Roberts and I were standing companionably side by side at the prow. I watched her eyes for any telltale signs of apprehension, but there was only the same deep mask she habitually displayed. The others must have been below packing, or perhaps toasting to the end of our voyage.

I asked her, "Excited about the mysteries we're about to take on?"

"I confess I was not thinking about the tomb at all. I was thinking of my children. I miss them so."

Since she had broached the subject, I asked her plainly why she had left them to make this voyage.

"We needed the money so desperately."

I raised an eyebrow at this. I wanted at first to ask her just how much money she was expecting. Holmes had mentioned an honorarium, but I wasn't expecting a remuneration of any size. But I sheared off from this sensitive subject and lighted on another one, probably just as sensitive. "Is your work lucrative?"

"I don't charge for my work. Or at least I didn't. Before the fire."

I looked at her in alarm.

"Sir Sherlock has told you about the fire, hasn't he?" She read the blank expression on my face. "No, I don't imagine he has. Discretion seems to be his watchword. Well, then, you may not believe certain parts of my story, but it is all true. It occurred only three months ago, when one night I woke up on the floor beside our bed. This was odd, because I sleep on the side of the bed next to the wall. My husband sleeps on the outer edge. I was too disoriented to make anything of it, though, and crawled back into bed, where I soon fell asleep.

"Only to wake up once again on the floor! I was bewildered, but I thought I must surely be dreaming and once again got into bed. At that point, fully awake, I felt myself rise through the air, only to be once again dumped on the floor. That was when I saw the smoke curling round the bottom of the door. The spirits were trying to save my life.

"The sitting room was already ablaze, but I shook my husband awake, and we were able to get the children out safely through a back window. By the time the fire brigade arrived, the house was already a ruin. We had nothing. So when Sir Sherlock presented his offer, it was a godsend."

I didn't know what to make of her story, but the fire was obviously real. Did my heart melt for her? I'm afraid not. But the tiniest window had opened into her soul. She had left her children for her children's sake. That I could admire.

On our port side slid into view the temples of Karnak and Luxor, breathtaking in their majesty, so old that they seemed wrought by time itself rather than the hand of man, as if those towering columns had been carved from sand by wind and water over the course of ten thousand years. I felt as a little child, staring up at the knees of giants. Tall obelisks reaching for the sky, hundreds of columns marching hand in hand with reticent sphinxes, doorways guarded by the gods.

On the starboard hand reared up hills of blistered limestone, snaggletoothed and bloody, which screened the Valley of the Kings. There waited at a mooring point, seeming very small indeed by comparison, a guide with camels and donkeys, and a crowd of boys alongside, to escort us on the last leg of our journey. We were going to explore the tomb, even before we registered at our hotel on the opposite bank.

It crossed my mind—indeed, made a great deal of sense to me—that perhaps Holmes had conceived of this elaborate charade wholly for Mrs. Roberts's financial benefit. It would be like him. And if that were true, perhaps he had insisted on my company for the purpose of healing the rift between us. That, too, would be like him. Since Reichenbach, of course. Not before.

"There's a barge coming up behind," Beauchamp's voice said. I turned to see him and his good lady wife staring back at a steam barge, low in the water like a crocodile, coming up on us fast astern.

"I'm not surprised. Carter may have moved up his whole schedule," said Lady Evelyn thoughtfully.

I had no clue what she meant by that, but I was too excited by our imminent arrival to give it much thought. Holmes arrived on the scene with an uncharacteristic scowl. I would learn soon enough what had angered him.

We were greeted at the jetty by a tall fellow with unkempt black locks and a cadaverous face. A heavy moustache was nailed to his upper lip. He introduced himself as Arthur Mace. I recognized the name as a member of Carter's team, but I could not recall what specialty was his. I didn't recall whether he had a doctorate or not, either, so I decided to refer to him simply as "Mace."

There were donkeys for the ladies—that is to say, for Miss van Vredenburch and Mrs. Roberts. I suppose a donkey would have been an insult to Lady Evelyn. She greeted her pony with a fond embrace and an apple she had brought all the way from Monte Carlo. They were old friends, these two.

There was some hilarity in mounting the camels. First they are made to kneel, and sitting astride them seems easy. But then they rear up on their hind legs first, in a perverse contradiction of every other four-legged animal on the planet, and if one is not leaning back as far as possible, one is liable to be pitched forward and wind up on one's bottom on the ground. All right, I wound up on the ground. Ha-ha. I still feel the bruises. Then they are impossible to guide in any one direction, whether because of the flies in their eyes or a natural curiosity to explore the unchanging landscape around them. Luckily the swarm of boys was supplied with sticks to keep them moving in the right direction. And the gorge we traversed was narrow enough there was only so far they could go astray. We were warned by Mace to keep to one side, however. There was a sort of miniature railway laid down in the center of the path, which was tricky for the camels to navigate. I was too busy trying to keep my seat to ask what the thing was for. I was soon to find out.

So we did somehow make progress, bumping along, however

slowly. We knew we were drawing close when we could hear a loud voice chanting in Arabic—midday prayer, I supposed.

Lady Evelyn sat up straight and proud in the stirrups. We descended into the valley. I would have said we descended gingerly, but the camels paid no attention to our directions and treated all ground the same, whether it was sloping or level. Once we came forth from the gorge, the boys were hard put to it to keep them in line. We descended into the wide Valley of the Kings and had our first sight of the of the tomb of Tutankhamun.

It wasn't much to look at. I hadn't expected a pyramid, exactly, but I had hoped for something more than what we were greeted with. It was a mound of dirt, not even a hill. It was backed by tall walls of limestone, brooded over by El Qurn, the highest point in the Theban hills. There was a rectangular hole cut into the rock, blacker than night, with an iron gate and a small sentry box beside it, nothing more. This was the famous tomb of Tutankhamun. Surrounding it were mounds of rubble on either side. There were a few more pockmarks in the hillside farther off—more tombs. Of course, there were the native workers, the fellaheen, all in ragged robes and tortured head wraps, standing staring at us with bald curiosity, while the muezzin had stopped in midchant. Weren't they supposed to be kneeling on prayer rugs, all facing—? I had no idea in which direction Mecca lay.

And onlookers, a whole crowd of them, which I had not expected at all. What they were doing there was not clear. Westerners by their clothes, they stood around aimlessly, or sat on flimsy folding chairs, mainly staring at the hole, as if they expected a dragon to issue forth at any moment. It was certainly warm as dragon's breath in that valley. Some examined guidebooks, some read newspapers, some shared food or drink from picnic baskets. Some were frankly napping in whatever meager shade they could find or devise. There was an endless clicking of little Kodak cameras, a sound so pervasive it might have been a plague of locusts. They could've been a crowd waiting for a cricket match to begin.

"Who are all these people?" asked Mrs. Roberts, echoing my thoughts.

"Tourists, gawkers, *newspapermen*." Mace emphasized this last with a definite sneer. "They're quite a nuisance, really. All wanting to be part of the Tutankhamun experience. They hope to get a glimpse of Tutankhamun's knickknacks. Or evil spirits." He darted a quick glance at Holmes to see if he was offended. "Plenty of treasure on display now at the Cairo Museum, but they seem to believe the best is yet to come. They've been coming here every day since news leaked about the discovery."

I am happy to report that I was able to dismount my camel with my dignity intact. The boys took the mules and the pony off, for shade or water, but the camels remained where they were, like mud bricks.

As we approached, I noticed the muezzin had a book in his hand. Was he a novice, still learning the prayers? I expected the fellaheen to get back to whatever work they were up to, perhaps sifting through those huge mounds of rubble. But they didn't move at all. They kept staring at us in a way that made my skin itch.

"I don't see any buildings at all," I said, looking around.

"What did you expect?" asked Mace.

"I understood from the papers that a great deal of work was going on right here. Cleaning and cataloging and such," I said.

"Indeed, I do most of the cleaning. I'm the conservator. But we don't do it out here in the sun. We've set up a conservation laboratory in the tomb of Seti just over there. Far more practical." He pointed to another cave, not far away, disappointingly like the first.

"You work in another tomb?" said Mrs. Roberts, plainly aghast at the idea.

"It's a big tomb, with lots of room, not like Tut's little squat," said Mace, as if that were her objection.

"And that is where we'll find Mr. Carter?" Holmes lifted his glasses, trying to get a better look in the glare of the sun. I felt in my pocket and withdrew my sunglasses.

The sudden wail of a whistle from the river made us all jump.

"Just wait a bit, he'll show. He's heard the barge's whistle."

"Is that why they stopped with the prayer? I imagined they must be glad to see you, Lady Evelyn," I proffered. "See how they stare?"

"What did you think Hassan was reading?" asked Mace, with an odd little smile.

"The Koran, I suppose."

He merely laughed at that, and I thought he was about to elucidate the matter, when we saw Carter indeed pop his head out of the other rabbit hole—the tomb of Seti.

"Ah, yes, here he is now," Beauchamp said.

In the far distance, a cloud of dust rose up. When the dust cleared, I saw a whole crowd of workmen gathered round the tomb's mouth. The crowd resolved itself into a line, and soon they were passing sealed wooden boxes from hand to hand and stacking them on low railroad cars, which I hadn't noticed before. This, I surmised, was the reason for the rails.

There was Carter among them, shouting instructions at the top of his voice till he was hoarse, gesticulating like a windmill. There was a string of armed guards there, too, keeping the onlookers at bay. It was all a bit chaotic. It seemed as if Carter was clearing out the tomb, from barrels to beads. A knot of workmen nearest us, though, was still just standing, staring at us, occasionally pointing and whispering to each other. They knew nothing of manners.

I had seen him in the newspapers often enough, stripped down to shirtsleeves, his watchful eyes and resolute mouth set against his sunburned face. The Carter revealed to us when the dust settled, stocky and rather short, in a three-piece suit and pomaded hair, looked more like a harried accountant as he knocked the dust from his homburg.

The distances seemed vast in the emptiness of the landscape. But it only took a minute for him to join us. Mace hailed him as he neared.

"Visitors? I haven't time for visitors today. Besides, Burton is taking pictures of the sepulcher." Then he recognized Lady Evelyn. With two steps he had her in his arms. "Evie!" He picked her up and twirled her.

Then he must have noticed the sour look on Beauchamp's face. He set her down gently and shook Beauchamp's hand gravely. "Good to see you, old chap," he said.

"It's *Lady* Evelyn," said Beauchamp sententiously.

"Sorry I wasn't there to greet you at the pier. Everything is running behindhand."

"We know. We just missed you in Cairo. Some new to-do with the government?" Lady Evelyn inquired.

"Outrageous. I wish I had your father still to deal with them. You'll be wanting to see the sepulcher. But surely you don't need me to lead you on a tour."

Carter seemed to take in the surroundings for the first time. "Why are those fellaheen standing around? What's happened?"

"They turned to stone as soon as these fellows appeared on the horizon. I think they're a bit overawed by our visitors," replied Mace.

"Nonsense, they've seen the Lady Evelyn before. Hassan, get these men back to work." He spoke to the tall black in the striped djebellah, who had been chanting.

"I meant Sir Sherlock. Hassan was just reading to them from *The Hound of the Baskervilles*. They are gazing upon one of their heroes."

Hassan nodded solemnly and clapped his hands. The men slowly came to life, but they still cast sidelong glances at Holmes.

"*The Hound* is the fellaheen's favorite story," said Mace. "They identify the hound with Anubis—whom many have claimed to sight in the darkness."

I'll admit this gave me a chill. I still remembered that spectral hound, black, silent, and monstrous.

As the men bent to their tasks, Hassan's clear voice took up the tale again in a singsongy manner. It didn't much sound like *The Hound of the Baskervilles* to me.

"I thought you'd like to meet our guests. This is Sir Sherlock and his associate, Dr. Watson," said Lady Evelyn, trying to get things back on course.

Carter's face went black. "Oh, yes, you're Holmes," he said in a clipped voice. He did not offer his hand, which took him down a notch in my estimation.

"Congratulations on your find," said Holmes, graciously, I thought, considering Carter had nearly bitten him.

But Carter was just getting started. "You're the one who's desecrated Lord Carnarvon's memory with your talk of curses and elementals."

"Howard, really—"

"No, they might as well know the truth, Evie. I was against you people coming out here at all. If it weren't for Evie—"

"As you have made abundantly clear, Mr. Carter, we don't need you for our undertaking. You have your work to do, and I have mine," said Holmes stonily. "I do hope afterward you'll be willing to entertain a few questions."

"Did you not receive my reply to your cable? As I explained to Eve, my dance card is full up the rest of this week. I've got more important things to do than entertain you and your ragtag bunch."

Ah, there was the reason for Holmes's scowl.

"I see your courtesy to the dead does not extend to the living," returned Holmes.

Then I was blinded. I suppose we all were, for I heard Carter shout, "Merton, get that bloody camera out of my face!"

As the flash faded, I could just make out the offending photographer by squinting.

"Let's have one of you together with Sir Sherlock, Carter. The great detective and the great excavator," said the photographer.

"Arthur Merton, the great pest," said Carter, by way of introduction. "*London Times*, my taskmaster." He was aggravated but eventually acceded to the photographer's wheedling, which surprised me. I didn't know at that time that the *Times* provided a significant portion of Carter's funding. The two men posed next to each other, scowling for the camera.

Arthur Merton gave off a patrician air unusual among newspapermen. His was a commanding presence. His bald head and round face were shaded from the sun by a homburg, but his penetrating eyes lanced through the shadow. He didn't mind laying hands briskly on people to pose them as he saw fit. He knew just what he wanted and was finished in only a minute or two, which was extremely fortunate. Any longer and Holmes and Carter might have come to blows.

"No pictures of us, Arthur," said Lady Evelyn.

"Right, right, you're not here. I am in receipt of your memorandum of the tenth."

Once he had exacted a promise of an interview from Holmes, he seemed to lose interest in us and began snapping pictures of the cargo loading, which was proceeding apace.

"And who might you be?" Carter asked, catching sight of Mrs. Roberts.

"Estelle Roberts. Consultant," she piped up bravely.

"Consultant on what? The supernatural? Should I pour milk and honey on the threshold? That's what one occultist advised."

"I suppose they'd appreciate the gesture, but it's not as if they actually eat," she replied saucily.

"Well, that's a relief, anyway," said Carter. He let his eyes travel over Miss van V., a little too long, I thought, but then he seemed to dismiss her. Her own eyes were hard and incurious.

"What's got you so surly, Howard?" asked Lady Evelyn.

"He had a crowd of a long-faced dignitaries to deal with at the opening just the other day," offered Mace.

"Nonsense. Their silly questions that would have you laughing in fits, Evie," remonstrated Carter. Every time he said "Evie," Beauchamp flinched. Rightly so.

"Oh, yes, I read in the papers, you've opened the sepulcher! That should be cause for celebration. Unless—" Lady Evelyn did not conclude her thought.

"The sarcophagus is a bloody mess," said Carter.

"Oh, no! But—the mummy is there," she said.

"Oh, he's there right enough. But some sort of black pitch was poured in all round him by the priests, and it's hardened. I don't know if we'll ever be able to chip him out. Come see. I ought to check on how Burton is coming along with his photos, at any rate."

As we turned to follow, Sherlock Holmes said under his breath, "It's not adoration in their eyes, but fear." And, looking at the workers, still staring underneath their lashes, their eyes bright and tracking our every move, I recognized the truth of his words.

"But why should they fear you?" I asked in a whisper.

"Not me, I think. Mrs. Roberts."

Estelle Roberts? How could *anyone* fear her? Although I'll admit she was a bit intimidating to the uninitiated. Those eyes of hers. But really—they *were* watching her. For heaven's sake, why?

"They sense her powers," he hissed.

Oh, piffle.

I was concerned as we approached the tomb that we would have to feel our way blindly down the shaft in the dark and cursed myself for not having bought a torch in the Cairo bazaar. But then I realized it must be well-lit if they were taking photos. It would all be all right.

I was right—and wrong. There were lights strung up all the way down. Blessed light. I strode over the threshold confidently. We were barely six steps in when all at once the lights blinked out.

I froze. In that dank, hot tunnel I felt a cold breath at the nape of my neck.

"Engelbach! Bloody hell!" exploded Carter. He did not apologize to the ladies for his language, which was gauche in the extreme.

I shot a look back at the entrance. There was still a square of light that marked the tomb entrance. I thought surely we would turn around and go back. We did not.

"It's all right," said Mace placidly. "We've got the mirrors aligned, more or less."

"Mirrors!" called Carter. "Where are the mirrors?"

And just like that, there was a whispering and padding, like the wind through the reeds, and I suddenly realized there was someone standing next to me, dark and tall, motionless and invisible, and for a brief moment the air was full of fairies, just as it had been in the Hodsons' compartment on the train, and then the light came flooding in from the outer world, honest sunlight, carried from one hand-held mirror to the next, punching through the darkness all the way to the heart of the tomb.

"Here are your mirrors, Watson. Perhaps we'll find the smoke farther down." Holmes spoke glibly, but if I'd known what lay ahead, I'd have quailed.

I was to learn that Burton generally preferred natural light for his pictures rather than using flashbulbs. So he had brought the sun in— with mirrors, all of them held in place by these tall, uncannily silent assistants, constantly in motion to catch the light, who barely seemed to breathe and had to be carefully stepped around to reach our goal. Each time we stepped in front of a mirror, the light blinked out, so it was slow and clumsy going with our group. All we had were those flickering beams to navigate by, so there was much tripping and muffled cursing. I think I may have even heard some from the ladies. My feet counted sixteen steps downward, sliding them along without ever picking them up, certain I was going to break my fool neck. I could feel that same claustrophobia welling up inside that had attacked me in the pyramid. I would have stopped, at least to catch my breath, but Holmes was behind me, prodding me forward with his stick in my back.

"Who's Engelbach?" asked Beauchamp.

"Rex Engelbach, chief inspector of antiquities," answered Lady Evelyn.

"He's in charge of electricity for the whole valley. Lately he's been playing these games with us," grumbled Carter.

"What about torches?" asked Beauchamp.

"Not enough air down here. We'd suffocate," came Carter's biting reply.

We paced some twenty feet farther down a corridor. Did I believe in curses after all? No, but the way was narrow, and the air had a sour, dead smell. The sweat pricked along my brow and slid down my nose. I felt panic bubbling up inside me. I was being buried alive. I pushed the feeling down, but it pushed back just as hard.

At last we reached—what? An empty room. Flashes of light danced about the walls like . . . like fairies! And at once it was revealed to me how Hodson had conjured his fairies on the train. The candle on the table. Mirrors, tiny mirrors, all arranged, so that if the candle was moved ever so slightly—ah, the cunning of it. A wave of relief passed through me as I put that puzzle to rest. Then there was a scream that put terror in my heart, and the lights went out.

"What happened?" Carter's voice.

"Oh, I stepped on Ahmed's toe, I think, and he ran off wailing like a banshee." That was Merton. I didn't realize he had followed us down.

"Burton, are you all right?" called Mace.

"I'd be doing better with a bit of light," came an answer from the far side of the chamber. The only thing I could see over there was a glimmer of a long stone box of some sort. It took me a bit of orienting myself to recognize it for what it was—Tutankhamun's sepulcher. The two bats' wings that brooded over it were reflectors on a couple of arc lamps—probably quite handy when there was a modicum of electricity on hand. The sepulcher was cambered to the left, where the mirror light could not quite reach.

"This is the antechamber," said Carter, as if he was showing us Versailles. His voice echoed in the emptiness. Then he did something that made me want to strangle him—he took a torch out of his pocket and shone it all about. *That* would have been useful on the way down.

The light revealed nothing but bare grey walls and bare floor.

"Where is everything?" asked Mrs. Roberts.

"We took over seven hundred items out of here," he answered proudly. "Most of it has been moved to the Cairo Museum, though some of it still waits in the laboratory."

Was Holmes sniffing the walls? Thank heaven it was dark.

"Will that stop your—?" asked Miss van V. of Mrs. Roberts.

"No, no—the spirit has not been removed," she vouched.

"Oh, for pity's sake," Carter erupted, dropping any semblance of patience.

"I heard you dabbled in spiritualism yourself, Carter," said Beauchamp.

"Oh, yes!" chirped Lady Evelyn. "Did I tell you about the time when my father held a séance at Highclere? Helen Cunliffe-Owen started speaking in tongues, and Howard swore it was Coptic!"

The Beauchamps laughed together, and I caught a glint of mirth in Holmes's eye.

"I was joking. It's only a party game to me, all that table turning and parlor tricks," retorted Carter.

Mrs. Roberts's disapproval was palpable, even in the dark.

"I'd be careful of party games if I were you," warned an asthmatic voice from the corner. "I nearly broke a toe last Christmas playing blindman's buff."

"Who's that?" said Carter, swinging his light on the far wall. I glimpsed a few heads bobbing up from behind the sarcophagus.

"Douglas-Reid," the voice drifted back.

"Ah, Sir Archibald, didn't realize you had got in."

"Yes, we've just been discussing your problem. Any idea how you'll dislodge your mummy from his casing?"

"It all depends on the resin's composition. Lucas is testing a sample now. We may have to chip him out if he can't devise some sort of solvent."

"That would be a shame. At any rate, I can't take X-rays till you've removed him from the sarcophagus."

"Agreed. I'm sorry you've come all this way for nothing," said Carter. His manner was far more collegial than with us.

"Not for nothing, sir. I've had a chance to renew many old acquaintances. And of course," he said, peering at Holmes's silhouette, "another chance to risk the curse of King Tut."

"I sincerely hope you may not fall under this sentence," Holmes returned with frigidity in his voice.

And then, when my eyes had finally acclimated to the darkness, without warning a dazzling light flooded the room. I was blinded once again. The arc lamps had popped on, as well as the bulbs, which were strung up haphazardly everywhere. We were granted light.

"Lady Evelyn, I didn't realize you were here." Two men emerged blinking from behind the sarcophagus, followed by three natives, whose arms were full, one with a camera and tripod, the other two with loads of glass plates. The sarcophagus itself was a heavy sandstone block, some seven feet in length. Above it, suspended from a sort of cat's cradle of ropes strung everywhere, hung the granite lid. Massive. I was not at all sure I wanted to risk my neck under that.

Burton was a natty little fellow with thinning hair and a perpetually nervous smile.

"Mr. Burton, yes, it's lovely to see you again. And this is my husband, Brograve Beauchamp."

"Oh, yes. Condolences on your father. And congratulations on your marriage. Off to the darkroom now. Oh, and this is our radiologist, Sir Archibald Douglas Reid."

Sir Archibald could have been Burton's brother, or his law partner, although I was informed later that he was one of the most distinguished pioneers in the field of radiology. He was, it is true, sallow of skin, and thin enough to be called wasted, but there was that same air of bland superiority and aloofness about him that the photographer displayed. Perhaps it was the identifying mark of the photographic specialist.

Carter did not bother himself with introductions, though both men eyed us with curiosity. How far had Holmes fallen in the estimation of society? How far had I fallen by association with him?

"You're finished, then?" Carter asked.

"Hardly. Hours yet to go," returned Burton. "But I'm off now to do some developing."

"There's a darkroom?" Holmes's curiosity was piqued.

"KV55."

I had read about these designations. *KV* meant King's Valley. The tomb we were standing in was KV62, the sixty-second discovered thus far. Not that they expected to find any more. But then, they hadn't expected to find this one, had they? Lord Carnarvon had been so dispirited he had very nearly packed it in. Or so the story went.

"Another tomb? It sounds made to order for a darkroom. Who was the former tenant?" Holmes asked.

"Akhenaten, near as they can guess," replied Burton.

"Akhenaten? The heretic king? But that tomb's surely cursed!" gasped Mrs. Roberts, blanching. She was hardly an expert on pharaohs, but Mrs. R. knew her curses.

"Well, it's certainly dusty, which is curse enough for my work. You must be Sir Sherlock," Burton said, offering his hand.

"And these are my associates, Dr. Watson and Mrs. Roberts." We shook hands all round, like polite society.

"Heard you were coming, of course. A bit of insurance against curses can't do us any harm. Now, if you'll excuse me."

Burton's little band filed out, leaving us to wonder whether his words were sincere or subtle mockery.

"Now you may view the sepulcher," Carter announced. "I suppose that's where your interests lie. Touch nothing! Do nothing that the lady Evelyn has not explicitly approved. As for me, I shall return to the laboratory. I don't think I could stomach the sight of all your shenanigans. Good day." With those frank and frankly brutal words, he left us.

"I'm sorry. He was close to my father. This talk of elementals has upset him badly," apologized Lady Evelyn.

"The atmosphere here lends itself to a certain moroseness," Holmes ceded.

"He's definitely cleared everything out. I didn't realize it would be so empty," said Mrs. Roberts wistfully.

"Oh, no, it's not empty at all. There's the annex"—Lady Evelyn pointed—"and the treasury there are as yet untouched. There are thousands of items yet to be cataloged."

I could just make out the cracks in the walls that confessed to those hidden rooms she had mentioned. I wondered whether there might be others, still undiscovered. What might be hiding behind them? Dogheaded men? A hellhound? The place was beginning to play tricks on my mind. I wondered about the quality of the air in this hot, stuffy little tomb.

We shuffled toward the burial chamber. I remembered that they had taken down a false wall that separated the two chambers, as well as the four nested shrines that had protected the sarcophagus. It was plain where the antechamber ended and the burial chamber began. Bare walls gave way to a torrent of frescoes in bright yellow, blue, and red, describing, so far as I could make out, the life and death of Tutankhamun. I suppose the afterlife as well, although on the western wall it appeared that the pharaoh had taken a boat ride to meet a delegation of baboons. The sarcophagus itself was a massive block of quartz. At each corner was carved some sort if winged guardian—an angel?

"Isis, Nephthys, Selkis, and Neith." Lady Evelyn traced over them caressingly with her fingers. That didn't leave me any the wiser. "Goddesses of protection," she added.

They hadn't exactly done a crackerjack job protecting their lad Tut, I thought, unless one subscribed to the whole elementals theory, in which all of us would die horrible deaths. I studied the walls. The entire room was incised with hieroglyphs, mainly eyes and birds—always Egyptian favorites. I wouldn't like to be the fellow tasked with translating them. Perhaps this was what had caused Hugh Evelyn-White to blow his brains out. I silently blessed the ancient fellow who invented the alphabet.

"Eve!" squawked Beauchamp. "It's solid gold!"

I heard gasps all around me. I stepped up beside the rest to peer inside the sarcophagus, still conscious of the lid hanging precariously over my head. At first I was too dazzled to make out a thing, then I thought of my sunglasses and donned them. The whole thing slowly came into focus. All I could think of were Carter's words, as reported in the *Times*, when he first set eyes on the interior of the tomb. Lord Carnarvon had asked him if he saw anything.

"It was all I could do to get out the words 'Yes, wonderful things.'"

Under the photographer's hot lights, it was almost blinding, even with dark glasses on.

I had thought he must have been an unusually tall pharaoh, since the sarcophagus was over seven feet long. But now I could see that there were actually one, two, no, *three* coffins, each set one within another, like Russian nesting dolls. Two were of gilt wood, but the innermost was indeed solid gold. The mummy's body was blackened, covered in the pitch Carter had mentioned, down to his feet, which were sheathed in golden sandals. He was in fact about my height, or shorter. He was the boy king, after all.

His face and shoulders were covered by a mask, which . . . Well, you must have seen the mask in the papers, so you'll understand how difficult it is to describe—the eyes of precious gems, the vulture and cobra sitting upon his forehead (the latter, I was told, poised to spit fire upon the pharaoh's enemies), the full golden lips. I have read since that Carter describes it as having a "sad but tranquil expression." He had neglected to mention that it was also a sight most unnerving, those large eyes staring up at you from centuries past, the oddly deli-cate, almost feminine features. I will never be quit of that unyielding golden face, nor the unasked question that seemed to hang upon his lips. It was a look of betrayal, such as I had witnessed on the faces of those whose last sight was their murderer's face. Could Tut have been murdered? If so, his murderer would be three thousand years beyond justice by now.

I made the mistake of mentioning those feminine features out loud, and Lady Evelyn launched into a long diatribe, telling me he was only nineteen years old when he died, a virtual child, and then going on to tell me everything that was known about his wife, his mother, his father, and his father's father. I kept expecting her to run out of steam. Several times Beauchamp interrupted, correcting her, which she did not appear to appreciate. She corrected him in turn, rather snappishly, and somewhere in there I drifted off. But I did notice out of the corner of my eye that Holmes had turned away from the coffin altogether and was meticulously scraping some sort of brown fungus off the wall and sealing it in an envelope, as if it were tobacco ash that he could analyze later to find out who'd murdered the boy pharaoh. I don't know that he even looked at the mummy. I also noticed Mrs. Roberts was looking none too healthy, wrung out and breathing hard, and it just occurred to me that she was about to faint, when she burst out with "Get out!" so loud it stunned everyone in the chamber to silence, which embarrassed her. "I'm sorry, but I need silence to concentrate," she crackled.

That brought Lady Evelyn's lecture to a merciful halt.

"Concentrate on what?" asked Beauchamp in a disagreeable tone.

"The voices. Can't you hear their tumult?"

It was quiet enough in that tomb that I could make out the breathing of seven separate souls. Nothing beyond that. Then Merton snapped a picture, and it sounded loud as an avalanche. Holmes glared at him.

"You wish us all to leave?" Holmes asked carefully.

"The nerve!" said Beauchamp. "We can't just leave a stranger—"

"It's why we've brought her here. Come, husband." Lady Evelyn leaned against him, shifting him toward the exit. Husband yielded. Merton backed away. Holmes and I moved after them.

"Except Dr. Watson. If you'll please stay."

What could I do but accede to her request? Perhaps I felt a little flattered. She knew I could certainly hold my tongue with the best of them.

"Shall I stay by you also?" asked Miss van V. Mrs. Roberts shook her head. The Dutch girl left, looking disconsolate. The others cleared the chamber.

Now what? I awaited her instructions.

"Please stay silent. Don't move, whatever you may see or hear," she told me.

Since I didn't expect to see or hear anything, compliance did not seem too terrible a boon to ask.

Mrs. Roberts herself stood perfectly still at the head of the sepulcher. She began mumbling to herself. She leaned over the mummy, pressing her hands upon its golden shoulders. Slowly she began rocking her head back and forth. Suddenly her head snapped back. I was startled to see the whites of her eyes.

"I can't hold her," she said, almost choking on the words.

She spoke again, but the voice was different, silken, with an accent. The voice I had first heard in the Aeolian Hall in London. Louise's voice.

And this is what it said: "John Watson? John? Where is Sherlock? You swore to stay by him. He's in danger! You swore!"

I was about to answer her, to comfort the mother, to reassure her. Then I remembered that Mrs. Roberts had sworn me to silence. But over and over, *you swore, you swore*—

I stepped back, distressed by her rebuke. I could feel the heat of the photographer's lamps on the back of my neck and the sweat trickling down my spine. Then I heard an unearthly sound, like an oak being riven by lightning. Mrs. Roberts cried out, shuddering as though racked with pain. But she had abjured me from moving. I stumbled and reached out.

Then the smoke came. And the flames.

They shot up from cracks in the floor, fed by a hot subterranean wind. The heat singed my eyebrows. The golden face in the sepulcher started to melt, the eyes swimming to either side, lips stretching, mouth gaping. The smoke rose, obscuring my view of Mrs. Roberts. There were flames all about her. Her head was thrown back so far I thought her neck would snap, yet she did not move, as though she were in a death rictus. I took a step toward her, and she threw up an imperious hand: stay where you are!

My coat had caught fire. I wrestled it off, blinded by the smoke.

Then there was blackness. And bitter cold.

Another voice, this time as old as time, terrible in its thirst for vengeance: "He has stolen the true name."

That was when I heard screaming. It wasn't Mrs. Roberts's voice. It wasn't like any voice I had ever heard. I remember realizing with a start that my hands were burning, watching in horror as they blackened and popped and withered away before my eyes. The smell of burning flesh was revolting. I must have fainted, though I am ashamed to admit it.

It was my voice screaming.

Chapter Ten:
Mrs. Estelle Roberts

When he came round, I breathed a sigh of relief, though he was still babbling about flames. His face was white as a ghost's in the light of Mr. Carter's torch.

Sir Sherlock turned to me. "Were there flames?"

"None that I saw, though there were plenty of sparks."

Dr. Watson's eyelids fluttered open.

"I knew I'd need someone as stouthearted as you," I said, leaning over him.

"Holmes isn't stouthearted enough?" he croaked.

Sir Sherlock broke out in a smile upon hearing his old friend's gibe.

"Sir Sherlock would have insisted on taking action. You have a talent for stillness."

He seemed to chew this over, not knowing what to make of it.

"On the other hand, I've never heard a man scream quite that loud before," jeered the baronet.

"Perhaps Mr. Holmes would not have been such a bumbling boob," Mr. Carter added unfeelingly. "I can't leave you people alone for five minutes." He had come galloping into the chamber ranting after the lights had gone.

"This will make the headline of the year," said Mr. Merton, all excited.

"Not if you ever want another headline out of me," answered Mr. Carter, crushing him.

"What happened?" Dr. Watson gingerly raised himself into a sitting position.

"You pulled the lights down around you. Looks as if you've broken a few. May have gotten a little shock. And of course you took out the power for the entire valley. Work has ground to a halt," said Carter.

"Yes, I'm all right, thank you," said Dr. Watson.

"You're the fortunate one. I'll have to write the reports explaining it all," scolded Mr. Carter.

At that, Sir Sherlock took a torch from his own pocket and flicked it on. Where were all these torches when we were groping our way down in the dark? He took the doctor's wrist and trained his light on it. "There is a burn mark on his cuff—indeed, the celluloid is nearly melted— but no cuts on his hands."

He turned his attention to the light cord. There were a number of smashed lightbulbs. He took no interest in them.

"Ah, you see?" There it was, a bare patch of copper. If Dr. Watson touched that—!

"Must be rats!" judged the baronet. It did look gnawed on.

Mr. Carter's face was a warring of emotions. For a moment I thought he was going to apologize. That moment passed in a hurry.

Sir Sherlock gave me a signal look, and I caught his meaning. What were the chances that Dr. Watson would reach out and make random contact with a live wire? No, it was a message from the elementals. Not a welcome mat, either.

Sir Sherlock tugged the doctor to his feet.

"I heard Louise—I mean, Mrs. Roberts, except it wasn't Mrs. Roberts—say my name," said Dr. Watson.

"Louise?" asked Sir Sherlock sharply.

"Well, I don't really have the foggiest idea what she sounds like—"

"It was she," I confirmed. "And then another woman. I don't know who."

Dr. Watson tottered over to the mummy. He stared down at it, his face bathed in golden light, as if he had lost something there. He turned back, mopping the moisture from his brow. "She said—the second woman—I think she said, 'He stole the true name.'"

I nodded.

"Exactly as Mynheer Gould says," Anna pointed out.

"What the blue blazes does it mean?" asked the baronet.

"It means we've just begun our investigation, I'm afraid," said Sir Sherlock.

"And it means something was stolen from this chamber. What?" I looked around at the dark emptiness. We had come to the tomb too late. Whose fault was that? Mine. My illness had delayed us too long.

"A cartouche box, perhaps?" suggested Lady Evelyn. "That would have the name of the pharaoh on it."

"The real question is, when? It could have been tomb robbers a thousand years ago," said Dr. Watson, muddying the waters further.

It occurred to me that there was something wrong in what Anna had said. Something wrong with everything said so far. I could not think what it was. My mind was such a muddle. My strength was at low ebb.

"Where has Carter got off to?" asked Sir Sherlock.

Everyone turned around. Carter had indeed disappeared. Perhaps he had had enough of our "shenanigans" for one day.

"I'd like to get out of this damned tomb myself, pardon my language," complained Dr. Watson.

"Yes, I think we've taken in enough sights for today," agreed Sir Sherlock. "Tomorrow I would like to see the laboratory, if possible, and ask Mr. Carter a few questions. If you can persuade him to sit down, my lady."

"I'll speak to him tonight. He'll come round."

"No one can refuse Eve in the long run," puffed the baronet proudly.

"Especially since my mother is still providing his funding. We're invited to dinner with him tonight. I don't think he'll need to be reminded."

"Does he stay at the Winter Palace?" I asked.

"No, he has a rest house just a stone's throw from the Valley itself," said Lady Evelyn.

"KV63, eh?" sniggered the baronet.

"Really, Brograve!" admonished his wife. But you could tell he felt he had scored. Perhaps he had. The other men laughed.

We were all staying at the Winter Palace in Luxor, right on the water on the east bank. The hotel was nearly as iconic as the ancient temple it stood shoulder to shoulder with. Our luggage had already been transported thither, and a good thing, as our dahabeah had virtually winked out of existence the minute we set foot on land. There was the barge instead, already heavy laden with crates of artifacts. The workers were still loading, standing in the shallows, passing parcels along. They did not chatter or even smile as they went about their work. Their silence was oppressive. Perhaps they were keeping their ears open for crocodiles.

There was a small felucca as well, its towering sail stretched out to capture any hint of a breeze. I boarded, as carefully as possible, and took a seat in the stern (the seats being nothing but rough slats). Here, with the hull low in the water, I felt truly baptized in the Nile. We had seen much larger feluccas on our journey, of course, but the little ones flew much faster. A gust of wind, like the blowing out of a candle, and we were across.

I would like to have explored the Temple of Luxor, and even Karnak, which stood so close by, so very inviting, but the truth was that every bone in my body ached. I was perhaps not quite as well as I had let on. I know nothing of the dinner that ensued nor who attended it. We definitely were not invited to Mr. Carter's little soiree, that much I do know. My bed was truly luxurious and called my name as surely as any spirit. I had some broth sent to my room and made an early night of it.

Yet when I sought release in sleep, none came. I kept reliving in my mind the strange happenings at the tomb. I had not expected Louise. Was she determined to follow her son everywhere? Could she find no peace? I felt certain she had not anticipated the advent of the other spirit, so powerful that she blotted out both Louise and Red Cloud. Why had it been a woman? If I had expected anyone, it was Tutankhamun himself. Whose spirit guarded him? Could it be his wife, or his mother? Had she that much solicitude in common with Louise? What was her name? Where did she lie? Too many questions. I had to shut them out if I were to get any rest at all.

It wasn't until I was finally drifting off to sleep that I realized what had really been bothering me. I sat bolt upright. The spirit had accused him of stealing the "true name." But surely Gould had said that *she* stole the true name. Which was it? I almost rose from my bed to tell Sir Sherlock of my conundrum, but a buffeting wave of sleep took me and I was carried away.

I woke the next day with the same thought still uppermost in my mind and relayed it to Sir Sherlock at breakfast. Dr. Watson, who appeared recovered from yesterday's brush with the elemental, admitted, rather reluctantly I thought, that he had heard the same thing. He seemed quite reserved this morning. Perhaps because he had come across something so uncanny he could not rationalize it away?

"So are we saying now that two items were stolen?" asked Dr. Watson, speaking with his mouth full.

"Perhaps, by Occam's beard. More likely it was one treasure stolen twice," Sir Sherlock clarified.

"But how are we to find out what that thing was when there are thousands of treasures to choose from?" I asked. "And most of them gone to Cairo."

"Carter assured us nothing had been stolen from the tomb," Dr. Watson reminded.

"I wouldn't put too much faith in Carter's word," said Sir Sherlock. "He has a well-documented history of dealing in stolen antiquities."

Dr. Watson was taken aback. "Well, there's news that never made the papers."

"You think Mr. Carter is the thief?" I asked, breathless.

"Perhaps. Or perhaps he never knew of the thing's existence;

therefore, he could never be aware that it was stolen. After all, Lady Evelyn was the first to enter the tomb, and alone. Only she was small enough to fit through the robber's hole."

Dr. Watson looked positively offended. "Surely you don't suspect Lady Evelyn of stealing anything from the tomb."

"Watson, as you are well aware, at this point in our proceedings I suspect everyone."

On that note we were joined by the Beauchamps, who had risen early to see sunrise from the temple. They had dined with Mr. Carter at his home the night before (along with Anna, whom the archaeologist seemed to have taken a fancy to). With some arm-twisting, he had agreed to an interview and a tour of the laboratory. We would have to wait till lunchtime, though; he couldn't accommodate us any earlier. So I did have time to explore Luxor Temple. I was delighted. And even more delighted when I discovered that Sir Sherlock was the only one who proposed to accompany me. It was wearying at times to have his shadow always with us, always questioning, always doubting, always suspecting, though I had high hopes Dr. Watson's shell had cracked after yesterday's events. But when I asked Sir Sherlock his opinion on the matter, he laughed. "Not such an easy shell to crack is John Watson. Last night he wanted to know all I could tell him about posthypnotic suggestion. He thinks you've been fiddling with his mind. 'How does she do it?' he asked over and over, dumbfounded. He's a man who stands on his dignity, and you made him look a fool, so he imagines. He thinks he's your pigeon, plucked from the audience because of his gullibility."

"You mean the visions he experienced he has decided I somehow lodged in his skull? That would truly be nothing short of sorcery." I couldn't help but laugh.

"Ah, but it falls under the rubric of science, therefore he prefers it."

I had wanted to see the temples of both Luxor and Karnak to the north, but Sir Sherlock assured me that Luxor alone was enough for several days' exploration, and he was right. I don't know what I had expected, perhaps something like Canterbury Cathedral, but the size of the thing, the sheer volume of it, was dizzying. It looked as if it had been built by giants, who had then deserted it, as a child does a sand-castle at the shore. It was a whole complex, begun by one pharaoh, then added on to by a whole list of names that fled my mind as soon as Sir Sherlock named them—except for Tutankhamun, of course—oh! and Alexander the Great, who had erected a chapel in the middle of it all.

It was not dedicated to any god but to the pharaohs themselves, though I suppose they considered themselves gods. There were statues of kings some seventy feet tall. There was a Roman fort housed within, and frescoes of Christian saints by early believers. You could have fit St. Paul's inside, and the Houses of Parliament, with room left over for Hyde Park.

We came to a mosque. Not the ruins of a mosque, but a living, breathing place of worship. It had once been a church, and a Roman temple before that, and even before that an Egyptian temple, where Tutankhamun had probably worshipped Amon-Ra and his gang. It was perhaps the oldest place of worship on God's good earth. I stared in wonder, trying to absorb it.

"Will you go in with me and pray?" Sir Sherlock asked earnestly.

I was honored to do so. We took off our shoes and entered. It was a mixture of classical Islamic and ancient Egyptian architecture, yet not inharmonious. There were a few others in the empty, echoing place, worshipping. We knelt and prayed: to God and Allah and Jupiter and Zeus, to Isis and Osiris and Horus.

"Estelle, do you feel anything?" he whispered.

Strangely enough, I did not. Though the place we knelt in was over three thousand years old, there were no presences, no voices. My mind was quiet and clear. I felt only a great peace. Then I realized why:

"All those who would speak with me wait across the river."

Along with the elementals, those deep resentments and jealousies and petty calumnies that had taken root, and something like form, like consciousness, like hatred, like desire. I could sense them, but they slept. I prayed they would go on sleeping.

Except one elemental. Stolen. Awakened. Unleashed upon the

unsuspecting world. To revenge. To murder. What form had it taken? How had it hidden itself?

In the end, I suppose we saw half of the temple complex before we gave it up and went back to the hotel for lunch. Anna finally joined us there, still suffering from the effects of too much wine the night before. She kept referring to Mr. Carter as a *varken*, which I guessed was not a complimentary term. Then we turned around and crossed the river once more.

When we entered the laboratory (I shall glide over the obligatory six-mile mule tide, which I found no more comfortable than the day before), I was sure we were in the wrong place, that we had stumbled into a tomb completely unexplored. As opposed to Tutankhamun's tomb, every inch was decorated, first with richly carved reliefs of kings and queens, gods and monsters, giving way to painted columns detailing the legend of Seti II and the pharaoh's journey through the netherworld, and the night sky painted on the high ceilings above. But we were in a laboratory for all that. The passage was lined with small trestle tables loaded down with King Tut's knickknacks, as Mr. Mace had called them, in various states of repair and disrepair, from timeless alabaster cups to sandals that looked ready to fall apart if breathed on.

There were three long corridors of this, and then the chamber of four columns. The chamber's effect was somewhat marred by the two large trestle desks, one on either side, sandwiched between the columns and the wall, covered with more detritus, where Mr. Mace and another fellow sat, hard at work—or asleep, it was difficult to tell, they were so still, concentrating on their work. Yet it made me realize how poor was the tomb of Tutankhamun by comparison. Mr. Mace looked up briefly from his work and gave us a nod.

And there was litter all over the floor, making every step awkward. Or treasure, I don't know which to call it. There was a golden goose, and a woman carrying a boy on her head, and a lovely black dog, his ears akimbo. There were wooden oars and a model boat that could have been a Christmas present for Tut when he was a boy. Mr. Mace's table was covered with jewelry, amulets, and other regalia. The other fellow seemed to be working on baskets and textiles, all ruined, with hundreds of beads literally hanging by their threads.

We found Mr. Carter at the very back of the tomb, down a set of steps, where the coffin must have once stood, but there was no coffin. Carter and a second fellow, heavyset, balding, carelessly dressed, were sitting at another cluttered trestle table in Thonet bentwood chairs, wolfing down something like Cornish pasties (they called them *shawarma*) and washing them down with hot coffee, which made me break out in perspiration just to see. I had grown fond of iced tea over the last few days, which I had always thought before was an American blasphemy.

Mr. Carter did not seem as savage as the day before. I sensed that he had come to some significant decision. I didn't think his decision had anything to do with us, though.

He said, "So you have had the tour," but a wry look from Her Ladyship brought him to his feet. His companion remained seated, dedicating himself to his lunch.

Carter began by explaining the pictures on the walls, Seti's journey though the afterlife in body, and spirit, and shadow, each protected by spells and counterspells, his encounters with Osiris and Anubis, his passages through gates and caves, his battles with foul creatures of the netherworld. Once he got started, Mr. Carter was a born story-teller. He led us back up the steps. Seti had only ruled for six years, he told us. Years marred by the rebellion of his half brother Amenmesse, who gained control of Upper Egypt and had Seti's tomb vandalized. Seti eventually defeated him and had his tomb restored. So we were standing in a literal battleground, in which the future of a pharaoh was decided for all eternity.

Mr. Carter began naming some of the treasures of Tutankhamun's tomb that littered the place.

"Were any of these treasures Seti's?" asked Dr. Watson.

"Oh, no, tomb robbers plundered this place thousands of years ago." He pointed out graffiti on the walls made by ancient Greeks and Romans who had ransacked the tomb. I wondered if any of them had met the same fate as Lord Carnarvon and Mr. Gould. He told us about the treasures we saw, most of which had been removed from the burial chamber. The antechamber's contents had all been floated to Cairo on barges. The annex, as the smaller room was called, and the beguilingly named treasury had barely been touched. There was still plenty of work to do of analysis, preservation, and restoration. This was the work that kept Mr. Mace and Mr. Lucas busy, he said.

His own table was loaded down with weapons, daggers and swords, and with writing implements, as if he were trying to discover whether the pen had always been mightier than the sword. There were life-size golden chariots, being assembled or disassembled, I'm not sure which. There was a collection of scarabs, lovely enough to make you forget that they were idealized beetles. There were the smells of paraffin and beeswax everywhere. Used as preservatives, Mr. Carter explained.

"And the tombs, they're all like this, all empty?" I asked, feeling a sudden sadness.

"All but Tutankhamun's. That's what makes it unique."

Sir Sherlock took this as his cue to ask the question burning in all our minds.

"Has anything been stolen from Tutankhamun's tomb?"

"The tomb suffered looters three thousand years ago. They didn't get much, although they made a mess of the antechamber and the annex. I have made certain that nothing has gone missing since we reopened it. Pecky here stood guard over it himself till we got the guardhouse up and running." He indicated the chubby fellow, just now wiping his hands with a handkerchief, his shawarma vanquished.

"Pecky" was introduced to us more formally as Arthur Callender, Mr. Carter's assistant.

"Me and my blunderbuss, all night long." He nodded, grinning.

"I'm sure of that," Sir Sherlock said tentatively. "But is there anything you did not find that should be here?"

"Such as?" Mr. Callender asked.

"I don't know. I'm hardly an expert on Egyptian archaeology," sidestepped Sir Sherlock.

"Well, you may be the only visitor I've ever had to make the admission. Most people who come through here are gifted with immediate expertise," Mr. Callender chuckled.

"Does it not seem strange? Sixty-two tombs and only one intact. Yet tomb robbers did discover the tomb, you aver."

"No doubt of it," affirmed Mr. Callender.

"Then why was it not plundered?" Dr. Watson asked.

Mr. Carter chose to field that question. "We'll never know for certain. Perhaps there were only two or three of them, unprepared for such a tremendous find. Then, when they were preparing to return, they could have been waylaid by other tomb robbers. Those were dangerous times."

"Or perhaps they were waylaid by elementals," I suggested. Mr. Carter laughed derisively. Callender looked at the floor, embarrassed, which I suppose I expected, but Dr. Watson nodded his head in agreement with me, which I most assuredly did not.

"Could there be another chamber with another body?" I asked.

"Well, of course there are the children," Callender brought up.

"The children?"

"Yes, the mummified remains of two daughters. Stillborn, of course. Tutankhamun's only heirs. Whether there may be undiscovered chambers I highly doubt, but we can't dismiss the possibility out of hand." Mr. Callender was a cautious one.

"It was no child who spoke to me," I whispered to Sir Sherlock.

But he was on a different track. "Would it not have been abnormal for a pharaoh to be buried with his unborn children?"

"There was nothing normal about Tutankhamun," Carter answered crossly. "But I don't mean any eyewash by that. I mean the shape and the size of his tomb, and many of the objects we've found therein. Relics that suggest Akhenaten more than Tutankhamun."

"Are you certain it *is* Tutankhamun?" I asked, still digging.

He turned to me. "Do you read hieroglyphics? No. Well, take a look at this." He slid a very old scrap of papyrus toward me, with these hieroglyphs drawn on it:

"This is the cartouche of Tutankhamun. Every one of those tomb seals is etched with it, proving beyond doubt that the occupant of the tomb is Tutankhamun. Nearly every object in the tomb was inscribed with his name. Why do you ask?"

"Because there's a spirit here. A very sad, very angry woman. And she keeps saying, 'He stole the true name.'"

"It's not a woman in that sarcophagus, that I'll swear to. Take a gander at this."

He took out a wooden box and opened it. Inside, on a bed of linen, was something black, long, but seemingly shriveled.

Callender chuckled again.

"That's his . . . uh. His . . ." Carter didn't know how to phrase it delicately. But I knew what it was.

"His male member," said Holmes gently.

"It's mummified, of course. When we unwrapped it, it broke off from the body, fully . . . erect and . . . regal in size."

I was speechless. I must have blushed down to my toes.

Sir Sherlock went off on another tangent. "Have you analyzed the fungus?"

"Fungus? What the devil are you talking about?" Mr. Carter was as mystified as I.

"The brown fungus that grows low along the western wall. Surely you have employed a mycologist to examine it."

Mr. Carter spoke in a low voice, almost gathering us in. "I have found the greatest hoard of ancient Egyptian artifacts that ever was or ever will be found." Then he roared, "Do you really think I concern myself with fungus?" He picked up a long, wide knife, which tapered to a wicked point, pricking himself and drawing a bright drop of blood. "Do you know what this knife is made of?" he asked, offering the blade to Sir Sherlock.

Sir Sherlock took it, hefting the blade in his hand. "Iron?"

"Very good. Iron it is. But Tutankhamun lived during the Bronze Age. Iron was so rare it was more valuable than gold. So tell me where the iron came from to make this knife, and then we can move on to your fungus."

Sir Sherlock handed back the blade. But the question was still in his eyes.

Carter huffed. "Anyway, fungus is Lucas's department, if it's anyone's. He's the chemist."

"Is this Mr. Lucas available?" asked Sir Sherlock.

Carter barked out the name, which echoed ringingly through the place. Soon we were introduced to Mr. Lucas, who seemed just as warm and welcoming as Mr. Carter. Men of science are apparently not bred for manners. He had a boxy face, with greying hair, a high, domed forehead, and bushy black brows like storm clouds. He squinted at Sir Sherlock through dusty spectacles, and his face took on the most alarming shade when told why he was summoned.

"What's this obsession with black fungus? Lawrence asked me the same thing."

"T. E. Lawrence was here? When the tomb was opened?" Sir Sherlock's face burned with a fierce light.

"He may have been, I don't recall. But he was here four days ago."

"Wait, you're talking about Lawrence of Arabia? The war hero? You do get all the famous people here," said Dr. Watson, rather gushingly.

"Wouldn't have given him the time of day, but he's an old friend of Lady Evelyn," Mr. Lucas said, frowning.

The name Lawrence stirred some memory in me, but I couldn't think what it was.

"That solves one riddle. There's evidence that a great deal of it had already been removed."

"Crumbled to the ground, then swept away," came the dismissive reply from Carter.

"No, I took a sample, of course," corrected Lucas. "Haven't sent it to be analyzed yet. Don't expect anything earthshaking, but I do try to be thorough."

"You have it here still? Did Lawrence ask to see it?" asked Sir Sherlock. Urgency kicked in his voice.

"That he did." Lucas shrugged.

"Might I see it?"

Lucas obligingly trotted upstairs and mucked around in the boxes behind his table till he came down with the vial of fungus. It looked like common dirt to me.

Sir Sherlock motioned for permission to open it. Lucas nodded.

He uncorked it. Sniffed it. Reached a finger in to scoop out a pinch. *Tasted* it. Shook his head and handed it back.

"Was there anything else? I really have a rather full schedule," said Mr. Carter, who had decided he had fulfilled whatever promise he'd made to Lady Evelyn under duress.

"Yes," said Sir Sherlock. "The lid of the sarcophagus is of granite, not sandstone."

"Is that a question, or merely an observation? We are quite aware of it," Mr. Carter responded pettishly.

"It has been cracked across the center and mended with gypsum."

"Again, this detail has not escaped our notice."

"Would you care to hazard a guess as to why the lid is in such a deplorable condition?"

"I would not. It is a capital mistake to theorize before one has data."

A smile burst forth on Dr. Watson's face. Sir Sherlock did not appear nearly so sanguine. He looked to be trying to stare Mr. Carter into cinders. Finally, Mr. Carter picked up his mail and began thumbing through it. It was a dismissal.

"Did your canary really get eaten by a cobra?" asked Dr. Watson, apropos of nothing.

"Oh, God, not that one again," Mr. Carter said with evident disgust. "Have you never heard of a thing called coincidence?"

Dr. Watson flushed, as though he had been caught at something naughty. "Just checking," he mumbled. Sir Sherlock smiled as at some private joke.

We had exhausted every line of questioning and gleaned little information for our troubles. Mr. Carter was what they call a hostile witness in the courts. As we came out into the bright sunlight, blinking, I felt positively vexed. We had been checkmated.

Chapter Eleven:
Dr. John Watson

———— ◆❖◆ ————

I stood at the mirror, examining my tongue, my lips, for any signs of discoloration. I checked my scalp for bumps or bruises. There were still no signs. I had fallen down, lost consciousness. I knew I was of an age when epilepsy often manifests itself. Had I experienced a seizure there in the tomb? It couldn't be ruled out entirely, and that made me fearful. I lived alone. My housekeeper was not a nursemaid. There were other explanations ready to hand for those symptoms, but the hallucination could not be so easily dismissed, if hallucination it had been.

On the other hand, could Mrs. Roberts really have hypnotized me? I had heard all sorts of wild rumors about the powers of mesmerism. But if she could accomplish such illusion without my willing it, without my even knowing it, she could do anything. I could still be in the Aeolian Hall, feeling the wet in my shoes, all unknowing. Little wonder then that the fellaheen should be afraid of her. It didn't bear contemplation.

I had just finished dressing for dinner when a knock came at my door. That would be Holmes, I thought, and went to answer it.

But it was not Holmes. It was Alfred Lucas, the chemist. Well, I had been told they all were staying in the hotel and were all curious about Holmes and Mrs. Roberts, but I couldn't imagine what he might want with me. I'm afraid I simply stared at him.

"Have you got a moment?" he asked brusquely.

"Of course," I said, and, remembering my manners, I ushered him inside.

I would swear the temperature dropped a few degrees once he was inside. His dark, deep-set eyes, thin mouth, and long, nervous fingers seemed made to order for the villain in a penny dreadful.

He looked about the room, as if assuring himself we were alone. Then he asked abruptly, "Is Sherlock Holmes mad?"

I was at a loss how to answer him. "Why, has he said something to you?"

"No, but you're his biographer, his Boswell, aren't you? All this silliness about spirits and elementals—has he gone round the bend? It's important that I know before I tell you anything."

What had he got to tell me? And how should I phrase my answer?

"Sherlock Holmes is as sound as he ever was," I said, choosing my words carefully. "He has merely chosen a larger map on which to draw his deductions." I nearly bit my tongue. I wasn't sure I believed my own assurances, but they seemed to allay the concerns of Mr. Lucas—for the moment, at least.

"Then tell him this—and tell no one else. Holmes asked today whether anything was missing. Do you know what a scarab is?"

"Sort of a bug, like a black beetle, only fashioned from jewels. Carter showed us a couple today, from the sarcophagus."

"Close enough, though I'm surprised he had the nerve to direct your attention to it. But one thing he did not show you was the heart scarab of Tutankhamun."

"Is it important?"

"It's vital. Because it doesn't exist."

"I'm sorry, I don't—"

"Every pharaoh was buried with a heart scarab. It was meant to bind his heart to silence so that it wouldn't bear false witness against him to the gods. But Tut doesn't have one. Holmes wanted to know what was missing. That's what's missing."

"Could it have been robbed by ancient tomb raiders?"

"You've seen the size of that lid. That thing weighs a ton."

"Perhaps it was an oversight when he was being buried?"

"Not bloody likely. Any mistake on that order could have meant the instant death of every priest involved in the funerary preparations if it were found out."

"Are you saying it was stolen by someone in your crew? Mr. Carter seemed to have complete faith in the probity of his men."

"Do I have to tell you what men are? There are always . . . trinkets pocketed in digs such as this. It was a sore spot for Carnarvon and Carter both that not a single item is to go to British museums. Completely against protocol."

I caught an undertone in his words that unsettled me, and I sensed that to question him further would put us both deep in quicksand.

"Well, thank you, Mr. Lucas. I shall be certain to relay your information to Mr. Holmes." A thought arrested me. "Would the heart scarab have had Tutankhamun's name inscribed on it?"

"Undoubtedly."

With that, our interview was concluded. He slipped out of the room as if he were afraid of being followed. I looked at the time and realized I was late for dinner.

I made my way downstairs, troubled in mind. I had seen the stymied look in Holmes's eyes that afternoon, after he had finished fencing with Carter and crew. Part of me couldn't help but hope he would throw up his hands and admit defeat. We could accept that we were at an impasse and simply go home. Admittedly, with our tails between our legs, but what else had I expected? On the other hand, I myself had heard that terrible woman's voice accuse someone of stealing "the true name." And now here was something stolen, something etched with Tutankhamun's name. Drat the man for confiding in me.

I traveled down the staircase, which was wide enough to admit a column of soldiers with cannon on either side, lit up by gargantuan chandeliers. England might be Georgian, but English possessions were still Victorian—that is, luxurious and ostentatious. There were the requisite Moorish accents, but subtly sketched in. No one preferred too much spice with their meals.

The Beauchamps had been invited for dinner to Carter's home again, as had Miss van V., whom he had exhibited a decided preference for. We of course had not, so there were only the three of us for dinner. Holmes seemed all at sea, and Mrs. Roberts looked bleak. The food and service were both excellent (especially the darne de saumon du rhin tzarine, which was some sort of salmon dish), but still we dined in gloom.

At last Holmes put down his silver and said, "You have to summon Red Cloud."

Mrs. Roberts looked even unhappier than before. "I don't think it wise," she said meekly.

"We are in dire need of guidance." I'd never heard that admission from Holmes before. He was truly at the ebb of the tide.

"I've tried to call him! There's nothing!" Her tone was so grieved that we were both shocked into silence.

"Since . . . ?"

"Since my illness struck me."

Holmes fell once more into a dejected silence.

"It's like being blind," she whispered.

"We are indeed in the dark," concluded Holmes.

I gathered up my resolve. "Perhaps Mr. Carter has not yet told you everything he knows," I said carefully.

"Mr. Carter has artfully managed to tell us nothing. His whole gang has conspired to tell us nothing. The dead could tell us more."

"Well, not quite everyone. I had an interesting tête-à-tête with Mr. Lucas just now."

A light sprang up in Holmes's eyes. His fingers dug into the table-cloth. Without so much as a word, he commanded me to speak.

It all came tumbling out.

By the end of my story, they were both on fire. And I was more daunted than ever. It all seemed to add up wonderfully for the detective firm of Holmes and Roberts. A valuable item that did not exist, stolen by no one, was the cause of four widely separated deaths. There was no budging them from their ill-considered, cobbled-together conclusions. Never mind that the tomb had been closely guarded since its discovery. Never mind that Carter himself had cataloged every item down to the smallest glass bead. I did my best to dissuade them. My arguments fell on deaf ears.

"You said yourself that Lucas accused his fellows of theft," said Mrs. Roberts.

"I did not say that. I may have inferred it. But it just isn't done."

"On the contrary," said Holmes. "Carter was already caught trying to squirrel away a priceless bust of Tutankhamun."

"What? I didn't see anything about it in the papers," I fairly yipped, then cast a quick look around the dining room to see if I had attracted attention. I had.

"And you never will. They kept it very much hush-hush. He made up an explanation, which no one really believed, but it passed muster. But that's only one reason the Egyptian authorities have been trying to sack him."

"You're saying that Carter took the heart scarab?" asked Mrs. Roberts, her mouth an O of incredulity.

"Possibly. But more than one person was involved. Perhaps even Lord Carnarvon had a dark hand in the deed."

"Why should there be more than one person?" I asked.

"Even with crowbars, it would have taken three or four to move the coffin lid, even fractionally. A ton of granite does not slide easily. As it was, they fractured the lid," Holmes explained.

"Ah. That's why you made a point of asking Carter about the lid," I realized.

"Yes. Of course, he may simply have wanted to be sure the mummy was within, but someone wanted the scarab once they saw it."

"Why would His Lordship have mixed himself up in the affair?" asked Mrs. Roberts, duly scandalized once more.

"To sell it. He had intended to sell many of his findings to Western museums. But the new government's interdiction made that impossible. He was out a large sum of money. Perhaps he decided to get some of it back."

"Lucas called it 'priceless.' Who could afford such a thing?"

"Gould?" suggested Mrs. Roberts.

Holmes slammed his fist on the table in triumph, which garnered more stares from nearby diners. I had to admit it made some sense. Gould was a well-known spendthrift. Perhaps a trinket for his new bride? On his first wife's death, her jewels were valued at a cool million, as the Americans say. Wife number two might have been looking for a head start on her own nest egg.

"And then it was stolen from Gould. By a woman," added Mrs. Roberts.

My mind was in a brown fog, trying to find its way clear. My two companions were already racing ahead. What they wanted to know now was about Gould's associates, especially anyone who might have visited him during his illness at Villa Zoralde.

"Lady Evelyn should help us there," Holmes said, as if she could remember the hundreds of visitors she had coddled on their tours of the tomb.

So far as I could make out, the reasoning was that since the voice in the tomb had said the "true name" had been stolen by a he, it must mean by Gould; since Gould's spirit had said, "she," it must have been stolen from him in turn by a woman. It seemed far too complicated.

"But if that's the case, wouldn't this woman have been struck down by the curse, too?" I argued, playing devil's advocate.

"Perhaps she has been," replied Mrs. Roberts.

There was that. Although she didn't supply any names.

"If only we had one more chance to speak to the lady of the tomb," said Mrs. Roberts.

That was her pet name for the shrieking fury who had knocked me flat. Her wish, luckily, was not to be granted. It had already been decided that tomorrow we would begin the long journey home, going the slow way by train to Alexandria and then ship to Marseille. We would have hours on the train to question Lady Evelyn about the Goulds and their intimates. We would not, however, have another chance to bother the "lady of the tomb," and for that I was thankful. At least we hadn't wound up attempting to exorcise the elementals, making complete and utter fools of ourselves, which I had feared would be the outcome. We had never aroused the hordes of newspapermen always on the hunt for a sensation, either, thanks in part to the sunglasses we always wore. I was beginning to understand why the film stars love them so.

"Perhaps we might have time to stop in at the Cairo Museum before we go? There could be important emanations from the treasures held there," said Mrs. Roberts.

Good heavens. Well, she wasn't insisting to interview the Sphinx. At least not yet.

That night, Holmes took up his violin again. It seemed that his three-pipe problems had become three-tune problems. As I have said, I find nothing more calming than to listen to his bowing. But perhaps his neighbor above or below did not share my fondness. I heard a knocking on his door. The violin ceased abruptly and did not resume. Probably a hotel official had dissuaded him from his late-night serenade. Just as well. We had an early morning ahead.

Then I heard voices. It wasn't difficult to make out whose they were: Holmes's and Mrs. Roberts's. Well, if they wanted to share secrets without me, that was all well and good. They could at least have kept their voices down, though. Some people were trying to sleep.

They kept droning on about the tomb, the tomb, the tomb ..

I snapped awake, only then realizing I had nodded off. The talk had ceased. But I could hear, plain as day, Holmes's door opening, then swinging shut. Locked. I leapt out of bed. What had she said? If only we had another chance ...

I rushed to my own door and cracked it open, letting the hall light flood in. I could see them together, just disappearing down the stair. Could it be? Of course it could.

Did I consider that I wasn't wanted? Not for a second. I threw on my clothes and was soon galumphing down the stairs. Where had they gone? Well ahead of me. They were hurrying, too. And they weren't going for a midnight stroll in the garden or a moonlight tour of the temples. The tomb, the tomb, that was where they were headed. Perhaps they intended an exorcism after all.

Which meant they had to cross the river. And so had I. Had they arranged their crossing beforehand? There was no shortage of small boats on the riverbank, but I soon found a definite shortage of pilots. They had wandered away for sleep or a late dinner or their own assignations. Some of them were asleep in the hulls of their boats, rocked to sleep by the waves. I attempted to wake one up and nearly got a dagger in my belly for my trouble. I did not repeat the experiment. Others I approached claimed to be reserved. Probably they were fibbing, but just as probably every one of them had a dagger or worse.

At last I found a fellow. He spoke no English, but I jabbed a finger across the river; that was plain enough. Of course, he flayed me alive on the cost of the trip, holding out his hand resolutely while I shoved pound notes into it. In the end I threw in my pipe. Then he had to raise the triangular sail. But once he weighed anchor, we skimmed across the water like silk. I would have instructed him to wait, but God knows what that would have cost me. Besides, there were plenty of boats still on this side of the river. I'd have no trouble getting back.

Of course, there were no mounts, no horses, asses, or camels in sight, so I'd have to ride shanks' mare through the Valley of the Kings. Then I remembered the heavy, barred gate in front of the tomb's entrance, and the guard. How did Holmes intend to defeat those?

Easily, it turned out. When I arrived, breathing heavily, the guard was asleep inside his box (or at least I hoped he was merely asleep). And both chain locks had been picked. So much for Carter's elaborate safety precautions. Still, if the guard should wake—

I slipped past the open gate. And stared into the dark, cursing myself for not having brought a torch. Had Holmes brought one? Of course. He was always prepared, because he had always planned his every move. And I was never prepared because he always kept me running after him in the dark, both literally and figuratively. Sometimes I think that he did it because it amused him to see me so blundering. Well, what of it? His eyes were failing him, his strength, his very breath. If he still needed his golden aura of superiority, he could lean on me; I would not deny him. Or I might have done him wrong in my thoughts; he may have simply assumed his mind was as transparent to me as mine was to his. Most of the time I refused to think about it at all.

I should simply turn back.

I didn't.

I crept slowly down the steps, holding on to the wall as though my life depended on it. The darkness swallowed me whole. Every step was slower, more uncertain, more full of doubt, till it became torture. But then, before I was even halfway down the passage, I heard the voices. I stopped dead, frozen in place.

Dozens of voices, all at once, from every direction, resounding from wall to wall, behind and before. Foreign tongues, none of them recognizable. Was I having another seizure? Or had all the devils in hell been released? My heart beat in my breast like a bass drum. I felt short of breath. My legs would not hold me up. I crouched down, still clinging to the wall, trying to steady myself.

"Lady, we shall return the heart. This we vow. Rest, spirits, rest. Elementals, be at peace." That was the voice of Mrs. Roberts, almost chanting.

The voices dulled and then dropped away, mingling with the sound of my breathing, which sounded louder than a train passing in the night.

Then Holmes's voice echoed, "'She paid for the name'? What did she mean?"

Then another voice, clear and strong:

"John Watson. John Watson." Oh, what a sweet voice. I could listen to it for hours. Louise's voice. At first I thought it was calling me. I would have called back, but my voice was trapped in my throat. Then it went on:

"Keep John Watson close."

"But why is Watson so important?"

It was Sherlock's voice asking. That hurt me.

"Keep John Watson by your side."

I felt my gorge rising. I had to steady myself. *Remember*, I assured myself, *it's only Estelle Roberts at her playacting, keeping Holmes in thrall*. I had to believe that. Why she was saying what she said, I couldn't guess, but I was sure it somehow worked to her personal benefit.

"Reichenbach."

What? Not that dread place again.

"You will need him at Reichenbach."

A wind swept through the place where no winds came. There was silence.

Then I heard a growl almost like a lion's in that echoing space, and a scream. A spasm of pure terror rocked me.

"Get behind me!" Holmes's voice came like a whip. And then I heard his stick, hammering away at something. I had to go to his aid! I stood upright. But my feet would not move forward.

Silence.

"Estelle, are you harmed?"

I could hear what sounded like muffled sobs from the woman. Then:

"Sherlock, Red Cloud spoke to me! He spoke at last! He warned me of the cobra! Did you . . . ?"

"It's quite dead."

"Who sent it?"

For that there was no answer. A light flashed. Holmes's torch! They were making their way out. I stumbled, trying to get away. They were going to find me, helpless as a child. My legs were leaden. I'd be humiliated. Was there anywhere I could hide? No. I didn't want to be in there when Holmes locked the gate behind him.

"The cobra! They'll know we've been here," hissed Mrs. Roberts.

That was something Holmes would have thought of as a matter of course twenty years ago. The torch swung out of sight. My legs were freed. I made my escape.

As I came tumbling out, I saw the eyes, but I could not stop. I slammed into the gate, throwing the man in front of it to the ground. The guard had awakened. And found the gate unlocked.

I threw myself on top of him. I rued the move as soon as I had made it. He was a head taller than I was and had muscles of iron. We rolled together in the sand. It was all I could do to hang on. Until he threw me off and dragged me to my feet. He peered at me in the gloom.

"Sharluk Hulmiz!"

He let go of me, then steadied me as I found my feet. It was the one called Hassan, the very one who had been reading aloud from *The Hound of the Baskervilles* the day before. He had not studied it very closely, I would guess, for he had somehow mistaken me for Sherlock Holmes. That was a bit of luck. I dragged him back into the sentry box. He tensed as we heard the soft clang of the gate. I put my finger to my lips.

"Moriarty," I whispered and sank out of sight. Holmes and Mrs. Roberts emerged. Holmes spent a few moments wrapping the chains around the door and locking up while Mrs. Roberts stood lookout. Then they both hustled away without even looking toward the sentry box.

"I thought Moriarty was dead," said Hassan in perfectly good English.

Curse all faithful readers. "Yes, of course," I scrambled. "But that is one of his most dangerous lieutenants."

"Then why do you go about with him as a companion?"

"He doesn't know that I know . . . who he is . . . Wheels within wheels, don't you know?" I trailed off, feeling a right duffer.

He stared at me blankly. "But what did he want in the tomb?"

I was fast running out of ideas. "Ah . . . spirits. Elementals. He seeks to control them."

That at least seemed logical enough to Hassan. After exacting his promise that he would tell no one of our midnight visit, I hurried away after my erstwhile companions.

I was in for the rudest surprise of the night. When I reached the river, the two had already departed, of course. But so had every single boat. Perhaps two in the morning was curfew for Nile boatmen. I had no choice but to sit down by the river, with my back against a palm tree, make myself as comfortable as possible (which was not comfortable in the least, as visions of cobras and crocodiles danced in my head), and wait till morning.

My thoughts kept going back to what I had heard in the tomb. Of one thing I was sure: Holmes would not be returning to the Reichenbach Falls. He had tried to explain it to me once. Although death was our handmaiden in many of our adventures, Holmes had never laid hands on a man and killed him before Moriarty. And though one might think Moriarty the most deserving of death of all the foes we had faced, seeing him plunge to his death had had a profound effect on my friend. For three years after he had wandered the earth, taking the name of Sigerson, seeking what could only be called absolution. He never found it. He'd plunged back into his peculiar profession, but more like a pack mule than a spirited stallion. Yet there was something softer about the man, a new hesitance to condemn, a look of regret to his demeanor when he'd laid some villain low. It was not unwelcome, but it was at times unfathomable—not that the man could ever be fathomed.

It was along about five, the light just smudging the sky, when I began to see lateen sails on the horizon. I rose and waved, jumping up and down. I would have called, but my voice had deserted me in the chill of the night, and I could barely whisper. But one eagle-eyed sailor saw me and lighted right in front of me. It was the same fellow who had brought me across. Reluctantly, I handed over my tobacco pouch.

Chapter Twelve:
Mrs. Estelle Roberts

Of course, it was a heart, a heart of stone. What more perfect vessel could there be for all the little hurts, the words locked away, the hopes never fulfilled, the love never shared, the desire never quenched? All roiling ceaselessly in the heart, in the fiery cauldron of the heart, till it must spill, it must flood, must rise up in waves to take out every living thing in its path. And I had promised to return the heart to the lady, to Tutankhamun himself, hoping they would sleep, merely on the strength of my vow. When I had no idea how I would fulfill that vow.

These were the thoughts chasing through my mind when I woke early the next morning. It was still dark. Our train was scheduled for six. It would be nine hours to Cairo, and we hoped to outrun the heat of the day, though it would inevitably catch up. It was the first leg of a long journey home—an awfully long way to have come for such a short time. Sir Sherlock seemed to think it was all worthwhile. And I missed my children so fiercely that I fell in readily. I was so impatient to see them that I wished to be to be home instantly. Where was a genie of the sands to grant my wish? But I was relieved at least that I wouldn't be getting on a plane ever again. Or so I thought.

We were making a frugal breakfast in the Beauchamps' suite. There was tension in the air. When was there not? Sir Sherlock hadn't touched his food. Lady Evelyn seemed snappish. Oh, and Dr. Watson kept falling asleep.

"It's time we had a talk, Lady Evelyn." Sir Sherlock seemed wintry. She did not meet his eyes.

"About T. E. Lawrence. And Captain Shaw."

This caused a sour look on both the Beauchamps' faces. Things were getting interesting. Dr. Watson started snoring. I gave him a good wallop on the back, and he reared up wide-eyed. Just then, a loud knock sounded on the door.

The baronet jumped up, seeming glad of the interruption, and opened the door to Mr. Merton, the *Times* photographer. He charged in without so much as a by-your-leave.

He tossed his head in greeting and turned on the baronet. "The Bugatti Torpedo? That's yours?"

The baronet dabbed at his lips with his napkin. "What the blazes are you talking about?"

"I heard you're leaving for Cairo today. I've got to go with you."

"I'm sure there are tickets available for the train."

"The train won't get me there on time. It's got to be your auto."

"I don't have an auto. Not here."

Merton scratched his head, looking overwrought.

A look of understanding spread across Lady Evelyn's face. "You mean Father's Bugatti. I'd forgotten it was here."

"Yes, beautiful car. If you're not using it, can I borrow it from you?" Mr. Merton pleaded.

The Beauchamps both looked horrified.

"Why the hurry, Merton?" asked Sir Sherlock.

"Something's come up, something big."

"Not another death?" I asked fearfully.

"She's come back. Princess Marguerite has arrived in Cairo. I've got to get the interview."

"The murderess? She's come to Cairo? Whatever for?" I asked.

"There's the little matter of two and a half million dollars. The prince died intestate, and the family is claiming his fortune. Did you think she wouldn't contest that? The only reason she married Fahmy to begin with."

"But she murdered him. Surely no court would award her the inheritance after that," Dr. Watson objected.

"I wagered no one could get her off in an English court of law, but Hall managed it quite adroitly," said Merton ruefully.

"She's a consummate gambler, and she'll play as long as she has a single card left," declared Sir Sherlock. "I'd be interested in posing certain questions to her myself."

"Now, that would sell some papers: Sherlock Holmes interrogates Princess Marguerite," mused Lady Evelyn.

"Would you let me publish it?" asked Merton eagerly, seizing on the idea.

"We're running away with ourselves. I can't just let you have the Bugatti—"the baronet began.

"We can't simply leave it here, Brograve. We're going to have to ship it home from Cairo."

"You could ship it to Marseille and Watson could drive it to Calais," suggested Sir Sherlock.

Dr. Watson was awake for that. He went deathly pale.

"Watson?" The baronet went saucer eyed.

"He's an excellent driver."

"*Ik kan rijden,*" interrupted Anna. She had been so quiet that morning I had almost forgotten she was with us.

"There you are, Brograve. Anna can drive them."

"Drive who?"

"Mr. Merton and Sir Sherlock. Oh, and Dr. Watson and Mrs. Roberts, too, I suppose."

"What about us?" the baronet asked, looking slighted.

"We can take the train, just as we'd planned. We're in no hurry."

That silenced the baronet, though I think he would rather have gone in the car.

And so it was decided, although I would have been happier on the train myself. The luggage was still going that way. I preferred to keep an eye on it.

It was ten hours by train to Cairo. Anna vowed to do it in seven, even though the baronet's last words to her were "Don't get the idea you're in a race, dear."

Just as we were about to disperse to our rooms, another knock came on the door. Mr. Merton opened it to Sir Archibald, the radiologist. He came straight to the point. "I've heard you're driving to Cairo. May I tag along?"

Thus we had a full complement. The Bugatti was a lovely blue, blessedly a four-seater. That meant I was wedged in the back between Dr. Watson and Sir Sherlock, but it also meant Sir Archibald and Mr. Merton were wedged into the front passenger seat, and they were neither of them petite fellows.

There was really only one drawback to the Bugatti—rather a fatal drawback for driving in the desert, as became evident in short order—no side windows. There were some yellowed sheets of cellophane hung as curtains, but these were a far from ideal stopgap. Which meant dust. Not a little dust: the dust was absurd, as if the clouds (there were no clouds) had opened up and, instead of sending cool, blessed rain, sent torrents of sand down on our heads, filling up sand rivers that flooded their banks, inundating the auto with sand. The men sitting next to the windows got the worst of it, turning into living sandcastles before my eyes. I daresay they are still finding sand in their pockets and their shoes.

We were lucky, according to Mr. Merton. In a few weeks the khamsin would begin, a desert wind so furious that it made driving impossible. I finally resorted to those silly sunglasses Dr. Watson wore everywhere. Anna, of course, had had the foresight to procure a pair of goggles and a flat cap from somewhere. Sir Sherlock looked uncomfortable, having wrapped a scarf over his mouth. I began to miss our slow, plodding dahabeah. Also, Dr. Watson snored like a band saw the entire trip.

"I suppose you'll have to board the early train tomorrow for the return trip to Luxor. I would have assumed the *Times* could allot two men to cover the land of the Nile," said Sir Sherlock.

"I won't let another chap elbow in on my turf. Besides, I may not be going back. Carter is threatening to shut down the entire enterprise," answered Merton.

"What are you talking about? It looks as if he's still loads to do," I objected.

"Oh, several years' worth, at a conservative estimate. Someone will have to do it. But not Carter. You haven't heard the rumors?" asked Mr. Merton.

"We've observed Carter in a very ill humor," said Sir Sherlock.

"He always is, but now he hasn't got Lord Carnarvon to intercede for him with the Egyptians. The new administration wants to horn in on the excavation. Well, they've always wanted their share of the glory. Carter's not having a bit of it."

"But don't the Egyptians own it? I mean, it's their land, isn't it?" I asked.

"Lord Carnarvon paid for the concession. Lady Almina renewed it. That gives Carter certain rights. But there's never been a find like this before. Lacau wants to throw out the rule book. The latest contretemps is on behalf of the ladies."

"The ladies? I don't understand." I felt myself sinking deep into the morass of politics.

"Carter had scheduled a tour for the wives of the staff to see the boy king in the flesh. Extravaganza. Lacau forbad it. It's made Carter furious. Straw that broke the camel's back and all that sort of thing."

"Carter can't see his way to a compromise?" wheezed Sir Archibald, who was suffering from the dust.

"Compromise is anathema to Carter, I suspect," said Sir Sherlock.

"True enough. He's spoiling for a fight. If Egypt rises up, Britain will bring the hammer down. Then Carter could have anything his heart desires," said Merton.

"Would the Egyptians stand for it? Aren't they supposed to be independent?" I asked, perhaps naively.

"In name only. Allenby's got them on a short leash," said Mr. Merton.

"'Lacau' doesn't sound like an Egyptian name," I said.

Sir Archibald cleared his throat portentously and turned toward me. "Pierre Lacau, French. A Jesuit, or at least trained as one. You know how some of those priests operate sub rosa. I wouldn't be surprised if he's working on instructions from Ratti."

"Ratti?" I echoed. This triggered a coughing fit in the man so loud that Dr. Watson shifted in his sleep. When Sir Archibald recovered, he explained.

"Pius XI. You know it's his ambition to make a state of the Vatican."

I didn't know anything about the Catholic Church or the Jesuits. "But why would they take an interest in Tutankhamun?" I persisted.

"To create unrest in Egypt. Ratti wants to spread his voodoo into Africa. Always easier to spread the faith during a time of crisis."

I had heard that exposure to radiation was dangerous. I was beginning to wonder if it had gotten to Sir Archibald.

Dr. Watson spoke up for the first time. "Murray!"

"Excuse me, Doctor?" I said.

The doctor only repeated, more emphatically this time, "Murray!" Then I realized, "Why, he's still asleep!"

"Yes," Sir Sherlock said parenthetically. "Watson always had a habit of talking in his sleep."

"Who in the wide world is Murray?" questioned Merton.

"His orderly from his days in Afghanistan. Saved him from certain death, so he tells it. He's saved him a hundred times over in his dreams, I suppose."

"Strange, isn't it, how our dreams always draw us back to those near-death experiences," mused Merton.

"It isn't strange at all," I replied.

"You really believe you can talk to the dead? It's rather macabre," stated Sir Archibald.

"They're not dead, simply passed over. Do you really believe you can see a person's insides?" I asked.

"It's science!" he sputtered.

"Fifty years ago, it would have been called black magic. Do you know what Röntgen's wife said when she saw the first radiographic picture he took, of her hand? 'I have seen my death.'"

His eyes slid away from me and fastened on Sir Sherlock, as if he were my sponsor.

"Oh, did you take her for a dullard?" Sir Sherlock asked him with a wry smile.

We were by this time in the heart of the desert, in a haze of dust. And yet out of nowhere, tall green reeds sprang up on our lefthand side. I wondered whether we were passing an oasis when, lo and behold, a giant ship rose up in the middle of the desert, gliding along as if that genie of the sands had it in tow.

"The Suez Canal. Nothing strange or macabre." Sir Archibald must have been reading my mind. Why was he still turned around staring at me?

"Of course not. Still, it is wonderful."

"More wonderful than the pyramids?" he asked, trying to spark a quarrel.

"Engineering and manpower, in both cases," I answered mildly.

"You don't think magic was involved in the raising of the pyramids?"

"I don't believe in magic."

Which promptly shut down that conversation. He stared at me a bit longer, then finally turned back, coughing.

It was nearly seven hours to Cairo, by which time the blue Bugatti was the color of sand. The noise of the city broke in on the silence we had fallen into. The odors of the city came out to greet us. The smells of jasmine and anemone lingered longest in the air, along with the dank onion smell of sweat from twenty million unbathed. I was ready for London and the smell of my daughters' hair and the baby's nappies. Or at least the smell of a solid English meal.

Chapter Thirteen:
Dr. John Watson

Lady Evelyn had refused to stay at the Savoy-Continental, where her father had died. But Holmes and I had no such scruples. He wanted to see the scene of the death (which the reader will remember I had suggested before) and perhaps unearth a few witnesses, so he and I decided to spend our last night in Egypt there.

"Whatever I say, simply stare and gawk." Holmes strode up to the desk and started speaking, for some reason, in an American accent. "We've just been to see King Tut. Marvelous! You seen King Tut?"

"Tutankhamun? No, sir, I have not had that good fortune," answered the clerk, as if by rote. He was brown enough to be a native, with curly black hair, but he spoke English with a pure French accent.

"Well, you need to go. 'Course, this is where he died, wasn't it? Sir Carnival? Right here at this very hotel."

"Lord Carnarvon. Yes, sir, very tragic."

"Hell, you musta seen a lot of famous people. Just come to court His Lordship."

"Yes, indeed, sir," he replied, drawing himself up with pride.

"Like who?"

"Well, one doesn't like to say—"

"They all stay at the Mena House?"

"The queen of Belgium stayed here," the clerk answered defensively.

"Say, didn't that wild lady that killed her husband stay here? What's her name, Mrs. Fanny."

"Fahmy? That incident did not occur here. That was at the Savoy in London."

"No murders here, huh? Well, don't feel bad." Holmes leaned over the counter. "I hear she's a looker up close," he said with a wink.

"She did visit His Lordship once," the clerk admitted. "Very well made-up."

"Alone? Her husband know about that?"

"He visited the next day."

"The husband, you mean?"

The clerk nodded discreetly.

"Oh, Lord, the shit musta hit the fan."

"I believe there were words spoken. With a wife like that, what can one expect?"

"You got that right. They said George Jay Gould visited King Tut. He ever stay here? You know, the American millionaire? Trains. I'd like to have his walkin'-around money."

"He did visit Lord Carnarvon. As a matter of fact, the day before Madame Fahmy."

"I bet his wife didn't visit. Not on her own."

"No, sir, I don't believe she did."

"American girls don't play around."

"How very unfortunate."

"Eh?"

"The boy will show you to your rooms. Enjoy your stay, messieurs," the clerk dismissed us diplomatically.

As we crowded into the elevator, Holmes asked, "What room did Lord Carnarvon stay in?"

"Suite four hundred, I believe it was, sir," reported the bellhop.

"Oh, a suite. Well, make sure my razor's sharp. I don't want to kill myself like he did."

The lift operator spoke up. "It wasn't shaving that he cut himself."

"Hush!" warned the bellhop.

The lift operator made a hissing noise and swiped at his face with his hand shaped like a claw.

"Oh, really? But wasn't no cat, I'll wager. Maybe a French wildcat," drawled Holmes.

Both attendants laughed at this.

"You are a man of the world," said the bellhop, grinning from ear to ear.

I had to ask. "You fellows don't believe all this nonsense about a curse, do you?"

Their faces drained of color. Finally, the lift operator answered, "Oh, yes. The lights went out all over Cairo the moment His Lordship died."

"The curse, it is real," the bellhop nodded.

At least they didn't blame the ten plagues of Egypt on the curse. Then again, I didn't ask them.

As soon as I had unpacked, I was knocking on Holmes's door. I could hear him speaking within, in a loud voice. He had never come to trust the telephone to convey his voice adequately and still preferred to communicate by wire. Thus I heard quite distinctly that Merton's interview with the infamous widow was scheduled for midnight—a strange time, I thought, as did Holmes himself. So much for getting here as fast as we could. The widow was obviously a night owl. So our race to get up here had been unnecessary. I was still finding sand in my pockets.

When I entered, I found Holmes at an odd endeavor. He had half a dozen bottles lined up before him, hotel amenities: scents, soaps, shaving necessities. He was sniffing them each in turn, which was strange, since Holmes normally avoided such emollients like the plague. "Plague" was what he called them, in fact, since they tended to interfere with his highly developed olfactory sense.

"Ah, Watson, just in time! Smell these," he commanded without explanation.

Since I was inured to his quirks, I did as he bade. I've had less pleasant chores. They were a bit more powerful than my tastes, however, the last one being so potent that I drew back and sneezed.

"Gesundheit, Watson. So you would say that one was the most overpowering?"

"Without a doubt," I replied, drawing my handkerchief and finding relief in it. "What is that?"

"Aftershave."

"I'll stay with Truefitt." I tucked my kerchief away. "Shall we inspect suite four hundred?"

"I've seen all of it that interests me. I'm ready for a long, leisurely dinner. I've hours to fill until I'm admitted into the august presence of the princess."

He would not speak another word about the case, which was equally frustrating and refreshing. We had the pleasantest meal of our entire trip and drank endless cups of coffee to keep ourselves awake until midnight.

And that was how Sherlock Holmes came to interrogate the murderess—not that I was allowed to be present. Merton didn't want her distressed by a whole crowd of people. Indeed, he would not allow Holmes to speak, presenting him as only a stenographer there to record the interview. But he took down Holmes's questions and promised to include them. Holmes wanted to be there to gauge her reactions. He could tell more from a raised eyebrow or a pursed lip than Scotland Yard could tell from a bloody dagger and a full confession.

Thus, when he joined me again, along about one in the morning, he was extraordinarily closemouthed. He only told me that I could read it in the paper the next day and that she was quite an accomplished liar.

We were at the breakfast table the next morning when Merton dropped down upon us with that day's *Times*. He threw it on the table.

Front-page news: "Master Sleuth Sherlock Holmes Grills Princess Marguerite." There was a picture of her at her most vixenish, and below

it a picture of Holmes that had to be from thirty years ago. I scanned
it, along with Mrs. Roberts and Miss van V. They had come over from
Shepheard's, promising that the Beauchamps would meet up with us
later. Miss van V. was about to leave us to return to Monaco, but the
two ladies had become thick as thieves. They crowded in on either side
of me to read.

Can you tell our readers why you have returned to Cairo?
This was where I met my husband. It is where I was happiest.
It's not to claim the 2.5 million dollars he left?
The money means nothing to me. But who should rightfully
have it if not his wife?
His murderess.
I only shot him in self-defense, as the court proved. He was
enraged.
**You shot him in the back. Three times. He could not have
been attacking you.**
He turned as I pulled the trigger. I was afraid for my life.
When you were here last, you visited King Tut's Tomb?
Ah, oui. Tutankhamun. Magnifique.
You must have met Lord Carnarvon then.
Who is this Lord Carnarvon? I do not know him.
**Did you not visit Lord Carnarvon in his room, in this very
hotel?**
Oh. Lord Carnarvon. One meets so many English lords in
Cairo.
You visited him alone.
What is that? More of your English prudery? We talked.
About the pharaohs. He was most knowledgeable.
What else did you discuss with His Lordship?
Only the treasure. Tres desirable.
**A very desirable treasure. Did you desire anything in par-
ticular?**
No. My husband was quite a generous man. I wanted for nothing.

I understand there were sharp words spoken. That you even scratched him.
No! Perhaps a little. He might have become too familiar. Englishmen are like that.
Did you tell your husband?
No! I did not wish to make him jealous.
Was he prone to jealousy? Is that why you shot him?
No. What we had was beautiful. Anyone would kill for it.
Then he sold it.

"Sold it? What's she talking about?" I wondered aloud.

"Mayday, mayday, mayday! She's just come through the door," Merton whispered urgently.

Indeed, there she was, framed in the doorway. With her smoky eyes and Clara Bow lips, she was perilous as a princess and just as imperious. She was, of course, with a male escort. The odd thing was that I recognized the escort. Her eyes studied the room. They settled on us, and her eyelids seemed to snap down like the guillotine. She advanced on our table. Her escort followed a pace behind. Her escort was Sir Archibald Douglas-Reid. His coughing broke the silence.

"Monsieur Holmes?"

"Bonjour, Madame."

"Monsieur Sherlock Holmes?"

"Oui, Madame?"

"Last night you did conceal from me that you are the Sherlock Holmes, the famous English detective. Last night you are only the silent stenographer."

"I was introduced to you as Mr. Holmes. I cannot be held accountable for any assumptions you may have made."

"You did not interview me. He did." She pointed at Merton, who reacted as if singed.

"No, I am not such an accommodating interviewer. Dr. Watson here can tell you that I do not tolerate liars."

I was fortunately not called upon to second Holmes in this.

Although his words were the unmitigated truth, I was reluctant to cross a trigger-happy Frenchwoman.

"I do not know why you have followed me to Cairo, but let me give you fair warning: stay out of my business."

She snatched up the article and crumpled it into a small ball. Then she threw it, rather surprisingly, at Mrs. Roberts, who seemed to come out of some deep meditation to register the assault. "Don't look at me that way!" the princess fairly screamed at her.

Mrs. Roberts shut her eyes as against a gale.

"And as for you"—she turned her blast on Merton—"never again shall I speak to the *Times*."

Merton clutched his heart in mock despair.

"Au revoir, Madame," Holmes said to her, but she had already turned stiffly and stalked away, Sir Archibald trailing behind.

"There is great evil about that woman," said Mrs. Roberts, opening her eyes.

It seemed an understatement. "After all, she did murder her husband," I reminded her.

"That's not what I mean," she said. "She is wrapped in evil, as though it were a dress she chose. It doesn't feel a part of her."

Even Sherlock Holmes seemed at a loss to answer this. Silence fell.

"What was the radiologist doing with her?" I asked at last.

"I wondered about that, too," said Merton. "You suppose that's why Sir Archibald was in such a lather about getting up here yesterday?"

"They obviously have a history," said Holmes. "I hope he does not let her get too close."

"Perhaps he intends to deliver the baby?" Merton conjectured idly.

"I didn't get a chance to read all of it," I complained, retrieving the balled-up article from the floor.

"It's nothing but more verbal fencing," Holmes assured me. "Then Merton asked her who made her clothes, which was meant to mollify her. Paul Poiret, by the way."

"The ladies clamor for those facts," said Merton in defense.

"You say that the evil does not come from her?" asked Holmes, reflective.

"Perhaps I would say that something draws forth whatever evil is within her. There's a bit in all of us, I'm afraid, though ofttimes buried deep within. In her case, cupidity drives her," said Mrs. Roberts, thinking out loud.

"Didn't have to dig too deeply there," I opined.

"I think we have not seen the last of the princess," said Holmes with a deep crease in his brow.

Well, I thought, if she wanted to see *me* for anything, she'd have to break down my door on Queen Anne Street, for we were going home that very day.

But first we had one more expedition to make that morning: the Cairo Museum. Mrs. Roberts could not be argued out of it. She, at least, had not given up on seeking out elementals. I feared she was due for a disappointment, but at least she was unlikely to run into any cobras there. We linked up with the Beauchamps at Shepheard's and took a taxi from there.

We were greeted at the museum by Monsieur Pierre Lacau, Egypt's director of antiquities, a long-faced, white-bearded old Jesuit, whom I gathered was Carter's bête noire.

"This can't be everything," said Mrs. Roberts, looking about the Tut exhibit.

It looked like everything to me. Cups of pure alabaster, chariots of gold, bows and arrows of gold, life-size statues, tiny figurines of Tut-ankhamun (in every pose), gods, monsters in every size, oars (but no boat), chests, scepters, crowns, wigs, vases, couches, beds, shrines, gold, gold, gold, everywhere, all in rows of gleaming glass cases. If he needed to pack this much for a trip to the underworld, who knew what he'd pack for a week in the country?

It made me pause and wonder whether the descendants of tomb robbers might not be tempted to become museum robbers. Although it looked well guarded, I wondered if the guards were well paid enough to fend off the enormous temptations that must come with the post.

"Certainly not," said Lacau in answer to Mrs. Roberts's question. "There's a great deal of work still to be done on restoration and mounting yet before we can display the entire treasure. And, of course, the main prize still awaits within the tomb—Tutankhamun himself."

"Oh, no, no more restoration. That won't do at all. It dulls the emanations. Can't we see the rest? Surely you can use your influence—" Mrs. Roberts urged.

"No, I'm afraid not. The state is very jealous of the treasure once they get their hands on it. And besides, most of is still bundled up and packed away," said Lacau.

"And some has gone to other museums, I suppose? The Metropolitan, the British Museum?" suggested Holmes.

"Oh, no, I've put a stop to that. Egypt's patrimony will remain in Egypt," he said proudly.

"Don't you have agreements with those institutions?" said Lady Evelyn.

"As I'm sure you're aware, Miss Herbert, the government has always reserved the rights to any tomb found intact. Just such a tomb is Tutankhamun's."

"But the tomb was not intact. It has been broken into, twice, we think, over the centuries," Lady Evelyn protested.

"We have decided that your proofs are insufficient. The agreement has been voided by the new government. No more of the British making agreements with the British." Lacau gave an unpleasant laugh. Did he think we would join him in laughing at the British?

I saw Lady Evelyn's face turn red as though she'd been slapped. But she said nothing to contradict him. She had already known of this turn of events, I realized. Beauchamp had his face hidden in a guidebook. He'd known, too, obviously. What a blow for science.

"Who are these?" Mrs. Roberts asked, screwing up her eyes at two statues as if just discovering them, though they must have been one of the centerpieces of the exhibit.

"Ah, the guardian statues. They were originally placed on either side of the door to the burial chamber," said Lacau.

They were certainly imposing enough to give any tomb robber pause. Both were life-size, carved of wood and painted black, with gilded headdress, sandals, and kilt, and burning obsidian eyes, ready to smite with their staffs and condemn any intruders to whatever hell the Egyptians believed in.

But Mrs. Roberts persisted. "Yes, but who are they?"

"Why, they're images of Tutankhamun," he replied.

She studied them closely, her breath fogging the glass. "No. I don't think so," she muttered, and she did that boring-eye thing that was so unnerving to him. "Too aggressive."

He blinked and turned away. Mrs. Roberts was at a loss. Whether she had hoped to find the revenant of Tutankhamun among the packing crates in the back, it was certain she felt no connection to the polished exhibits on display. Her nerves were strained. I caught the look of concern on Holmes's face. While there were certainly many other wondrous exhibits and mummies aplenty on view, we would never see them. We were done.

We retreated to a place just off Tahrir Square, where they served real English tea, a much-needed restorer of equanimity all around.

Holmes leaned back, templing his fingers in his lap, and said, "Now, Lady Evelyn, if you'll tell me about your dealings with Colonel Lawrence, or Airman Ross, or Captain Shaw, as he's now calling himself."

I couldn't decide who was blushing brighter, husband or wife, but the two of them could have lit up a tomb quite comfortably. What the dickens was Holmes talking about?

"I didn't want to deceive you," said the lady meekly.

"I most assuredly did not wish to deceive," added her husband.

Holmes simply waited, his heavy-lidded eyes flashing quicksilver.

"Tom was an old friend of Uncle Aubrey. They were much alike—men of a different age, men of vision, adventurers. Much like yourself."

Ah, flattery. Holmes's Achilles' heel. Well played.

"After the war, he felt betrayed. So many promises he had made to Emir Faisal and his father, which were completely ignored by those now in charge of the fate of Arabia. He felt disgraced."

"So many promises he was not authorized to make," said Holmes.

"Perhaps. He tells it differently. At any rate, he was sick to death of the famous Lawrence of Arabia. He's really an intensely shy person. So he went into hiding, enlisted in the RAF as Airman Ross—"

"That was where I first tumbled to him."

"Ah! I didn't realize. Believe me, he only wants to be left alone."

"Believe me, he's up to more mischief. He's already upset the apple cart in Iraq and Syria. Now he's got his sights set on Palestine and Egypt."

"He's gained the trust of the Arabs," said Lady Evelyn.

"Yes, yes, and lost it twice over. You know that he murdered one of his own men in cold blood? Shot him in the head while two lieutenants held him down."

"He said he did it to keep a blood feud from splitting his men apart," Beauchamp protested. "Besides, where did you learn that? It was supposed to be hush-hush."

"From his own writings. He planned on publishing a book. *Seven Pillars of Wisdom*, I think he wanted to call it. It was full to bursting with official secrets."

"But he didn't publish it," Lady Evelyn said.

"Not after we lifted the only copy of his manuscript, no. I hear he's planning to rewrite the whole thing from memory. He cannot take a hint. Now he's intending to 'liberate' Egypt."

"What makes you so certain?" broke in Beauchamp.

"I know dirt from fungus," answered Holmes gnomically.

"You certainly haven't solved the riddle of the so-called curse!" Beauchamp's temperature was rising.

"It might help if you tell me what you know," said Holmes placidly.

"I don't know what you're talking about," said Beauchamp, suddenly turning cagey.

"Perhaps you could assist me by telling me about your dinner with the Fahmys and the Goulds."

Beauchamp sighed heavily. "So you're determined to follow this to the end?"

"My friend Watson here can tell you what I'm like once I have the bit between my teeth."

I nodded emphatically.

Beauchamp seemed to be ruminating, as if he saw things in a new light.

"All right, then, I'll tell you what I know. It's not much, and it may be of no help whatever, but you can take it for what it's worth."

Holmes gave him an encouraging look.

"Eve and I left early that night. She complained of a headache, but Eve doesn't get headaches. I think she was embarrassed being seen in public with Marguerite Fahmy."

Lady Evelyn nodded, pinking.

"Anyway, I got to my room and realized I had left my demmed cigarette case. I went back down for it. They were still there, Herbert, Fahmy, and Gould.

"He showed them something. No, I don't know what, and not one of them would tell me—Gould said they'd taken a vow of honor, and he made me take a vow not to reveal even that much—but they were mightily impressed with it, whatever it was. That's all I can tell you. No, not because of the vow I took; I've already broken that. But I did hear Herbert say, to both of them, 'Which would you choose, beauty or power?'

"'Is this your idea of a game? Or can you grant these things?' said the prince.

"'I can,' replied Herbert . Then they noticed me and fell silent. I excused myself, retrieved my cigarette case, and went up to bed."

"Perhaps one of the widows could tell me more," Holmes conjectured.

"The women weren't present. After dinner, brandy and all that rot," said Beauchamp.

"So, no one living knows what was said," I said.

"I realize it's not much to go on," said Beauchamp falteringly.

"On the contrary, it clears up one puzzling riddle," said Holmes.

"What's that?"

"Why you are not dead."

Beauchamp's eyebrows shot up.

That afternoon we said goodbye to Cairo and to the Beauchamps. We took the train to Alexandria to board the ship to Marseille. I was half afraid Mrs. Roberts was expecting to visit the great library of Alexandria, but she merely looked glumly around her at the dreary port town. Most of the ancient city has long since foundered under the sea.

She had not spoken all through the train ride. She was furiously busy catching up on letters home. She had held a long, private conversation with Miss van Vredenburch before they parted. It seemed a strange pairing of friends, but no stranger than mine with Holmes, I suppose. They both liked doing things that were ordinarily the province of men, and we both liked sticking our noses into problems ordinarily left to Scotland Yard.

Holmes and I were standing in the stern of the ship, watching the wake cream out behind us. For once we had shed the company of Mrs. Roberts, who had retired to her cabin in a sulk. Well, it's said witches can't cross water. For my part, I was wondering whether we two would ever go hunting together again. What a shambles this journey had proved!

I cleared my throat. "Holmes, you know you have my services to the end."

"I never doubted it."

"And I promise, no matter what the outcome, I shall not record this case."

"Don't be so hasty with your store of promises. I might want you to publish this one."

My heart was eased. I didn't have the slightest grasp of this tangle, but I knew the look on Holmes's face. I had confidence in that look. Somehow, whether with the aid of his medium or without, he would untangle every strand.

"I was shocked to learn that Shaw was really the hero T. E. Lawrence—how has he fallen from colonel to an ordinary pilot?"

"That unfortunately falls under the Official Secrets Act, but I'm afraid he's up to some skulduggery. Frankly, he's a bit of a loose cannon, more inclined to safeguard the interest of his Arab allies than those of king and country. And he's got a special grudge against yours truly."

"Then you've met before?"

"Not in person. But I was the one tasked with discovering his whereabouts when he went to ground before. Intelligence likes to keep an eye on him. Airman John Ross, he called himself that time."

"What was he doing as Ross?"

"It wasn't part of my portfolio to unearth that. Probably spying. Or plotting."

"With the Arabs?"

"No, he'd finished with them, or they with him. Too many promises broken. Perhaps for the Egyptians?"

"Aren't Egyptians Arabs?"

"You have a great deal to learn about that part of the world, Watson."

I really had no desire to learn anything more about that part of the world. But I was worried about Holmes. He obviously knew more about Colonel Lawrence than he could reveal. I only had the vaguest idea of what Holmes had done for Intelligence during the war. There were times when I thought his travels as a spiritualist might be merely an elaborate ruse to disarm his enemies. I still recalled vividly the time he pretended to be dying—pretended even to me!—to catch an enemy unawares.

Which brought me back to where this had all begun. "How do you think Evelyn-White's death figures into the puzzle?"

"Who?"

I was astounded. Sherlock Holmes forgetting? Sherlock Holmes without every aspect of a case at his fingertips? Age brings even great minds to ruin.

"Hugh Evelyn-White?" I gasped. "The suicide?"

"Oh, the lecturer, you mean. Nothing to do with it at all."

"But wasn't he one of the first to enter the tomb?"

"I suppose, depending on your definition of *first*. I did spend an afternoon at Leeds examining the evidence. Plain as a pikestaff."

"He claimed there was a curse upon him."

"Aye, the oldest curse in the world. He had got mixed up with a girl, a music teacher named Helen Nind. How seriously I can't say, but she definitely thought it was serious. When he spurned her, she ended her life by swallowing carbolic acid. Evelyn-White was scheduled to testify at her inquest. Whether it was shame or remorse, he took his own life rather than attend."

"Could she have been . . . with child?"

"Very good, Watson. The coroner said otherwise, but I consider it likely."

"Then it had nothing to do with the curse."

"Of course not. Did you think all deaths were attributable to elementals?"

You cannot imagine how cheered I was by that statement. I only had one more question to ask: the most difficult one. "Holmes, your father . . . ?" I didn't know how to phrase it.

"I didn't think you'd let that one go. But I've already given you the only clue you need to solve that riddle."

Of course, I had no idea what clue that might be. I looked at him, beseechingly.

"All human wisdom is contained in these two words, 'wait and hope.'"

And with that Holmes strode away, signaling the subject was closed.

Chapter Fourteen:
Mrs. Estelle Roberts

I was being a termagant again. I knew it, but I couldn't help myself. A woman has to shout sometimes to be heard. Once I'd seen the guardian statues at the Cairo Museum, I wanted nothing but to go back to the tomb. The answer was staring me in the face, if I could only see it. Those guardian statues were wrong, all wrong. But the doctor told me I was too weak; he said my pulse was beating like a hummingbird's wings. What caused my pulse to race was worrying over the riddle! No doubt that was why I couldn't sleep, either. But Red Cloud had returned to me. I knew I was in no danger as long as he was by my side. If I could only get the lady of the tomb to tell me her name, I could commune with her anywhere in the world. But the farther I traveled from Luxor, the more strained became the ties between myself and that troubled spirit.

I was too sick to go up on deck much. From what Dr. Watson told me, it was cold and rainy most of the time, anyway. He seemed well pleased with the weather. A true Englishman, I must admit.

I was terribly relieved when we made landfall in Marseille, even though it must be the ugliest city in the world. At least that is how I remember it. Grey and muddy. Sir Sherlock made sure for some reason to point out the Château d'If, a rocky island just off the coast, which was famous for its prison fortress. I suppose such things are interesting to detectives. As we traveled through France, I stared out the train window as the two men discussed the "case," as they referred to the chaos we'd left behind in Luxor, and it was like traveling from summer to autumn to winter. In Paris it was raining as if it had never stopped.

We had left the Beauchamps behind in Cairo, along with the Bugatti. Anna would drive it to Highclere Castle in Hampshire. On her way back she promised to attend one of my demonstrations. I looked forward to seeing her again. She would never make a sensitive, but she had a fierce heart.

Sir Sherlock had assured the Beauchamps before we left them that we would yet supply the resolution Lady Evelyn sought. His promises rang hollow. How could I, in the rain and cold of London, call up the furious soul imprisoned in the tomb of the pharaoh? And how else could we discover the answers we sought?

Since having seen him laid out in his coffin, I had begun thinking of Tutankhamun as the boy in the golden mask, staring up for centuries at the lid, waiting to be freed. I had posed the detective a simple enough question: Where was the pharaoh's wife buried? But it appeared, as was often the case with Sir Sherlock, that there was no simple answer. I marveled sometimes at Dr. Watson's patience with him.

Tutankhamun's wife was named Ankhesenamun, he said, and she was his half sister. I thought that utterly disgraceful, but he claimed it was customary in ancient Egypt. Their father, Akhenaten (if he was their father) had turned the Egyptian world upside down by dumping the Egyptian gods in favor of one god—not the true God, but the sun god. After Akhenaten died, Tutankhamun ascended the throne at the tender age of ten. He turned around and welcomed back all the old gods, the Ennead, as they were called. Which long-winded discourse still didn't answer my question.

Then Sir Sherlock rambled on about Nefertiti, who may have been Tutankhamun's mother or may not but was definitely the power behind the throne until she vanished in a puff of smoke when Tut-ankhamun came of age. It all made me cross-eyed. The upshot was that Ankhesenamun's tomb had not yet been found, which was what I had suspected from the start. Nor had Nefertiti's. There positively must be a hidden chamber in the tomb where one of them, wife or mother, was buried, I decided. One of them must be the lady of the tomb.

I pressed my face against the window again and let my mind wander. Where was Madame Louise? I couldn't simply summon her. She was too powerful, too capricious, too hurt, for even Red Cloud to call her if she did not wish to be called. She seemed still bathed in the flames that had taken her away from this plane of existence. But she had contacted me in the first place because her son was in danger. Had that danger passed? Was my part in this drama finished? I had not exactly covered myself in glory up to that point.

The men were talking now about interviewing subjects. Dr. Watson spoke with confidence, as if he'd finally found the ground solid beneath him again. How could I contribute? I had tried to summon the souls of Colonel Herbert and Lord Carnarvon at the very beginning of our investigation, to no avail. They refused to speak to a stranger, perhaps. That was often the case. Or sometimes those who had died recently had not yet got their bearings. Some were still unconvinced that they had passed over. In death, as in life, we have a great deal to learn, and to learn to accept.

Should I attempt them again? Would they even know who had murdered them, or how? Oftentimes it is as great a mystery to the victim as to the detective. How does it feel to be poisoned, to be stabbed in the back, to have one's skull split open? Can one take such a brutal memory to the other side? Would they have simply told me, as George Gould had, that she had—or he had—stolen the true name? Was the true name to be found in the heart scarab? If so, why had they not simply said so? In spite of depictions in the sensationalist press, those who've passed speak plainly, not in riddles. What could be more pressing than the name of your murderer, Mr. Gould?

It was all for the best, perhaps. I had neglected my husband and children, rushing off to Egypt to impress this man with my talents. No, for the money, which we sorely needed. I was grateful to Sir Sherlock for the opportunity. But it was over, finished.

What had happened at this mysterious dinner the baronet spoke of? All three men were now dead. Perhaps I had been spending too much time at the Marylebone Spiritualist Association. I had made more money as a housekeeper, and no one ever questioned my credentials with a broom. My mind could not rest anywhere. It kept buzzing around like a—what? A bee? No, like a wasp, a maddened wasp.

When I stepped off the train at Victoria, I fairly flew into Arthur's waiting arms. I didn't even make a proper farewell to Sir Sherlock or Dr. Watson. Of course, there was no one waiting at the station for those two lonely old men.

When I arrived home, I hugged the children till I almost squeezed the life out of them, and the girls hugged me back just as hard. The baby just let out a hearty burp. Then I put on the tea as the rain pattered on the window. Of course, it was a new home, with new things since the fire. Rather bare. Shoddy. It would take some time till I could make it truly a home.

After I saw the children off to school the next morning, and Arthur off to work, I sat in the rocker with Terry asleep in my arms. I felt a ringing sadness, as though a chapter of my life had come to an end. I was desolate.

Three days later I received a wire from Sir Sherlock. I was to please attend him at the Queen Anne Street address of Dr. Watson, to prepare to visit the home of Mrs. Mary Gertrude Herbert, widow of the late colonel Aubrey Herbert. My heart soared. I threw on my shawl and tied my bonnet and went skipping out into the world with a light heart. Stupid woman. I ran back to tell Bea that I would be gone for a few hours, and to look after the baby. Luckily, my reputation as a sensitive had always overawed her. She did not ask questions. She only nodded.

Chapter Fifteen:
Dr. John Watson

Once Mrs. Roberts appeared, greeting us as if we hadn't seen her in years, and her hair looking a fright, we were ready to decamp. We took a cab to Bruton Street in Mayfair. It was a fine, imposing house, as one would imagine, with a ruthless Georgian facade. We were fortunate in that Mrs. Herbert had just come up to town. She had been cloistered in Somerset since her husband's death late last year. She was overseeing the construction of a rather elaborate tomb to house his remains. No scarabs included, I hoped.

"Now, Mrs. Roberts, a bit of theatre will be in order," said Holmes, and he sketched out his plan as we rode along.

We rang the bell, bringing to the door a clockwork butler who insisted we were tradesmen and we should use the back entrance. White tie and tails must have been the order of the day, at least to pass muster with this stiff-necked functionary. I'm afraid I disagreed with him and was soon raising my voice to such a pitch (wholly unconsciously) that we attracted the attentions of a constable and the lady of the house, a formidable if slender personage in her thirties, with a hard face and calculating eyes, dressed in black bombazine for mourning.

Luckily, the lady recognized Holmes right off. Indeed, I was to learn later that he had often been a dinner guest during the war, when-ever Colonel Herbert was at home and not off in some far-flung corner of the empire. She sent both the butler and the bobby about their busi-ness and guided us into the parlor herself. The room was unrelentingly modern, all chrome and glass, with Bibendum chairs in which one could do nothing but slouch. We were soon slouching with the requisite tea and Mrs. Herbert was staring at us inquiringly. She did not slouch.

"If you're here to console me, I'm afraid the bloom is off the rose on that one. If Aubrey owed you money, send in an invoice like everyone else. You look tired, Mr. Holmes."

There was a disappointed set to her lips, but her eyes were far-off, enjoying themselves in the mountains, or perhaps by the sea. Anywhere but the here and now. She was well equipped for disappointment.

"I have some questions regarding a matter your husband was involved with just before his unfortunate demise."

"Then you're here in an official capacity?"

"I'm here representing a client."

"I thought you only sleuthed for king and country nowadays."

"This is for God," said Mrs. Roberts meekly.

Mrs. Herbert stared at her in wonderment, as if a pet canary had spoken.

"This is my associate Mrs. Roberts," Holmes hastened to interject.

"Ah. And this must be the famous Dr. Watson. I should have known you were on an investigation as soon as I saw him in tow."

I merely nodded, uncertain whether I should take umbrage.

"You realize that most of what my husband was engaged in falls under the Official Secrets Act. That means he didn't talk to anyone about it. Even myself."

"You know that I did some work for the Egypt Office during the war," Holmes said.

"I do."

Holmes pounced. "Then the colonel did tell you some things."

Mrs. Herbert colored. "For which he swore me to secrecy," she countered.

"But now he is dead."

"That does not release me from my vow."

"No . . . " Did Holmes have another move? "But it surely releases him. This lady, Mrs. Roberts, is a talented medium. Should you consent, she can ask your husband certain questions, which he can answer as he sees fit—through you."

Her eyes narrowed. "I understood you had taken up spiritualism. It seemed odd at the time. Now I begin to understand."

"Do you consent?" he pressed.

"You're as sly as Aubrey was. All right. I shall don your fig leaf. Ask me what you will."

Mrs. Roberts looked at Holmes for her cue. He nodded. She would remember what we had discussed in the cab.

"Colonel Herbert, what was your relationship with Ali Fahmy Bey?" she asked tentatively.

"Don't we extinguish the lights and join hands?" Mrs. Herbert put on a scandalized mien, which I assumed was merely to protect her reputation.

"We can dispense with the theatrics. Mrs. Roberts is a powerful sensitive. Just answer her questions as the spirit moves you," said Holmes, dropping a wink.

"Keep calm and let the spirit flow through you. You can close your eyes if you like," added Mrs. Roberts in a reassuring tone.

Mrs. Herbert did as she was bidden. She took a long, deep breath and then began.

"Prince Ali was conflicted. He wanted to be loved by his people but respected by the British. He wanted a typical Islamic marriage, though he'd married a French tart."

"In other words, he was the perfect subject to turn into a spy," said Holmes.

"For the British, perhaps. Certainly for the Egyptians. Probably for anyone who greased his palm."

"And you ran him," Mrs. Roberts said, sounding like an old intelligence hand herself.

"My husband . . . I saw a certain potential in him," she responded, keeping up the fiction.

"For access?" Mrs. Roberts ventured.

"For secrets. Aubrey was a great collector of secrets. He stored them up for a rainy day."

Now Mrs. Roberts consulted with Holmes in a whisper. "And he had something to sell Ali Bey," she put forward.

"I don't know what it was, though."

"A thing of beauty? Or a thing of power?" Holmes broke in.

"My dear sir, beauty is power. Even with your reputation, you must be aware of that. Perhaps you should talk to Princess Marguerite."

"But will she talk?" I asked.

"She'll talk to anybody that wants dirt on her husband. After the things she revealed in court about their most intimate moments in the boudoir—well, it's enough to make one blush. She might need the incentive of a few quid, of course. She's trying to get hold of Ali Bey's fortune—over two million pounds—but for some reason the family has objected. They're fighting her for it."

"What about Guinevere Gould?" asked Holmes.

"Harder to read. Definitely the distraught widow. Married less than a year. Of course, she was his secret lover for years before his first wife died. Had three children by him during that time. So she might have shared his secrets. And she might not be inclined to give them up. But I've found American women rarely concern themselves with their husbands' business affairs. Foolish."

Mrs. Roberts leaned into Holmes again to receive whispered instructions. "One more question," she asked. "How were your relations with Lord Carnarvon?"

There was a prolonged silence. At last Mrs. Herbert opened her eyes with a dramatic flutter and said, "I'm sorry. The spirit has left me." She slumped back as if exhausted. A pretty little performance.

But Holmes was not to be denied. "Then let me ask you. Was there bad blood between your husband and Lord Carnarvon?"

Her back was up. "Not in the least. They were brothers."

"No jealousy?" Holmes probed.

"They were both ambitious. George made the biggest find in the history of archaeology. Aubrey was offered the crown of Albania—twice. They both reached the pinnacle of their chosen fields. They cheered each other on lustily."

"The dispute between Carnarvon and the Egyptian government must have been ticklish for your husband."

"The dispute was, as you say, between the government and George. My husband did not concern himself in any way with it."

Holmes's eyebrows did not go up. But I recognized the effort to keep his face immobile. It meant that he had encountered a lie but could not find his way around it. "Well, that should be all, then." He rose. We followed suit. "Thank you for your cooperation, Mrs. Herbert. Or your husband's, I should say."

But if Holmes was satisfied, I was not. I spoke up. "One question: Who told your husband to have his teeth pulled?" A question so obvious I assumed it had been overlooked.

"I don't really know. My husband was desperate. His sight, which had always been weak, was failing entirely. He got the doctor's name from a friend in the service. I'm afraid they're rather fanciful in the service, begging your pardon. Still. He never should have listened to that man. I told him so. But he'd rather listen to some Oriental quack than his loving wife."

"Oriental?"

"Oh, yes, I'm fairly certain the doctor was Arabic, though his practice was here in London."

"Do you know the friend who recommended him, at least?"

"Certainly. Lawrence. Tom Lawrence."

Holmes, who had been moving toward the door, stopped and turned around. "Lawrence? Are you certain?"

"Have you ever met Mr. Lawrence? Well, then, you know he's hardly forgettable."

"Thank you, Mrs. Herbert," said Holmes crisply.

"And again, we're sorry for your loss," Mrs. Roberts added as a sop.

"Well, apparently I can call on you anytime I need to consult with him." Whether it was meant as a harmless joke or to sting, it definitely landed. Mrs. Roberts cast her eyes to the floor and did not raise them again until we were well clear of the house.

We filed out, hardly knowing what we had achieved. I went to whistle up a cab, but then I realized the clockwork butler was there before me. He had a cab in hand and was even holding the door open for us. This was such a turnabout that I felt it was necessary to ask, "Is this for us?"

He gave the briefest of nods, all the contrition we would get from the fellow. We settled into the cab and soon cast off the gloom of Bruton Street.

"Mrs. Roberts, you were tremendous. I know you have scruples against that sort of playacting, but be sure, it was necessary." Holmes was usually not so free in handing out compliments. "Watson, your question was particularly incisive. I don't know why I bothered to put in an appearance at all. I could sit at home, listen to the gramophone, and wait for the clues to come in."

I felt pleasure burn my cheeks, although I wasn't sure what we had learned on our outing.

"Shall we try our luck with the grieving widow of Ali Fahmy Bey?" Holmes said.

"The princess?" I stared in wide wonder. "She's in Cairo, isn't she?"

"According to this morning's *Times*, she's at the Savoy."

"The Savoy?" Mrs. Roberts's hand flew to her mouth. "Isn't that where—?"

"She slew her husband, yes. And trust me, the Savoy is soaking up all the publicity it can. They've even concocted a drink named in her honor, the Three Shot Killer. Brandy, curaçao, and bitters."

I put my hand to my temple. "It's appalling. Why on earth—?"

"She has an announcement for the fourth estate. It seems she's given birth to the child."

"No!" said Mrs. Roberts. "Does she intend to produce the infant?"

"Can you purchase a child on the black market in Paris?" I asked, only half joking.

"I don't think she'll go that far," Holmes assured us. "It's obviously a further ploy to bolster her claim to her husband's fortune. Or she's gone mad, which is a distinct possibility."

"Why did she come to London to announce it?" Mrs. Roberts asked.

"I think she expects a more receptive audience," I offered.

"Yes. Watson, you brought along your camera, as I asked?"

I nodded. I had bought an Autographic after the war and taken hundreds of pictures before I became bored with the thing and sick of the smell of darkroom chemicals.

"Excellent. We'll freshen things up a bit. You will be the intrepid journalist, Mrs. Roberts the stenographer, and I shall be the photographer. That should make her hungry to see us."

Holmes reached into his own bag and produced a false beard and spirit gum right there on the spot. He began to apply it. Mrs. Roberts held up her compact mirror to help him. There was a service I'd never thought to afford him. I busied myself with the settings on the camera.

"Holmes, what you intimated about trouble between Lord Carnarvon and Colonel Herbert . . . ?" I hinted.

"There was naturally a dispute when the Egyptian government went back on their agreement to divide up the spoils from the tomb, and the English government—read one Aubrey Molyneux Herbert as their representative—sided with them. Herbert was chosen as a peacemaker, but of course Carnarvon as the older brother thought he was being betrayed. They nearly came to blows."

"Surely you don't think he killed his own brother," I tutted.

"Half brother. I cannot rule it out."

"But who killed Colonel Herbert? Or did he simply die of blood poisoning?"

"Perhaps Princess Marguerite can shed some light on the subject."

But we were not to speak with the lady that day. Though we came into the lobby of the Savoy with Holmes clicking the camera shutter for all he was worth, we were too late.

"She's checked out, sir. Just this afternoon," a clerk informed us.

"Didn't she have a meeting with the press scheduled?" I asked, scanning the deserted lobby.

"The reporters and rubberneckers have all decamped, begging your pardon. Word leaked out that that the princess's midwife, a Madame Champeau, has confessed to the Paris police the forging of a birth certificate for Princess Fahmy. The first question from the press today was on that subject. There was no second question."

The shutter ceased clicking. Holmes scratched his beard.

"Surely she must have left a forwarding address," he demanded.

"Oh, yes, sir, the Ritz. In Paris."

We made an ignoble retreat.

"Who's for a quick trip to Paris?" I said, only half joking.

Mrs. Roberts looked up hopefully, then said, "I have to be there when the children get home." She looked downcast at the prospect.

"I think that's enough for today. We'll resume the hunt tomorrow," said Holmes.

We dropped Mrs. Roberts (who was anxious to be home before her children returned, as if she were a truant hoping to avoid a scolding), and we made our way home, only to find a cable from Lady Evelyn.

He had done it. Carter had shut down the dig and had refused to turn over the keys to the proper authorities. Now the fur would fly.

After dinner, Holmes was restless and went out once more, whether with some definite purpose in mind or merely to feel the streets of London beneath his feet again, he did not say. I sat down with a spot of port and endeavored to finish John Buchan's *Greenmantle*.

The next morning, Holmes was brimming with news; unfortunately, none of it was hopeful.

"We won't be taking any overnight trips to Paris. I cabled the Ritz. She was there for one night and checked out. No forwarding address. I should have taken your advice and pursued her while we had the opportunity."

"Well, there's Mrs. Gould."

"Who is in America. No one can hazard a guess as to when she'll return. Or whether."

"Well, then, what about this Lawrence chap?" I knew I was reaching.

"He has literally dropped off the face of the earth."

"My, you have been busy. What about a spot of breakfast, then?"

"Good old practical Watson. Bring on the kedgeree and buttered brown toast."

We sat at the breakfast table in our dressing gowns eating a good English breakfast and talking of nothing. Forty years were wiped away and we were young again, making our way in the world.

Chapter Sixteen:
Mrs. Estelle Roberts

L ouise came to me that night in a dream. Her voice was so hopeless, her warnings so terrifying, that I am surprised I did not wake up howling, beating Arthur's chest. I think she must have held me under, the way one drowning person will another when she loses her head and panics. Sir Sherlock was swallowed by holes, traps, pitfalls, crevasses, graves, endless abysses. Only he was not a man of sixty-odd years in my dream. He was a child of three or four, a baby rocking in his cradle on the edge of a cliff. How I wailed for mercy for that child, tried to reach out and save him, but each time I did I discovered anew that my own limbs had been lopped off, leaving horrid bloody stumps. I only brushed his stricken face, his tiny fingers. Above all there was the endless roar of waters.

I knew, even as I dreamed, I was witnessing every mother's fears for her child, played out in excruciating detail. I couldn't tell if it were prophecy or only maternal anxieties. Every mother has these terrors; everyone has imagined her child dying in every conceivable fashion, falling, burning, drowning, cudgels, knives, one moment laughing and alive, the next crushed beneath some shapeless falling thing—but we do not speak of it.

I wanted to comfort Louise, to hold her close, but I could not make myself heard above the waters. When I woke in the smeared morning light, it was to headache and exhaustion.

I got up, put on my bravest face, and made breakfast for Arthur and the children, as in the olden days. The olden days? What was I thinking of? It was but a month or so ago. The fire had created a great gulf in my life, a chasm that seemed impossible to bridge. My own dear ones were so vulnerable. I'd never feel safe again. The eggs looked up from the pan at me with sickening false smiles. I felt nauseous.

To make matters worse, the dream did not fade from my consciousness, as dreams mercifully do, but stayed with me, stepping on my shadow, clawing at me with phantom fingers, whispering voices. I was scheduled to give a demonstration for the Marylebone Association that day, but I doubted my ability to hear any voice but that of endless cascading waters. Perhaps I should put it off for a day or two?

I expected a wire from Sir Sherlock as to whether he was interviewing Mrs. Gould that day, but the morning wore on and no message came. Should I call him, tell him Louise had predicted imminent danger? But he knew all about imminent danger; he'd always lived with it. He needed to know what form the danger would come in. And that I could not tell him.

I had the dream again. I woke in terror in the middle of the night and fled my bed, Arthur's calm breathing. I sought shelter in the baby's room and the rocker there. But I did not dare sleep. I had not heard a word from Sir Sherlock. I would have to seek him out—if he were still alive.

He may have returned to Sussex. Dr. Watson would know. But when I called, Dr. Watson was not at home. I talked to his housekeeper instead. Fortunately, she was the garrulous type.

"Gone to Paris, he has. Never home—how can I cook his dinners?" she squawked.

"Well, at least you'll have some time to yourself." I was hurt. They had gone to the continent without me. Not that I could have gotten away. But still, they might have asked me. They must be seeking out Princess Marguerite. It was dangerous to beard her in her own den. Oh, everything was dangerous! Even sleep.

"No such fortune," said the housekeeper, bringing a merciful halt to my tumbling thoughts. "Mr. Holmes is still here. He's even worse. That man eats like a bird for days on end, and then he has the appetite of a horse. Never know how much to prepare."

"Is Sir Sherlock in now?" I asked hopefully.

"No, he's at Barts."

"Barts? Hospital? Has something happened to him?"

"Couldn't say. Just left a note this morning. He was looking peaked last night. Of course, he does, most days. Doctor should prescribe a paregoric."

I was too late. My nightmare had come horribly true! I took a cab to the hospital, hang the expense. I had failed Madame Louise. Why, oh why had I waited?

There was no record of him having been admitted at St. Bartholomew's. Had he gone to another hospital? I couldn't check them all. He *must* be there. They had made some sort of mistake. I'm afraid I made something of a scene. I found myself facing the head of the hospital, a doddering old fool named Stamford, trying to calm me down.

"Now, what was the name of your friend again?" he asked, waving a noxious pipe around.

"Sir Sherlock. Sherlock Holmes."

He laughed long and heartily at this. I hardly thought it seemly given the circumstances.

"Come," he said. "I'll take you to him." And he padded away. I followed, all at sea.

We walked down one long hall after another, till we left the clamor of the hospital far behind. The halls were dark and empty. I began to be a little afraid. After all, how old was this hospital? Nearly a thousand years. How many had died here, in loneliness and pain? I could feel them gathering behind me.

Then we came to a door, the only door that had a light underneath.

He knocked, and I heard a muffled voice say, "Enter." He opened the door to a long table filled with gleaming glass—glass tubes, glass vials, glass retorts—and through it all, the stony face of Sherlock Holmes was reflected.

"What is it, Stamford?" he growled.

"Someone to see you, Holmes."

Sir Sherlock glanced up and, recognizing me, broke into a smile. "Mrs. Roberts! Welcome to my world. To what do I owe the honor?"

"She was afraid something had happened to you." I would rather Dr. Stamford had not mentioned that detail, but I could at least breathe again.

"Something *has* happened. I haven't had my tea yet. The hospitality of your hospital has fallen on hard times, Stamford," Sir Sherlock scolded.

"All right, I'll have tea sent. You'd think you were the only person I have to look after around here."

Stamford shuffled off, muttering to himself.

"So what is all this?" I asked, trying to make sense of the scene.

"Chemical analysis. You remember I took a sample of the fungus growing on the walls of the tomb."

"Yes, I remember that Carter dismissed it out of hand."

"I found what I was looking for. *Aspergillus flavus.*"

"Which is what?"

"The prime suspect in the deaths of Lord Carnarvon, Colonel Herbert, and George Gould. It's an airborne fungus that causes symptoms from allergic reactions to congestion to bleeding in the lungs."

"And it's fatal?"

"Usually not. But when introduced directly to the bloodstream, through abrasions—"

"Like a cut on the cheek?" I guessed.

"Precisely. The question is, who introduced it?"

"One of Lord Carnarvon's team? I mean, a visitor wouldn't just collect fungus from the wall. Except for you, of course. Who else would know it was deadly? And how would he administer it to all three of our victims?"

"All good questions, which must be considered in turn."

"You don't believe it was elementals anymore?" I asked, trying to keep the defensiveness from my voice.

"It was you who showed me how elementals can work through people. I think that is precisely the phenomenon we are dealing with in this case."

There it was, out in the open. He believed someone had murdered Lord Carnarvon. And Aubrey Herbert, and George Gould, and who knew if there were more? There was still a murderer out there somewhere. It was easier for me to believe in ancient powers seeking revenge for violating a pharaoh's tomb than a warm-blooded human ready to take lives without compunction, even if that person were acting under the influence of an elemental. I told him the story of my dreams.

A dark cast spread across his face as if night were falling on his soul. "If you dreamed that I was in danger, then you must have realized you are in danger as long as you associate with me. Perhaps I was wrong to involve you. This is no holiday in the sun."

"I never thought it was," I answered roundly.

"Then you'll not take it amiss when I tell you, go home, Mrs. Roberts."

"You involve Dr. Watson in danger constantly."

"Watson is an old campaigner. And he does not have a spouse and four children waiting for him to come home to them."

"I can't get the roar of the waters out of my head."

"You didn't mention any waters."

"It was in the background of all my dreams. Why, does it mean something?"

Sir Sherlock sat staring into space, his eyes fixed on a point far away. He looked about to spill whatever was in the test tube. Then he snapped back. He set the tube down. "Don't need to get that on any open cuts. I do not want to go the way of the other victims of the curse."

"Who would have known it was deadly?" I repeated.

"Someone who'd had experience with it. An archaeologist."

"Carter?"

"Not unless he's a remarkably fine thespian. But there have been any number of archaeologists working in the Valley of the Kings for over a century. Any of them might have experience with this fungus. And perhaps have been jealous of Lord Carnarvon. One certainly falls under suspicion."

"Lacau, the Jesuit?"

"Ah, if he were truly a Jesuit, we could never know what was in his mind. But yes, Lacau."

I didn't want to speculate on these Jesuits, who seemed terribly dangerous in their own right. I went on to another question bothering me.

"Why did you send Dr. Watson to Paris?" I asked.

"Watson in Paris?"

It seemed I had stolen a march on him at last.

"So his housekeeper informs me."

"You're certain Mrs. Colfax said Paris?" He seemed genuinely perplexed.

I was becoming anxious now. An orderly came in with tea, and that calmed my nerves a jot. Sir Sherlock promised me that he would wire me as soon as Dr. Watson returned. "Watson is a prudent fellow, not given to caprice. He may simply have experienced an overwhelming desire for *viennoiseries*."

I knew he was only trying to jolly me along, but sometimes jollying is just what I need. I bade farewell to Sir Sherlock and returned home, somewhat relieved.

I didn't hear from him all that day or the next morning. At least the dream had not returned. I had rescheduled my demonstration for that day, but my nerves were still shot.

I began the demonstration so distracted I had to strain to concentrate. I was finally able to fall into a blessed trance and relied on Red Cloud to carry the day. Dr. Gordon Moore was there once more, desiring to speak with a patient who had passed over only a week ago. Dr. Moore was so solicitous of his patients that he wanted to be sure they were comfortable in the afterlife. These were always pleasant conversations.

Then I felt a cold wind on the back of my neck, and all my muscles locked up. I felt a burning in all my limbs. I was gasping for air as if my lungs had forgotten how to expand. I forced my eyes open. At the back of the hall were Sir Sherlock and Dr. Watson just entering, neither the worse for the wear. I knew that some truly malevolent being had seized me, almost throttling me. I tried to fight, to call out, but it was no use. I prayed for Red Cloud, but there was no answer. I felt my posture become bent and broken, my voice taken by a voice at once musical and deadly:

"Mr. Holmes?" A thin, biting, truculent voice.

He stopped and looked up. He knew the voice at once.

"Moriarty?" he whispered. Both men froze in their tracks.

Though I was unwilling to move, he had command of my limbs. I started down the steps, trying to keep from tripping over my own feet. "You really must come to the falls. It's been so long since I've seen you. We must catch up."

"The one place in the world I never wish to see again is the Reichenbach Falls. I took a life there. It was many years ago, but still it plagues me."

"Why not give me a second chance, then? You may be able to atone for your sins." I approached the two men. I felt like a snake crawling on its belly toward its prey.

"I don't fear you, Moriarty, alive or dead. Now, leave this woman!" he answered with steel in his voice. He struck the floor between us with his stick with such force that it split in two.

His words cut through my heart like a knife. I heard a long wail. I stumbled and would have fallen, save that Dr. Watson stepped forward to take me in his arms and stop my headlong momentum. There was a gasp from the crowd. I knew I was released when I heard that gasp. It took long minutes to get my breath back to normal, but Moriarty had left me. I soon washed up on a familiar shore.

"Mrs. Penderecki, are you here?" I called out. It was my voice, my own.

Mrs. Penderecki let her hand creep up.

"Mrs. Penderecki, I have a message for you from your husband."

"I'm not in any danger, am I? I was going to go to the theatre tonight."

I noticed Dr. Watson smirk as they settled into their seats. Good, I was going to find out why he had gone to Paris. If I could make it through the afternoon.

You'll wonder why I decided to go on that day. Because I knew Red Cloud had been ambushed, bested by a force more powerful than he. Because he needed healing. I let the Pendereckis be my penance.

Chapter Seventeen:
Dr. John Watson

W e were seated in a tea shop, though I would have much preferred a pub with a pint of bitter in front of me. It had been a long twenty-four hours. But Holmes was solicitous of Mrs. Roberts after her strange ordeal. We did not speak of it, though, and I was of such divided mind that I was content to let it lie, for now.

"Whyever did you go to Paris, Dr. Watson?" asked Mrs. Roberts.

"Yes, whyever, Watson?" Holmes chimed in. I put a scone in my mouth. After all that time away, I had a new appreciation for plain English cooking. Especially when it involved clotted cream.

She peered at Holmes. "He hasn't told you?"

"We met at the door," Holmes explained.

"How propitious."

"Didn't you see the paper I left on the table? Open to the news?" I asked.

"There was no paper on the table." He moved the scones out of my reach.

"Blast, the one time Mrs. Colfax tidies up. Excuse my language."

"What was in the paper?" Mrs. Roberts asked irritably.

"Princess Marguerite returned to Paris yesterday, as you know. I knew you still wanted to question her, so I decided to hunt her up before she went to ground."

"So you were able to get there before she disembarked?" she asked, obviously confused.

"Oh, no. Impossible. But yesterday's paper noted the name of the ship she traveled on. So I took a valise along. One of yours, Holmes. They're nicer than mine."

"And?" Holmes by now had probably anticipated all my moves. But I continued for the benefit of Mrs. Roberts.

"I went up to the left luggage desk. I told them I was from the front office and that I had a valise that belonged to the Princess that had got waylaid. She was fit to be tied and I'd promised her a personal apology. So I was able to winkle her address out of him. A place in the Rue Georges-Ville, a little elbow street on the Right Bank. I thought about ending my quest there, save that I had passed a camera shop along the way. Well, it brought to mind your dodge with the *Times*."

Sherlock Holmes was smiling broadly. "You didn't."

"I did. I wired her. Said I was from *Antiques Quarterly* and I'd love to get some pictures of her Egyptian collection. She fell for it like the vain little thing she is."

"You weren't worried she'd recognize you from our encounter in Cairo?" Mrs. Roberts asked.

"I think all her attention was on Holmes and, begging your pardon, yourself. Besides, I had my reading glasses on that morning, which I'm told make me look quite different."

"They make you look like a sleepy old owl," volunteered Holmes.

"I don't believe there is an *Antiques Quarterly*," said Mrs. Roberts.

"Be that as it may, I purchased a new camera—I have the receipt here for Lady Evelyn—and I presented myself at her door. I had to make it through a formidable secretary and the princess's sister, Yvonne, but I was finally ushered into her orgulous presence. She did have quite a collection of Oriental whatnots, and I took pictures from every angle except standing on my head. One of the new single-lens reflex cameras—they're a dream. She seemed to cotton to me, though I'm old enough to be her pater. So I started dropping a few pertinent questions into the mix:

"'I heard you toured King Tutankhamun's tomb. That must have been thrilling.'

"'Mais oui. We had the private exhibition, of course.'

"'Which of all those treasures would you own if you could have your pick? One of the couches perhaps?'

"'You both remember that couch we saw at the museum. Body of a lion, head of a hippo, tail of a monkey or whatever.'

"'Indeed? I would have guessed something more intimate would be to your taste. Perhaps the heart scarab.'

"'There was no heart scarab found upon the body.'"

I slammed my fist down the table, so the tea things jumped in unison. Holmes and the lady seemed to jump as well.

"That's when I knew I had her; for she had visited the tomb long before the sarcophagus was opened, and there had been nothing in the papers about it. Then I turned up the heat on her."

"'You know what I can't figure out? Where do you suppose your husband got to the night he died? The newspapers said he was gone for hours in the pouring rain.'"

"Well, her nostrils flared at that one, but I tried my best to look harmless to pacify her."

"An effect which he does quite well, considering. You know he received a V.C. for his derring-do in Afghanistan? You won't find that in any of his narratives. Harmless he is anything but," Holmes interposed.

I tried not to blush at that one. "Well, she stammered a bit, and cleared her throat, so I poured it on:

"'I suppose he was with some boy. Orientals like those little boys, don't they?'

"'He wasn't with a boy. He was with a woman, and if I told you which woman, a woman fully five years older than myself—'

"But there she clamped her mouth shut."

"'Oh, please. I've got to know. Strictly off the record. My hand before God. You'll never hear a peep out of me, Princess.'

"It was plain that she was dying to tell me."

"'Natacha Rambova.'

"She said it as if she was pulling the veil off a magic trick. Well, I gasped, to go along with the mise-en-scène, though I have no idea who Natacha Rambova is. But she must be at least somewhat famous from the way she said it, and—"

"I know who she is. I've met her. And she's more than five years younger than Princess Marguerite, not five years older," said Mrs. Roberts.

I must have been staring cross-eyed at her. Even Sherlock Holmes had his mouth open.

"She's the bride of the Hollywood actor Rudolph Valentino," she added.

"*The Sheik*?" Holmes asked.

"He's a sheik?" I asked, confused.

"He starred in the film *The Sheik*," Mrs. Roberts corrected.

I don't see many films. As in, any. "And how do you come to know a film star?" I asked, rather piqued that she had stolen my thunder.

"Oh, she's devoted to spiritism. They both are. Their last time in London they wanted to meet Sherlock Holmes's medium. So I made their acquaintance."

I have never seen Holmes laugh so hard. I thought he would choke on his tea.

"Well, could you write Mrs. Valentino and ask what her business was with Ali Fahmy on the night of his death?" I asked squarely.

"Oh, no, that wouldn't do at all, especially if she were guilty of an indiscretion. Some questions are better asked tête-à-tête, over tea and biscuits," said Mrs. Roberts firmly.

"Well, would you care to fly out to Hollywood and chat her up?"

"Don't be so flippant, Doctor. It doesn't become you. Besides, there's no need for such drastic measures. They're preparing another film. All about El Cid, I think. That means she'll be back here shortly, trawling the shops for costumes and props. Then it will be perfectly natural of me to ask her to tea."

"Then we shall await the advent of Mrs. Valentino. We may finally discover what was the thing of beauty and what the thing of power," said Holmes, "provided she knows."

"I thought we had determined the first one was this heart scarab," Mrs. Roberts sallied.

"We as yet have no proof that there *is* a heart scarab," Holmes reminded her.

An idea hit me: "Mightn't what's his name, Burton, have gotten a picture of it while it was still on the body?"

"Even if he did, Carter would likely have destroyed any such photo by now."

"So, Carter did steal the scarab?" Mrs. Roberts asked, trying to nail Holmes down.

"I'm not convinced of that, either. But he must be aware of the theft, if theft there was. He would hardly be willing to admit such an abstraction took place under his watchful eye."

"Then how on earth can we prove it?" she asked.

"We must follow the trail of the thing of beauty. We do have one advantage, if it is indeed the heart scarab."

"And what might that be?" I asked.

"The scarab itself. It cannot be that it wanders idly from hand to hand. It must have a specific gravity."

Mrs. Roberts and I exchanged sidelong looks of perplexity. Then her dark eyes lit up. "Of course!" she said. "It's an elemental, after all. It has its own desires. It seeks its center."

Now I was more baffled than ever, and said so.

"The same principle guides the elemental as for a magnet that seeks true north, a moving object comes to rest, or water seeks its own level. The elemental must have a resting point," said Holmes.

This was a bridge too far for me. Even if I were to accept all their wild ideas up to this point, this mishmash of physics and the meta-physical I refused to follow. But once again, I held my peace. I could hardly walk out on them now. They would need a rational mind on their side.

"But then the scarab may kill while attempting to return to Tutankhamun," said Mrs. Roberts, dismayed.

"It may kill and kill again," said Holmes in a doom-laden voice.

I saw an opening. "But didn't you say it was the *aspergillus* whatever that killed them?"

"The fungus was merely the means to hand. The scarab was the force majeure," he replied.

"But we still don't know that it was the scarab that was stolen," I said. "There were thousands of items in that tomb, and most of them had Tutankhamun's name etched on them somewhere. Carter said as much."

"We can wipe a few thousand from our rolls. The item must perforce be both small and extremely valuable," Holmes pointed out.

"And it should be something dear to the pharaoh, which the elemental would logically attach itself to," chimed in Mrs. Roberts.

"I'll grant you that, but don't you see what I'm driving at? If it's so valuable, perhaps there's no spirit involved at all. Men have lusted for gold since Midas. What great gem does not have its story of a trail of death left behind it? There was enough gold in that tomb to sink a Spanish galleon," I rejoined.

Mrs. Roberts's eyes rolled in her head, but Holmes gave my argument the consideration it was due. I thought for a moment he would be forced to stand and pace the floor. I even considered offering him my pipe. But I could feel something rumbling within him, something about to erupt.

"I've been a fool! I've been approaching this problem the wrong way round. The item wasn't stolen, but appropriated!" he said triumphantly.

I was frankly hoping for something with more teeth. "I really don't see the difference."

"It could only be appropriated by someone who thought they had a rightful claim to it."

"You mean one of the Egyptian officials?" Mrs. Roberts asked.

"I mean Lord Carnarvon. Remember that he went into the affair with the understanding that he would get an equal division of the spoils. The Egyptians reneged. It wouldn't be a question of the value of the thing. It would be a matter of retribution, of justice, as he saw it."

"But he was a man of sterling reputation. I'm sure he wouldn't dream of taking some trophy just to display," I said.

"Indeed not—the one thing he could never do is display it in any way. But remember he was an avid collector. Such wealthy men as he hold their secret treasures as dear as the picture of Dorian Grey."

He was still pondering, his fingers drumming the tabletop louder than the trooping of the colors.

"If we give Watson's theory its due—" he began.

"What theory was that?" asked Mrs. R., now thoroughly muddled.

"That it's simply a question of avarice. We must look for opposites that attract," he announced.

"I don't follow you at all," I confessed.

"What did Gould and Fahmy have in common?"

"They were both rich as Croesus."

"Besides the obvious, Watson."

I got rather huffy at that remark. "I don't know! What did they have in common?"

"Absolutely nothing. What brought them together?"

"The scarab," said Mrs. Roberts, still championing her scarab theory.

"The scarab. Either its desire to change hands, or their desire for plunder, brought them together. We must look for other unlooked-for associations. There shall we find the scarab," Holmes said with finality.

"Then we just wait?" That did not suit me at all. "What if your spirits strike again?"

"We must hope that they don't strike at one of us."

There was cold comfort indeed.

"Have patience, my friend. The pieces are falling together," he said.

My patience was exhausted. "May I have another scone, please?" I begged.

Chapter Eighteen:
Mrs. Estelle Roberts

———◆◁◆▷◆———

I prepared dinner—or rather, I burned dinner—in a hurry that night. Though we had by tacit agreement avoided the subject entirely in our discussion, I was still deeply shaken by my bruising encounter with Moriarty. One thing I was sure of: I had no wish to ever come near the Reichenbach Falls.

Sir Sherlock had said that all the pieces of the mystery were falling together, but they seemed more jumbled than ever to me. If there were a heart scarab, who had stolen it from the tomb? Lord Carnarvon had died, so it must have been he. Next had come Mr. Gould, who had somehow stolen the scarab from Lord Carnarvon, from his cold, dead hands, even as the elemental passed to him? And then had Aubrey Herbert killed him to avenge his half brother, coming into possession of scarab and elemental both? And then Ali Bey must have killed him for it. I could imagine him in a fit of madness, pulling the teeth from the blind Colonel Herbert's open mouth, one by one, all the while making soft clucking noises to throw him off guard. And then the elemental must have passed to the princess upon his death. But that was not the order the spirits had hinted at.

Ouch! I'd burned my finger.

Well, what then? Had the princess stolen it from the lord and the prince stolen it from the princess and the colonel—oh, it was maddening! Where had the spirit fled to? What was its purpose? To be reunited with the pharaoh? Or to poison whoever came into possession of it? If they came too near, could it possess Sherlock Holmes or Dr. Watson? Was that what Madame Louise had been warning us about all along—that her son might add another death to the scarab's score? Was I safe from possession? Surely Red Cloud would protect me. If he could. He hadn't been able to defend me from Moriarty's onslaught.

Salt. It needed more salt.

If we were to return the scarab to the tomb, would Mr. Carter even take it back? He had already denied its existence. And what if he took it back, returned it to the pharaoh? Wasn't it his intention to remove the mummy from the tomb? Would the elementals strike him down if he attempted it? It might serve him right. Oh, I wished that they had never found the tomb, no matter how fabulous the treasure. What is gold to the lives of innocents?

The family crowded into the kitchen, but they seemed far removed, as if I viewed them through a spyglass. My beloved Hugh, and my three daughters, Ivy, Evaline, and Iris, all at the small deal table, smiling up at me, but with that guarded look that meant they knew I was in another world. No, not Hugh—Arthur, my second husband. Hugh was gone, but I often saw him sitting there at the table, watching over his girls. Of course, I never told Arthur.

Yes, I had burned the bottom of the stew. No matter. The girls were used to it. They probably thought it was supposed to be that way. Arthur was patient. Where was baby Terry? My heart stopped. Oh— Bea was with Terry. He was asleep. He was safe. I wish that I could sleep so soundly. Ever since the spirits had begun visiting me at the tender age of three, my sleep had been invaded by the dreams of others.

None of the girls had yet manifested my gift. Would Terry be the one to inherit it? I hoped not. But what was it like, to be alone in one's mind? It seemed lonesome. Was it only emptiness, with one solitary soul rattling around in there? I could not remember a time before the voices. They were part of me. I would be lost without them. I would be incomplete. I remember when my brother Lionel, who had died before I was born, first appeared to me. I was only five. He was a child then, too, but I watched him grow to maturity along with me. He still comes to visit me in the quiet hours, bringing soft words of encouragement.

"Look for the unlooked-for," Sir Sherlock had said. There was something—

I dished out the stew. Iris, my picky eater, took a tiny spoonful into her mouth. "Stew's burnt," she said, with a look of disgust. The other two girls nodded in unison. They hadn't even tasted it yet.

"It's not. It's fine," said Arthur. Bless him for lying so valiantly.

"There's bread and butter," I said.

"What about bread and chocolate?" Iris begged.

Bread and chocolate? Where did she ever get an idea to mix—?

Princess Marguerite and Sir Archibald!

Chapter Nineteen:
Dr. John Watson

That night, I met one of Holmes's elementals. Or, not precisely met, and not precisely an elemental. But he was unquestionably a creature of ill omen. Let me explain. Holmes had disappeared on some secret fact-finding mission, and I was feeling fidgety. I went down to the pub for a pint and some chips. It was a bit more crowded and a bit louder than I liked, so I decided on having only one. I was taking my first sip when a sudden slap on my back knocked my teeth against the glass and sent bitter flying in all directions. I swung around to find myself facing—what was his name?—Shaw—no, Lawrence. The plucky pilot who had flown us to Cairo. That was how I placed him at first. It was hard, even with what I now knew, to picture him in flowing white robes. How could he even ride a camel, short as he was? Not exactly the hail-fellow-well-met kind, I would have thought. He wanted something.

"Well, what are you doing here?" he cried, which is exactly what I had intended to say to him.

"I live just round the corner," I said defensively and immediately wished I had not volunteered that information. Still, I could not help but think of Holmes's directive to look out for the unlooked-for. This meeting definitely qualified. Silly, perhaps. But was this meeting a coincidence? Doubtful.

"Well, imagine that. By the by, did you ever find what you were seeking in Tutankhamun's tomb?" he asked. I noticed he didn't have a drink in his hand.

"Looking for?" I remembered all too well Holmes warning me about the man. Although he could hardly be causing the Egyptians much trouble in a pub off the Marylebone Road.

"That's what your companion said. He was looking for some explanation for all those unnatural deaths connected to the unsealing of the tomb. Or was he just having me on? All that blather about a curse."

"He makes such a pother. You don't believe in supernatural curses, do you?" I said, trying to put him on his back foot.

"I don't know. One sees a great number of outré things in the Orient. Especially poisons. I've seen men die the most excruciating deaths because someone shook a drop or two of something wicked in their waterhole."

"That doesn't exactly fall under the definition of the supernatural, though, does it?"

"Quite natural. But nothing says those ancient Egyptians couldn't have devised a poison that would activate when someone opened their tomb three thousand years later. They were far more sophisticated than we give them credit for."

"*Aspergillus flavus.*"

"What's that?" His face colored an alarming shade.

"Oh, nothing. Just something I heard." From Holmes, who had finally explained his fascination with fungus to me. I bitterly regretted mentioning it to Lawrence. We old men tend to prattle on too much.

His eyes narrowed. "Take heed, Dr. Watson. You should know I have nothing but the greatest respect for Mr. Holmes. And yourself, for that matter. But there comes a time in every man's life when he loses a step or two, finds himself short of breath at the top of the stair; he can't remember crucial facts or important dates anymore. Perhaps the mind wanders in the undiscovered country. That's when the time comes for him to leave the stage to younger men who can play the roles a new drama may require. Don't you agree?"

"I suppose that's true of some, sometimes," I answered guardedly.

"May I buy you another pint?" he asked, with just the semblance of a smile.

"No, no, I think I'm headed on home to bed. If I can remember the address."

"You'll pass that message along to Mr. Holmes, won't you? Let him know his bees are lonely for him down in Sussex. He's inconvenienced me once already. I would be most unhappy if he crossed me again." His tone was friendly as ever, so that you might not even notice the threat implicit in his words. No, explicit, I suppose. He was young and vital. I don't think I could have taken him. Nor, I thought, could Sherlock Holmes, not at this late stage in life.

I was still up when Holmes came in, on toward one in the morning.

"Watson, old friend, you look as tired as I feel. Don't tell me you waited up for me."

"Tell me about T. E. Lawrence," I demanded.

"That's a peculiar request, since I've spent the evening combing the city for Lawrence. I received a tip today that he's been seen in London."

"Oh, he's here all right. I just had a drink with him down at the Barley Mow. We exchanged some words."

Holmes poured himself a brandy, drew up a chair in front of me and straddled it. "I would very much like to know those words. Exactly."

"And he made me promise to repeat those words. But first: he alluded to dealings you've had with him before?"

"The Official Secrets Act—"

"The Secrets Act be hanged!"

He considered. "I can tell you that I have faced him once before, although from a distance. It was really Gertrude who tumbled his apple cart."

"Gertrude?"

"Gertrude Bell, the most brilliant mind in all Arabia. The bravest woman in the world. Of course, he could not accept being stymied by a woman, so he shifted the blame to me. More than that I cannot tell you."

"But did he not help defeat the Ottomans, or the Turks, whatever?"

"By unleashing an Arab jihad."

"Jihad? Could we stick to English, please?"

"A holy war. An uprising. And I fear he thinks that uprising has just begun. He wants to nurture it until it is a full-blown conflagration. Now, tell me about your conversation in the pub."

So I recounted to him everything Lawrence had said.

When I got to Lawrence's reaction to the word *aspergillus*, Holmes sat upright. He said not a word but was plainly excited. Finally, he let out a sigh as I finished my tale.

"I think you should not go out tomorrow," he advised.

"Holmes, I hardly think such precautions are necessary."

"Not necessary for you, perhaps, but necessary for myself. I need you by my side. My arthritis—"

He hadn't mentioned arthritis before, but I had suspected it. The finest single-stick fighter of an age was no more. Old age is cruel.

"What about Mrs. Roberts? Is she in danger?"

"I'll have a private word with her husband. I think she'll be all right as long as she keeps clear of us."

"But why was he so wrought up about the *aspergillus*?"

"When I inspected the fungus in Dr. Lucas's possession? It was not fungus. It was common dirt."

I digested that. "Lawrence switched the vials?"

"Racing ahead of us by aerophane to do so."

"Lawrence was the poisoner?"

"I doubt it, but I suspect he is the one who taught the poisoner the deadly effects of the fungus. He's an archaeologist himself. No doubt he's come across it before. And if he passed that information on, he must have had a reason to do so. He always has a reason."

He downed his brandy.

"And I received confirmation today—there *was* a heart scarab."

"Burton replied?"

"Not exactly." He removed a cable from his pocket and handed it to me. I unfolded it and read it eagerly. It wasn't what I expected at all.

It was from Carter. It read, "NO HEART SCARAB. STOP. CARTER."

"Definitive confirmation that there is indeed a heart scarab. Carter saw my name and took the extraordinary step of intercepting my cable."

"But does Burton have a photo?"

"Carter will likely have destroyed any photos by now. But Burton may still have the plate stowed away somewhere safe. In which case, he may be in danger."

"We must get word to him."

"We shall, as soon as I can track down Lady Evelyn. She and her husband are unfortunately incommunicado at present. Honeymooners have a regrettable inclination for privacy."

I did not sleep well that night. I finally left my bed and rejoined Holmes, who was obviously in the middle of one of his three-pipe problems, which had become a three-bumper problem. I joined him in a brandy, drinking until the decanter was empty and I was in a stupor. I fell asleep before the dying fire.

I awoke the next day to an aching head and stiff bones, and Holmes asleep in the chair across from me. Mrs. Colfax had come in and was scandalized to find the empty decanter between us. She started thrusting the windows open and letting the cold air pile in. I asked her to please work quietly and to fry up every egg she could lay her hands on. Holmes looked old, old and worn-out. I reminded myself that I was two years older than he.

The day passed away. We did not go out, more from torpor than fear, and we got no word from the outer world, except the papers. These we practically bathed in, especially the *Times*, with its news of the continuing wrangling between Carter and Lacau. This inaction continued for three solid days, while Holmes gathered in and sifted through what information he could from contacts. But he was sorely hampered. We knew no one at the Yard anymore. If he had wanted to recruit new irregulars, they were all in school nowadays. It was a new day. So we stewed, till news came from an unexpected source.

Mrs. Colfax answered a knock on the door and announced Mrs. Roberts. We exchanged frowns—so much for keeping her safe—but there was nothing we could do but let her in.

"Oh, Sir Sherlock, I have a message for you from Madame Louise, but it doesn't make any sense at all," she burst forth without even a greeting.

"Bring some tea, Mrs. Colfax, make it strong," Holmes ordered.

"You look all in," I said. Perhaps it was ungentlemanly of me to even notice.

She caught her breath and continued. "She wants you to go save Sir Archibald. The radiologist. The man we saw with the princess. At Meiringen. I know!" she cried before we could even get a word out. "She's warned you over and over not to go to Meiringen, and now she wants you to speed there. At once."

Holmes asked quietly, "You're fully certain it was my mother?"

Mrs. Roberts accepted a cup of tea from the housekeeper and sipped at it. She nodded her head. "There are no emanations remotely like your mother's."

"I'm sorry," I asked. "Where is Meiringen?"

"Have you forgotten? We've been there. Meiringen is the town next to the Reichenbach Falls."

And with that, he started packing. I tried to talk him out of it; I talked till I was blue in the face, but he only said brusquely, "You're the one who doesn't believe in all this mumbo jumbo, have you forgotten? Commence packing or you will surely be left behind." Mrs. Roberts stayed silent, obviously conflicted.

Then the telegram came. I opened it and shouted to Holmes, "It's from someone named Marie-François Goron."

"Princess Marguerite has left Paris for Switzerland," he boomed back.

Which is exactly what the cable said. I started packing.

"Unlooked-for associations," Mrs. Roberts said mysteriously.

"Mrs. Roberts, could you secure a cab for us?" I called.

She returned, "I have one waiting in the street! With my luggage."

I poked my head out the bedroom door. "I don't think it wise for you to accompany us. It could be dangerous."

"Luckily, I am going with Sherlock Holmes and Dr. Watson," came her steady reply. "I think I'll be safe enough." This prediction would prove as wrong as wrong could be.

From his bedroom, Holmes bellowed, "Pack, Watson, pack." So I supposed it meant she was coming. We had all taken leave of our senses. I returned to my packing. At least I knew where we were going this time. My woolen things would be perfectly welcome.

"Who is Goron?" I asked.

"An old friend from the Paris police. Retired, of course. Writes detective novels now. Once you supplied us with her location, I asked him to keep an eye on her."

"Would this be the same mustachioed fellow you employed in Monte Carlo?"

"Pack, Watson."

In short order we were dragging our bags down the stairs to the street and heaving them into the back of the cab. We piled into the back seat all higgledy-piggledy. Soon we were roaring toward Victoria Station.

"Why is the princess headed for Switzerland?" asked Mrs. Roberts.

"More specifically, Meiringen. Not the falls, which we should have no reason to visit. I'm afraid Sir Archibald may have made the mistake of trying to blackmail her. And we know she doesn't like to be threatened."

"So the princess was the poisoner?"

"She was always the most logical suspect. She did kill her husband in cold blood. But does she have the scarab? Or does Sir Archibald?" His forehead wrinkles creased as he juggled the possibilities in his mind.

"I can't imagine what else would draw her so promptly," said Mrs. Roberts.

The cab turned onto Wigmore. We settled in, each to his own thoughts. Mine were full of misgivings. Of course, I *was* the one who had called it all mumbo jumbo. But sometimes the snark *is* a boojum, you see. I glanced out the window.

"Wait, we've passed Victoria Station! Driver—"

"Let him be. We're not going by train. We're going to Biggin Hill," Holmes put in.

"Biggin Hill? Is it still open? I thought after the mutiny there—"

"It is very much open. I made the trip down there only yesterday, searching for Lawrence's plane. Fell into a conversation with one of the pilots. I told him to be on the lookout for a pilot named Lawrence, or Shaw, or Ross. I told him I might need his services one day if he was amenable. I rang him up while you were still packing. We haven't time to waste."

Mrs. Roberts winced. Two aeroplane flights in the same month must have chilled her blood. She would have to grit her teeth and bear it if she were coming with us.

"And this fellow is a qualified pilot? Truly?" she asked, almost pleading.

"This fellow is Billy Bishop."

That made my eyes light up. "Billy Bishop? The war hero?"

"I've had my fill of war heroes," she said acerbically.

"Billy Bishop! Hell's handmaiden. He brought down something like eighty Fokkers during the war! He's a legend. How did you get him to pilot us, Holmes?"

"I'm a legend, as well."

Point to Holmes.

Biggin Hill wasn't much to look at in those days, rows of canvas hangars holding mainly Bristol flyers, already out-of-date, some rough-shod barracks, and a few anonymous concrete buildings that Holmes said were for advanced research, though he did not elaborate. It was cold on that windswept hill. Luckily, Colonel Bishop was waiting for us at the gate. I tried not to look too awestruck. Mrs. Roberts tried not to look too distrustful. We all tried to avoid the mud.

"Junkers F-13. German make," said Bishop, introducing us to our flying steed. "Isn't she a beauty? She'll hold four comfortably."

"A German aircraft?" I asked, disturbed.

"We're studying it," he said with a wink.

"And it's made entirely of metal?" said Mrs. Roberts, gazing in wonder.

"World's first aluminium aircraft," he said, petting its side as if it were a horse.

Mrs. Roberts looked pleased, although she probably would have been more comfortable with brick, to ward off the big bad wolf. Looking back, I might have preferred it myself.

"Are we ready to take off, Bishop?" asked Holmes, who was not in awe of man or machine.

"Let me just kick the tyres and light the fires."

We entered the plane, which actually had proper, upholstered seats. Mrs. Roberts surprised us all with blankets—which I recognized were taken from my own linen press. What would Mrs. Colfax think? I hoped she wouldn't bring in the constabulary. The blankets turned out not to be needed, as the cabin was sealed and even heated, more or less. She did offer mine to the colonel up in the open cockpit, who gracefully refused it.

"Ceiling and visibility unlimited. Nice day for a flight," he called back to us. "Should be over the Channel in a little under an hour." Then he lit the fires.

We took off, only to find that metal was even louder than wood. Still, it was a good deal warmer. And Paris in two hours. Flying was a marvel. If we didn't crash. I surreptitiously knocked on metal. Mind you, we had Bishop in the cockpit. And weren't about to engage any German Fokkers. Things were looking up for a change. I sat back and watched the boats chasing each other across the Channel below.

We were in the middle of the Channel when Holmes jumped up

and threw open the cockpit door, sending cold air whistling through the cabin. "There's another plane out there. Port side."

We peered through the windows. Surely it wasn't that unusual to see another aeroplane crossing the Channel, not in this day and age.

"Yes. She's an Avro. Wave," said the major. Obviously, nothing to worry about.

Mrs. Roberts and I waved obediently, but Sherlock Holmes stood in the cockpit doorway, staring suspiciously at our friend in the sky.

"Bishop, does the Avro have any weapons capabilities?" he asked.

It was getting cold inside the cabin. Mrs. Roberts reached for her blanket.

"Not that one. Looks like a . . . Type G. There was only one made, and usually she's sitting on the runway right next to this bird." His voice seemed to lose a bit of its cheery Canadian confidence.

The plane was rapidly closing the distance between us.

"Then it's strange that she should be in the sky right next to us, don't you think?" said Holmes.

"Well, now that you mention it—there, she's climbing."

"Why is she climbing?" Holmes's voice was urgent.

"She's climbing awfully slowly," I chimed in.

"That's why there was only one of them made. Poor rate of climb. But as for why, she probably wants to take advantage of our draft." Was that worry creeping into Bishop's voice?

"Could you outrun her if you had to?" questioned Holmes.

"Probably not. She's a much lighter body, spruce and canvas, and he's the only one weighing down that plane—"

"What's that noise?" shouted Mrs. Roberts.

"That's the sound of her engines. She's right above us now. A little too close, really," replied the major.

"Yes, far too close," shouted Holmes.

Then there was a shudder and a terrible scraping sound above us. The roof began to buckle. Holmes threw himself into the copilot's seat.

"What the—" I cried, stunned.

"She's trying to land on top of us!" barked Bishop.

"What for?" asked Mrs. Roberts.

"She's trying to kill us!" said Holmes.

Mrs. Roberts's face turned green. Our nose dipped as the weight settled on us.

"You've got to outrun her!" I shouted.

"Can't do that. But I can do the next best thing. Hold on!"

I felt the sudden wallop of my heart against my rib cage. There was a tearing sound; I thought the roof was going to peel off. Then all at once we popped up, and the Avro was filling the cockpit window. Then it rolled off and disappeared from our view.

"What did you do?" I called.

"I just throttled back. I can't outrun her, but I can stop on a dime if I have to. She's pranged us good, though."

"Is he gone?" Mrs. Roberts asked.

"Who *is* he?" I shouted.

"It's Lawrence, of course. He must have been watching your place. And no, I fear he is not gone."

"If Princess Marguerite is the killer, why is Lawrence trying to kill us?" I asked.

"I never said she was the only killer."

Perhaps he might have mentioned that before we were in the air over the Channel, I thought.

"Well, you did say it might get dangerous," said Bishop.

"He didn't say it to me," muttered Mrs. Roberts. I *had* said it to her, though I had never anticipated anything quite like this.

Holmes craned his head out the side of the cockpit. "He's behind us. Coming up fast."

"How crazy is the man?" asked the major.

"He's desperate," said Holmes.

"He's Lawrence of Arabia!" I said.

"Then she's going to try to ram us," Bishop concluded grimly.

"Won't she do more damage to herself than to us?" I asked.

"It doesn't matter. If she can shear off our empennage, we'll lose any maneuverability."

"What can we do?" Mrs. Roberts asked, peeking from behind her blanket.

"I've got a few tricks up my sleeve. As for what you can do—pray."

"Why do you keep calling him 'she'?" asked Mrs. Roberts.

"Brace yourselves. She's coming up on our tail," said Holmes, still hanging out the port side.

"That's luck!" Bishop gave a little whoop. "Hang on!" He tugged at the wheel and we went spinning. I nearly lost my breakfast as we went barrel-rolling, one, twice, three times, each time battering the nose cone of the other plane. Then he broke away, veering off, and we rose into the clouds.

"Good show, old man," said Holmes. He had found a pair of goggles and put them on. His hair, blown by the wind, was standing straight up. He looked rather like a praying mantis.

"She'll be climbing up our tail soon enough. Didn't biff it as much as I'd hoped," reported the major.

"But don't you see?" Holmes cried. "That's it! The rate of climb."

"You might have something there. All right, yank and bank."

So began a strange chase. As soon as the Avro appeared on our tail, we would plunge till we could almost smell the salt waves beneath us. The Avro followed fast enough, but as soon as it attained our level, the major would turn up the F-13's nose and rise above the clouds. The Avro, with its deficient climb rate, would struggle to follow, then once we spied the pursuit, he would once again plunge. Lawrence seemed stymied by the maneuver.

Then the Avro simply disappeared.

"Did he give up?" asked Mrs. Roberts hopefully, opening one eye.

Just at that moment, a roaring filled our ears. "Roll, roll!" cried Holmes. And Bishop put us into a snap roll just in time to avoid by a cat's whisker being sliced in two by the Avro attacking at almost a sheer vertical from below. I date my neck problems from that moment.

"He's downright mad!" roared Bishop. "But a damned foxy pilot."

"We can always hear him coming," I reminded.

"That's probably what he'll pull next," said Bishop.

"Kill his engine and try to spin into us?" Holmes asked.

"That's what I'd do if I didn't care if I lived or died."

"Oh, he doesn't think he can die," said Holmes.

"Who the hell taught him to fly? Beg pardon, ma'am."

"I believe he taught himself," said Holmes in a matter-of-fact way.

Bishop groaned. "We'll just have to get fancy, then."

And he did get fancy, with simultaneous half rolls and half turns, snap rolls, and half loops, and something he called a wingover, in which he seemed to be going every direction at once. Holmes spied the Avro behind us twice, but each time our pilot made a dizzying array of evasive maneuvers. I could see why the Germans had never brought him down.

"Well, we can keep this up forever," I said cheerfully.

"Can we keep this up forever? No, we'll run out of petrol. And before he will. We're one plus zero to splash. And by splash I mean buy it, because we've got land in sight."

"Do you have parachutes on this aeroplane?" asked Holmes.

"Check behind your seats."

We searched. We came up with two parachutes. Two.

"I've got one behind my seat," offered the major.

"Keep it. Have you parachuted before, Watson?"

"Never," I replied glumly.

"Count this as your first lesson. Under no circumstances land on your feet. Drop and let your whole body absorb the brunt of your impact. Mrs. Roberts, you'll hold on to me. Imagine, if you will, a waltz."

Mrs. Roberts did not look convinced. Nor did I feel it. But I donned my parachute, as Holmes did his.

"Don't we have any weapons on this aeroplane?" asked Mrs. Roberts. Her face was the color of curdled milk. Bishop just laughed in response.

"The devil we don't," I said, remembering. I made my lurching way back to where the luggage was piled. I found my bag and pulled out the revolver. Had I remembered to load the thing? Yes. Six bullets. I would have to make them count.

"Level out," I barked. "It's about to get colder in here, friends." I took the revolver and smashed one of the windows out. Glass sprayed everywhere, and the wind rushed in like a slavering dog.

"When was the last time you fired that?" Holmes asked.

"You've dropped enough hints about all your activities during the war. You never asked me what I did."

"You performed surgery, did you not?"

"And I gave lessons in marksmanship."

"Fire away."

I got out my reading glasses and set them on my nose.

"He does look like an owl," commented Mrs. Roberts.

"Here he comes," called the major.

"I see him. Let him get right up on you, Major," I replied tightly.

"Righto!"

I could see the whites of Lawrence's eyes. We hit turbulence. I fired.

And nearly lost the gun as I lurched backward. Holmes caught me. "I missed him."

"He didn't even notice your shot," agreed Holmes.

There was a sickening thud as he hit us. We both fell back.

"He's right up on us now. Are you boys going to do something or will I?" shouted Bishop.

I was angry now. I took my roost in the window again. I braced myself. Holmes put his hands to my shoulders. She banged against our tail again, but Bishop held the plane steady, and I held myself ready. I squeezed the trigger and fired.

Damn, damn, damn, I muttered to myself. I had seen the wood of her wing splinter. But now at least I had my range. I fired again. My aim went true! The glass of the pilot's window cracked. But did it hit him?

"Fire again!"

I fired. The glass shattered into a spiderweb. The Avro twisted and fell out of sight.

"Did I hit him?"

"He still seems to be in control of his craft, but you made a mess of his windscreen. He wasn't wearing any goggles, and his cockpit's enclosed. He's blind."

"We've won!" I crowed.

"Not exactly. He's chewed up my rudder but good. With these crosswinds, I'm going to have to land as soon as possible."

"Where?" asked Holmes.

"Le Bourget, just north of Paris, if I can make it."

"And where will he make for?"

"The same—if he can make it" was the major's verdict.

"Then I'd ask you to drop us off at Gare de Lyon," said Holmes, as unflappable as ever.

"This isn't a taxi, man!"

"No, fly over the train station. We'll parachute. Once we're gone, you won't have to worry about Lawrence, I think."

"Do you know what it's like trying to make a jump in the middle of a large city?" he asked, incredulous.

"We have no choice. Time is of the essence. Of course, if Watson or Mrs. Roberts wishes to remain—"

"With you to the end," I said.

"You're not leaving me behind," said Mrs. Roberts.

"You're all mad. All right, Gare de Lyon it is, but be ready. I can only take one shot at this," warned Bishop.

"Uh, just one thing," I asked. "How do I open this thing?"

Holmes showed me how the rip cord worked. "Lesson two," he said with a wink.

"I'm going to climb, so you'll have room for your chutes to open properly."

The wind was still screaming through the shattered window, but it was nothing to the mighty rush of air that almost knocked me down when I heaved the door open. We had already passed the towering spires of Rouen. Soon the banlieues of Paris would come into view. We only had a few minutes to make our plans.

"If we become separated, make your way by the first train to Meiringen. What was the name of the excellent hotel we stayed at there?"

"Englischer Hof." How could I forget that name of ill omen?

"That's it. If we've gone out, and we almost certainly shall have, we'll leave a message with the landlord."

"There's the Seine," I said. Glittering in the sunlight. So close. I felt sick.

"Hold on tight, Mrs. Roberts. Major Bishop, we're forever in your debt."

Bishop gave a backhanded salute. Then he shouted, "Jump!"

They jumped.

"Jump!"

My stomach twisted in knots.

"Jump!"

I jumped.

Chapter Twenty:
Mrs. Estelle Roberts

First there was the terrible sensation of falling, and then a kick that put my heart in my throat, and then a suspension, when my heart stopped altogether, and the parachute opened like a tulip unfurling above us. Then we began floating, so peacefully, so quietly, with just the air feathering my skin. I was afraid to look down, but I stared into the gray eyes of Sherlock Holmes, his strong arms about me, my hands clasped tight round his neck, and in that moment, he wasn't an old man nor I a wife and mother, but we were two dust motes spiraling together in the wind. For a moment I thought I would kiss him.

"When you hit the earth, don't tense. Let your muscles go slack, fall on your side and roll. Let the earth take you in its arms. We may land in a crowd, so there could be a panic."

But the first panic was mine, when I looked down and saw that we were drifting toward an enormous clock tower at one end of the railway station that reminded me of Big Ben. I wanted to shout a warning, but all I could get out was a sort of mewling.

"Yes, I see it," he said as though he'd read my mind. Though how he could see it with his back to it, I had no idea. "The wind is blowing us straight toward it. Luckily, it's 11:59."

He said it as if we had a luncheon date at twelve. Then the minute hand ticked over and the clock began to toll.

The noise was tremendous, as we were directly in front of the clock face. I could feel its vibrations shuddering throughout my entire body, hammering at my heart. But something else was happening. With each stroke of the clock, the vibrations drove us farther away from the clock tower. For a moment I thought we might land in the Seine, but we were wafted backward by the wind. We were going to land directly in front of the station entrance, thronged with people coming and going. Would the crowd part for us?

A sea of faces turned toward us, a sea of hands pointing. I tried to remember everything Sir Sherlock had said, but hands were reaching for me, all over my body in the most personal way, and then the parachute landed on top of us and I got separated from Sir Sherlock, and for a few moments I feared the intentions of my rescuers until the parachute was lifted and there I was in a wide clearing of men, with Sir Sherlock calmly folding the parachute, and the crowd broke into a round of applause. Not that I could hear it. The bonging of the clock had deafened me.

I wished then that could wear trousers like Anna, but I smoothed down my dress as modestly as I could. Sir Sherlock bowed and I made a little curtsy, and we made our way inside to the ticket counter with a thousand eyes upon us.

"But what about Dr. Watson?" I asked, scurrying along behind him.

"If he jumped—I'm sure he did; he has the heart of a lion—there's no telling where he landed if he hesitated even for a moment. I only hope he hasn't broken his neck. We'll purchase three tickets and hope for the best," he said.

I felt somehow bereft but knew there was no arguing with Sir Sherlock. We boarded the train and took our seats, but my eyes strayed to the windows and the crowds outside. I could communicate with the dead across the ages, but there was no knowing about the living. Perhaps that meant something? That he was alive still? But then, if he were dead, he might be in no mood to chat.

Then I noticed a disruption in the crowd outside. Someone was burrowing his way through the thick of it. I slammed open the window and waved the ticket at him. It was John! Then he was swallowed by the crowd again. The whistle shrieked, and I fell back as the train began to chuff away from the platform. I put my head out the window and was greeted with a wreath of steam and soot. He was gone. Had he seen me? Had he made the train?

"Should we search the train for him?" I suggested timidly.

"He saw you. He knows where we are. We will remain here until he joins us."

"But what if he didn't make the train?"

"He made it from the Place de la Bastille in ten minutes' time. He was determined not to miss this train. When Watson is determined, he does not fail."

I was glad to hear he was so confident, but still felt quite unsettled. And how he knew that Dr. Watson had landed in the Place de la Bastille, wherever that was, I didn't dare ask.

Then a shadow fell across his face. He heaved the door open and Dr. Watson entered, or rather, lunged across me and into the seat, looking bruised and battered and thoroughly disreputable. For some reason he had hung on to his parachute, which he had balled up as best he could against his chest. He was breathing heavily.

"Dr. Watson. You poor thing," I uttered. "What happened?"

"Bad luck, old man. You got caught on the July Column."

Dr. Watson merely grunted.

"All right, if Dr. Watson won't ask, I will. How did you know he landed in this Place de la Bastille and got caught on the—what do you call it?"

"Yes, Holmes, how did you know? Entertain us," Dr. Watson croaked.

"The plane was turning into a north-by-northwest course. The largest open space by far in that direction is the Place de la Bastille. As I'm sure you know, the prison that once stood there was the touchstone for the revolution of 1789. The prison was taken down brick by brick, leaving only an empty space behind. Later at its center was erected the July Column, crowned by a gilded statue of the spirit of liberty. Rather gaudy, really."

"Inconvenient place to put a statue," said Dr. Watson, as if personally affronted.

"Your right ankle is swelling. You fell on it when they cut you down. You were cut down with a meat cleaver. You still have your harness on, but of course the lines have been cut. Notice the lines were cut evenly on each side, two chops of the cleaver. You can see the blood, which I am happy to report is not Watson's—more likely that of the fatted calf. There's an open-air market just north of the square, including a boucherie. The crowd must have rushed toward your descent even as they did ours, and the butcher obligingly cut you down with the cleaver still in his hand. Then you were lowered—"

"They pulled me up," said Dr. Watson. "They didn't cut me down."

"Ah, of course. I forgot about the staircase inside and the platform on top. A magnificent view, wouldn't you agree?"

"I twisted my ankle going down the stairs. The bottom stair, if you want to be exact," the doctor said dryly.

"Even so, you could never have made it here in ten minutes by taxi, not with the noonday traffic," Sir Sherlock continued, undaunted. "But there is the Gare de la Bastille, which, though it only makes local stops, connects with the Gare de Lyon, only five minutes away by train. Why did you bring the parachute, by the way?" Sir Sherlock concluded by asking.

"Well, I couldn't very well leave it in the middle of the square."

"Souvenir, then? Or were you planning on dropping off a cliff?"

"Don't even mention such a thing," I said.

"Indeed, the reading public would never believe you plunged to your death from the Reichenbach Falls." It was a gallows sort of humor, but both men cracked a smile.

"Well, we have six hours to Meiringen. I don't believe Watson is fit for the dining car, but I think some sandwiches would not go amiss."

"Our luggage! We left it on the plane!" I wailed.

"It would have been rather an encumbrance on our jump," Sir Sherlock said.

"I suppose so, but I do look a fright. Oh, I don't even have my powder box mirror."

"In that case, you look as rosy as the dawn," said Sir Sherlock, tongue firmly in cheek.

"Oh, pshaw!" But I must have gone bright red at the compliment.

"Meiringen is a town of not inconsiderable size. How do we go about finding Sir Archibald?" asked Dr. Watson.

"Tell me, Watson, why did we originally pick the *Englischer Hof* to stay in?" Sir Sherlock asked in return.

"Well, all we really had to go by was the name. We thought with a name like 'English House,' it might be owned by an Englishman, or at least cater to the English."

"And we were half right. Old Peter Steiler looked like Geppetto, but he spoke perfect English, and most of the guests were Anglo-Saxons."

"So?"

"So why should not Archibald Douglas-Reid reason along the very same lines? We shall begin our search at the *Englischer Hof*. If he's not there, we may get wind of him from one of the guests. The English are a small, clubby set."

"Have you considered that Sir Archibald and the princess may be meeting for a perfectly harmless fling?" Dr. Watson asked. I flashed him a ferocious look, I'm afraid. Flings are never harmless.

"If we only find them in flagrante, I should breathe a sigh of relief," Sir Sherlock replied. His waxen face belied the possibility.

Chapter Twenty-One:
Dr. John Watson

Meiringen was not at all as I remembered. For a quarter century I'd had it lodged in my brain as shrouded in darkness and dread. We walked out of the train station, a gingerbread concoction such as only the Swiss can construct without being laughable, into the bright Alpine sun. A jingling pony-driven cart painted red waited to take us to the hotel. Normally we would have walked it, but Holmes took mercy on my swelling ankle.

The hotel, in turn, which I remembered as a Gothic monstrosity, was instead a bright thing in Art Nouveau style, curled like an orange peel. Why, it must have been nearly new when first we visited. Yet I felt chilled to the marrow when I crossed the threshold.

Holmes dispensed with the preliminaries as soon as he arrived at the desk, actually shouldering another guest aside. "Is Sir Archibald Douglas-Reid staying here?" he demanded of the clerk, who was not old Peter Steiler but spoke English quite as well.

"Did you have an appointment? No? I'm sorry. Sir Archibald is otherwise engaged."

"With whom? It's a matter of life and death."

"Calm yourself, sir. If you must know, he is entertaining a young lady. A rather fascinating—"

Holmes swung the register around to read it. "What room is he in?" He leafed through, scanning the pages.

"Please sir, it's most irregular—" The clerk tried to scrabble the register back.

Holmes grabbed the clerk's collar and pulled him close. "What room?"

"Three oh five!" squeaked the clerk.

"Call the doctor." He shoved the telephone in front of the clerk. "Tell him it's urgent."

We ran to the lift, threw the attendant out, rammed the cage closed, and punched the button for the third floor.

The door to 305 was standing open. We burst into the room. It was in disarray, with drawers open and clothes tossed hither and thither. A man was lying on the bed. His skin was grey and his eyes distended, his limbs flailing helplessly. It was Sir Archibald, knocking at death's door. There was no sign of any fascinating woman.

I leaned over him, sniffed his breath, and took his pulse. "His heart is beating like a trip-hammer. He's been poisoned."

"We've got to pump his stomach," said Holmes.

"It'll do no good. Look at the deep scratches on his cheek. It's gone straight to his bloodstream, the same as Lord Carnarvon."

Holmes picked up an empty vial from the floor, examining it. "A much more powerful dose, it would seem."

I spied Mrs. Roberts, looking small and frightened.

"Mrs. Roberts, go downstairs. Make sure he's called the doctor. Tell him it's blood poisoning," I shouted.

"Aspergillosis," pronounced Sherlock Holmes.

"Immediately," I said as she stood stock-still, watching the man in his agony.

Mrs. Roberts regained her senses and clattered out.

"I had to get her out of here. She looked as if she were about to faint," I said.

"She reminds me of you when we first started. You recall the murder of Enoch Drebber?"

Of course I remembered. It was the first account I had written up of our adventures together. But I hadn't been as green as all that. I had seen plenty of death in Afghanistan. I didn't see any reason in arguing it at this crisis point.

"The princess made a thorough going-over of this room," I remarked instead.

"And found nothing, I'll be bound," Holmes observed.

"She can't have gotten far."

Mrs. Roberts appeared in the doorway, fairly panting for breath. She appeared to fill the entire doorway, darkening the entire room like a thunderhead.

"You know where to find her," she said. "You're the only one who can save her." Her voice was deep and harsh and seemed to come from somewhere far away. I felt an icy hand grip my heart.

"Why? Why would she go there?" I asked, petrified by the very thought.

"To end her life."

"Well, then, let her go," I said coldly, despite my medical vows.

Mrs. Roberts drew back from me as though repulsed. But she hadn't seen Holmes perish once already at the bottom of that cauldron.

"I shall go to the falls," Holmes said solemnly.

"Holmes, for God's sake, why?" I begged.

"Because my mother asks it of me. Because I still have business with Professor Moriarty." And that was that. The resolve in his eye, ah! I knew it so well—it was unconquerable.

"Then this time I shall go with you," I said.

"No, you must stay by Sir Archibald's side and lend him what succor you can, at least until another doctor arrives."

He and Mrs. Roberts went out together. I looked daggers at the dying man on the bed. I'm sorry, but I did. Then I set about making his last moments as comfortable as possible.

I waited and waited, the tall clock in the corner eating up precious seconds, whole minutes. Finally, a young fellow came through the open door, far too young to be a doctor. He looked exasperated. He went straight to Sir Archibald.

"I knew we should never have discharged you from the clinic," he said, laying his hand along the fevered forehead.

He *was* a doctor.

"*Aspergillus flavus,*" I said in his ear. "Blood poisoning."

"This man has just undergone abdominal surgery. Radiation poisoning is what he's got."

I did not care to hear it. I went after Holmes. I went banging down the stairs, shouting his name. The clerk met me at the bottom of the stair.

"He left, he and the lady," he said calmly.

"I'm going after them. Check us in."

"I see that you are lame. It will not do to assail the mountain in your present condition."

Till he mentioned it, I had forgot all about my swollen ankle. Now the pain came throbbing back. I winced, but I was determined. I strode out through the front door without another word.

"Here, take my staff." The clerk ran up to me and presented it. It was good, stout oak. I thanked him profusely, touched by his good heart. I might look like a decrepit old man with it—I certainly felt like one—but I wasn't jolly well going to be deterred by the falls this time. I tottered off with a renewed sense of vigor. Holmes and the woman were already far ahead of me.

Chapter Twenty-Two:
Mrs. Estelle Roberts

The clerk had told us it was only a fifteen-minute ramble to the path that that led to the falls. "Then you can take the funicular to the top."

"The funicular?" Holmes repeated in disbelief. "There's a funicular now?"

"Oh, yes, sir. The falls have become a very popular tourist attraction. You know, the famous detective Sherlock Holmes slipped and fell to his death there."

Holmes gave him a frosty look. "Don't believe everything you read." He stalked out the door. I struggled to keep up.

"The station is next to the clinic in Willigen. Do you know it?" the clerk called to Holmes.

"I think he knows it," I said apologetically, turning round and round.

I don't think Sir Sherlock had any intention of taking the funicular. He had climbed the mountain path thirty years before and intended to do so again.

But that had been thirty years ago. After a brisk ten-minute march, he began wheezing, and I was laboring hard. I had heard something about lighter air—or lesser air, thinner air—in the mountains. Believe me, it's true.

I was entirely out of breath by the time we reached the funicular. The high mountain air was paper-thin and clear as crystal. I feared my lungs might shatter like glass. Sir Sherlock looked done in. When I saw the climb the funicular would make, I was amazed that Sir Sherlock and Dr. Watson had once hiked their way up. Without even consulting one another, we settled in on the cold wooden seats. I tried to look as calm as Sir Sherlock did. He was positively somnolent.

I didn't feel calm at all. I was about to face the elemental, to test my power against its malevolence. I had to free the woman from its poison. If I should fail—it didn't bear thinking about.

A tall man came in and sat across from us. His face was grey and haggard, and the look in his eyes so haunted that once I had seen them, I did not want to meet his gaze again. His clothes were of good make, but in a style of the last century, as if they had been handed down to him from his father. His hair was gray and lank and oily with some foul-smelling pomade in it. He did not speak, but his eyes drifted toward me and made me feel so unclean that I shuddered all over.

That was when I realized that Sir Sherlock did not see him.

He spoke to me. "Estelle, how nice to finally make your acquaintance." Then he entered me. I choked. Sir Sherlock eyed me with concern. He laid a hand on my forehead. I could feel the slime of his flesh.

"He's here," I managed to get out. "Moriarty."

His eyes narrowed to fierce grey slits. "What does he say?"

I wanted to slap Sir Sherlock's hand away. I could only manage to wave my hands helplessly. "He's waiting for you. He's been waiting for you a long time."

He removed his hand, but I could still feel his fetid breath on my face.

With a jump, the funicular started up. Dr. Watson was not coming.

"Oh. Let's get off!" I cried. The few passengers aboard turned my way.

"Calm yourself. It's only bluster. What else does he say?"

"You must stand clear, Mr. Holmes, or be trodden underfoot," I said in a thin, serpentine voice.

"Ah, he's said that before. And rued it, I fancy," Sir Sherlock said.

We began climbing toward the sky. I had never felt such evil coursing through my veins before. Nausea came in waves.

"I'm glad you killed him, God forgive me, but I am glad," I breathed.

"God forgive me, for I never meant to kill him. It preys upon my mind."

"And now you will kill a woman. Let that prey upon your mind," came that voice, clutching at my throat, wagging my tongue.

Did he mean me? Did Sir Sherlock mean to murder me? Did he have the pharaoh's heart already? I had never suspected, fool that I was. There was nowhere to escape to.

I struggled for release as Moriarty poured his bile into me, cruel words, crueler thoughts, with a tenuous, mocking laughter behind them. My mind was at war, and I was no match for him. Red Cloud could not hear me over the roaring waters. But I never repeated another word to Sir Sherlock. I let him think that Moriarty had left me. I would wait, and watch, until my moment came.

At last, we reached the top. Moriarty's voice abated, as if I had left him in the lower depths, but I felt ground down like meal. The falls were roaring in my ears ceaselessly, half-human, reminiscent of my dreams. It came to me that Moriarty wasn't the only one who had died here. Adventurers, spurned lovers, ruined traders, lost souls had all cast themselves or been cast onto the rocks below. Whether they were benevolent spirits or malevolent devils I couldn't begin to tell. But they were all calling to be heard. I could not but pity them.

Sir Sherlock led the way to a narrow rocky path. It was slick and icy in places with the spray of the falls. I could have wished for a railing or a walking stick or . . . something. Sir Sherlock ahead of me seemed sure-footed as a mountain goat.

My first sight of the falls up close snatched away what little breath I had left. They were awesome, turning and churning in a widening gyre. What was it about this old man that made me follow him down that path? I don't know to this day. But I followed. The sun was shining like a gold coin on fire, but there was a heavy mist all about, soaking me, coating my face and limbs with ice. I looked down for only a moment into that seething cauldron, feeling it would reach out with awful tentacles and drag me under. There were eyes in that black pool and malice in those eyes. From then on, I trained my eyes only on Sherlock Holmes's narrow back. It was when he stopped abruptly, and I almost ran into him, that I saw her at the end of the path.

There was nowhere for her to go but into our waiting arms. Or down—down into the dark tumult. For a moment, just a moment, I was so maddened by the sound that I thought of throwing Sir Sherlock off the edge. Or was it a moment? Time seemed suspended. If I threw him over, I could go back. No one need ever know. The temptation was sore.

As for her, she looked like one already drowned. Her hair was streaming down her back, her collar wrenched open as if she could not breathe, her grey gown bedraggled. Her imperious ways were fled, replaced by a look of deep desperation. She stood trembling like a windblown leaf, perilously close to the edge.

"Marguerite." His voice was soft and low, like a lullaby. I felt the strings of my own mind go slack. All the horrid thoughts of throwing him over the edge blew away, as if driven by the wind. Moriarty passed from me—into her? Was Moriarty dancing in her head?

Sir Sherlock's voice rose a breath. "Marguerite!"

With that her eyes came into focus and she started. I held my breath until she spoke.

"Have you got it?" she breathed.

There was no doubt what she meant. She didn't have it. She had come all this way, only to be cheated.

"No," he answered. Her face darkened. He quickly added, "But I know where to find it."

"Where is it? Did he have it? I searched everywhere."

"He doesn't have it. He never did."

"He said he had it!" she screeched.

"It was a lie, and you knew it. You know who has it."

"Who?"

"Come away from here and I'll lead you to it."

"No, no, it's down below. I can hear it calling."

"You showed it to someone. After your husband warned you against it."

"No."

"You did, Marguerite."

"It was his fault," she whined. "He boasted first."

"Who did you show it to?"

"I showed it to no one!"

"Who?" he thundered, and my legs quivered.

"That woman. The girl with Valentino."

"Natacha Rambova. She is the one who has it."

"No, you're lying. I hear its voice calling."

I heard that voice, too. Sweet and sinister. I couldn't make out the words, but it was seeking to snare me again.

"What did the voice tell you?" I asked, my voice brittle.

"It told me it's at the bottom, the very bottom." She cast her eyes longingly into the void.

"No. That voice is full of deception, Marguerite." Sherlock's voice was laden with suasion. "That voice only wants to torment you, to destroy you. Believe me, I know that voice. It has haunted me for years." His voice so passionate that it forced her to listen, to reconsider. Light slowly spread across her face.

He eased toward her, almost imperceptibly, narrowing the gap between them. If I could only keep her distracted. Or was it him I wanted to distract, to lure him over the edge? The desire suddenly was overwhelming. I reached out—

It was then that Louise came to me, filling my blood, burning the shadows from my heart, freeing my tongue, banishing Moriarty. I don't remember everything she said through me, but they were words of consolation, bright drops of mercy, words to break the heart and forge it anew.

But the waters drowned her voice. Even her words were not enough. Words would not suffice. The woman took a deep breath and leaned over, as one leans over a lover. Lost her balance.

And fell.

Sherlock Holmes lunged for her. He grabbed hold of her arm. He went to his knees with the sudden weight. His bones cracked against the hard earth. Still, he held on to her somehow, though he was sprawled on the cold, wet stone. He slipped, inch by inch, being dragged to the edge. Was it only her weight that was pulling, or had Moriarty grasped her by the legs, pulling her down? He didn't care about the woman at all, I saw that now. He wanted to drag Sir Sherlock into the teeming waters. I looked on, trading horror and ecstasy back and forth. I went to my knees beside him. I didn't think to help at all. I didn't think to harm. I could only watch, held at bay by all those drowned spirits.

"Let me go!" she cried, twisting and turning in his grasp.

"I'll not let go. Though it be forty days and forty nights, I will not let you go."

She went silent, pouting like a little girl who cannot have her way.

So he lay there, motionless. I could hear his breath next to me, and the occasional sob of the girl. From far away I thought I heard Moriarty's laughter. Sooner or later Sherlock Holmes must tire and let go.

"Let go, old man." Did I say it aloud? Did I whisper in his ear? In a moment there is time for visions and incisions, which a moment will erase.

Then I heard a stamping, and a new voice, clear as day. Not one of my voices.

"Grab hold of my stick, Maggie. Sherlock Holmes has wrists of steel. He will not let you go. You shall not die today—be reconciled to that. Take hold."

Hearing that voice, the plain, steady syllables of John Watson, Moriarty fled the earth as though he were no more than a sparrow. I found myself again staring into Princess Marguerite's eyes.

Her gaze flickered over me. She looked at me searchingly, beseechingly, and something seemed to go out of her face, something hard and cruel in the lines around her eyes and lips. She was left with the face of a sad, lonely woman.

"Take hold," commanded Dr. Watson, in a voice that would not be denied.

There was a moment of indecision. Then she raised her free arm, flailing at the stick. He lowered it farther. She clamped her hand around the base. His knees buckled slightly. He must have felt the pull of her weight stabbing at his bad ankle. Yet he held. He gritted his teeth and slowly began to raise her. Holmes strained with every fiber of his being and grabbed hold of her by the shoulder. Together, scrabbling for every sweet inch, they lifted her to safety. She collapsed into my waiting arms. My arms, not Moriarty's, nor Louise's, nor even Red Cloud's. I held her like a daughter.

Sir Sherlock stood, creakily. He turned to Dr. Watson. Both men were out of breath. "How did you get here so soon? The funicular is thirty minutes each way," he said, huffing and puffing.

"I walked," the doctor replied simply.

"You walked. You are a marvel."

And he wrapped his arms around his friend in a great bear hug. I'd never seen two men hug, and I'm not sure Dr. Watson was entirely comfortable with it.

"Can you help me with her?" I called.

Sir Sherlock broke off from his embrace and came back to me. Together we lifted the woman, who was nearly catatonic, to her feet. She seemed to revive a little in the warmth of the detective's arms. Together we carried her away from that dangerous place, with Dr. Watson limping behind like one of those St. Bernard dogs one always hears of.

Soon we saw the funicular humming up the cable, growing big

like a child's toy become real. We deposited her in a seat safely away from the window.

"The scarab, do you have it?" she uttered faintly.

"Forget about the scarab. You flung it into the falls," said Sir Sherlock.

"Did I? Oh, good. It was heavy." She seemed to collapse in on herself.

"I think it's leaving her. I can feel it ebbing. All the voices have been silenced."

"I did not save her from the falls to see her hanged," said Sherlock solemnly.

Chapter Twenty-Three:
Dr. John Watson

We left her laid out on Mrs. Roberts's bed, Mrs. Roberts holding her hand tight. Both of them looked like driftwood washed up on the shore. We had hot cocoa sent up.

"Holmes," I whispered in his ear. "The doctor could do nothing. Sir Archibald is dead."

"I hope he may be the last victim of the curse."

"The curse? She murdered him in cold blood," I protested.

"I think I would like to partake of a drink in the lounge. Will you join me?"

Of course, I acquiesced.

We argued it through three brandies, till I was quite frazzled. Holmes, of course, remained unperturbed throughout, though on occasion I'd swear his temper almost flared. We were about to begin round four, with what might have been disastrous results, when we were joined by Mrs. Roberts. So we switched to sherry and cooler heads prevailed.

"It all came pouring out. She's told me everything, or everything she remembers. I'm afraid it's all mixed-up in her head like a bad dream.

"She says it all began with that strange honeymoon dinner hosted by Colonel Herbert. She wasn't there for the offer made by Colonel Herbert, having been relegated to being bored to tears by Guinevere Gould, but she heard all about it when her husband came to bed, deep in his cups, as was usually the case.

"He'd given them a choice between power and beauty and gave the first choice to Ali Fahmy Bey, knowing, I suppose, that the Oriental will always choose power first, anticipating beauty would follow in its train. Ali chose accordingly. Gould was content with beauty."

"One would expect of a man who marries his mistress," Holmes commented.

"Then Colonel Herbert made the abstract concrete, like a magic trick. He offered Ali Fahmy a vial of poison from the dust of Tutankhamun's tomb, both lethal and undetectable, for a thousand pounds. And to Gould, for that same thousand pounds, he offered the heart scarab of Tutankhamun. He set them out on the table, like a merchant bargaining his wares in the bazaar.

"The scarab was a thing of wondrous beauty, so that for a moment Prince Ali regretted his choice, but he eagerly eyed the black liquid in the vial. The power of life and death—ah, that were power indeed. The colonel asked them whether they would like to trade, but each was enthralled by his own choice. So, they made their deal and checks were forwarded to Colonel Herbert that same night.

"Ali told her all this, and she praised his choice. But as she lay there in bed, her thoughts went to the scarab, and the thought grew in her mind until she had to see it, just once, just for a minute. She didn't sleep that night."

"When the dawn came, she called Mrs. Gould and invited her to lunch that day," Holmes surmised.

"Oh, no. To breakfast."

"'Oh, yes, what foolishness,' Guinevere Gould said when the princess broached the subject.

"'Still, it must be very beautiful,' Marguerite said longingly.

"'Beautiful, but quite impossible. I do wonder how Colonel Herbert got hold of it at all.'

"'Could I see it? Just for a moment?'

"'Oh, I'm sorry, you don't understand. I had George return it to Lord Carnarvon. He told me how relieved His Lordship was to see it. I don't need any stolen baubles.'

"Princess Marguerite looked at her as if stricken. What a fool the woman was! She hurried through the meal."

Holmes saw it all in his mind's eye. "She must have assumed Lord Carnarvon had given the scarab to his half brother to sell. He had to get some of his money back, after all. If he had sold it once, he would sell it again."

Mrs. Roberts took up the thread again. "Yes, she determined to go to Lord Carnarvon. He'd sell it to her for half the price, or she'd take his secret to the Egyptians. First she would go home and put on a new frock, perhaps touch up her hair. The flapper look wouldn't do for a man like Lord Carnarvon; something softer and fuller was required—"

"I don't think it will be necessary to detail her wardrobe," Holmes cut in.

Mrs. Roberts did not appreciate the intrusion. "You must understand that she was dressing with the intention to seduce."

"Her normal intention. Do go on."

"Well. She got up her nerve with a couple of cocktails and went to his room. She knocked on his door, possibly a little too loudly. He opened the door with a puzzled look on his face.

"'Princess Marguerite, I believe it was?'

"'Lord Carnarvon, it is imperative that I should speak to you. Alone.'

"'Your husband?' He looked up and down the hall.

"'Is not with me. May I come in, please?'

"He admitted her and shut the door behind her.

"'To what do I owe the unexpected pleasure of this visit?'

"'I will come right to the point. You are trying to sell a precious item. I should like to buy it.'

"'I have no idea what you're talking about.'

"'Don't be coy. I've seen the heart scarab.'

"'There is no heart scarab.'

"But she could see the fear in his eyes. She, of course, had never laid eyes on the scarab, but she described it, just as her husband had described it to her.

"It must have been too much for him. He grabbed her by the wrists and began shaking her. 'Who told you? Who told you?' But she knew how to handle herself in a fight with a man. Long fingernails raked his cheek, drawing blood. He threw her onto the bed. She expected him to throw himself on her, but instead he turned away. The deepest cut of all. 'Get out,' he told her."

Holmes interposed again. "He was signing his death warrant. She went directly to her husband and told him Lord Carnarvon had tried to have his way with her. Did he believe her?"

"Not really, but he made sure to be in the hotel dining room the next morning when Lord Carnarvon come down to breakfast. Fahmy noted the scratches on his face."

"Would he really have cared?" I asked.

"Perhaps not, but he knew what was expected of him as a man. And besides, he had purchased the poison. He was eager to test it. It seemed the perfect opportunity. He knew any number of people who would like the Englishman out of the way. So while Carnarvon was having his toast and marmalade, he crept up to his room. Getting a maid to unlock the door was easy, with his brilliant smile and a claim that he was meant to wait for Lord Carnarvon.

"Once inside, he swiftly found milord's aftershave and added a few drops of the poison to it."

"The aftershave! Of course," I said, remembering Holmes's testing of the scents.

We looked to Mrs. Roberts to take up the tale again.

"Then he searched everywhere for the scarab. But it was nowhere to be found. Nowhere! He slipped out and down the stair just as the lift opened and Lord Carnarvon stepped out.

"She was bitterly disappointed when he told her he had not found the heart scarab. She berated him for not searching till he found it. It was nowhere to be found, he insisted. But Gould had returned it! She was certain.

"Did his wife see him return it? He'd never brought it back to Lord Carnarvon, Ali reasoned. He wouldn't pay a thousand pounds just to throw it away. Gould had lied to his wife."

"Ah, so that was when she realized Gould still had it," said Holmes.

"And the more she brooded over it, the more convinced she was that she was right: Gould still had the scarab. He must have it. He would give it up, or he would die, too.

"No, he would not kill again, Prince Ali vowed. Gould had done him no dishonor. 'Very well then,' she threw back at him. She would get the scarab herself, by hook or by crook.

"Her husband didn't believe her; he thought she wouldn't have the courage to act. But oh, she had the courage, *and* she had access to the poison. That meant Gould's death. She was able to introduce a few drops into his drink at a rather somber farewell dinner. It was risky, but she had already discovered that it was a slow-acting poison: Lord Carnarvon had taken three days to die once he'd shaved himself.

"Gould apparently felt their mutual experience of Lord Carnarvon's death had created some sort of bond between them. He invited them to his villa at Cap Martin. Foolish man."

"Things did not go as she had planned," said Holmes. "Gould came down with a fever, and his wife rushed him to Cap San Martin the very next day. He was far more robust than Lord Carnarvon had been. There was nothing to do but follow them, pretending they were concerned for Gould's health."

"By the time they arrived at Villa Zoralde, she told me, they found Guinevere Gould worn-out with worry. Marguerite offered to look after him while Guinevere took her rest. While he moaned in his sleep, she searched his room from top to bottom. At last, she found the scarab, hidden away cunningly among his papers. She was transported by the sight of it.

"Of course, the scarab would never be safe as long as there was a chance that Gould might rally. So she administered another few

The Strange Case of the Pharaoh's Heart

drops in his tonic to finish him off. Then she begged off, saying she had received word that her sister in Paris was ill. They would return as soon as ever they could. She kissed Guinevere lovingly on the cheek. So it was from the comfort of the Savoy that she read of Gould's death two days later.

"And all would have been well, had they not met Valentino and his new wife, dancing one night at the Savoy. She immediately sensed an attraction between her husband and the Russian girl, Natacha Rambova. He even invited the couple to dine with them, a sure sign that he was smitten.

"He'd warned her that she must never show the scarab to anyone, but she so badly wanted to make the Russian girl jealous. Somehow the conversation had turned to Egypt and Tutankhamun. The little Russian girl was eaten up with jealousy that they had toured the tomb. The princess could feel the heat of the scarab beneath her clothes, burning between her breasts on the golden chain she had fitted it with. In fact, she had not been parted from it since she had first donned it in the Villa Zoralde. She showed it to the Russian girl, only briefly. What harm could there be in it? And Rambova had gushed over it so.

"Ali was furious. That would pass. She knew how to manage him. But she was not prepared for the row that came later. She locked herself in the bathroom to avoid blows and decided to take a bath to still her pounding head. When she came out, tranquil in mind, he was gone."

"And so was the scarab." Holmes and I arrived at the conclusion together.

"It was pouring outside. The hours ticked by. What if he didn't return? What if he was with that woman? Or with both of them? She knew her husband's predilections quite well by then. Could he have hidden it somewhere in the room as a nasty trick? She searched diligently. All she found was the gun. She felt it smooth and cold in her hands. Luxurious. She checked to make sure it was loaded. She loved the perfume of the bullets. She even rubbed them on her neck, just below the earlobes."

Holmes hurried her to the ending. "When he came back, it was after two in the morning. He told her he had sold the scarab to Valentino. So, she shot him."

End of story.

"And Sir Archibald?" I asked after a bit.

"She didn't even remember Sir Archibald."

"Didn't remember murdering him? That's cold-blooded," I said.

"I think I can enlighten you with regards to Sir Archibald. I found this in her coat pocket. It's from him." He pulled a paper from his pocket, unfolded it, and gave it to me to read aloud.

Dear Lady,

I believe you have in your possession an item of interest to us both. You see, I am the radiologist who was brought in by Mr. Howard Carter to examine and scan Tutankhamun's mummy. Examining it, I made a rather interesting discovery: the definite impression of a heart scarab, though I had been told definitively that there was no heart scarab. When I questioned Mr. Carter on the matter, he admitted that there might have been such a scarab, but it must have been plundered a thousand years ago. I accepted his explanation, even though I knew it wasn't the truth. The marks around the scarab's impression told of a far more recent plunder—nor was it hard to guess by whom.

For, you see, I had heard the rumor of a very special dinner, and a disquisition afterward concerning power and beauty. No one seemed certain what those talismans representing power and beauty were, but I could guess what beauty was, though not to whom it had been sold. There are two of you whose husbands were privy to that discourse. One of you has the scarab. The other one is innocent. If the scarab is returned to me, I shall see to it that it is returned to the proper authorities, and nothing more need ever be said about it.

"Then he gives the date and place for their rendezvous."

"Did he really intend to return the scarab?" I wondered aloud.

"No," said Mrs. Roberts, with all the certainty of women's intuition. "But why did she go? She didn't have the scarab by then."

"No, but the letter made her doubt her husband's final words. She thought perhaps he had sold it back to Guinevere Gould. She had never believed that lady could give it up so blithely. She hoped the other woman would bring it."

"Then he sent a letter to both of them?" I asked.

"The identical letter, I should say. It was only because she is out of the country that Mrs. Gould did not receive it, else she might have come today as well, if only to disabuse him of the notion that she had the scarab in her possession. She might have been the sixth victim of the curse."

"Shall we go to the police now?" I asked.

"I don't think the police will be necessary," said Mrs. Roberts, rubbing a finger along her lips as if she meant to wipe away the story she had just related.

"Pah! Now you sound like Holmes."

"You're a medical man," said Mrs. Roberts. "Think of the elemental as an infection, passed on from one host to another. The infection caused her to lose her balance, badly. But now the infection is fading. She has righted herself."

"And who is she? A money-grubbing little—"

"I know something of what it is to be a woman grubbing for money," she replied dryly.

"So we blame her actions on what—elementals? Because if that's the case, the scarab is still out there, in the hands of this Hollywood actress. Should we expect to hear of a rash of murders in Hollywood?"

"Not necessarily. The elemental has a different effect on each person, just as an infection does. It had no effect at all on Guinevere Gould. Still, I think it would be safest if the scarab is returned to its rightful owner."

"The Egyptian government," I said.

"Tutankhamun."

She saw the look of disbelief on my face. "Surely you have seen enough to shake your disbelief at last."

I think I grunted. It was the only cogent answer I could make. I didn't know what I believed any longer. I had yet to work it all out logically. But I didn't want to admit that to her.

"Surely the police will want to know who poisoned Sir Archibald," I cried.

"I've discussed that with the clerk already. Did you know that he is Peter Steiler's son?" asked Holmes. "He said that the doctor has already signed the death certificate, giving cause of death as hepatic abscess."

I threw in my cards.

I went to bed a little tipsy that night, but sleep eluded me. In the morning we would take the train to Paris. We would deposit Princess Marguerite at her home. Holmes and Mrs. Roberts kept assuring me it was the right thing to do. Every fiber of my being told me I should go to the Meiringen police and tell them everything. I could not bring myself to believe in all this spiritualist pap that Holmes so voraciously dined on.

Yet I had seen things that I could not explain, it was true. How had Mrs. Roberts known that we would find Princess Marguerite at the falls? Could she really have practiced hypnotism on me? I could still remember the heat from the flames in the tomb, my skin crackling and blackening. But what if I cracked the door open to the "other side"? Would I then be forced to believe in philandering fairies? Or could I believe in just a little of it? Must it be all or none? Where to draw the line?

Murderess! She'd ruthlessly murdered four people for a mere bauble. Wait, then who had murdered Colonel Herbert? He seemed to have been forgotten. Holmes had said not every death could be attributed to an elemental.

What time was it? Would the kitchen staff still be working? Perhaps a glass of warm milk would soothe my jangled nerves. I must have fallen asleep with that comforting thought in mind.

Thus, the next morning at breakfast, it was I who looked as if I'd murdered someone. As for Princess Marguerite, she seemed perfectly normal, if a little vacant. Her eyes were unfocused and the blood at her throat pulsed like a metronome.

Conversation was tepid. I decided not to take up the argument again, not there in front of the lady herself. To what purpose? Mrs. Roberts was convinced that the princess was well on her way to a cure of some sort, that the scarab itself was entirely to blame for her sins, that she could heal the woman with soft words. And Holmes, once the paragon of logic, merely parroted her arguments. Was there some logic beyond logic that I was missing? Oh, I had been all over this a hundred times. I could either go to the police, who had already declared Sit Archibald's death a result of a failed operation, or I could keep quiet.

I kept quiet. As the tomb.

The princess did mention at one point that she was anxious to get home to her husband. Whether she was serious or shamming, I couldn't tell. No one seemed comfortable reminding her that she had put three bullets in her husband's back. Where he was buried, I didn't know, but he certainly was not waiting for her at the Rue Georges-Ville.

She and Mrs. Roberts sat next to each other whispering the whole way back to Paris. Her sister had by now alerted the authorities since she had left without a word or even a note. It was rather a job to call off the dogs, and her sister seemed disappointed that she had not returned with a pack of reporters at her back. We booked rooms at the nearby Hotel du Bois and repaired thither. Mrs. Roberts chose to stay with the princess till the wee hours of the morning. I feared for her, alone with that woman and her sister, who might be as mad as she. But I admired her courage.

I sat with Sherlock Holmes again that evening in the hotel lounge, though I was careful to drink sparingly this time. My unresolved feelings made conversation a burden. But then I recalled the question that had been pushed to the back of my mind. Who had killed Colonel Herbert?

"I'm afraid I was the cause of Colonel Herbert's death."

"What—?"

"At least in part. By placing the blame for Lord Carnarvon's death on the curse, I emboldened Colonel Herbert's assassins, who knew that many would jump to the conclusion that it must be the work of the curse, as well. Even Scotland Yard was lulled."

"Assassins?"

"Oh, yes. Lawrence never works alone. The Arab doctor who performed the operation was as guilty as he. I suspect he has disappeared deep into the curtained desert by now."

"Did Herbert really steal the scarab from his own brother?" I asked.

"I think not. Far more likely he was given the scarab to smuggle out of the country. Herbert was a remarkable man, but remarkably unprepossessing. He aroused suspicion in no one. He often traveled around dressed as a tramp. It made him a superbly effective spy."

"But why did he have to die? Because he knew about the poison?"

"No. Because he was a man of reason. A peacemaker. You know how he negotiated the release of prisoners from Mustafa Kemal after the battle of Kut? By offering himself in their place.

"But there is a faction among the Egyptians who don't want reason; they want independence above all. The charming Zaghlul Pasha is their chief. The voice of reason is a hindrance to them and must be stilled. Far better to deal with firebrands. And those few who have proven entirely sympathetic to their cause, like Lawrence."

"Lawrence killed Herbert? And that's why he tried to kill us?"

"Had him killed, or had a hand in the planning. Lawrence knows better than to sully his own hands. And he didn't try to kill us because of what we knew, but to keep us from stopping his next move."

"He's got more deaths planned?"

"You remember what you said upon meeting General Stack? That he seemed a reasonable man?"

"Lee Stack is his next target?"

"I believe so. A reasonable man might bank the fires of the Egyptians."

"You've got to warn him."

"I've already made my report to Intelligence and to Colonel Stack personally, but I'm afraid I've been met with disbelief. Lawrence is still adored in some quarters. As for me, I'm the man who believes in fairies."

"You're bitter," I ventured.

"I'm not bitter, strangely enough. I saved a life at the Reichenbach Falls yesterday. I can't help but feel absolved to some degree for the life I took there thirty years ago. I am at peace. I am willing to let the world go on as it will, for good or ill. It will anyway, you know."

"You never could have saved her without Mrs. Roberts."

"And you, my doughty friend."

That night I was plagued by nightmares about leaving my hotel room for something, the newspaper, perhaps, and being shot in the back, thirty times, by Mrs. Roberts. Would Sherlock Holmes absolve her of my murder, blaming it on the scarab?

I was ready for my own bed at home. Hadn't we solved the case?

Well, no. For there was still the matter of the scarab. Scarab, scarab, who had the scarab?

Of course, there was another loose end to wrap up, one which had been entirely driven out of my mind, although I'm sure my readers have by no means forgotten it. I was reminded painfully of it as soon as I entered my sitting room the next day, with Holmes at my heels.

Sitting there, in my best chair, was T. E. Lawrence.

After I got over the initial shock, and realizing that he was not armed and that Mrs. Colfax had seen him in and that Holmes had situated himself in my second-best chair, I busied myself making tea and bringing in the low stool from my examining room. Neither Holmes nor Lawrence seemed inclined to speak of any matters of importance until I was settled and they'd had a few bracing sips of blue tea.

"First," said Lawrence, clearing his throat, "I suppose I owe you both an apology."

"For trying to kill us?" surmised Holmes, as if he might have been referring to Lawrence's dropping in on us unannounced.

"Just so."

"So you could kill the sirdar," I said flatly.

"What? No, of course not. To keep you from taking the caliph."

"The who?" I asked.

"Abdülmecid II, the caliph of the Ottoman Empire. Or he was

until three days ago, when the caliphate was dissolved and he was banished from Turkey. He had to flee for his life to Switzerland. He will be the last caliph."

"What's that got to do with the price of onions?" I asked.

"There was a plot, devised by Harington and his boys, to bring Abdülmecid to England and prop him up as caliph in exile. When you took off for Switzerland in such a hurry, I thought you were part of it. They failed in the end. He had no wish to be a puppet."

"I begin to understand. Without the caliph, the sharif of Mecca becomes the sole voice of Islam," said Holmes.

"Sharif Hussein has already taken steps to have himself proclaimed caliph," Lawrence replied.

"Which would strengthen the hand of Faisal and pan-Arabism. You're still in Faisal's corner after all this time?"

"I made promises," Lawrence said solemnly.

I couldn't follow all the twists and turns of politics. But I had not taken my eyes off the main point. "And did those promises include the murder of Aubrey Herbert?"

Lawrence looked at me as if I were mad. "You lay that at my door? He was my bosom friend."

"Yet you were the one who recommended the doctor who pulled every tooth out of his head," I exploded.

"He was desperate! He was going blind. Can you imagine what that meant to a man like Herbert? I'd heard that clearing out bad teeth can help with cataracts. He had a mouthful of rotten teeth. It was a risk, but one he was willing to take. I had no idea he'd have every tooth in his head pulled! And it did him absolutely no good."

"So you poisoned him. Aspergillosis." I wasn't letting go.

"Ah, I should have known you'd recognize the symptoms in Lord Carnarvon. Your friend is not as perceptive as you, however, Holmes. But then, what is he but a stenographer? I came here today to ask you about this letter, whether I should put it in the hands of Mary Herbert." He took an envelope from his pocket and threw it on the table. Then he stood.

"I'll leave it in the hands of the good, saintly doctor. Only know that if you had insulted me a hundred years earlier as you did today, I'd have put a bullet through your brain."

He strode out the door and slammed it behind him.

"The gall of the man! Shall we at last call Scotland Yard?" I roared.

"My eyes are tired, Watson. Would you do me the favor of reading Colonel Herbert's missive?"

I picked up the envelope. It was indeed from Colonel Aubrey Herbert. I put on my reading glasses, opened it, and read aloud.

My dearest Tom,

When this reaches you, I shall be no more. I'm afraid the curse of Tutankhamun is real, at least for me. I fear I should never have visited the tomb with you, nor asked you about the fungus on the western wall. Certainly I should never have collected it, never had it distilled. I thought to turn two of the wealthiest men in the world into informants. It would have been quite a coup. Instead, I am certain my actions led inadvertently to the death of my brother, and likely Gould's death as well. I cannot expiate these crimes, except by one means.

Night is closing in on me. The operation was a failure. I thought that I was brave, but I cannot go on with the shame of either my spiritual or my physical afflictions. I still have enough of the aspergillus solution to provide my quietus.

Tell Mary, tell Mary . . . whatever you think is best. But tell her that I have loved only her and shall love her beyond death and to the end of time. I am sorry to lay this burden on you. I have no one else, and I know that you are brave beyond all reason.

Your loving friend,
Aubrey

By the time I finished reading, my voice was hoarse.

"I apologize. I have led you badly astray" was all Sherlock Holmes said.

I did not speak for several minutes. Then I mumbled, "He did try to kill us, remember."

"True. Of course, that's hardly an exclusive club."

Chapter Twenty-Four:
Mrs. Estelle Roberts

Yesterday I received a letter from the princess. She was full of woe. She had miscarried Prince Ali's child, she said. I was at first stricken by the news, until I remembered that she had never been pregnant, that it had only been a ruse. She was still in a state of shock and confusion from which she might never fully recover. Perhaps she had convinced herself she had been pregnant, as she had believed her husband still alive. She needed someone to love. It was part of her makeup, her very being. It is a curse to be beautiful. As for the murderer that had once dwelled within her, there was no trace remaining. It was as if it had lost its footing, slipped through Sir Sherlock's hands, and perished in the waters below. One sincerely hopes so.

But I soon put her out of my mind. Today was the day. Today I would meet with Natacha Rambova. I would have been nervous enough dealing with such a celebrity, but today I had a mission. I had to learn how she had been affected by the scarab—*if* she truly had the scarab. Sir Sherlock and Dr. Watson would be close at hand, awaiting my verdict. At least her husband, Valentino, would not be present. He had an interview with *Film Monthly* to attend.

Sherlock Holmes had written to Mrs. Gould, who confirmed that she had told her husband to return the scarab to Lord Carnarvon. She also confirmed that she had received the same letter as the princess from Sir Archibald—just after reading in the papers that Sir Archibald had died.

I had been cleaning house all day. The children would not be home for hours. Holmes and Watson were in the baby's room with the door firmly shut. I was afraid they would wake the baby, but they had practice at sitting quiet as church mice for hours, they assured me. I turned down the gas, more to hide the shabbiness of the furniture given to us by friends than to set a mood. I had met her before, had a brief conversation with her, but I had never before held a séance with her. She had smarts, though, I was immediately impressed by that. She was not some brainless Hollywood starlet. I would have to be careful.

A knock came at the door. I froze for a second, then recovered myself, smoothed down my hair, and moved to answer it.

She sailed through the door like a swan. Her dress left me tongue-tied. So chic, so lovely, so—Egyptian (a gold metallic lace dress with silk lamé and handcrafted floral ornaments). Her eyes were questioning—no, questing. Her hair was parted in the exact center, throwing the severe planes of her face into stark relief. I recovered myself and invited her inside. Except she was already seated, exactly where she was supposed to be, puffing carelessly on a cigarette. I suppose that poise came with being an actress. I could learn from her.

I sat down across from her at the small table. A candle was lit between us. Unaccountably, I was reminded of the Hodsons on the train. I muffled a giggle. She must have thought me deranged.

But sensitives are excused their little eccentricities. Soon we dropped into a more somber mood. She wanted to talk to Heber C. Kimball, her great-grandfather. (The "little Russian" confessed to me that her given name was Winifred Kimball Shaughnessy; she was born in Utah).

I thought it an odd request, wanting to commune with a relative from so long ago, but she explained that no one else had been able to reach him. He had been a lion in his time, and she badly wanted his advice. She'd heard Sir Sherlock lecture in New York, remembered that I was the only sensitive able to put him in touch with his mother. She said she was afraid that her relative was reluctant to speak because he was a Mormon. Indeed, one of the first Mormons, counselor to Brigham Young himself, if I knew who that was (I didn't at the time but later educated myself). He most definitely did not believe in spiritualism. So he might be embarrassed to admit he was still alive, so to speak. Of course, he had wed forty-three wives during his lifetime, so perhaps he simply preferred to keep a low profile in the afterlife rather than be plagued by them throughout eternity.

I said that I would relish the challenge, but that he might not appear if his beliefs interfered. I called Red Cloud to my side easily enough, and after a longish search he said that Kimball was there with us, but whether he could get him to speak he doubted very much. He was a closemouthed one, even to his fellow spirits. Did she have any specific questions?

She thought for a bit. "Is death the way you imagined it would be?"

There was silence, but I could feel a rumbling, like faraway thunder.

"Will you not speak to the daughter of your loins?" I asked.

"No," came the roar. "I'm waiting for the last judgment."

"But the world hasn't come to an end," she answered meekly.

"My world has. I should be exalted."

"I'm so confused, Grandfather. Where can I find peace?"

"Didn't you find peace in Egypt?"

I was flabbergasted by the words coming out of my mouth. I had been thinking desperately of a way to shoehorn Egypt into the conversation. Now the spirit of her ancestor had laid the groundwork for me.

"I've never been to Egypt," she replied.

"You haven't been? You look like you've been. Go to Egypt and leave me in peace."

"It's strange you should mention Egypt, because—"

"What's strange about it? Don't bandy words with me—spit it out." He was a fierce old goat, impossible to restrain.

"It's just that I've received a rather strange gift from Egypt. Something that feels—powerful."

"Thought you said you hadn't been to Egypt," he snapped.

"No, I—"

"Leave me be." And just like that, he was gone.

No amount of coaxing would get another word from that proud, defeated spirit. At last, I shook my head and admitted failure. She was obviously disappointed, though she assured me that I was praiseworthy for being able to summon him at all. "What do you suppose he meant with all that about Egypt?"

"Well," I said cautiously, "your interest in Egypt is obvious from your dress. And you said you had received a powerful gift—"

"Yes, well, I really should be going. I have to meet my husband." She stubbed out her cigarette and rose. I had gone too far, too fast.

"Perhaps some tea to refresh you?"

"You English with your tea. Charming. I think a cocktail at the hotel might be more my cup of tea. But thank you. You're a magnificent medium. I'll tell everyone about you." She kissed me on both cheeks too quickly for me to dodge. She moved toward the door. That was when the baby's door opened, and Sherlock Holmes and Dr. Watson issued forth. She looked askance. "I didn't realize you had another client waiting."

"Mrs. Valentino, Sir Sherlock and Dr. John Watson," I struggled to get out.

"Well, I'm honored." She actually made a little curtsy.

"It might not be such an honor as you wish. If you'd care to take a seat?" said Sir Sherlock.

"This sounds ominous. I really do have to meet my husband."

"It's about your scarab."

"Scarab? I haven't any scarab."

"You do. You're wearing it now." I could feel the heat of it as soon as she had stepped in the door.

A look of calculation came into her eyes. She retired to the sofa. "Perhaps I shouldn't have chosen a medium who mingles with a world-famous detective."

I took a chair as well. Dr. Watson positioned himself in front of the door. Sir Sherlock remained standing, hovering over his subject. It struck me that if he were a pharaoh, he would probably have to be entombed standing up.

"Surely you knew where the scarab came from," said Sir Sherlock.

"The princess was very coy about that. I suspected, but then I thought, how could she have come by such a thing? Not that I cared overmuch. It was beautiful, and I wanted it."

"She came by it through treachery and murder. It is steeped in the blood of innocents."

"If it came from where I suspect, there can be no innocents involved," said Natacha, facing him down.

"You speak the truth. But the scarab is cursed and will curse anyone in the chain till it is restored to its rightful place. You have felt the power of its allure."

"So it *is* from the tomb of Tutankhamun," she said.

"It is the heart scarab. It must be returned," I replied.

She lit another cigarette at that, leaned back and puffed on it thoughtfully. "Oh no, I don't think they'll want it back. I think Carnarvon's greatest conundrum must have been how to get rid of it," she said nonchalantly. "Do you read hieroglyphics?" She looked toward each of us in turn.

"Very badly," admitted Sir Sherlock.

"I've been studying them lately. Fascinating. But perhaps you've seen the cartouche of Tutankhamun?"

"That I have." We nodded in tandem with Sir Sherlock. I could see it in my mind's eye: the bird, the flame, the ankh, the crook, the . . . what else? I would know it if I saw it.

She reached into her bosom and produced the heart scarab. She had had it on a chain around her neck the whole time. It was a beetle, oval in form, of emerald, and etched with dozens of tiny hieroglyphics in gold. I stared at the hieroglyphs as if they might suddenly become plain to me.

"This is not Tutankhamun's cartouche," said Sir Sherlock, confounded.

And then the scarab spoke to me with the voice of the Lady, and all became plain.

"It's Nefertiti," I said quietly.

"You expected it, didn't you?" said Sir Sherlock, turning to me with an appraising look.

I nodded. "Who else would have her stillborn daughters by her?"

"That's what all that writing says?" asked Dr. Watson, his eyes nearly crossing at all the tiny symbols.

"No, indeed," Natacha replied. "It's etched with an entire chapter from the *Book of the Dead*. I won't translate it all for you, but the last line reads, 'May I endure on earth, not die in the west, and be a blessed spirit there.'"

I reached for the scarab. She handed it to me willingly enough, a good sign. It was almost hot to the touch. I felt a great welling of desire within me. I closed my eyes, concentrating on Terry in the next room, and my three girls. The yearning slowly subsided.

"That's why he stole the heart scarab. Because it was Nefertiti's tomb, not Tutankhamun's," said Dr. Watson.

"No, I don't think it was quite like that," said Natacha. "I think Tutankhamun *was* Nefertiti. Or rather, I don't think there ever was a Tutankhamun as such. Remember, she was trying to rule a kingdom that had always been a patriarchy. She needed a young, virile male to hold her kingdom together. Someone she could trust. Who better than herself?"

"You're saying Tutankhamun was Nefertiti in trousers?" Dr. Watson asked.

"Why not? She needed the authority that only a male ruler could command. But she couldn't risk another male who would commit the folly of her former husband, Akhenaten. There must have been a few priests in on the impersonation, sworn to secrecy. She needed the cooperation of her daughter Ankhesenamun, of course, who gave it wholeheartedly. The daughter desired no male to rule over her, either."

"That was why the voice in the tomb was a woman's," said Sir Sherlock.

"So, you see, I think Carter would not welcome the return of the scarab," said Natacha. "He'd look a fool."

"But it needn't go back to Carter, or Egypt," I blurted out.

They all turned to me. What had I said? It had dawned on me; the scarab had spoken to me again.

"It should go where Lord Carnarvon intended—to his widow. His queen."

"Is this true? This was his intention?" She directed her gaze to Sir Sherlock. He was taken by surprise. We had never taken Lady Almina into account at all. He looked to Dr. Watson, who merely shrugged his assent.

"He meant it as an act of love. An act that was never fulfilled. That's what awakened all the wretched evil in the elemental."

"You believe it would break the chain of blood?" Sir Sherlock asked me.

I nodded. "If it is freely given."

"You're asking a great deal of me. To give is one thing, to freely give quite another." Natacha sat quietly for a few minutes, gathering her thoughts. Finally, she said, "I should be the one to take it to her."

You could feel an exhalation around the room.

"Shall I escort you, Mrs. Valentino?" asked Sir Sherlock.

"Surely you trust me to do what I say I will do," she replied.

"I trust you. I do not trust the scarab."

"Rest assured, I don't feel like murdering anyone. Not even my husband."

And such was the force of her personality that Sir Sherlock bowed, both literally and figuratively.

"Natacha, you really should visit the Valley of the Kings," I urged.

She nodded. "Someday. And someday, Mr. Holmes, we would like to make a movie based on one of your adventures. Rudolph is very interested in playing the great detective."

"Oh, but there's already been a Sherlock Holmes film, featuring William Gillette. I hardly think there would be interest in another."

Epilogue:
Dr. John Watson

id Natacha Rambova fulfill her promise? There was no way
to be sure. She indeed took a trip out to Highclere. Sherlock
Holmes shadowed her thus far. But, of course, he could not question
the lady Almina. The heart scarab still legally belonged to the Cairo
Museum. But the murder trail died there—though the trail of death
did not, not quite. Every time anyone associated in the slightest with
the tomb died what were seen as unnatural deaths (such as when Lord
Carnarvon's secretary, Richard Bethell, was found smothered in his
room in 1929), the press presented themselves at Sherlock Holmes's
door. They were always greeted by a curt "I have nothing to say on the
subject."

Sherlock Holmes met privately with Lady Evelyn and her husband.
I do not know how much he told them, or whether he collected his
thousand pounds, but they were satisfied. Both Mrs. Roberts and I
were remembered for our roles in the investigation, although the lady
refused to pay for my camera. Aristos! I was not asked to pronounce
an opinion on the existence of elementals, for which I was grateful.
Holmes issued a patently insincere retraction in the *Times*, which was

promptly buried in the back pages. The papers preferred to print the legend of the curse rather than the facts of the case.

Holmes tapered off his lectures on spiritualism and sank into obscurity. But he never flagged in his belief in spiritualism and the marvelous. Nor, after our encounter with the pharaoh's heart, did I ever again try to turn him away from his beliefs. I think that this world had become too small a stage for him to practice his craft upon. He required a larger arena, a more inclusive set of data. I, for one, would not deny him that larger stage on which to perform his arias.

Mrs. Roberts went on to relative fame as a medium, although she never allowed herself to be tested by independent experts. I still have not made up my mind about the events of 1924, or the source of her extraordinary talents. I should like to think I keep an open mind, but if you tell me man can fly, I shall require proof. If you tell me pigs can fly, the bar of proof is that much higher. When you have eliminated the impossible, Holmes used to say, whatever remains, however improbable, must be the truth. But the devil is in separating the improbable from the impossible. One thing is certain: I do not believe in fairies.

We did have a treat in July of that year, when Howard Carter came to London to deliver a lecture on Tutankhamun to the Royal Asiatic Society. He was still deep in his dustup with the Egyptian government, so he had plenty of time on his hands, I suppose. The lecture was to be given at the aptly named Egyptian Hall, Mansion House. Lord Chalmers was indebted to Sherlock Holmes for his many services, so we were able to secure seats, although we did not actually stay for the lecture. You must imagine Mr. Carter's look of surprise to find us waiting for him on his arrival backstage.

"Now," said Holmes in his most reasonable tone, "will you tell us about the theft of the heart scarab, or shall I tell your audience how I deduce it occurred?"

I was standing in front of the door, my arms crossed. All the fight drained out of Carter's face. "At first, we only wanted to know whether the mummy was actually in the sarcophagus. Lord Carnarvon was mad with anticipation," he said miserably.

"So you broke through to the burial chamber?" Holmes drove him.

"There were four of us—His Lordship, myself, Callender, and Hassan. Bloody little room to maneuver inside the shrines, but we needed to move the lid only a few inches, just enough to see inside. Even with crowbars it was hellish."

"You cracked the lid," Holmes reminded him.

"That was unfortunate, but we could always blame it on tomb raiders. We'd done that before."

"Most convenient."

"If we hadn't done it, Lord Carnarvon would have gone to his grave without ever meeting Tutankhamun face-to-face. That was our entire aim."

"But then you spied the heart scarab."

"His Lordship saw it and fell in love. He wanted it for the lady Almina. He adored that woman. No one there could say boo to him. But it was the devil clawing it out of that muck. So he gave it to her as a love token. I for one am glad of it."

Holmes did not inform Carter of the crooked road the scarab took to Highclere Castle.

I do hope he had a spare dress shirt for his audience. When we left, the one he had on was drenched with sweat.

On a suitably cold night in November, with the rain driving hard, I was listening to the Kutcher String Quartet playing Mozart on the BBC when an announcer interrupted to report that the sirdar of Egypt, General Lee Stack, had been ambushed by Egyptian extremists and had died in a hail of gunfire. His aide, P. K. Campbell, was injured. Members of Parliament were already calling loudly for repeal of the grant of independence that Great Britain had given to Egypt, and that Egypt had now proven itself profoundly unworthy of. King Fuad and Prime Minister Zaghlul had both expressed horror at the murder. Crocodile tears. Egyptian nationalists, Russian Bolsheviks, even British radicals all came in for their share of the blame. Did Lawrence have a hand in the deed? If he did, he was careful to wipe his fingerprints.

Seven men were hanged, and harsh penalties were imposed upon the Egyptian government. Zaghlul was forced to resign. Egypt will remain a thorn in England's side. But we shall never give up the Suez.

There was still one question that haunted me. The answer came to me, quite by accident, on February 19, 1925. I was reading the obituaries in the *Times*. (When one reaches a certain age, one follows the obituaries to catch up on old friends.) I came upon a name that arrested my notice. George Sigerson was laid to rest that day in Glasnevin Cemetery, Dublin. He was a great man, the paper said, a physician, writer, politician, and poet. The mourners at his funeral comprised a who's who of the Irish literary movement, or the Irish Rebellion. They were too often one and the same. But there among the Casements, the Hydes, the Stevenses, the Yeatses, the Pearses, McDonoughs, and the de Valeras, one name stood out to me: Sherlock Holmes, pallbearer.

Sigerson!

Epilogue:
Mrs. Estelle Roberts

I was at John Watson's funeral in 1932. I was not invited to speak, of course, as I had been at Sir Sherlock's Albert Hall memorial. His skepticism of spiritism was well-known, especially his scathing repudiation of Mr. Hodson's fairies, published in *The Strand* in 1930.

What was known to only a handful was the story of our investigation of Lord Carnarvon's untimely death. And even fewer knew that we became fast friends afterward. He would often visit my public demonstrations, unannounced and incognito. I would spy him at the back of the crowd, scratching his head, looking flummoxed, and a little thrill of satisfaction would go up my spine.

Sir Sherlock never got up to London again, so far as I knew, though I did visit him in Sussex once or twice for séances. These were small affairs, barely a handful of people. But I would never again feel the powerful presence of Louise Vernet-Lecomte Holmes, nor indeed did he ever call on me to summon her. He seemed wholly at peace with himself. I do not believe he was ever asked to take on another investigation. The last time I went down, he had turned over his bees to a neighbor; he knew he was about to die.

Dr. Watson's funeral was well attended, especially by his fellow authors. I was surprised to see the esteem in which he was held in by his fellow scribes, some of them quite famous. The eulogy given by his friend J. M. Barrie was especially moving. He said of him "I have always thought him one of the best men I have ever known, there can never have been a straighter nor a more honorable."

After his funeral, I went out directly and bought all of Dr. Watson's books and read them, marveling at the way he captured Sherlock Holmes on the page. I wish there could be many more books. Perhaps he is still writing.

Was he an unbeliever to the end? I went to visit his grave once and found a Latin inscription on his headstone: *Non omnis moriar.* I had no idea what it meant, but I found a very learned sexton who could translate it for me:

"I shall not all die."

The sexton proposed it meant that his books would live after him—and indeed they have. But I wonder. I wonder very much indeed.

There is of course, this book, which is meant to be published post-humously. When his publisher approached me asking for a release, I insisted upon reading the entire manuscript. One must be careful of one's reputation. I will acknowledge that I was not entirely pleased and insisted several lengthy addenda of my own composition be added. Whether they may cause the publisher to abandon the project alto-gether, I cannot say. Whether other players in our drama may threaten legal action if the book is released at all, I have no idea. It could be a very long time before the story sees the light of day. As the *Book of the Dead* says, "May it endure on earth, not die in the west."

T. E. Lawrence died of a motorcycle accident in 1935. Britain mourned his passing.

In 1932, Natacha Rambova, long since divorced from Rudolph Valentino, visited Egypt for the first time and found her true calling. She has since edited and published several volumes on Egyptology and religious symbolism. She is at work on another, I hear, having to do with scarabs. I hope in this one she will propound her theory of

Tutankhamun/Nefertiti (without, of course, mentioning the heart scarab). I am certain her ideas will make scholars sit up and take notice.

Princess Marguerite lives quietly in the same apartment on the Rue Georges-Ville. We still correspond. She seems such a gentle soul. The elemental, I think, drained her of all cupidity. She never shared in her ex-husband's fortune. Occasionally, she sends me his greetings.

The Lady Evelyn gave birth to a daughter in 1925. I sent her a letter of congratulations. I was surprised to receive a letter back, not from Lady Evelyn, but from her mother the lady Almina. She said that her daughter was resting after a difficult birth; she was nursing her back to health. By way of addendum she wrote: "If ever my tomb is dug up three thousand years from now, they will find me with my heart scarab intact. Thank you." I treasured those words.

What you will want to know is whether I have ever been in contact with Sherlock or John since they have crossed over. I can only say that after a lifetime of notoriety, they have begged their privacy, and earned it. I shall not speak of them again.

The End

P.S. There is one error on Dr. Watson's part I should unquestionably set to rights: George Sigerson was *not* the father of Sherlock Holmes.

Acknowledgments

I'd first like to thank my editors, Dan Mayer and Rene Sears, for their steady guidance, along with the entire staff at Seventh Street, particularly cover artist Jennifer Do and copyeditor Sara Brady.

Special thanks must go to my readers, Laura Dragon (if she hadn't hated my original ending for my first Holmes book, this book would not exist); everyone's den mother, Betsy Hannas Morris; and Professor Elizabeth Liebert, expert in all things British.

Thanks to all my family, but especially to nephew Sean Bos and his father, Frits, for their help with the Dutch language. And thanks to Terry Ward for his excellent renderings of the cartouches.

Thanks to the Griffith Institute at Harvard University for so generously making their wealth of research accessible online, including Howard Carter's journals, which were essential to this novel (even where I fudged facts). Thanks to Daniel Hånberg Alonso for the Conan Doyle press quotes that open the novel.

As always, a number of books were ground up in the writing of this novel. *Fifty Years a Medium* by Estelle Roberts, *Seven Pillars of Wisdom* by T. E. Lawrence, *The Tomb of Tutankhamun* by Howard

Carter, *Fairies at Work and at Play* by Geoffrey Hodson, *Making Monte Carlo* by Mark Braude, and *Scandal at the Savoy* by Andrew Rose are just a few. *Lawrence and Aaronsohn*, by Ronald Florence, provided a very different view of T. E. Lawrence. *The Complete Tutankhamun* by Nicholas Reeves put me inside the boy king's tomb, and *Cook's Tourists' Handbook for Egypt, the Nile, and the Desert* (1878) guided my steps.